LOOK BEHIND YOU, LADY

What a pickup line! Bruce Flemish is getting ready for his magic act at the Hotel China Seas in Macao when the girl sits down next to him at the bar and offers her room number. But this casual meeting is anything but. Donna Van Deerlin is looking for a hero. Her father was killed trying to get information to Hong Kong about a local opium ring. Donna has her father's notes in code. But getting them out of Macao will take courage. Bruce is sure she must have the wrong guy— he's just an itinerant magician. But before long Donna is working her magic on *him,* and Bruce is trying to stay one step ahead of a gang of murderers who want to get their hands on the notes as well.

THE VENETIAN BLONDE

Skelly stumbles into Venice with a gangster on his tail and his card dealing confidence blown to hell. He feels washed up. That's when he runs into Viola, a young blonde in a black swimsuit sitting at the end of the bar. He can't shake her. And he needs to, because Skelly is in town to hit up his old friend Rinny Jim for some quick cash. Instead he finds Rinny's beautiful wife Maggie, and a very sweet deal—a million-dollar con to bring a rich da⌐   e dead. Now he's got two   hat sweet green tempti   D1247728   Skelly's problem

A. S. FLEISCHMAN BIBLIOGRAPHY

NOVELS
The Straw Donkey Case (1948)
Murder's No Accident (1949)
Shanghai Flame (1951)
Look Behind You, Lady (1952)
 [aka Chinese Crimson, UK, 1962]
Danger in Paradise (1953)
Counterspy Express (1954)
Malay Woman (1954)
 [aka Malay Manhunt, UK, 1966]
Blood Alley (1955)
Yellowleg (1960) [aka The Deadly
 Companions, 1961]
The Venetian Blonde (1963)

SCREENPLAYS
Blood Alley (1955)
Goodbye, My Lady
 [as Sid Fleischman] (1956)
Lafayette Escadrille (1958)
The Deadly Companions (1961)
Scalawag (1973)
The Whipping Boy
 [as Max Brindle] (1995)

As Sid Fleischman

Mr. Mysterious & Company (1962)
By the Great Horn Spoon! (1963)
Ghost in the Noonday Sun (1965)
Chancy and the Grand Rascal (1966)
McBroom Tells the Truth (1966)
McBroom and the Big Wind (1967)
McBroom's Zoo (1969)
Longbeard the Wizard (1970)
Jingo Django (1971)
McBroom's Ear (1971)
McBroom's Ghost (1971)
The Wooden Cat Man (1972)

Mr. Mysterious's Secrets of Magic:
 21 Tricks (1975)
McBroom Tells a Lie (1976)
Kate's Secret Riddle Book (1977)
Me and the Man on the
 Moon-Eyed Horse (1977)
Humbug Mountain (1978)
Jim Bridger's Alarm Clock
 and Other Tall Tales (1978)
McBroom and the Beanstalk (1978)
The Hey Hey Man (1979)
McBroom and the Great Race (1980)
The Case of the Cackling Ghost
 (1981)
McBroom the Rainmaker (1982)
McBroom's Almanac (1984)
Whipping Boy (1986)
The Scarebird (1987)
The Midnight Horse (1990)
Jim Ugly (1992)
McBroom's Wonderful One-Acre
 Farm (1992)
The Charlatan's Handbook (1993)
The 13th Floor: A Ghost Story
 (1995)
The Abracadabra Kid:
 A Writer's Life (1996)
Bandit's Moon (1998)
The Ghost on Saturday Night (1999)
Here Comes McBroom!:
 Three More Tall Tales (1999)
A Carnival of Animals (2000)
Bo & Mzzz Mad (2003)
Disappearing Act (2003)
The Giant Rat of Sumatra:
 or Pirates Galore (2005)
Escape! The Story of the Great
 Houdini (2006)
The White Elephant (2006)

Look Behind You, Lady

The Venetian Blonde

By A. S. Fleischman

STARK HOUSE

Stark House Press • Eureka California
www.StarkHousePress.com

LOOK BEHIND YOU, LADY / THE VENETIAN BLONDE

Published by Stark House Press
2200 O Street
Eureka, CA 95501, USA
griffinskye@cox.net
www.starkhousepress.com

ISBN: 1-933586-12-5

Text set in Figural and Dogma. Heads set in Celestia Antiqua.
Cover design and book layout by Mark Shepard, shepdesign.home.comcast.net
Proofreading by Joanne Applen

The publisher would like to thank Sid Fleischman for all his help on this project.

PUBLISHER'S NOTE

First Stark House Press Edition: December 2006

0 9 8 7 6 5 4 3 2 1

Contents

LOOK BEHIND YOU, LADY: CLASSIC NOIR
By Steve Lewis

Albert Sidney Fleischman, known to his friends and colleagues as Sid, was born in 1920, and at 86, thankfully he's still around to see Greg Shepard bring a couple of his old Gold Medal paperbacks back into print.

His career in the adult mystery field was relatively short, beginning with a couple of Phoenix Press mysteries in 1948 and 49, then shifting to Gold Medal for five paperback originals between 1951 and 1963, with one from Ace making an appearance in 1954.

After that he became an author of children's books, winning the Newberry Medal for *The Whipping Boy* (1987), and the creator of Bullwhip Griffin – the movie about his adventures was based on the book *By the Great Horn Spoon* (1963).

Greg always does a great job in adding material to his books about the authors he publishes, so I won't try to come up with any more background like this on my own. Nor will I say anything about *The Venetian Blonde*, one of my favorite mystery titles of all time, and I love the cover as well – they go hand-in-hand together as a truly great match-up.

To introduce you to *Look Behind You Lady* (no comma on the first edition, and I'm not sure why), you might pretend that you're at the newsstand in 1952, or the drug-store spinner rack, and you'd see the cover, designed to catch anyone's eye, 100% guaranteed. (Truth be told, I was 10 at the time, so it had to have been the 1956 reprint that snagged my attention.)

Then once in the would-be purchaser's hand, he would have looked inside the front cover to read the following blurb:

She dipped the coal of the cigarette in the water and it died with a thin sizzle. Then she rose from the tub like a mermaid, turning her back to me, and held her arms up. I wrapped the towel around her, sarong-like. Her hands closely softly over mine as I tucked in a corner.

"I was mad at you when you walked out," she whispered, "but I like the way you walked back in."
I turned her around and kissed her lips.
"You're getting wet," she said.
"Stop talking," I said.

Not a word wasted, and if you could pass this up, you're a better person than I, or your tastes are so different from mine that you should be reading the introduction to some other book anyway.

But just in case a quarter was all that you had in your pocket, back in 1952, and you needed just that one extra nudge to tip the balance toward paying the storekeeper and on your way with the book, all you would have had to do was to turn two more pages and start reading from the top of Chapter One:

She said, "May I sit down?"
I looked up from my vinho e licores *at the girl standing beside my table. I was on the marble terrace of the Hotel China Seas in Macao, killing time between shows, and feeling a little surly. Along the hotel wall a Filipino swing band was giving the week-enders from Hong Kong something to dance to.*
"Talking to me?" I muttered.
"Talking to you," she said.
She was wearing a smart white dress, and her dark hair was cut short, with bangs. I didn't like the bangs. The dress had a mandarin collar, which was a shame, because a plunging neckline would have been something worth plunging for.
"You can sit down," I said. "I was just leaving."
"Please —"
I looked at her and smiled only to myself. Sure, I thought, there's not much paradise left in the Orient, but there's Macao. Don't bring your wife unless you're just interested in the view from the old Portuguese fort on the hill. Macao attracts the finest tramps in the world, its streets are paved with gold, and gambling is a way of life. If you can't enjoy yourself in Macao, there's something wrong with you — not Macao. Or you brought your life.
"Look," I said. "Is every woman in Macao on the make? Every time I buy myself a drink some girl comes along and wants to muscle in on the act."

Ka-ching! Sold, am I right, or am I right? If you can't read this story and hear the voices of Humphrey Bogart as rather world-weary stage magician Bruce Flemish and Lauren Bacall as Donna Van Deerlin, the lady above who has both a room number and a proposition for him, you haven't been watching as many of the movies of the 1940s and early 1950s as is good for you. Something's been missing from your video diet that you ought to remedy as soon as possible.

More. The owner of the Hotel China Seas is Senhor Gonsalves, a gentleman who is missing both his thumbs, and he also has a small task for Flemish to perform as part of his act, a task involving the not-so-small sum of $10,000 Hong Kong dollars. Sydney Greenstreet.

One of Senhor Gonsalves' many assistants is a mousy sort of fellow named Josef Nakov, who is handy with a gun. Peter Lorre.

From page 144:

I was on my feet now and had a cigarette going in my fingers. Gilberto held Donna's arms behind her. Phebe sat on the edge of the bed, like an outcast, her head buried in her hands. Nakov held a fresh, big gun and looked supremely happy. "O.K.," I said, "so you're going to murder us."

"We can find another word," Gonsalves said, his hands stuck in his pockets. "Eliminate. Murder is for your Chicago gangsters. In politics, we eliminate. It is death on a higher social level."

"We'll appreciate the difference," I said, "but why bother? We're not very clear on what the hell your game is. You must be getting damned scared to want to murder everyone in sight."

Nakov says something about the intelligence of Donna, who had who walked back into Gonsalves' hands after a brief escape.

I turned on Gonsalves angrily. "Make him shut up," I said. "If he licks your boots once more in public, I'll puke."

You can cast Gilberto, young punk working for Gonsalves, and Phebe, a somewhat shopworn stripper whose act follows that of Flemish on stage, yourself.

The plot has something to do with the Communist Reds and/or the opium trade, and it matters not very much in the long run. But there are twists to be had, and thrills of the nature above, and what more could you want of a book of exotic Oriental danger and intrigue like this?

NEWINGTON, CT
SEPTEMBER 2006

INTRODUCTION
By Sid Fleischman

When I first took it into my head to become a writer, I decided to begin with a mystery novel or two. After all, what could be easier? All you needed was a dead body and a detective. I could find those in the yellow pages.

The mystery itself would be a piece of cake, for I had been making a hardscrabble living as a magician. I knew about misdirection and pulling red herrings our of my sleeve and back-palming props.

Those beginner novels, hastily written to pay the rent, (post World War II veteran housing, $21.00 a month) were published and went out of print almost before I could rush the advance check to the bank before it bounced. But those noirs were literary anvils. Pounding them out on a Royal portable, I discovered a visual imagination. I hammered out a style of my own and formed a cocked eye for whimsy.

My timing was good. When Gold Medal Books decided to move the publishing furniture around and offer advances on print runs, not sales, I was ready for the feast. For the first time, writers were being paid royalties up front and could get their shoes shined now and then.

I had landed in Shanghai as the war ended and used the fabled city as a setting for my big time debut, *Shanghai Flame*. Gold Medal dispatched a check for $2000 for the first printing, followed by checks every few weeks as the novel went back to press. I felt freshly dipped in gold dust and soon went off to Europe for a while.

How about a night club magician as my next hero? I knew the scene: I'd done my share before the war. And there was that sinful island, Portuguese Macao, hanging like a necklace of simulated diamonds and paste rubies off the neck of Hong Kong. A title popped into my head: *Look Behind You, Lady*. Well, that was a start.

I had already learned not to plan out my novels in advance. I worked best in the dark, so I jumped into the first scene. There stood my heroine. To the regret of my hero, she is wearing a mandarin collar... a shame, because a plunging neckline would have had something worth plunging for.

A bit daring for those *Saturday Evening Post* days. But I was off and running, improvising villains and shenanigans and cliff hangers galore. I've never lost a novel because I was unable to figure out the ending (more sensible novelists often figure out their endings first). But I worry a lot.

In Shanghai I had stumbled across a narrow cobbled street of low dives and high crime declared out of bounds to us sailors. It was nick-named Blood Alley.

It struck me as a strong title for a novel of the far east. Back in civil-ian life, I wrote it. My life changed as suddenly as a snap of the fin-gers.

John Wayne bought the film rights and would act in it. The direc-tor was one of the Olympians, "Wild Bill" William A. Wellman, who made *Wings* way back in the silent days and won the first Academy Award.

Bill found my work to be instinctively dramatic and he offered me the opportunity to write the screenplay. I have been a screenwriter ever since.

Several years later, as a refreshment from undistinguished film work (*Lafayette Escadrille; Goodbye, My Lady: The Deadly Companions*, etc.) I returned to Gold Medal for the sheer fun of it. (Come to think of it, *Goodbye, My Lady*, with Walter Brennan and Sidney Poitier, was dis-tinguished, but did no business.)

Enter, Charlie Miller. He was a magician and a friend, who was dei-fied within the shadowy world of tuxedoed wizards for his art and astonishing skill with cards. He could deal from the bottom of the deck as effortlessly as the top. Despite this mastery of the pasteboards, he grew tired of starving to death and crossed the line. He became a crooked gambler.

Charlie took a bus to the Midwest, bought a suit of overalls and in his hotel lobby, scraped dirt under his fingernails from the potted palm. Then he went looking for a card game. You can imagine the rest. He got well in a hurry. But as if to flail his sense of guilt, Charlie devel-oped asthma.

I wanted to put him in a book and *The Venetian Blonde* was it. My original title was *Abracadaver*, but the publisher trumped me.

Like most magicians, on the shelf or on stage, I rant and rave by how easily otherwise intelligent people can be taken in by the nitwit hoax of raising the dead in the magic shows of spiritualism. Every conjuror knows how the tricks, redressed in white sheets, are done.

So there was the raw material of my plot: good ol' Charlie Miller, his hands confounded by guilt, caught up in a cunning and theatrical caper of chattering ghosts. Almost before the ink was dry on the novel, the film rights were bought by a producer who has since vanished from sight.

You'd think, with the advance of years, I'd have the decency to quit. But the screenwriters' strike of the early 60s, dooming us ink stained wretches to twiddling our thumbs, backed me into a field I barely knew existed: children's books.

I wrote a book for my kids (about a magician— who else?). I assumed it was a one shot affair. But something strange happened.

When I wrote for adults, it was rare for anyone to drop me a note, except to complain about some wretched point of grammar. It was much like a comedian who never hears any laughter.

But with the publication of *Mr. Mysterious & Company*, letters by the dozens, by the hundreds, dropped through the mail slot in my home. I was astounded and overjoyed. I answered them all.

And still do. Book after book followed. I went on to win the Newbery Award, the Pulitzer Prize of children's literature, and just about every other award in sight.

Unlike novels for adults, that may go out of print in twenty-minutes, children's books are apt to have long lives. I can hardly believe that I have novels for young people that have been continuously in print for forty-five years. I am hearing from kids whose *grandparents* read me.

As a committed writer of fiction, I recall saying in the past that the only way I would write non-fiction was with a gun at my head. It turned out to be a cap gun, for my most recent book is *ESCAPE! The Life of the Great Houdini*, about the hero of my youth.

When I look at my long shelf of books, I am touched with embarrassment. I'd retire, but I'm too lazy.

SANTA MONICA, CALIFORNIA
JULY 2006

Look Behind You, Lady

By A. S. Fleischman

Chapter One

She said, "May I sit down?"

I looked up from my *vinho e licores* at the girl standing beside my table. I was on the marble terrace of the Hotel China Seas in Macao, killing time between shows, and feeling a little surly. Along the hotel wall a Filipino swing band was giving the week-enders from Hong Kong something to dance to.

"Talking to me?" I muttered.

"Talking to you," she said.

She was wearing a smart white dress, and her dark hair was cut short, with bangs. I didn't like the bangs. The dress had a mandarin collar, which was a shame, because a plunging neckline would have had something worth plunging for.

"You can sit down," I said. "I'm just leaving."

"Please—"

I looked at her and smiled only to myself. Sure, I thought, there's not much paradise left in the Orient, but there's Macao. Don't bring your wife unless you're just interested in the view from the old Portuguese fort on the hill. Macao attracts the finest tramps in the world, its streets are paved with gold, and gambling is a way of life. If you can't enjoy yourself in Macao there's something wrong with you—not Macao. Or you brought your wife.

"Look," I said. "Is *every* woman in Macao on the make? Every time I buy myself a drink some girl comes along and wants to muscle in on the act."

Her green eyes worked themselves into an honest little smile. "Sorry I wasn't a little more original."

"At least, you're better stacked than most."

Her eyes turned faintly chilly. "Now, that's what I call an original remark."

"I couldn't help noticing," I said. "It sticks out all over."

She sat down.

I felt trapped by her eyes and I didn't get up. She had something on her mind, and it was obviously me. "I'll do you a favor," I said. "I'll tell you all you'll want to know about me. I'm broke. Flat. Busted. The fan-tan tables spotted me first. Sorry."

The waiter came over, but I shooed him away. I had spent my last pataca on the drink I was dawdling over. I looked at my watch; I still had half an hour before the midnight floor show went on. The girl watched me, and she seemed faintly amused now. I began to wonder if I were making a fool of myself.

"You don't seem impressed," I said.

"I'm not interested in your money," she said, "Mr. Bruce Flemish."

I put down my glass and eyed her curiously. I wasn't *that* famous. "Anything else you know about me?"

She smiled dryly. "You're the magician upstairs in the Magellan Room. I've never cared for magicians. You drink too much, you gamble too much, and women fall all over you because you're so well stacked—for a man, that is."

"Say," I said, "you're a real bright kid."

A breeze was coming in off the harbor, but the night was still hot and sticky. She was looking straight into my eyes and it made me uncomfortable. I guessed she was about twenty-four, but there was something flinty in those eyes that told you they had seen plenty for their age. After the first couple of minutes, I had realized she was an American, but it didn't cut any ice with me. There are all kinds, and this was Macao.

"Well," I said, trying to get back to the beginning. "See you around."

She gave me a new look. The calmest, laziest eyes you ever saw. "Can you remember a number?"

I sensed it coming, but I decided not to head it off. "Like what?"

"Like three-six-two."

"Sounds like a room number."

"It is."

"What's in Room Three-six-two that could possibly interest me?"

"Me"

"I'm lousy at remembering numbers," I said.

She got up. "It's an easy one," she muttered. "Room Three-six-two. Try. You'll remember it. After the floor show."

"I've forgotten it already."

She turned and crossed the terrace into the hotel. I watched the interesting movement of her legs and hips, but reminded myself she wasn't for me. I could never get used to those bangs.

I stuck around for a last cigarette, watching the Britishers from Hong Kong dancing with the Eurasian hostesses. Beyond the terrace, Macao harbor was a black stretch of night except for the bobbing lights of the fishing junks. They weren't fishing, of course; they were smuggling. It's one of those open secrets you get used to in Macao. Gold, opium, military supplies—anything worth the risk. The colony was Portugal's only flyspeck of empire on the China coast, a small, lush peninsula within spitting distance of the Reds. You only had to spit a couple of miles.

I was putting out my cigarette when a waiter came over and picked up my glass. *"Outro, senhor?"*

I told him to forget it, but he just stood over me smiling. He was a half-caste in a starched white jacket. He bent closer and his smile bore down on me.

"Senhor, I bring fine advice from fine gentleman. He say tell American man to keep much distance from American girl. He say American man better keep nose clean or end up with neck broken."

I felt a chill on the back of my neck. I glanced around the terrace, but no one seemed to be paying any attention to us. The waiter straightened to leave, but I grabbed his small wrist.

"Who the hell's giving out free advice?" I snapped.

"Not free, senhor. He pay me."

"Who sent you?"

The waiter smiled stupidly. The only thing that wised these boys up was dough, and that left me out of the game. I felt like flattening his nose, but Mother Nature had beaten me to it. The American girl didn't interest me, but I didn't like anonymous people telling me where to get off. "You can tell the fine gentleman to go to hell," I said.

The waiter paused uncertainly. "You pay—I carry message," he said.

The guy had a sense of humor. He got lost before I lost mine.

I took a last glance around the terrace and then entered the hotel. I had my act to set up and I was a little late. The express elevator seemed forever in coming, but when it settled to the lobby there were two of us waiting.

We got in. The other passenger was a big man in a floppy seersucker suit, and he nodded amiably to me as the doors closed after us. If he had looked a little more like a fine gentleman I'd have told him to go to hell. I hadn't noticed whether he'd come in from the terrace or not. We stood silently as the elevator rose and he kept popping toasted watermelon seeds into his mouth. The sounds of his heavy jaws grinding up the seeds bothered me. He looked like the British army, retired, and he must have been living in Macao quite a while. It takes time to develop a taste for toasted watermelon seeds.

The elevator moved slowly, even though it was marked express, and I began feeling a little anxious about time. Strictly speaking, innkeeping was only a lesser activity of the Hotel China Seas. Two of its nine concrete stories were fancy gambling layouts, one floor was a high-class brothel, and there were rooms where opium was included with room service. Whichever floor you chose, the elevator was never in a hurry.

I was going to the top floor, the Magellan Room, and so was the other guy. The elevator landed, and as I passed through the club's rich red and gold entrance the two hat-check girls smiled eagerly.

It was funny about the Hotel China Seas. I was a sensation on the ninth floor. I was a stranger to everyone below, because every story was its own little world. But I was on the ninth floor now, and to this pair of Chinese dolls I was Senhor Sensation. I smiled back and walked along the heavy carpet into the noisy semidarkness of the Magellan Room.

I cut along one side of the tables to the dressing rooms behind the bandstand. The air rumbled with talk and laughter and the steady clink of glasses; the place had jammed up since I'd left after the ten-o'clock floor show. It was Friday night and the week-end crowd was in—from Hong Kong, from Red Canton, from God knows where along the southern coast. Smiling Chinese boys in crisp white jackets were all over the place, either carrying drinks or running bets to the fan-tan and dice casinos below. Right over the bandstand hung a large electric board that flashed winning numbers from the gambling floors. Senhor Gonsalves, who owned the night club as well as the two gambling casinos, made it as convenient as possible for you to lose your money.

Or spend it. The Magellan Room printed the most expensive liquor menu this side of the Philippines, it had the best dance band left in the Orient, and its customers had nothing but money.

I was in my fifth week in the Magellan Room, booked in from Hong

Kong, forty miles across the mouth of the Pearl River. It gives a guy quite a charge to be a sensation in the place he's working. I might have written home about it, except that I had no address to write to.

I went through the door to my dressing room, forgetting about the American girl with the bangs and completely dismissing the man in the seersucker suit. I had a show to do and I felt the small anxiety any performer feels before going on. When you're a magician, like me, you always wonder if anything in the act will go wrong tonight. It seldom does, but you always worry about that. I flicked on the light.

It was my dressing room, all right, but it wasn't exactly the way I had left it. I had company. He was sitting on my chair with his feet propped up on my wardrobe trunk and he had a look on his face as if he owned the place. He did.

"*Boas noites,*" Senhor Gonsalves muttered. "I have been waiting for you."

"Make yourself at home," I said, moving into the room and hanging up my sport jacket. "You pay the rent."

"I will not disturb you," he said. "I will talk to you while you set up your act."

"I like to do that in private," I said as casually as I could. "Like sex."

"Perhaps you will consider me a privileged visitor."

I didn't answer him. He held the purse strings, which made him pretty privileged, but not that privileged. Yet I was broke until payday, Wednesday, and I warned myself not to queer my chances of getting an advance. I slipped out of my shirt and tie and began to wash up. "Why don't you see me after the show? I'll come to your office."

"After the show, senhor, will be too late."

I came out from behind a face towel and looked at him. He was still in my chair and his feet were still on my trunk. He was wearing a fresh suit of whites and immaculate two-tone shoes. His sideburns were thick and curly and he had a face you could literally read like a map. There was China in it and Portugal and maybe a distant strain of Africa—especially in the lips, fleshy and pink, and in the coloring under the eyes.

Senhor Gonsalves, I had heard, was Macanese. The Macanese trace their ancestry back to the Portuguese who settled Macao more than four hundred years ago, and in the colony that's like being a Daughter of the American Revolution in Boston.

"Look," I said, putting aside the towel. "Maybe you've got something on your mind. but you're going to have to clear out of here. I've got a show coming up fast, I'm late, and I've got some gimmick to slip into. I don't like an audience for that."

He smiled, but it wasn't really a smile at all. It only looked like one. "We shall delay the show, then." he remarked. "What does it matter, Senhor Flemish?"

I stood impatiently across from him. I didn't like the way he dismissed the problem, even though the floor show was strictly his toy. It was my life. "You're the boss," I snapped.

"*Sim, sim,* I am the boss." He smiled. He kept his hands jammed in his pockets; I'd heard about his hands. "But you are becoming angry, Senhor Flemish. That is the way of you entertainers, eh? You are high-strung people."

"Don't worry about me," I said. "I just don't like guys barging into my dressing room because they pay the rent or juggling show time because it's not very important—except to us high-strung entertainers. You've got something on your mind. I'm waiting."

For a moment I thought he was going to take his hands out of his pockets, but he didn't. He had to get awfully wound up for that, and I'd never seen him that wound up. Both of his thumbs were missing, and he was sensitive as hell about it. He looked like the kind of guy who had learned to talk with his hands, and keeping them under control must have been quite a trick.

The way I'd heard the story, he had been kidnaped about six months ago and his French wife refused to pay the ransom because it was a half a million Hong Kong dollars. While she bargained for a better price his captors got impatient, so they sent her one of his thumbs to express their haste. Somehow she got it into her head that they had already killed him, and decided to hold onto the dough. But when the second thumb came along with a note from her husband promising to beat hell out of her, she paid, and when Senhor Gonsalves got back he beat hell out of her anyway and shipped her back to Indo-China, where she came from. Since the kidnaping he hadn't set foot outside the Hotel China Seas, and had doubled the Mozambique guards that all the gambling hotels in Macao keep at their doors. He wasn't going to let it happen again.

"I must ask you a simple favor, Senhor Flemish," he was saying. "I do not often ask favors, even simple ones. You can understand something important has come up."

"Never mind softening me up."

He grinned and swung his feet off the desk. "There is an Englishman in the club tonight, an importer from Hong Kong. Would it not be possible, Senhor Flemish, for you secretly to place something in his pocket?"

I lit a cigarette and thoughtlessly offered him one. He refused, of course. He gave up smoking when he gave up his thumbs. "All right," I said. "It would be possible—if I wanted to do it. But I don't like the sound of it."

"For three hundred patacas, perhaps you will like the sound of my proposition."

"That's a nice piece of change. What do you want slipped in his pocket?"

"A packet of Hong Kong dollars."

Through the wall, the muffled sounds of the orchestra suddenly cut out and I knew it was the three-minute break before the floor show. But I didn't let it bother me. I just listened to my master's voice, and tried to make some sense out of what he was saying.

"In other words," I said, "you want to hire my hands to drop some English money in your friend's pocket. What is he, one of your charities?"

"My reasons need not concern you. I said it was a simple favor, and I offered to pay you well."

I took a drag on my cigarette. "Would you be insulted if I said your deal smells as fishy as your Macao water front?"

"You are entitled to your opinions."

"Thanks for that, anyway."

Three hundred patacas for about three minutes' work. I could use the money, all right, but saying yes to the deal made me feel uncomfortable.

I said yes anyway. What the hell, there was no law against giving money away. I put out my cigarette. "Let's get down to details."

He rose with a grin and produced a crisp packet of Hong Kong bills. He tossed it on my dressing table. It was funny how he had learned to hold his hands, the fingers curled almost to a fist, so you didn't miss the thumbs. Then he brought out his wallet and extracted three hundred patacas for me.

"Who's the guy?"

"He is seated at table eleven. It is on the right, beside a pillar. Just before you go on I will have a camera girl stop at his table. She will start a small argument with him. You watch."

"I'll watch for him," I said. "Do you want to tell me his name?"

"His name, senhor, is not important."

I looked at the money he had thrown on my dressing table, and tried to talk myself out of the deal. But I couldn't think of any good reasons for not earning some easy money. All I had to go on was an uneasy feeling that I was being played for some kind of sucker.

"Tonight, during your performance," Senhor Gonsalves asked. "you can accomplish it?"

"Tip off Lascal to hold the floor show on your way out."

He nodded with that thin smile of his, and I watched him close the door as he left. I stood there getting a little mad about the whole thing. Then I sat down and rubbed on my make-up.

Chapter Two

I was pulling on my boiled shirt when I heard the fanfare from the orchestra, which meant I had five or six minutes. As the headline act, I was entitled to close the show, which was a three-act affair in the Magellan Room. But when I tried it I fell flat as the closer, for a damned good reason, and switched myself to second place. The reason: a Greek strip artist had been booked in months ago, and in the Magellan Room, where it was expected, she peeled right down to her talcum powder. No magician can follow the facts of life, even when the stripper has lost the first bloom of youth, and our Lady Godiva was no eighteen-year-old chicken. So I let her close the show, which made me pretty popular with her, and gave myself a chance with the audience before the trauma of sex set in.

It was silent out there now, and I knew Lascal was introducing the opening act. I hooked on my tie and slipped into my tails. The packet of Hong Kong dollars still lay where Senhor Gonsalves had tossed it on my dressing table. I broke the paper band and counted the money. There were ten crisp $1,000 bills. The whole thing amounted to a little less than U.S. $2,000 at the current rate, and that struck me as a tidy sum to give away.

I paused for a moment, planning the best way to manage the loading problem. Then I rolled the money into a tight tube and fixed it with a rubber band. That made it about the size of a king-size cigarette, and I tried palming it. I used a finger grip, and it palmed smoothly.

I went to my wardrobe trunk and picked out a wire gimmick that would hold it. I pinned the gimmick under the tail of my coat, out of sight, and loaded the tube of money. Half the battle was over.

Through the wall I was getting a little music and sensed that the opening act, a Chinese tumbling team, was approaching its finale, I checked my other gimmicks, slipped into white gloves, and put a deck of cards into my pocket. I looked in the mirror and got my top hat on at the jaunty angle I liked. My face, in the reflection, looked suddenly strange to me. Was that really me, a guy with dark, nervous eyes and a cleft chin? You look tired, Flemish, tired and lonely. Even the make-up won't cover it up, will it? Hell, that can't be you. It's just a trick. It's done with mirrors.

I shrugged my shoulders and stopped talking to myself. I wheeled my props out of the dressing room.

When I got to the doorway that opened into the night club, I found Phebe Bion checking the audience from between the golden drapes. She wore a kimono loose from her shoulders, she was barefooted, and she wore a snakeskin costume that was covered with sequins. Phebe was the stripper.

We had found a common language, French, which she spoke effortlessly and I spoke like a third-year tourist. She was trying to learn English and kept practicing, at least on me. *"Bon soir,"* she said, turning when I came up behind her. *"Mon dieu, la jeune fille—she* is *très jolie,* but very pretty, m'sieu."

I looked down at her. "'What girl?"

She smiled coyly. "On the terrace. I saw. *Quelle jolie jeune fille!* I am jealous, m'sieu."

Maybe she was trying to be amusing, but her remarks rattled me. I hadn't noticed her on the terrace, and I thought it a little odd that she had paid any attention to an American girl who had invited me to her room. I hadn't made a play for Phebe, mainly because the first time I saw her she was naked under the spotlight. I didn't like playing around with public property.

"You know her long, m'sieu?"

"Let's forget it," I said. "And I wish you wouldn't call me m'sieu. Call me Bruce or Flemish or hey, you."

"I will call you—*mon chéri.* O.K.?"

Nothing sounds stranger than "O.K." on a foreign tongue. I said, "Suit yourself."

The Chinese tumblers were going into a series of fast spins and it was a matter of seconds before they would be through. I tried to see beyond them to the tables in order to pick out my mark, but the spotlight cast everything but the tumblers into blackness. I would have to wait. Then a young Chinese waiter came toward the drapes and I let him through. I used him to wheel my cart of props out on the floor after I made my entrance.

Finally the tumblers finished, the band held them there for their bows, and the floor lights came up. The applause was general, but only polite, which was all you could expect from a drinking crowd in Macao unless you really worked for it. Lascal stepped to the floor mike, and I was next. He doubled in brass as band leader and m.c., a lanky Swiss just rounding out a solid year at the Magellan Room.

The tumblers passed by us in a happy sweat, breathing heavily and smiling big. Phebe and I smiled back as if they were terrific, despite the crowd. I could hear Lascal's nasal voice giving me a build-up, something he did in a mixture of languages to accommodate the mixed crowd. I peered out over the floor now that the lights were up. My eyes started to roam, but stopped almost at once on a fleshy guy in a seersucker suit. He had come up on the elevator with me, chewing those damned watermelon seeds, and it bothered me to see him out there. He was alone at a ringside table looking very pleased with himself.

Then I spotted the camera girl moving down the table aisle on my right. I watched her and felt like a damned conspirator. She stopped at a table near the bandstand, and even before she started her little argument, I felt as if I had walked into a crazy house.

There were two people at that table. I was prepared for the man, the British importer. He didn't bother me. But the girl sitting with him at the table did.

It was the brunette who had approached me on the terrace. Miss Room 362.

My mind went into a fast spin as Lascal's words blared over the amplifiers.

I checked over the Britisher fast, but from the distance he was just a tall guy in a summer tux. I had expected an older man, and probably bald at that, but he looked somewhere in his early thirties, and his dark hair had an impeccable part that I could see across the room. My hands clutched the drapes for my entrance and I fought off an attack of nerves. I tried to think about those three hundred patacas, easy money, forget the girl, forget the warning about her. I tuned in on Lascal.

"And now, ladies and gentlemen, *minhas senhoras e meus senhores*. I give you that light-fingered gentleman, straight from a record-smashing European tour, the great magician, *o ilustre prestidigitador*—Bruce Flemish! Watch your wallets!"

Great little joke.

The floor lights faded and the spotlight caught me as I broke through the gold drapes. There was some enthusiastic applause from the regulars who had seen me before and the Chinese waiters who loved me because Orientals go crazy for magic. I reached the mike with all my pretty teeth showing. I had to keep that smile going for the next ten minutes.

I got into my act, but all I could see under the blazing spot were my hands manipulating coins in a Miser's Dream routine. For the first time in years, my hands had a slight tremble to them. That made me angry, because they were telling me I was a lot more disturbed than I wanted to be. What the hell kind of deal had I walked into? A strange girl makes a pass at you on the terrace and then turns up with a guy on the receiving end of an anonymous gift of Hong Kong dollars. I went through my routine mechanically. At least this part of the act was pantomime and I could think about other stuff.

I was frying under the spot and perspiration soaked through my shirt. I finished the Miser's Dream and a ripple of applause came back at me. I wasn't doing so hot. I usually got a burst of applause.

My hands became restless, and my muscles felt tight and unreliable. I was going to have to relax if I was going to get through the rest of the act without a slip.

I picked up a fancy silver dagger from my cart of props, balanced the deck on the blade, and tossed the cards into the air. They scattered and cascaded. I lunged with the dagger, and when the cards had fluttered to the floor, I showed four of them impaled on the blade. They were the four aces.

I showed my teeth and got a good response from the crowd. Hell, all they need is warming up, I thought. I'm doing all right.

Within a few minutes I'd reach that part of the act when I could load that money, and I played with the idea of letting the opportunity pass. It wasn't too late to walk out on the deal. Give Senhor Gonsalves back his dough and tell him to go fly a kite.

I kept playing with the idea right up to the last minute. The floor lights were on for my feature trick, a bar act, and I asked people to call out the names of drinks. I poured about a dozen different drinks from the same cocktail shaker.

Suddenly I heard from the man in the seersucker suit. "If you please, ol' man—a spot of gin."

He sat there grinning on my left. I began to hate that guy, and I didn't know why. I poured his gin, walked to his table, and set the drink down.

"Bravo, my lad," he muttered. "Bloody clever."

I managed to hold onto my smile and returned to the mike. This was where I earned the three hundred patacas. I looked around at the Britisher. "Anyone can do this trick, ladies and gentlemen," I said. "I'll prove it to you."

I worked over to the edge of the table where he sat with the American girl. The Britisher watched, unsmiling, and twirled the stem of his glass. The spotlight followed me to the table, and the three of us were all lit up. The girl glowered, and he looked daggers at me.

I held out the cocktail shaker for him to examine and he put his feelings in words. His voice was a firm whisper.

"Get lost, brother. Leave me out of this."

We traded glances, and something jarred in my head.

This guy was no Britisher. The voice was strictly American.

I shoved the cocktail shaker into his hand. "Examine it," I said. "Here, get on your feet so everyone can see what you're doing."

I'd look silly if I let him turn me down and I forgot about everything but getting him into the act. I got a tight grip on his arm and felt his muscles tighten as I helped him up. He knew he was licked and put a makeshift smile on his face. O.K., he was in the act.

I went into a few hits of business, and pretty soon he was pouring drinks from the shaker he thought was empty. I asked for champagne, but all he could get to come out was milk. It was a laugh.

My fingers fell behind the tail of my coat and I took a grip on the roll of Hong Kong money dangling from the gimmick. I palmed away the dough, but even as I did I began to realize I couldn't go ahead with it. Maybe I got the money in my hand to satisfy my professional pride: I was skillful enough to do it if I wanted to. But I sensed now that Gonsalves' deal was more than irregular; there was a vague element of personal danger in this thing. As I had worked in close to the guy, getting him on his feet, I had brushed against something hard and unmistakable under his coat.

It felt snug and small in a holster slung over his shoulder. The gun didn't frighten me; it only made me feel like a sucker. Gonsalves' sucker. Let him go fly that kite. I crumpled the tube of money in my fist.

Then I jammed it into my pocket and remembered to keep smiling.
No one had seen a thing.

The American got back to his chair and there was a good bit of
applause for both of us. Then I cleaned up my act. I could feel the girl's
eyes on me, and they weren't the same eyes she had given me on the
terrace. They were smoldering.

When I got off the floor the applause told me I was a sensation. I
disappeared through the golden drapes and ignored Lascal's call for
an encore.

As soon as I got into my dressing room I closed the door, lit a cigarette, and tried to think. What the hell was going on in this hotel? I
didn't particularly like the looks of the guy with the razor-sharp part
in his hair, but he was an American, and so was the girl and so was I.
As far as Gonsalves knew, I had delivered for him. I put out my cigarette quickly and decided to have a talk with the mark. I felt I owed
him that. And the girl had seemed to me suddenly rather interesting
with anger in her eyes.

When I got some idea where I stood I'd know what to do about
Gonsalves.

I peeled off my coat and got into my street jacket. I didn't take time
to change trousers and left on my stiff shirt, even though it was limp.
Then I went back out front.

The club was black now, with only a lavender spot following Phebe
in her strip. The band was silent except for the pulse beat of a jungle
drum. I felt my way along the aisle between tables and hoped to avoid
Gonsalves.

I glanced at Phebe every few seconds because it was hard not to. She
was no Greek goddess—in fact, she stripped with about as much
grace as a country girl on a dare—but someone had built an act for
her. A real act, and even a third-rate stripper like Phebe could put it
over. Her costume was this sequined snakeskin affair, and one of her
hands was slipped into a glove up to her shoulder. The glove was decorated like a serpent, and the jaws, operated by her fingers, slowly dis-
robed her.

The crowd was very still. Right now that arm was weaving around
her bra, trying to undo it.

I moved along the carpeted path until I came to the table the two
had been sitting at.

It was empty.

I don't know why it made me angry that they had skipped out. I stood for a moment and decided the smartest thing to do was sit down and watch Phebe.

Chapter Three

I sat in the darkness. Under the lone spotlight, Phebe's small breasts swayed rhythmically with her shoulders as she fought that snake hand of hers. In another moment the jaws made strikes at her G string. The drum heat faster and louder and the crowd held its breath.

My eyes were riveted to her movements, but my thoughts wandered. Why not just hand the dough back to Gonsalves and resign from the whole crazy mess? Why bother tipping off that pair of Americans? Let them look out for themselves.

Then it happened. Against the drumbeat in my ears, I hadn't heard movement near me. But I felt it.

A hand brushed my shoulder and then a cold strip of wire touched my throat—and tightened. My hands went for it. My God, some bastard was trying to cut my throat!

I felt the guy's quick breath on the back of my head as the garrote burned into my skin. I clawed to get my fingers under the wire, but there wasn't any slack. God, this was murder in public! I tried to let out a yell, but I didn't have a voice.

My hands lashed out behind my neck and grabbed two thin wrists. He was in a hurry, all right; in a minute Phebe would be finished and the lights would come up. I couldn't take a breath and my head felt swollen. I strained to pull those wrists against me to ease the pressure of the wire, and prayed for lights, but they didn't come on. I was heading for a blackout of my own.

The wrists suddenly disappeared and the garrote relaxed on my throat. I choked for breath and pulled it free. I grabbed for the guy but there was nothing around me but darkness. The ringing in my ears died away and I heard the swelling sounds of the hand. Phebe's act was almost over and the guy knew he had to get out of there.

I stumbled out of the chair and tried to hook onto him, but he had vanished. I stood, weaving on my feet, and clenched the small wooden handles of the garrote. All I could think was: I'll kill you. I'm going to kill you. Phebe was stripped down to her bare feet and the guy at the spot whirled a color wheel on her. There were people at the tables around me and the bastards hadn't seen a thing but Phebe. When the lights came up I was still standing there with the garrote in my hands.

I looked around quickly, but there was no one but me in the aisle. There were wealthy Chinese at the tables, and Portuguese colonials and Hong Kong British, and they were all applauding Phebe. I was aching to throw that piece of wire around someone's throat—but whose?

I gave it up angrily, rubbed my neck, and decided to keep that date with the girl in Room 362.

The door was bleached mahogany and the upper half was louvered. The hall was richly lit but deserted, and as I leaned on the buzzer that lone feeling came over me again. For the past three years I had wandered from Europe to the Middle East and now the Far East. I had been hanging my top hat among strangers and telling myself it was a great life. But there were moments, like now, when I knew I was kidding myself.

Footsteps sounded inside the apartment and the door finally opened.

"Hello," she said. She wasn't smiling.

"I remembered," I said.

"Yes," she muttered. "Men always do, don't they?"

"I don't know," I said. "I'll take your word for it."

I came in and she bolted the door after me. The garrote was coiled up in my pocket, and I couldn't help taking a look at her wrists. That's all I had to go on, a pair of wrists, and I wondered if I'd really recognize the feel of them again. She wore thin silver bracelets, which put me at ease. It had been crazy to think *she* had tried to kill me, but I reminded myself those wrists had been thin and they *could* have been a woman's.

The place looked like a small suite, expensively furnished, with what must have been a nice view from the windows in the daytime. I spotted a bar in the corner and ambled toward it. "Mind if I make myself at home? Where's the guy?"

"Help yourself to the liquor. The guy's not here."

"I can see that. Fix you something?"

"No, thank you."

"I'll fix you something anyway. I don't like to drink alone—unless I'm alone."

She stood in the center of the room, and I could feel her eyes on me as I mixed the drinks. When I finished I carried them to the coffee table and helped myself to a cigarette from a cloisonné box. She followed my movements with a cold stare.

"Sit down," I said.

She stood where she was. "Why did you pick on Phil tonight?"

"Funny," I said. "I've been wondering why everyone's picking on me. Who's Phil?"

"The guy." She held herself erect, and I noticed again she had quite a bit to hold erect. It was really time I took a good look at her.

"I had reasons," I said. "This is fine whisky."

She had slim ankles and her legs were long and willowy like America grows for the whistle trade. She came forward and sat down in a gold brocade chair opposite the coffee table. Her hips had a very fine movement and I admitted to myself they said class. I had learned long ago that a woman tells you more about herself by the way she works her hips than with her mouth. I should have recognized it on the terrace, but her boudoir come-on was blinding. Her green eyes probed me in small glances as she lit a cigarette. Her eyelashes were very black. It was a nice ensemble, but I reminded myself it was all beside the point.

"What reason?" she asked.

"We'll get to that," I said. "You've got a name."

She hesitated. She was a long time answering. "Donna Van Deerlin," she said.

"Nice name," I replied, picking up my glass. "Sounds phony."

"Think what you like."

"Just visiting in Macao?"

"A couple of weeks."

"This place looks lived in. Where are you from?"

"Hong Kong."

"Oh," I said. "Then you're Chinese."

"I grew up in Nevada. Any more questions, Mr. Flemish?"

The whisky warmed my stomach and relaxed my nerves. I wondered why I hadn't noticed her before. With those bangs she was very noticeable. She faced me coolly, as though she wished I hadn't remembered her room number after all.

"Sure," I said. "I've got a lot of questions. I'd like to know what there is about you that makes people want to cut my throat."

She didn't seem surprised. But she was nice enough to say, "I'm sorry."

"Why did you make a pass at me on the terrace?"

Her eyes softened. "I knew you were an American and I had an idea you would help me. Now I'm not sure I'd trust you."

"Now that's sweet," I said. "*You* don't trust *me*."

"When did they—try to kill you?"

I told her about the warning, and I told her about the garrote. I got the wire out of my pocket and showed it to her. "Do you know anybody who carries one of these things?"

"No."

"You don't have a crazy husband in the wings, do you? Are you married to Phil?"

"No. Look, I'm sorry about all this. Why don't you leave and try to forget the whole thing?"

"I never walk out on good whisky," I said. "And I *never* take good advice."

She smiled faintly. I was letting myself get a little angry, or at least show it, and it seemed to amuse her. I got the feeling she really wished I'd get the hell out, so I made up my mind to stay.

"All right," I said, "let's take it apart piece by piece. You trusted my looks out on the terrace, but now I'm no good. Why?"

She killed her cigarette. "Mr. Flemish, there's something odd in the way you pulled Phil into your magic act. Out of all those people you went straight for him. He was probably the one man in the club who really didn't want to get under a spotlight. All right, I'll ask you. Why?"

"Money," I said. "I got an offer of three hundred patacas to do a job on him."

"Who paid you?"

"A guy named Gonsalves. Know him?"

She nodded. "He was a friend of my father's."

"Where's your father?"

"Dead, Mr. Flemish. He was murdered here in Macao several weeks ago."

"Oh."

"Why did Senhor Gonsalves want you to do that to Phil?"

I put down my empty glass. "I was hoping you could tell me. I was supposed to drop some Hong Kong currency in your friend's pocket. Does that make any sense to you?"

"Did you do it?"

"No. That's one reason I came here. I thought Phil might be here with the answers. By the way, does he have a last name?"

"Jordan. You could be lying."

"Look, sister, if I wanted to lie I could think up a better story than that."

She rose and started walking around, her jaws tight and her eyes low and preoccupied. I don't know why I hadn't detected it earlier, but I saw now that Donna Van Deerlin was frightened. She had been scared all the while I had been sitting here, but now it finally showed. It showed in the way she seemed to forget I was in the room, it showed in the way she cradled and stroked her arms, as though she were cold. I felt myself drawn to her, and that made me feel uncomfortable. This kid went around giving guys the kiss of death. Making a pass at her would be cuddling up to a high-voltage wire.

"Well?" I said.

She turned absently. "Your glass is empty. Let me fill it."

"Never mind that. Gonsalves' dough is burning a hole in my pocket. Sit down and tell me where the hell I fit into what's going on around here."

"Do you have any idea who Philip Jordan is?" she asked.

"How would I know?"

She sat down. "He's supposed to be an American. I wish I knew for sure."

"He talks like an American. Isn't that enough?"

"No, not in this—business."

"What business?"

She hesitated. I couldn't tell if she were beginning to trust me or get her claws into me. "Espionage. You know this hotel is full of spies."

"No," I said, "I didn't know. But I think I'm beginning to lose a taste for your whisky."

"I've got something they're after."

"Are we talking about sex?"

"Please—"

"What do you expect me to do? Go out and buy myself a cloak and dagger because you made eyes at me on the terrace?"

"I *had* to find an American to help me. I couldn't trust anyone but an American."

"Jordan's an American."

"Maybe."

"O.K., maybe. For all you know I'm a Commie myself."

She picked a cigarette out of the box and lit it nervously. "I'm willing to take a chance," she muttered. "I've got to. I got a little frightened of you when you picked Phil out of the crowd. I'm not frightened of you now."

"Listen, you're so goddamned scared of something, if I yelled boo you'd have to head for the bathroom."

Her green eyes flashed with quick anger. "*Must* you be rude?"

"Yes," I said. "I must."

I was having a strange reaction to her, as though she were two people. One I wanted to know better and the other I wanted to stick pins in. As a nice kid with crazy black bangs, she stirred something in me. But as a nervous *femme fatale* she made me a little sick.

"You don't have to stay," she said.

"I'll listen until it gets too deep."

Her eyes avoided me. Her lips parted, but she seemed to be having trouble deciding what words to use. She said finally, "There's something I want taken out of Macao. To Hong Kong."

"And you elected me."

"Yes."

"My, but you've got a sense of humor."

"I know I'm making a mess of this," she added in a quick, desperate voice, "but I'm doing the best I can. My God, stop laughing at me!"

I rocked the ice cubes in my empty glass. I began to see why someone was attempting to discourage this kid from making friends and influencing people. "All right," I said, "I'll stop laughing."

"I'm an amateur at espionage," she admitted softly. "My father wasn't. He discovered something in Macao, and he was killed. I came here to find out why. I found out. He made a report, and I want to get it out of Macao. Jordan was helping me, but I've stopped trusting Jordan."

"So you don't want to hand this report over to him."

"Thanks for saying that," she muttered. "At least you're listening to me."

"But me, I'm just a perfect stranger—you trust strangers?"

"Don't you, Mr. Flemish?"

"You're pretty strange. I don't know whether I trust you or not. What is this gimmick you're in an uproar over?"

"Just—some information."

"That's telling me, baby."

"I'm sorry."

She got up and walked to the open window. I should have left long ago, I told myself. Espionage was for the other guy, not me. It still wasn't too late to pull out. But I sat there, because something wouldn't let me ditch this kid. I didn't like the idea that someone was trying to scare me away from her. If I pulled out, it would make that bastard think I could be pushed around.

"Why would Gonsalves want me to stick money in your friend's pocket?" I asked. It seemed as though I'd been asking that question all night.

"It sounds like a pay-off. My father trusted Gonsalves, but I'm not sure I do."

"Isn't that an elaborate way to make a payment?"

"Yes. They do things that way."

"Is Gonsalves a Red?"

She turned away from the windows and faced me. "I don't know. Gonsalves is very close to the governor general of Macao. But he could be playing a double game. He used to give Dad tips. But times are changing so fast here, you can't be sure of anyone. He doesn't know I'm Robert Chandler's daughter. Dad made a mistake somewhere and was killed. I'm trying not to repeat the mistake."

"So your name's Chandler, not Van Deerlin."

"I'm using Van Deerlin in Macao. I'm trusting you with my real name. I hope you'll—"

"Sure."

"Don't you see, if Jordan told anyone I was bringing the report Dad made to the hotel tonight, I'll never get it out of Macao."

"You have it *with* you?"

"Yes."

"Baby, you *are* an amateur. How did you get it?"

"That's not important. Take it to Hong Kong. Turn it over to the authorities. No one here would suspect you as a courier."

"Does Phil know you're carrying the thing?"

"At the moment, he thinks he has it."

"Let's play that over again."

She came across the room to her straw bag on the coffee table. She poked around in it, her face set, and withdrew a red firecracker. "They make firecrackers in Macao," she said. "But this one is different."

I put out my cigarette and took the firecracker out of her fingers. I bounced it on my palm. It was a funny feeling. Dry, light—explosive. "What exactly is in it?"

"My Dad's report. It's coded, so don't bother trying to read it. I turned a fake one over to Phil during your act. He told me he would take it straight to Hong Kong. He was on the verge of leaving when you got the spotlight on him."

"No wonder he was sore about it."

"He may have taken it straight to Senhor Gonsalves—or someone else. Before very long he's sure to discover I deceived him."

It was a wild story, from beginning to end, but I believed it. I believed it because I didn't like Gonsalves, I didn't like Phil—and I did like Donna Chandler. It was a crazy sort of logic, but I closed a fist over the firecracker and said to hell with logic.

She watched my fist and smiled faintly. "Thanks—Bruce."

"Don't jump to conclusions," I snapped. "I'm swallowing your story, but I'm not going to be your errand boy to Hong Kong. You're forgetting someone made a pass at me with a garrote just because you flapped your eyelashes at me. I'd never get there, baby, and neither would your firecracker."

"I'm *desperate!*"

"Sure, for a sucker. For God's sake, use your head. I'm already marked."

She sat down and seemed to get a cold grip on herself.

"All right," she muttered. "I'll manage myself. I'm sorry I bothered you. May I have it back, please?"

I stared at her a long time. I think I'd have liked to slap her around. She sat there calling me a coward with her eyes and I knew there was no sense trying to make her understand. I asked myself what difference it made to me what she thought. It made me angrier still that I felt it did make a difference. I liked some hidden part of her that I could barely see for the spies and firecrackers. Hell, why couldn't she be a nice, simple kid with nothing more complicated on her mind than sex?

I got up and I stopped thinking clearly. "All right, sweetheart," I snapped. "You've found yourself a sucker."

They don't come any bigger, I added to myself.

I got out my pack of Chesterfields and juggled things around until I had the firecracker concealed under the covered end. I walked to the door. I had no money for a fast trip to Hong Kong, unless I held onto the dough Gonsalves had left with me, but I hadn't earned it and I wanted to wipe my hands of it. I was damned if I was going to ask *her* for money. I turned at the door. She stood beside the chair, watching me. "Phil is liable to be a little rough when he finds out you slipped him a phony, isn't he?" I asked.

"I suppose so."

"Well?"

"I'll think of something."

"Whatever you think of, he won't believe you."

"Please—you'd better go before he gets back."

"Baby, I'm going to come back from Hong Kong just to find out what makes you tick."

Chapter Four

I felt like a guy who wandered on the stage of a puppet show and discovered someone attaching strings to him. It's a weird feeling, and makes you want to run like hell.

Walk, don't run, to the elevator, I told myself.

I got out on the seventh floor. Gonsalves' offices were there.

The seventh floor was one expansive gambling casino. The air buzzed with voices in crosscurrent, and the busiest tongues of all were those of the Chinese croupiers at the fan-tan and three-dice tables. Most of the patrons were in summer evening dress, except some of the rich Chinese refugees, who stuck to their silk gowns. The floor itself was a bright mosaic of tiles, and my heels made a racket as I crossed to the offices along one side.

I wanted to see Gonsalves. I wanted to return his money, play it innocent, and tell him to get off my back. I needed dough, but I didn't want his. I had no idea how much it would take for the trip to Hong Kong. The steamer didn't leave until tomorrow noon, so that was out. I'd want to go right away, just after my two-o'clock show, and that meant hiring some fishing junk to make the forty-mile crossing.

I paused with my hand on the doorknob and gazed out over the gambling scene. The idea came with a bang. Why not? Take a chance with a couple of those Hong Kong bills. I might be lucky. I was already risking my neck: what difference would it make if I risked some of Gonsalves' money? If I got a break, I could win enough in five minutes to finance a quick round trip, and Gonsalve would never know the difference.

It was a crazy idea, but I couldn't shake it.

I left the door and looked around for an empty chair at one of the fan-tan tables. I found one by the windows, and got out the crumpled tube of Hong Kong bills. A game had just finished, and I looked at the silver plate inlaid before me in the table. You place your bet along one of the four sides. One chance in four to win.

I pushed one of those bills along the Number One side of the plate, because I felt lucky about that number. H.K. $1,000 isn't peanuts, but in the Hotel China Seas it's not enough to raise anyone's eyebrows.

The croupier started his tongue going again and overturned a large rice bowl of Chinese cash. He began detaching the brass coins four at a time with an ivory rake. You've got to guess how many he'll be left with on the final stroke to win—one to four. It's a lousy way to gamble when you could be playing poker or blackjack, but they don't play poker or blackjack in Macao.

I got out my cigarettes and watched the pile of cash dwindle. I hadn't felt any particular sensation at carrying the firecracker until then. I pulled out a cigarette quickly and felt a tremor of panic. Good God, I thought, get that pack out of sight. Give up smoking for a few hours, if you have to.

"American cigarettes, yes?"

The voice came from the guy on my left. He had a thin, deeply lined face, and his suit fitted him as if he'd recently lost a lot of weight. His smile bore down on me through perfectly round glasses in steel rims.

"What about it?" I said. The croupier kept chattering, his rake flicking at the cash.

"I would like to smoke an American cigarette. I like everything American. Are you an American?"

"The cigarette girls carry American brands," I said. "I'm almost out."

He shrugged his narrow shoulders amiably. "It doesn't matter. My remarks were only by way of introduction. I am Josef Nakov. A Russian name, of course, but you understand, White Russian. Formerly of Canton, now of Macao,"

I turned back to the game and ignored him. But he kept talking to me.

"I am a writer, you know. One of my books has been translated in your country."

"I don't read," I muttered.

"But of course, you are joking. All Americans can read."

I turned on him angrily. "Am I bothering you?"

"No, no." He grinned eagerly. "Would you believe it, I write your Western story. They have quite a popularity in this part of the world. I would like very much to visit your Arizona. Do you come from Arizona?"

I tried to tune him out, but his voice kept going through my head. The croupier was reaching the end of his count, and attention around the long table was sharply focused. No one seemed to be talking except the croupier and Josef Nakov.

"You would like a drink? Let me buy you a drink."

"*I don't drink,*" I shouted.

The game was over. Three brass coins remained before the croupier. The table broke into noise as the cashier began raking in the bets and paying off the winners. I was not one of them.

I watched the curled Hong Kong bill move toward him under the sweep of the rake. I decided to try one more time.

"Perhaps you would like—"

I spun on him. "Will you shut up!"

I hadn't meant for my voice to burst *that* loudly, but I couldn't help it. The little guy was driving me crazy with his yapping.

His eyebrows rose and his brown eyes, enlarged grotesquely by the lens, turned a crushed look on me.

"I'm sorry," I said suddenly. "Why don't you just leave me alone?"

"It is my fault."

"I hope you get to Arizona someday."

He was betting patacas, and he had lost too. He turned now to his money and considered a new bet.

When I glanced at the cashier, I saw he was examining the curled bill I had lost. He held it very close to his eyes, almost like a jeweler looking at the bowels of a watch. One thing about Chinese money handlers—they don't trust anybody's dough. I watched him as he rubbed the bill between his dark fingers. He passed the bill to the croupier, and they conferred. I knew something was wrong and my heart began to react. The next game was being held up, and everyone at the table was noticing now.

It happened.

The cashier clamped the gimlet eye on me and pushed the bill at me with his rake. "Money no good," he said in a tight little voice. "Coun'feit."

My mind spun. If this guy said the bill was phony, it was phony. What sort of pay-off was Gonsalves making with counterfeit money?

"Sorry," I heard myself say. "I didn't know."

Someone at the table laughed.

I got up, and saw that the cashier was going to let me pick up my homemade marbles without making trouble. I jammed out my cigarette and a dozen pairs of eyes grinned at me.

"Please." Josef Nakov smiled. "I shall be honored to make it good."

"Forget it," I muttered. I folded up the bills and stuck them out of sight in my pocket. I goddamned Gonsalves and felt mad enough to kill. What sort of chump had he played me for?

When I turned to leave, I was burning with anger.

So was Senhor Gonsalves.

He was standing behind my chair, his hands jammed in his pockets, an ice-water look in his eyes, and his heavy lips trembling with controlled rage.

All right, so he knew. He knew I had double-crossed him, he saw I hadn't stuck those Hong Kong bills in Jordan's pocket. "How about that, senhor?" I grinned contemptuously. "Someone slipped me a batch of job printing and told me it was money."

"That's a pity," he answered softly. It was clearly an effort for him to keep his voice under control and his hands in his pockets. He had to play it nice and smooth until we got out of there, or create a scene. The game at my table had resumed, and I could hear the croupier's strident voice carry it along. Gonsalves gave his head an almost imperceptible nod in the direction of his office. "We will talk privately."

It was all I could do to keep myself from throwing the money in his face. "Let's," I said.

We crossed the casino to the entry door and I followed him along a hall that served half a dozen busy rooms—the brain cells of Gonsalves' financial empire. We passed through a heavy door at the end and entered his private office.

The yellow Oriental rug was so thick you felt it needed mowing. The walls were pale green under indirect lighting. There were lots of pictures around the office, all of men in white military uniforms, with dates engraved on brass plates set in the frames. I assumed this was a gallery of Macao's governors general, past and present. The office was spacious, but very sparsely furnished. "Let's get it over with," I said.

"Sit down," he snapped in a brisk voice.

"I don't plan to stay that long."

He had taken a green leather swivel chair behind a heavy desk and stared up at me. "Senhor Flemish, you are a man without honor."

"Never mind the lecture," I said. "Here's your dough. Your British importer had an American voice, and he carried a gun. Those were two reasons why I changed my mind. I don't like pulling things on Americans."

He hardly glanced at the money I dropped on the desk. He said in a taunting voice, "Do you like Macao, senhor?"

"What's that got to do with it?"

"You may stay forever if you don't watch your step. Forever."

"Are you threatening me?"

"Warning you, only. I am not a murderer, senhor. Others in Macao are. You have made dangerous friends."

"I haven't made any friends," I shot back.

His anger was coming under control; his dark eyes steadied on me, like a scientist watching for reactions in a laboratory animal. "I have observed an interesting friendship develop between you and the Senhorita Donna Van Deerlin—or rather Chandler."

"You don't miss a lick, do you?"

"It is my job, senhor, to keep informed."

"Are you the bastard who's been trying to persuade me to lay off?"

"I do not understand."

"I'll bet. Look, there's your money. I don't blame you for being sore that I went back on you, but think about it and maybe you'll understand. Now keep out of my hair, and if it's all the same to you, I'll pick up with anyone I feel like."

"I understand, senhor."

"That's swell."

"It is you who does not understand."

He folded up the money and slipped it into a drawer of his desk. I was ready to leave, but his words had a sharp cutting edge. I couldn't walk out on them. I wanted a cigarette badly, but I couldn't bring myself to take out my pack. "All right, I'm listening," I said.

"You must appreciate my position, senhor. I am Macanese. My ancestors settled Macao. We Macanese, we have a great responsibility to the colony. There are a few patriots in Macao. We Macanese are the patriots. Sit down, senhor."

It seemed the thing to do now. I sat down.

"Once, senhor, the Japanese stood across the Porto do Cerco, ready to invade our small colony. Macao remained free by using its brains, while even Hong Kong fell. So now we are threatened again, but this time it is the Communists. And again we must resort to wits instead of guns. How long would our garrison of five thousand last against the Reds?"

"What are you getting at?"

"Senhor, as you know, I am a friend of the governor general. He honors me by entrusting to my hands the espionage problem here. The Reds need us as an open door through which the products of other nations may flow. It is vital that we give no cause for the Red dragon to grow angry at us. Your friends, senhor, are making us trouble. It is dangerous for us to harbor spies working against our *kun-chan* neighbors."

"Doesn't anyone have a conscience in Macao?"

"Of course, senhor. It is desirable that all espionage activity be stamped out here—against your country as well. Macao is like Switzerland. We must fight to remain neutral. My job, as counterespionage chief, is to aid in this fight. I ask for your help."

"Aren't you forgetting? I'm a guy without honor."

"The senhorita has approached you for good reasons. She and Jordan are a very clever professional team, senhor. They work, as you say, both sides of the street. And they have chosen to make a fool of you."

"Thanks for the tip." I let him keep talking, but cautioned myself against falling for his line. He had reasons for talking so freely to me, and it wasn't because he was naturally talkative.

Gonsalves leaned back in his chair, his eyes firmly on me. "Until a few minutes ago, senhor, I did not know the senhorita was Jordan's accomplice. Had I known that earlier, I would not have troubled you to place money in his pocket."

"Are you making sense?"

"Nothing makes sense until you have all the pieces. Jordan is a spy. He lives in the hotel, but he cannot pay his bill. The man is without funds. He has no country behind him. I prefer keeping him in the hotel, where I can keep an eye on him, you understand. So I have his credit extended. I do not own the hotel itself, but I have influence." His eyes didn't leave my face and his voice fell into a monotone, as though he had told his story a dozen times. "It would have been simple enough to remove him from the colony, but I wanted to discover his accomplice as well. Both, I assume, are without funds. So I employ you to place money in his pocket. Does he wonder where it came from? Of course. But does that keep him from using it? No. Some he gives to his accomplice. The moment that person attempts to spend the counterfeit money, I learn of it. In the East, one must match cunning with cunning."

"You expect me to believe his partner is Donna Chandler?"

"I can prove it, senhor. Then I ask you to do me a favor."

"What? Drop dead?"

"You seem unwilling to give up the dangerous friendship you have acquired. I ask you only to drop it—for your own sake."

"Everybody is full of good advice tonight."

His fleshy lips parted in an impatient grimace. "I told you, senhor, I discovered the senhorita's role a few minutes ago—unexpectedly. I was dumfounded. I knew her father. He was a very honorable man." He took a hand out of his pocket and pressed a lever on an intercom box on the desk. "Gilberto, bring the recording in here."

I was dying for a smoke, and I felt uncomfortable sitting around his office when I had that loaded firecracker in my pocket. I didn't want to hear any more from Gonsalves. He was knocking himself out trying to put the chill on Donna, and I was still uncertain enough of her so that I knew he might succeed. I didn't like to consider the possibility that she and Jordan were a professional team free-lancing secrets. I started to rise.

"In a moment you can leave, senhor. As you say in your business, the finale is coming up."

A tall Portuguese came in. This would be Gilberto. He ignored me and handed a flat spool to Senhor Gonsalves. It looked like a tape recording, and my mind began to reach out for possibilities. The Portuguese left the office silently, a guy who carried himself with the muscular poise of an athlete.

Gonsalves slid open a panel in a wall cabinet and threaded the celluloid tape through a recording machine. He flicked on the playback, and settled back in his chair.

My jaws clenched as I looked from him to the machine. And then the recorder began to speak.

A woman's voice: "Hello."

A man's voice : "I remembered."

"Yes. Men always do, don't they?"

"I don't know. I'll take your word for it."

My pulse leaped with the words. That was Donna's voice. That was my voice. Gonsalves had tapped our conversation in Room 362, right from the beginning.

That meant he knew I had taken the firecracker—that I had it with me!

My fingers tightened involuntarily along the arms of the chair. That Portuguese muscle man would be standing outside the door, waiting for trouble. Gonsalves wasn't through with me, by any means. He had been putting me through the softening-up process with his talk.

The recording played on, our voices filling the office. Gonsalves listened intently, studying it as though for things he might have missed on an earlier hearing.

Think fast, I told myself. Gonsalves will ask you to hand over the firecracker. You won't be able to deny what you have agreed to half an hour ago in Room 362—not with the evidence on tape. What had I said? "All right, sweetheart. You've found yourself a sucker." Had I put in words that I was slipping the firecracker in my cigarette pack? No. I thought not. I hoped not.

Our conversation droned on, flurries of argument, long silences, the clink of our glasses against the coffee table. Gonsalves must have planted a dozen microphones in that room. Our strange, recorded voices went on saying familiar things. I wanted to jam a foot in the machine, but it was too late for that. I searched my brain for some way out of the office.

Gonsalves was concentrating on what he heard; his eyes, even when they weren't on me, told me he was confident of the position he had me in.

There was only one door out of the office, and I knew I'd be stripped to my skin and searched if I tried to play hero. I sweated out the recording—and grabbed at an idea.

I got out my pack as casually as I could and withdrew a cigarette. I twisted up the pack as though it were empty and tossed it in the wastebasket beside the desk. Then I lit the cigarette, and tried to keep a quietly smoldering expression on my face.

Had Gonsalves noticed? Wasn't it natural to smoke a cigarette when you wanted one, wasn't it natural to toss the empty pack away?

"Gonsalves is very close to the governor general of Macao," Donna was telling me over the recording. "But he could be playing a double game.... He doesn't know I'm Robert Chandler's daughter."

Gonsalves grunted when he heard that.

I drew on the cigarette, dreading the moment the tape would end and Gonsalves would face me with an outstretched palm. Four fingers, no thumb.

A couple of minutes later it ended, and Gonsalves switched off the machine. He looked at me a long time before speaking. The thing to do, I decided, was put up a fight getting out of the office. Force him to think I had the firecracker on me, then let him wonder how I had concealed it so well. As far as I could tell at the moment, he had dismissed or hadn't consciously recorded my small action in discarding the cigarette package.

"You can understand now," he said slowly, "why I said she was making a fool of you."

"What are you trying to hand me?"

"Senhor, you do not understand after all. Hasn't it occurred to you that the senhorita knew the room was wired?"

"Like hell!"

"She knew the conversation would he overheard by me. She planned it exactly so."

"You'll have to take it away from me, Gonsalves."

"Don't be a child. Why didn't she take you to her own room? Instead she used Jordan's, which has been wired for some time. Do you suppose that firecracker you carry has anything in it but powder? You are their decoy. She believes now we will follow you, while she and her partner slip away. But she underestimates me."

I was on my feet. Maybe he was making sense, but I fought against believing it. "I might as well go," I steamed. "You know all the answers."

"Shall we open the firecracker and see? It is a simple thing to prove."

He was giving himself away, I thought desperately. He wasn't sure of his own reasoning. And he knew I could have ditched the firecracker before coming into the casino. This was the easy way out, easier than having Gilberto work me over. Talk me into giving myself away.

I jabbed out my cigarette in a polished ash tray that looked as though it had never been used. "Let's get it over with," I snapped. "Do I walk out of here, or fight my way out?"

His eyes peered at me between short, dark lashes that seemed almost never to blink. "It is for your sake, senhor, that I have taken so much trouble with you. If you wish to continue playing the fool, you are free to go. There will be no fight. I am experienced at these things; you are not."

"Thanks."

"Adeus, senhor."

I felt suddenly reluctant to leave. My brain was on fire. I wanted to dive into that wastebasket and break open the firecracker. The answer was there. Gonsalves was so goddamned sure of himself he was letting me walk out of his office. Or did he suspect the wastebasket?

I got to the door, afraid to make any decisions. He *could* have out-foxed himself on the recording; the firecracker might be dynamite.

His voice stopped me when I got my hand on the knob. "I understand, senhor. It is difficult for Americans to distrust each other. That is too had, for your sake."

Gilberto was not waiting outside the door, as I had expected. The hall was clear. I opened the door into the casino and wondered if I knew what the hell I was doing. At least Gonsalves had been nice enough not to fire me.

Chapter Five

It would be easy, I told myself. Let the firecracker go out with the morning trash, and say to hell with the whole lousy business. Let Donna worry about it, let Gonsalves play his angles.

By the time I reached the elevator I had shaken off everything but a sense of humiliation. I asked myself what there was about Donna Chandler that had suspended my judgment. She had thrown a pretty face at me, a shape, and a nervous voice. She had said jump, and I jumped. Why?

I felt like a guy who had been lured to a dark alley and rolled—with his eyes wide open.

I got out of the elevator on the third floor. I wanted a final talk with her. It wouldn't be a long talk. Just long enough to tell her to go to hell.

I paused outside Room 362. Gonsalves had been cool and logical; I found myself hating him for being so persuasive. Some part of me wanted to believe in Donna, but he made that impossible. As I knocked I asked myself if I had really come back to watch Donna's face when I told her what I had done with the firecracker. Her expression would tell me whether or not that firecracker was loaded.

I knocked a couple of times. I waited around. After a few minutes I gave it up. I stood outside the door and told Donna Chandler to go to hell. She was probably on her way to Hong Kong, I thought bitterly. Why kid myself? Gonsalves had called the shots. Exit Bruce Flemish.

On the ninth floor I was back in my element, the Magellan Room, and began to feel myself again. God, Flemish, I said to myself, that was a close shave. Next time a pretty girl flaps her eyelashes at you, kick her out of there. You've been around; stick to the beautiful-but-dumb variety. Keep your nose clean. The domestic life isn't for you. Don't go around looking for someone to fall in love with. *That* was the trouble with Donna Chandler, wasn't it? She was a kid you might have tumbled for. Forget it.

Lascal's band was taking a break and all I could hear was the breezy rustle of voices and laughter. The sounds and smells of the club refreshed me. I looked at my watch: forty minutes before my next show, the two A.M. I looked around, absorbing the scene hungrily, like a prodigal son coming home. I must have been crazy to fly off into espionage. I passed through the gold drapes into the relative quiet of the dressing room area.

The short hall was deserted. The door on the left, the one directly behind the bandstand, was mine. It was closed, as it was supposed to be. Opposite mine was another door, and it was ajar. Phebe's door. And Phebe's friendly brown eyes were looking at me.

"M'sieu—"

The door opened a little wider and my eyes did the same. I couldn't see all of her, but I could see enough to know she was wearing nothing but skin all the way down. It startled me because I figured her for the frigid type.

"Baby, you're getting punch drunk," I said. "Every time you see a man you take your clothes off."

There was a nervous smile on her face, and I think she was a little embarrassed to be standing there that way. I reminded myself of my recent resolution, but Phebe was quite beautiful, she wasn't very smart, and it looked to me as though she had nothing but sex on her mind. Half of her figure was concealed behind the door, but there was enough showing to keep me there.

She smiled testingly. "You are shocked? *Je vous demande pardon de*—"

She wasn't entirely nude at that, I saw. A lavender ballet slipper was on the one foot showing.

"You don't have to apologize," I said. "I probably wouldn't know you with clothes on."

"Let us speak French," she said. "It is more suitable, *n'est-ce-pas?*" She opened the door wider to let me in. I paused with what must have been a cynical smile on my face. I envisioned Donna standing in the door that way with nothing on her mind but me. But this was Phebe, and that made it amusing. I walked in. Phebe might be no Greek goddess, but she was diverting.

She closed the door after me and spoke French. "I only want to talk to you." She was smiling vaguely.

"As long as we stick to the birds and the bees," I said, "I'm for it."

When I turned she was standing in a sort of pose against the door—all of her.

There was no color wheel flashing on her now, and visibility was perfect. But even as a nude she wasn't very professional. Her breasts were small and shy. Her hips were fine and her skin was a pale olive, but she lacked the usual voluptuous charge of the professional. I sat at her dressing table and lit one of her cigarettes. I kept looking her over, because I'm human. But she stirred no impulses, and I found myself trying to talk myself into the thing.

"Are you through looking?" she asked in a small, warm voice.

She stood there posing, and I realized this was her idea of being seductive. She was just standing there like a picture, and pictures never excited me. That was Phebe's trouble, I decided. She *did* have something to show, but she didn't know how to show it. Someone had built her a nice act, but take that snake glove away from her and all you had was a girl taking her clothes off for pay. Nice kid, but no talent. "You need someone to routine your act," I said.

"What?"

"Never mind. Let it go."

"You are not—interested in me?"

She didn't wait for an answer. She turned her back to me suddenly, as though embarrassment had overtaken her, but even then a mirror on the door threw all of her nakedness back at me. I asked myself how I could sit there smoking a cigarette in a tight little room with that standing a few feet away. It was easy. Maybe she thought stripping first should have inspired a grand passion, but she was realizing now she wasn't being seductive at all.

My eyes looked over her dark hair, haphazardly done up on top as if she were ready to take a shower. I began feeling sorry for her and angry at myself. My eyes followed the graceful lines of her back and hips. I got up and turned her around.

"Phebe, baby," I said, "you're funny. You're got some pretty good equipment, but you've been hanging on that door as if you're afraid I'll walk through it." I picked up her face and kissed her lightly. Her response was hesitant, her arms limp at her sides. "I've been across the hall from you for a month, and suddenly, with a show coming up in half an hour, you can't wait." I pulled her up closer. "Baby, you're funny."

She wore a faint, lazy perfume, and it was only now that I caught it. Suddenly her arms came up my back and her eyes began to smile.

"You made me feel so cheap—just looking. Like a streetwalker."

"Streetwalkers aren't cheap any more." I smiled back.

She laughed, and I felt we were getting somewhere. "There is still time now," she whispered. "If we hurry."

My hands traveled along her back to her waist and I separated her from me. "Hurry, hell. Why don't you relax? Put a little something on, and we'll start over again. It might be more fun that way. Keep the smile, baby. Let's stage this act right."

She kept the smile, and it helped. She went behind a large rattan screen that only came to her shoulders and I watched her arms twist to fix her bra in place, and then her head bob down as she slipped into her panties. I took the kimono off her wardrobe trunk and threw it over the screen to her. I turned on a small portable radio plugged in beside her make-up case and got some dance music from Radio Hong Kong. She stepped from behind the screen, lit a cigarette, and gave me a hell of a comehither smile.

I came hither.

I caught her hands, pulled the cigarette out of her lips, and kissed them long and hard. She clung to me during those seconds and her whole body trembled. My hands pulled the top of the kimono over her shoulders and stripped it down to the sash. Then I worked at the rest of what she had on and before very long she was right back where she started, but I wasn't. I was feeling real human.

She broke away from me finally and pulled her wardrobe trunk apart. She began throwing silk garments to the floor, yards of colored veils and scarves she used in other strip acts, and pretty soon that floor looked like a sultan's bedroom. Except for chairs, there was no furniture in the room, and I had to hand it to the kid. She had imagination. Finally she turned her eyes up to me and told me to turn out the light.

I did.

A few seconds later she was back in my arms, and it was nice. But in the blackness of the room a weird feeling began to intrude. Even as her breath touched my neck, I felt that something was wrong.

I sensed another person in there with us.

She bit playfully at my ear and I tried to ignore the idea. Moments passed and the silk rustled against us like a friendly breeze.

Then I caught it again—a silent movement in the room. Phebe was hugging me jealously. When I tried to pull back I found myself suddenly trapped in her arms.

A panic shot through me. I tore myself loose from Phebe and threw my arms wildly into the blackness around me. I head Phebe cry out a warning.

My hand caught a strange wrist, and my heart vaulted. Phebe's fingers tried to claw me, holding me back. I shook her lose and held tightly to that wrist. It writhed frantically; it was thin and I knew suddenly I had felt it before.

The guy who had attempted to garrote me—it was his wrist.

I struggled to my feet against the animal fight of the two of them. I swung my free fist where I thought the guy's head ought to be. My fist rocked against hard skin and bone and the force tore him loose from my other grip. I heard his body crash against the dressing table and the wild scatter of perfume bottles. A chair overturned and struck my legs. Phebe was yelling at me.

I got to the light and snapped it on.

He was lying with his face against the floor, one knee folded under him. His position was deathly still, and I looked at him with murder in my eyes.

It was the White Russian. Josef Nakov.

Phebe's eyes were on him and she seemed almost hypnotized by his motionless form. Then she sprang to him almost like a frightened cat and picked up his wrist. I saw that he had been in the act of collecting my clothing in the dark. I realized now what their game had been. They thought Donna had given me the firecracker. Nakov would examine my things while Phebe kept me occupied. No wonder Gonsalves had let me walk out of his office. He had a surprise party all set up for me.

Phebe's eyes caught mine. She said very slowly, and very clearly, in English, "He's dead."

I didn't believe her. The guy would be unconscious from cracking his head on the floor. I ignored her and picked up my clothes.

"He tried to kill me tonight with a garrote," I said finally. "Why?"

"He did not try to kill you," she protested. "He meant only to warn you."

"He'll come around in a couple of minutes. Tell him to lay off me. Tell him I'll beat his brains out if he gets in my way again." I got myself back together and picked up my coat.

She was getting herself under control. "You have already killed him."

"Don't be ridiculous."

She was holding his wrist. I bent down and felt the pulse for myself.

It was beating, and I didn't think I had even knocked him out. The guy was only playing possum.

But Phebe wasn't. She had risen beside me. She was still naked and maybe that made her seem harmless. I don't know what she struck my head with, but it dropped me with a single blow.

The last thing I remember as my eyes stopped seeing were her painted toes.

Chapter Six

There was something in my hand. It was the first sensation of consciousness. There was something in my hand, and I knew what it was. It had the cold, polished surface of the handle of my dagger, the one I used in the card trick. My fingers were closed into a fist around it.

The second fragment of understanding that cleared my brain was that my chest was under a weight. There was something vague and heavy over me, my arm was around it, and my hand held a dagger in it.

I got my eyes open, but there were long moments before I could make sense out of it, and when I did, it still didn't make sense.

I was in my own dressing room, I was stretched out on the floor, there was a man's body across me, and I held a dagger sunk in his back.

A flash of light in the room brought me sharply awake. I turned my head and saw two people standing nearby. My head ached violently, but I didn't let myself think about it. Hovering over me to grab another flash picture was Nakov. Grinning down at me was Senhor Gonsalves.

I rolled the heavy form off me and got unsteadily to my feet.

"You must forgive me for this arrangement," Gonsalves said. "It has become necessary."

I was too confused to say anything. Then the shock of reality hit me. Nakov, using one of the photo girl's cameras, had taken pictures of me in the act of murder. That guy I was posed with was dead. That guy had a sharp part in his hair, hardly disturbed now, which I had once seen across the night-club floor. That guy was Philip Jordan, Donna's partner.

Nakov hurried to the door now that I was on my feet, the camera in his hand. "Two excellent shots," he said to Gonsalves, "In half an hour they will be developed."

Gonsalves nodded for him to get out, as a wave of nausea came over me. I knew I ought to tear the camera apart, destroy the film, but I was heading for the washbasin. The last I saw of Nakov, he had turned a big smile on me, his eyes enlarged buglike by the heavy lenses of his glasses.

I heard Gonsalves lock the door and rustle around the room as I threw cold water in my face. I felt like a guy in a crazy house; every time I thought I had my feet on the floor someone would give the room a spin. I gripped the washbasin and was sick. The intimate memory of that dead body heavy across me tugged at my mind with the intensity of a nightmare. A crazy house. I had hurried toward the door marked exit, Phebe's door, but it wasn't the way out.

I straightened finally and dried my face. I found cigarettes on my dressing table and lit one hungrily. Gonsalves watched me patiently, his hands stuck in his pockets.

"You understand, of course," he said, "the value of the photographs we have just taken. It is true, you appear unconscious in them, but the police will find no trouble believing you struck your head in the struggle as the two of you went down. We were fortunate enough to come in, and thoughtful enough to take pictures. *Sim, sim,* it is perfect evidence."

"You're the best friend a guy ever had," I said weakly. "Go to hell."

He smiled warmly. "Senhor, I do not want you to worry. I shall not turn the film over to the police—unless you make it necessary."

"What have I got to do with it? I go around letting everybody make a sucker out of me. I do it for kicks."

"Senhor, do not think badly of me. Earlier this evening I did everything in my power to discourage you from becoming involved in this unfortunate affair. Now, I discover, I need you. Forget the pictures. I promise they will not be used against you. They are merely a guarantee that you will not attempt to work a double cross, as you Americans term it."

I kept seeing Jordan's body out of the corners of my eyes, even though I tried desperately not to see him at all. He lay on the floor between us. Gonsalves calmly ignored him.

"What are you going to do with the guy?" I asked. "Stuff him and hang in your office?"

"If you choose to co-operate he will in time be discovered floating in the river. An unsolved murder. It is a commonplace thing in Macao."

I learned heavily against my dressing table and worked on that cigarette like a fire-eater. This whole business was so goddamn sickening I couldn't quite believe it was happening. Happening to me. "How do I get off the hook?"

"I will explain," Gonsalves replied, pacing slowly by the door. "It is as I suspected. The Chandler woman deceived you and her partner, Jordan, as well. It was necessary for him to die for other reasons, reasons that do not concern you. I took steps instantly to recover the— the secrets from her, but she was not so stupid as to actually bring them into the hotel. She has been thoroughly searched, senhor, and her apartment too. I hold her prisoner there, but it does no good. She will not talk. She is a very stubborn young lady."

I felt a moment's flash of anger as I imagined the steps he must have taken with her, but I wouldn't let the anger take hold. What he did to her was his business. "I'd just as soon be dealt out," I said. "I don't give a damn about the whole bunch of you. You all make me sick."

"Again, senhor, I apologize for taking these steps. I am a peaceful man, but others make trouble for me. Within a few hours you will be free to leave Macao as you came, and I shall provide a bonus for the trouble I have put you to. But first, you must help me with the young lady. You must go to her. You must help her escape from the hotel. I will co-operate in that. Even though she is stubborn, she is frightened, and when she sees how you aid her, she will trust you. She needs your help as much as I do, Senhor Flemish. Once out of the hotel, tell her you will help her escape from Macao. Go to the water front. You will find a fishing junk tied up at Wharf Thirty-one, an oil pumping dock. You cannot miss it. The name of the junk is the Shan Yu. Remember that, senhor."

"You own it?"

"The captain is friendly to me. Before the young lady leaves Macao she will either tell you where she has hidden the secrets or insist upon getting them herself. But we can be sure that once she is aboard, she will have the secrets with her. We will take over from there, and your job is done. I shall let you have the pleasure of burning the films."

"But—"

"But if you find the Senhorita's charms irresistible and attempt to double-cross me, you know what I must then do."

"The police get the films and I'm wanted for murder."

"*Sim,* exactly."

I jabbed out my cigarette. I didn't like being blackmailed into doing anything, but it would almost be a pleasure handing Donna over to the wolves. It hurt to have a woman make a sap out of me. Let her look out for herself; I had myself to worry about. The idea of clearing out of this mess *and* Macao seemed suddenly appealing.

Gonsalves' brown eyes hung on me. "Well, senhor?"

"Hell, yes," I said. "I know when I'm over a barrel."

"Again, I apologize."

"Don't bother. Have you canceled the two-o'clock show?"

"Of course."

"Then I'll get going. What's her room number?"

"It adjoins Jordan's apartment. Room Three-six-four." Gonsalves bent clown to the dead body at his feet and removed the gun from Jordan's shoulder holster. It was a .32 Colt automatic. Gonsalves slipped out the magazine, ejected the shell from the chamber, and handed me an empty gun. "I have left one man to guard her. He will not argue with you if you surprise him with a gun. Make it look good so the girl will be convinced you rescue her. My man will hurry to tell me what happened, as he does not understand my plans. I will see that no one troubles the two of you in your escape. Until you board the Shan Yu."

I nodded and got out of my dress shirt and trousers. I put on my street clothes and a windbreaker. The gun was only a prop, but I liked the feel of it. Inwardly, I was mad enough to shoot the place up just for the hell of it. Gonsalves stepped aside and I went through the door. He locked it after us, and we walked together through the club.

He left me at the seventh floor, returning to his office. I stayed in the elevator and got out at the third. When the doors opened there was a man waiting to get in, and just seeing him gave me a prickly feeling.

It was the man in the seersucker suit. He was still munching watermelon seeds; and he gave me a friendly smile as we touched shoulders. The doors closed after him and he went down with the elevator.

I walked along the hall to Room 364.

Chapter Seven

I knocked with the tip of the gun, and began to feel like a bastard. They were ganging up on Donna, and I was one of the gang. I didn't like the company I was keeping, but for all I knew she had it coming. Whatever the secrets were, espionage was out of my line. And so was Donna. I tried not to let my conscience get me down.

The door opened and a pair of suspicious brown eyes looked out at me. I kicked the door all the way open and stuck the gun in the guy's face.

I felt a little silly doing it and even sillier when I said, "Stick 'em up."

He was so startled, he didn't do a damned thing. Looking over his shoulder, I saw Donna sitting on a divan. She had a pale blue sheet wrapped around her. They must have stripped her clothes off. The guy, a dudish Portuguese in a tux, finally came to and decided to show some muscle. He made a lunge for the gun, and I decided to make the act look real good. I clipped him with my free hand and threw him off balance. I kicked the door shut and piled into him. He had a gun of his own and he looked pretty mad because he hadn't answered the door with the thing in his hand. He rolled out from under me and reached for it. He never got it. I connected with the empty butt of my gun, and it rocked him senseless. I felt good.

I took his gun, and it was loaded. When I looked up Donna was on her feet, the sheet clutched around her, and amazement in her eyes.

"Hi," I said.

I put both gums in my pockets and walked toward her. When I got closer I saw that it wasn't amazement in her eyes; it was anger.

"What are you doing here?" she snapped.

"Do you want to go as you are, or is that what the best-dressed spies are wearing these days?"

"Don't try to be funny. I thought you were on your way to Hong Kong. Why did you come back?"

"I'll be damned," I said. "I'll be goddamned. Who are you trying to kid, sweetheart?"

"Bruce—"

"Bruce, my fanny. Your boy friend's room was wired for sound and

Gonsalves heard the whole deal, as you damn well knew he would. He wasn't fooled about the dud firecracker you handed me, but me, I fool easy. Get some clothes on and let's clear out."

She swept toward me, her green eyes burning with intensity. *"What did you do with that firecracker?"*

"Let's forget it and get out of here. I don't like Gonsalves any more than I go for you, but I thought maybe you'd say thanks if I were chump enough to get you out of this mess."

She didn't say thanks. She stopped very close to me, her shoulders naked above the toga she'd made of the sheet. Her voice turned very soft. "Bruce, I don't understand. My God, believe me! I've gone through hell in this room to keep them away from you."

"Sure," I said. "Sure."

"I was praying you'd be halfway to Hong Kong by now—with the firecracker."

"I wish you'd do something about those bangs. They drive me nuts."

I enjoyed it. I enjoyed making her squirm, but it was making me a little sick, because I began to squirm. Her eyes looked up at me with the injured pride of a lost animal's, and somewhere in the back of my mind I was seeing a possibility that scared me stiff. The possibility that Donna hadn't deceived me at all.

"Bruce, *where*—"

I clapped a hand over her mouth. Hell, I was putting on a rescue act, but was she acting? Why would she make such a fuss over the firecracker unless it was the real article? "Listen," I whispered harshly. "I haven't got you figured out yet, but *this* room could be wired too. You're going to talk and talk plenty." I twisted her around and hustled her into the bathroom. I went over it quickly, but found no hidden mikes. I turned on the shower for the noise it would make, just in case, and cold so the room wouldn't steam up. Donna hugged the pale blue sheet around her and I told her to sit down. She rebelled at the suggestiveness of it, so I got bold and shoved her on the seat. I sat on my haunches in front of her and told her not to give me any more trouble. "I'm probably signing my own death warrant, baby," I said, "but I'm going to listen to you. I want to know what's in that firecracker and exactly what the hell's going on. If you make it good enough I might frame myself for murder, but it won't be your fault. Let's have it."

The shower was a strong, steady whisper beside us and I hoped it would foul up our low voices if I missed a mike. Donna's eyes avoided mine. "I did lie to you, Bruce," she muttered, "in a way. This isn't espionage. I was afraid if I told you what it was, really, you wouldn't want to help. I'm sorry."

"Never mind softening it up," I snapped. "Make it fast—just what's important."

"This thing is—opium smuggling."

Her eyes watched for a reaction, but I wasn't being surprised any more. I was doing a crazy thing, straying from Gonsalves' script, but if she had really given me the gimmick they were after, I wouldn't be able to let it go out with the morning trash. I wouldn't be able to throw Donna to the boys, no matter what the cost.

Opium. I didn't like the sound of it. Gonsalves had talked espionage too, but I made the reservation that he might only have picked up the lead from our conversation on the tape recording. It looked as if they were fooling me all over the place. "O.K., opium," I said.

She bunched up the sheet tighter around her. "My dad was a Treasury attaché in Hong Kong. The customs service cabled him that opium has been flooding into the States for the past six months and they thought it was coming from South China. As undercover man in the Orient, his job was to find the source and tip off customs who and what to look for."

"Never mind the family history."

"Dad traced it to Macao. He was killed in an automobile accident before he could get off his report. That's what's in the firecracker— the one I gave you."

I reacted to that. I flinched.

"I was in Hong Kong when it happened," she went on. "At first I believed Dad had died accidentally. Then I became convinced he hadn't—that he had been murdered. We had known Gonsalves for years. In the past he always co-operated with Dad, giving him tips. It was funny—when I came over here I met Gonsalves in the casino, and he ignored me completely, as though we had never met before."

"Having his thumbs cut off must have done something to his memory. No one in his right mind could forget your bangs."

"I decided then to use a different name. Dad had made a mistake somewhere, and I knew I'd better not make the same mistake. Dad trusted Gonsalves; I don't."

"Where does Jordan fit in? I notice you have connecting doors."

She gripped the sheet in her hands and her eyes turned away from me. "Must I tell you that?"

I stared at her for a few seconds, and then rose. "No," I said. "Not if you don't want to. Forget it. Maybe that's your private business. Now listen to me, baby. That firecracker is sitting in a wastebasket in Gonsalves' office. I'll have to figure some way of getting it out, so for God's sake if you're just handing me a line, get smart. Don't let me break my neck—"

She got up and the sheet touched me as she held it to her. "Bruce, please, Bruce—believe me. I'm sorry I got you into this. You don't have to help me. I'll find a way myself, now that I know what you've done with the firecracker."

"Don't be a sap. Look, Jordan's dead. These boys play rough. The first thing to do is get you out of the hotel. Then I'll worry about getting the firecracker out."

She was startled, and she stood in front of me looking suddenly very mixed up.

"I'm sorry," I snapped. "I could have broken it to you with hearts and flowers, but he's dead and that's that. Did he mean a hell of a lot to you?"

The shower hissed like something alive beside us. It was the only sound in the room for a moment. "No," she said. "I just wasn't prepared for it."

"Tell me—why the hell did you ask me up to Jordan's apartment in the first place?"

"I didn't want you seen coming into mine, in case you were followed."

I decided to go along with that, but decided not to tell her about the frame-up I was waltzing myself into. I took her shoulders tightly in my hands and made her listen carefully. Even as I began to talk, I realized I had never before touched her bare skin, and the contact disturbed me a little. "Gonsalves sent me here," I said. "Never mind why I came. I'm supposed to help you make a phony escape, only we're going to make it a real one. Once I get you out of the hotel I'm going to put you on ice somewhere until I can get the firecracker, and I want you to say put. Somehow we'll get out of Macao—as long as you don't double-cross me or get fancy ideas of your own."

"You still don't trust me, do you?"

"When I open that firecracker, I'll tell you. Now hurry up and get into something less conspicuous."

She opened the door as I reached to turn off the shower. "Bruce?" she muttered.

"What now?"

"I'm glad I picked you."

"Don't call me a sucker to my face. Move."

She got something out of the closet and returned to the bathroom to dress while I looked over the Portuguese. He was showing signs of coming to. I shook him until his eyes were open, put my gun in his pocket, and hoped he wouldn't notice the switch. By the time I had him on his feet, mumbling to himself in a daze, Donna was out of the bathroom in a jade-green dress that I could have kicked her for putting on. It made her as inconspicuous as a billboard.

I opened the door and shoved the Portuguese through it. "Go on, scram. Get lost."

He was confused as hell. He walked the wrong way for the elevator.

Donna was slipping into shoes when I came over to her. "Have you got any money?" I asked.

"In my purse, unless they've taken it."

"They weren't after money." I found her purse in a pile of lingerie and other stuff they had gone through. I picked up a number of Hong Kong bills, divided them, put some in my pocket, and gave the rest to Donna. "In case we get separated, we've got to eat."

"Don't apologize. You told me you were broke."

"O.K., O.K. Let's get going."

Chapter Eight

Just to make it look good, we avoided the elevator. We took the back stairway to the ground floor, passed through a deserted reading room, and came to the patio doors. There were guards there, of course, but they weren't the uniformed blacks used for show and protection at the front doors. They were Sikhs, and they let us through without even a nod. I took Donna's hand and led her through the dark patio, where a giant banyan tree rustled in the breeze.

"We're probably going to be tailed from the hotel," I whispered. "From here on it's luck."

If there had been anyone waiting in the gardens behind the hotel, I didn't spot him. We worked our way to the Avenida Almeida Ribeiro and hurried along the arcaded sidewalks. Even at this hour the streets bustled with life, and I felt a sharpening danger with every step we took away from the Hotel China Seas. We brushed past shadows that thrust lottery tickets at us, and ignored the ricksha boys who shouted to us from the curbs. I kept glancing behind; I knew Gonsalves wouldn't let us leave the hotel without a tail, but I couldn't spot the guy.

We turned into a cobbled side street. At the far end of the block, carbon light from an all-night gambling dive painted the street an eerie, flickering white. I pulled Donna toward it and we went through the doors.

Inside, the air was thick with smells and smoke and noise. Street coolies were packed around the single fan-tan table, and money baskets in play lowered and rose by strings from the several balconies that circled the walls to the ceiling. From the higher balconies we could see Europeans leaning over the railings, watching the game below. I nodded toward the stairway and Donna hung onto my hand as we hurried to the top.

We found a couple of seats and I looked down, across the gambling table to the open doorway. A couple of Portuguese officers from the Macao garrison were gambling noisily beside us, dropping their bets by basket to the table. But I kept my eyes on the doorway, and finally spotted our tail. He crossed slowly, looking into the dive, and came back a moment later. He was a bullish-looking Chinese in Western dress.

I turned to Donna, and noticed that the two officers were sizing her up with alcoholic grins. I tried to ignore them. "This is where we separate," I whispered. "I'm going back to the hotel. Gonsalves put only one man on us, and he can't follow us both. I think he'll follow me. He'll figure I'm leaving you here for safekeeping."

The Macao army let out a laugh between themselves, and from the look on their faces, Donna was the sensuous butt of it.

"Bruce, I'll be all right."

"I don't like the looks of those guys," I said.

"I can take care of myself. If they try to get fresh, I'll toss them off the balcony."

I took the gun out of my pocket and slipped it into her bag. "O.K., you're armed," I muttered. "If they try to move in after I leave, just give them a flash of metal. The gun ought to scare 'em away."

"Are you sure?"

"A gun won't help me too much. Anyway, I'm liable to kill someone. I'm better off. Listen, after I leave, stick around about five minutes and then high-tail it to the red-light district. I don't think Gonsalves would figure I'd take you there. We might have to hole up for a day or so. Don't ask me how I know, but the girls can rent cribs from a joint on the Rua da Felicidade—by the hour, week, or year. All right, I met a Portuguese girl when I first came here and she turned out to be a whore. So I know. The joint is called Charlotta's. Any objections?"

"No."

"Get the best accommodations you can. All the rooms are on the ground floor along an alley. In about half an hour you can start watching for me. But keep the door locked and don't take in any stray customers."

"I'll try to get twin beds."

"They've never heard of them." I got up and gave the officers a mean scowl. I'd have felt better leaving Donna with the coolies on the ground floor. The higher you went in these joints, the better class of people you were supposed to meet, but in outfits like this it was a joke. They wouldn't let coolies in the balconies because they had a way of dropping lice on the players below. So you got drunken officers dropping nasty glances instead.

"Use the gun if you have to," I muttered.

"Don't worry about me."

We said good-by, and I left.

The tail picked me up, and that was fine. I led him to the lobby of a nearby hotel, where I bought a couple of packs of cigarettes. I saw him slip into a phone booth, and I didn't like that. But Donna would be out of the gambling joint before Gonsalves could send out another man.

Back on the street I bought a small package of firecrackers from a street vendor. Then I turned into the black doorway of a godown and let Gonsalves' man cool his heels while I got fixed up. I emptied one of the packs, separated a firecracker from the bunch, and stuck it in the empty cigarette pack. Then I twisted it up and tested it for palming. It palmed O.K. I stuck it in my pocket and headed back to the Hotel China Seas.

When I started up the broad marble stairway to the front doors a chill took hold of me. I dreaded going back. I wasn't the hero type; what the hell was I doing sticking my neck out for a girl? A girl with a firecracker full of opium secrets. She was right about one thing: If she'd tipped me off originally that I'd be walking into opium, I wouldn't have tumbled. For a moment I had at least been aroused at the idea of espionage.

When I reached the top of the stairs I faced the two Mozambique guards at the revolving doors, but I knew I wasn't going to have any trouble getting into the hotel. Getting out again would depend on luck. I brushed by one of the guards, and all I got from him was a tired glance and the hot breath of garlic.

I stood for a moment inside the doors, and saw the tail move up the stairs. I took my time crossing the lobby to the elevators. I spotted a few high-class professional women back on the prowl before the night wore out. A drunk in a spotless tux was trying to conduct himself out of the adjoining bar. People, faces, nobody.

I told the elevator girl to take me to the seventh floor.

The casino was bright and alive even though dawn would break in a couple of hours. I crossed the tile floor to the offices. The entry door was locked. The Portuguese whom I had seen earlier, Gonsalves' lieutenant, answered my knock. From the look on his face, they were expecting me. I figured the Chinese had tipped them off from the lobby that I had returned to the hotel.

Gilberto walked down the short hall with me, silent and unhappy, to Gonsalves' door. He knocked. I waited.

Senhor Gonsalves appeared. *"Bom dia,"* he muttered coolly. "Come in. Gilberto, wait outside the door."

"Sim."

I glanced around at the gallery of governors general on the green walls, and took a chair across from the desk. While Gonsalves returned to his own chair, I glanced at the wastebasket. It hadn't been emptied; a Hong Kong newspaper had been discarded there since I last had been in the office.

"Senhor Flemish," Gonsalves muttered between tight, angry lips, "you leave me completely puzzled. Does your own life mean so little to you that you risk it so unnecessarily—for a girl?"

"What I do with my life is my business. I came here to deliver the plans."

"Senhor, you have altered my instructions. What am I to make of you?"

"Look, you told me to find out what she did with the plans. I found out, and I'm reporting back to you."

"I have had you watched. I observe the American double-cross coming to fruit."

"You're nuts. Damnit, she swears she gave me the plans in that firecracker. The trouble with you is you outwitted yourself. You gave her credit for more cunning than she had. All right, I ditched the firecracker and I left Donna to wait for me in a gambling dive. I don't know the name—ask the Chinese boy you tagged us with, if he hasn't already tipped you off."

"I told you to take her to the fishing junk."

"I forgot the name."

"That is unlikely."

"Go to hell, will you? I don't give a damn what you do with the girl, it's my neck I'm worried about. I'll lead you to the firecracker in return for those negatives."

His black eyebrows lowered thoughtfully. "All right," he said. "Let us see if you tell the truth." He used the intercom on his desk, and we sat staring at each other, waiting for the films to be brought in. He gave his instructions in Portuguese, which worried me a little, because I couldn't be sure what he had said.

Gilberto finally came back into the room and handed his boss an envelope. I used those moments to reach into my pocket for the cigarette pack I had gimmicked. My fingers closed around the twisted pack, jockeyed it into a finger palm, and came out again. I crossed my wrists over my lap. Look natural, I warned myself; watch your timing. Gilberto returned to his post just outside the door.

"All right," Gonsalves muttered, "we will go now."

"We're not going anywhere," I said. "Let's have a look at those negatives."

He smiled indulgently, slipped them out of the envelope, and held them to the light. I rose and stuck my face near them. He was too impatient to let me have more than a glance, but I saw arms and bodies, and that was enough. I faced him.

"Get ready to trade," I said. "I ditched the firecracker in your office."

Gonsalves straightened his shoulders against the leather back of the chair. His expression was critical, as though he felt I were on the verge of making a fool of him.

I stepped to the side of the desk, the back of my hand toward him, and reached into the wastebasket. My finger joints felt stiff, even though the sleight I had to perform was child's play. It was the difference between performing for laughs and performing for blood.

I kept talking, patter to support the sleight. "When you started to play that tape recording I knew I was in a spot. I had hidden the firecracker in my cigarette pack. In your office. I lit my last cigarette, twisted the package, and tossed it in your wastebasket."

My hand was buried, fumbling, searching for the other twisted pack.

"I congratulate your cleverness."

My fingers touched slick cellophane. I thumb-palmed it quickly and got the dummy pack to my fingertips. I withdrew my hand from the wastebasket and tossed the dummy pack to the desk. The switch was made. "It's all yours." I said. "Let's have the negatives."

"One moment." His hands came back out of his pockets, leaving the envelope behind. Thumbless hands, fingers that looked like short brown tentacles, untwisted the pack and ripped it open. A red firecracker stared back at him.

He looked up at me, but his expression told me nothing. Then he twisted the firecracker to break it.

"Hold on," I said angrily. "Put the film on the desk. I want a chance to grab for it if you decide to double-cross me."

"Senhor, if this indeed holds what I have been searching for, I shall burn the film for you myself."

He broke the firecracker. I bit my lips and managed to drop the switched pack into my pocket. He separated the two pieces and over-turned the raw ends. Silver-black powder flowed out.

We stared at each other.

"Senhor," he said huskily, "either the girl has deceived you, or you are deceiving me."

I did my best to look grimly surprised at what I saw. "I'll go back and break her neck," I said.

"You are an actor, senhor. I am sorry that you have chosen to work against me. I admire your skill. I saw nothing. But my mind tells me what my eyes cannot see. Give me the other firecracker, senhor."

"You're off the deep end, Gonsalves."

He called for Gilberto in a loud, angry voice. I picked up a side chair, spun, and slammed it into Gilberto's face as he came through the door. Blood gushed from his nose as a yell of alarm died in his throat. I turned. Gonsalves was on his feet, the telephone in his hands. I dove for him across the desk.

He fell against the leather chair. It teetered and spilled us to the floor, the telephone cord entangling us. One four-fingered hand hooked onto my neck like steel. He still had the phone in his other hand and he tried to bash me with it, but there wasn't enough slack in the cord to complete the blow. In another moment he rolled over on top of me, and I began to feel the power of his body. I got a hand in his face and shoved, but he held. I finally worked a knee under him and broke his hold. I got an arm free and lashed out with my fist. He rolled with it, but was back on me before I could get to my feet. I twisted away, but the next moment he was working a flat palm and four curled fingers into my face. I broke loose and shoved a haymak-er at him. It made hay.

I rested on my knees, looking at him as he rolled over with a moan. Then I went to his pocket, took out the envelope, and paused to tear the telephone out by the roots. I found a pack of matches and set fire to the negatives. They made a nice little blaze.

I glanced at Gilberto, bleeding badly in the doorway, and figured I was lucky the adjoining offices were deserted. But as I glanced, I saw more than Gilberto.

Standing behind him, grinning broadly, was a heavyset man with a gun in his hands.

It was the man in the seersucker suit.

Chapter Nine

"Good show, my lad, good show." He stood there with the gun on me, and popped watermelon seeds into his mouth. "But I say, you've a bad temper."

"I eat revolvers with my bare teeth," I said. "Are you going to give me any trouble?"

"This chap's rather in a bad way." He stepped over Gilberto's body and kicked the overturned chair aside. "Name's Wilkerson. We were destined to meet, my lad." He stood looking at the mess in the office, his florid face weighted with fat. A brown scalp shone through short-cropped gray hair and his puckish eyes danced with a sort of malevolent humor. He had the look of a retired British officer gone to fat, and worse, gone Asiatic.

"I'm just leaving," I said. "But you can stick around if you like."

"I'm a great believer in the open door." He smiled. "It's what made China what it is today. But I believe I'll close this one and we'll have a bit of a chat." He handed over a business card and rolled Gilberto out of the doorway with his large foot.

Was this guy crazy? I glanced at the card quickly, crumpled it in my fist, and tossed it to the floor. It told me he was Colonel Percy Wilkerson, proprietor of the Chan Tom Firecracker Works, Macao.

"I say, that's the good Senhor Gonsalves immobilized behind the desk. Find yourself a chair, my lad. Sit down."

"If it's all the same to you, I'm in a hell of a hurry."

He sat down heavily in a chair, but kept the gun and the grin on me. "Surely you've a moment or two for an old party such as myself."

"Where do you fit into this mess, Wilkerson? Every time I turn around you're there, breathing down my neck."

"I say, you and the girl have led me on a merry chase." He spotted the remnants of the firecracker, part of the shell on the floor. He examined it briefly and tossed it aside. "One of my competitors' brands. Too much clay. I use more powder, less clay. You can't beat the Chan Torn brand for quality."

"I'll pass the word along."

"Splendid. Now, information slipped into a firecracker—that, my lad, is something to whet a man's interest. The device has a special virtue. There are so many firecrackers in Macao, it amounts to hunting a needle in a haystack."

"Is everybody in this goddamned colony onto the thing?"

"Only a select few. I come to offer my humble services. I shall be delighted to relieve you of the burden of transporting the secrets to Hong Kong. It is the least I can do, after you and the girl have done so much."

I nodded toward the desk. "Look around. You'll find the rest of the shell and maybe even some of the powder. We thought we had the right one, but it turned out to be a dud."

"That's a pity. You know, my man Jordan turned out to be a dud as well. One must always provide for disappointments."

"What do you mean—*your* man Jordan?"

"A scoundrel, but really a man of singular abilities. Manager of my plant these last six months, he was. A jolly lot of trouble he's causing me."

"Look, the secrets aren't here. We've all been on a wild-goose chase. Any objection if I leave?"

"I say, you could be telling the truth. But it isn't likely."

"Look around. If you find anything, it's yours."

I started toward the door, but the gun took on a fresh gleam in his hand. "Come, come, don't be foolish. Did I tell you I enjoyed your magic? Good act. Bravo."

I stared at the gun. "Yeah, I know. I'm knocking 'em dead in Macao. We're wasting our time, Wilkerson."

His lips parted in a fresh grin and he started in on the watermelon seeds again. "Quite so. How does this strike you as a line of action, my lad? It would be perilous for an old party such as myself to search an impetuous person, full of tricks. But consider the consequences if I press this trigger. You, first of all, are regrettably dead. I have the freedom of your pockets. If they prove to be empty, I shall be conscience-stricken for having acted with such finality. But at least I shall be able to mark you off the list of our select few."

"I deliver, and you let me walk out, is that it?"

"A splendid alternative."

"I don't have it, and I don't think even you would kill a man in cold blood."

"That, my lad, is a romantic notion. I quite disagree. I have much at stake, and death in the Orient is such a commonplace, one learns to accept it with only a shrug of the shoulders. Come now, hand it over and we shall part warm friends."

My mind wanted to reject the gun in his hand and the murder on his lips. I thought of Donna holed up in a shabby alley off the Rua da Felicidade, waiting for me. Was any woman worth looking into the wrong end of a gun? All I had to do was hand over the firecracker and walk out of the whole deadly business.

"Well, my lad?"

I glanced at Gilberto and saw a chance, a bluff worth trying. "O.K., Wilkerson," I muttered, "you win."

The grin left his face quickly and nervousness came into his eyes. He hadn't been sure I had it; now he was. "I shan't abide any tricks."

I tossed him the cigarette pack. "There's a firecracker inside. I hope it's your brand."

"Thank you."

"O.K. if I leave now?"

"Cheerio."

I started for the door and heard him rip open the package. I looked down at Gilberto. "You'd better call a doctor before he bleeds to death."

"The Portuguese are a sturdy race. He won't even have a headache tomorrow."

I bent to move his body. With my back to Wilkerson, I brushed Gilberto's pockets and prayed for a shoulder holster. There was none. But I felt what might have been a knife in the breast pocket of his coat, behind the crisp white handkerchief. It was. "See you around," I said with pretended calm.

I withdrew it as I rose, a short stiletto in a sheath sewn to the pocket. My eyes gazed at the sparkling goldstone handle, the blue-white blade.

I straightened. Wilkerson was big enough and he was close. It would be like hitting the side of a barn. I heard him get to his feet.

"I say—"

I wheeled and flung the blade.

Wilkerson lurched heavily when the knife struck. Then open astonishment burst over his face and his eyes fell disbelieving to the sleeve of his coat. The rust-colored handle quivered from his forearm. He held the gun, but he couldn't pull the trigger.

I rushed forward. He stumbled back and tried to get the gun into his other hand. I got there first, twisted and brought the butt in fast against the side of his head. He hit the floor like a ton weight.

I stood over him, breathing fast. His left hand was a tight fist. I bent down and pried it open. The firecracker rested in his palm like an innocent charm. I took his gun, too.

Then I got out of there.

I ran into trouble at the elevator. When the doors opened for me, Nakov stepped out of the car. He eyed me sheepishly through the heavy lenses and slipped by into the casino. If he walked into the office, he'd have a fit, and all he'd have to do was notify the door guards and I'd be trapped. But I didn't see how I could stop him. I couldn't show Wilkerson's gun with all the people around; I'd just have to take a chance. At the moment he believed I was co-operating with Gonsalves, thanks to the pictures he had snapped. I let him go, and stepped into the elevator.

It started down at a slow drag, the cables snapping above us. I got a cigarette going. The car stopped at the fourth floor to pick up a drunk and I thought I'd break out of my skin at the delay. We got going again and I tried to figure my timing. Nakov could be entering the office now. We moved past the third floor without stopping. There would be a phone in one of the other offices. He'd know I'd been there. He'd be smart enough to try to stop me. The elevator stopped at the second floor, and I couldn't stand it any longer. I pushed my way out and let a pair of waiting Chinese move in. I started for the stairway and reached it as the elevator doors behind me closed.

I tossed away my cigarette and hurried down. As it emptied into the lobby, the stairway curved around a thick pink column and passed through a sort of botanical garden. There was a pair of rococo fountains flanking the lower platform where a tight little forest of green plants and tropical vines began.

I stopped behind the stuff and checked over the lobby. The only activity was at the bank of elevator doors, where several people clustered, waiting to go up to the gambling floors. I glanced across the lobby to the revolving doors. The uniformed guards were still outside the doors and my hopes rose. I straightened and decided the thing to do was walk down, across the lobby, and out.

But I took only a couple of steps. A bellboy cut across the lobby from the desk and hurried through the revolving doors to the guards. In another moment they came trouping in with their guns. They were all muscles and all black. I saw the bellboy point to the lobby display that carried my picture. "Bruce Flemish, performing nightly in the Magellan Room." That was great. They knew exactly whom to look for.

I dodged behind a cluster of vines. Hell, they'd never let me through that front door. I looked above me to a stretch of naked stairway. I'd have to go back.

I didn't stand there arguing with myself. I started up and I didn't stop when I heard a yell below. Someone down there looked at the right place at the right time, and my blood chilled, but I kept climbing those stairs.

When I reached the second floor I was afraid to stop. Shoes make a racket on marble, and those boys didn't try to be quiet. I strained to increase my lead on the sharp clatter behind me, taking the stairs by threes. My own room was on the fourth floor, but I saw no point in heading for it. When I reached the third-floor landing I headed for the fire-escape window, but when I looked down I saw a police van careen to a stop on the street below. I wheeled and raced down the carpeted hall. To Room 362.

The cops below worried me as much as the guards on my tail. Had Gonsalves come to, and called for help?

When I reached the door I tried the knob. The door was locked. I moved to the adjoining room, Donna's room, unlocked. But even as I slipped inside, I knew I was spotted.

I pushed the door closed and slipped the bolt. It was only a matter of seconds before they were hammering on it. I snapped on the light and looked around desperately. There was the connecting door to Jordan's apartment and I hurried to it. It was unlocked. I pushed through and locked it after me. I heard a shot, and knew they were coming in next door. It wasn't going to take them long to search through Donna's apartment, and get wise to the connecting door. They didn't need a key, not when they could blast the lock.

I hurried to the windows and looked out. Occasional lights shone dimly in the harbor. Beyond, in the darkness, lay the hills of Red China. And on the street below, Sikhs in striped turbans were piling out of the police van. My eyes picked out the narrow ledge about five feet below the window sill.

I heard them try the connecting door. There was only one way out for me. I slipped over the sill, turned on my stomach, and let myself down to the concrete ledge. It was lower than the five feet I had estimated. My toes just reached it, with my fingers hooked onto the sill. The ledge jutted about nine inches from the wall, but felt as narrow as a bad crack. My feet got an uneasy purchase, and my breath caught. It was now or never. I had to release my fingers and trust my sense of balance.

I held on for a final moment, fighting a sudden dizziness. Then I let go with my fingers and glued my palms to the surface of the wall.

I heard another gunshot, and that meant they'd be scurrying through Jordan's rooms in another moment. If they decided I might have gone through the window, I'd be a sitting duck. But they might figure I had slipped back out the front door and into the hall again. I counted on it.

It was dark out here, and that might help if luck ran against me. My legs started to move, and the dizziness turned to sharpness and all my senses became alert.

I edged to the left, toward the back of the hotel. My palms shimmied along with the movement of my feet. I wasn't breathing. I couldn't. I just moved.

Three flights down. Not much when you're looking up, but try looking down. My heart beat wildly. An early-morning breeze was riding in over the harbor and I felt as delicately poised as a feather.

When I had gone about three windows beyond Jordan's apartment, I stopped and tried to figure a way off the ledge. There was an electric sign at the front of the hotel, but I wasn't headed that way and it would be too bright there. Then I remembered the old banyan tree set in one corner of the large patio out back, and tried to visualize whether its branches touched the wall.

I couldn't remember, but it was the only chance I saw. My feet moved unsteadily, each flat against the wall. I fought the breeze that plucked at me. It seemed almost human, taunting me with gentle pulls, and I fought back with silent curses.

I looked back once, to the window I had left, but no head poked out. I could feel the echo of my heartbeats against the cold concrete.

When I reached the sharp corner of the building, I knew I was looking into the eyes of eternity. The muscles in my shoulders were locked
and my calves were stiffening. I reached an exploratory hand, and
then a foot, around the sharp angle. I edged my way in agonizing slow
motion, but even then I thought I'd never get my body shifted around
that knifelike corner without losing my balance and falling.

But I did. When I got back to flat surface I had to stop and close my
eyes and wait. The breeze chilled the perspiration that covered me.

Finally, I looked to my left. There was the banyan tree. It touched
the wall, all right, but it didn't grow three stories high. My heart
almost stopped.

I leaned against the wall, wondering what to do.

Jump. I don't know where the idea came from. Jump into that tree
below and pray you can grab something before you reach bottom.

I didn't hang there trying to make up my mind, because I knew I'd
talk myself out of it. My palms were moist and I had passed the cli-
max of my energies. I wasn't going to last on that ledge much longer.
I shimmied along the ledge until the branches of the tree were directly below me, about nine feet of thin air away.

Then I jumped.

My blood felt as if it was bursting free of my skin as space opened
up for me. I struck a small high twig that snapped instantly, and then
my feet scuffed off a heavier branch. My arms flailed for something to
catch, but I kept dropping like a plummet. Leaves brushed like lightning across my face. My arms caught a branch, lost it, and caught
another—and got it. I could hear the snapping, brushing noises closing over me and my heart was a cold pain in my chest.

I held, and my breath came back to me. I clung to that branch with
every muscle of my body.

Then I heard the answer to the noises of my fall. Sharp voices from
below. A pair of voices.

My face was screwed up tight and it went tighter. My feet dangled
for something to get hold of and they found a heavy limb.

I strained quietly to let myself down. Then I flattened myself like a
lizard along the surface of the thick, swollen branch. Flashlights were
already beginning to poke up into the tree, and I made myself a part
of the limb. My fingernails dug into the soft bark, and I didn't move
anything but my lungs for three or four minutes.

I don't know what they thought below. Maybe they dismissed the noises as the snap and fall of an overweighted limb. Let them think what they liked. I hung there long after the flashlights went out and the two guards returned to the back entrance of the hotel.

Then I moved again. I moved slowly, slithering by inches down the tree toward the tangled trunk far below.

I had forgotten the gun in my pocket until it worked itself out and began to clatter through the branches. It struck the brick seat that collared the base of the tree. It hit with a sharp crack, but it didn't explode.

"Olá!"

I froze. The two guards trotted over, guns and flashlights aimed. I stood at the high joint of the trunk, about ten feet above ground.

Two beams of light crossed on me, and all I could do was sag. They had me.

"Alto as mãos. Descenda devagar."

The taller man was speaking, the bearded Sikh that Donna and I had seen as we left the hotel together. His voice surprised me. I got the idea he wanted my hands up, but his voice was more curious than demanding. They had been alerted for me, of course, but they probably couldn't make much sense of finding a guy in a tree.

I came down, and we looked each other over cautiously. The older man bristled with sudden authority, and I could see he was going to impress his side-kick in handling affairs like this. His turban was seedy-looking and his black beard had the look of polished steel wool.

The other was a gawky boy in a uniform that was too large for him. *Mão arriba!"* the kid howled as I dropped my arms.

"Relax," I said. I reached slowly into my trousers pocket. The bearded man lurched with his gun until the cold nose was buried deep in my stomach.

"Listen, you bastards," I snapped. "I don't have another gun."

English wasn't their language, but maybe Big Boy read my thoughts. He let me get my hand out of my pocket with the wad of bills I had taken from Donna. You never know about a bribe in the Far East. Either it takes or it doesn't, but the odds are with you. The bearded guy looked to me as if he'd taken plenty, and maybe he'd like to break the kid in on the ways of a smart guard.

I held out the money. "Buy yourselves a bathtub. You're both fragrant."

Big Boy glanced at the kid and put up a hand protestingly. *"Não, não, senhor!"*

But even in the darkness his eyes had an oily gleam. I fanned the bills out, and let him feast on them.

The kid started jabbering, and it earned him a smack from the boss. My heart raced, but I made myself stand very calmly, as if I bribed cops every day. The boy shut up. Hell, he wasn't even old enough to grow a beard.

Suddenly that big paw swiped over my fingers and collected the bills in a fist. The boy stood watching, his eyes wide and frightened. Then an open hand slammed against my shoulder, and I got the point.

I turned and ran.

Chapter Ten

I stayed off the main drag and worked my way to the Rua da Felicidade by the darkest streets I could find. I gave the Hotel China Seas a
backward glance as I hurried along; it stood as an evil giant, towering
over the inner harbor, its gambling floors brazenly lit up. The chill
breeze came in small gusts and smelled of rain to come. I looked at my
watch. Dawn would break over the colony in another hour.

Forty miles to Hong Kong. The steamer was out of the question.
We'd have to hire a junk, and I knew that would be a tricky business.
But if we stuck around Macao we'd make the trip by air. Some accom-
modating bastard would pin wings on us.

Happiness Street. The Rua da Felicidade. I worked my way past dis-
mal alleys where soldiers and Chinese seamen off the smuggling
junks wandered boisterously. Oriental and Eurasian girls eyed me for
business as I hurried along. I brushed past an occasional Red sailor in
tennis shoes, off the power boats down from Canton to pick up supplies at Macao's wharves.

From the hill, the moon was beginning to rise off the South China
Sea. It lit up the empty facade of the São Paulo cathedral ruins, now a
gray shadow that watched over the jungle of tile roofs, the city half
asleep, half awake.

I turned into the cobbled alley where Donna would be waiting.
Charlotta's place. Under a light at the end two Portuguese Eurasian
girls were gossiping between customers. From the open door of one
of the cribs a tall Russian in a kimono showed herself off and gave me
a cut-rate glance. I walked. A garrison officer and a girl who looked
nonprofessional and embarrassed left another door and hurried out of
the alley.

I reached the end and turned back. Hadn't Donna reached the
place? Had Gonsalves been able to pick her up before she got out of
the gambling dive?

I kept walking. And then a door hardly ajar opened wider.

"Bruce."

Her voice was only a whisper, but it sounded big to me. My muscles relaxed and I went toward it. I stepped over the threshold into a darkened room and Donna closed the door after me.

She fell into my arms, as relieved as I was. "Bruce, I was getting terrified. You've been so long."

Her body was tight against me. How many hours had we known each other—only four? Violence had thrown us together. I found her chin in the dark, raised her head, and kissed her lips. It seemed right. Her response was natural and gentle and willing. I was glad, suddenly, she had picked me.

I broke away and reached for the light switch. "I was detained by a couple of Sikh friends," I said. "Let's see what kind of lodgings you picked out."

It wasn't as bad as it might have been. The bed was an old four-poster and the walls were a faded pink. There was an old-fashioned cabinet radio near the bed. The room was obviously one of Charlotta's plushier rentals. The ceiling was very high and some artists had been up there to do a fresco of cherubs and angels, so that you felt you were in an old converted church. And I saw there was a bathroom with an ancient zinc tub.

"Home." I smiled.

"There's no place like," she said.

"Did you have any trouble with those officers?"

"They scared off easy. Did you get the—"

"Yes." I sat on the edge of the bed and got the firecracker in my hand. "Do you know a guy named Wilkerson?"

"Jordan worked for him."

"I know that."

"Wilkerson's mixed up in the smuggling."

"He's a cute guy. Mind if I open this firecracker? Not that I still don't trust you, you understand."

"If we're going to Hong Kong, hadn't we better get on our way?"

I watched her curiously. What the hell, I thought. Was she afraid to spend a few hours locked up in a room with me? "That's going to take smart planning, baby. By this time Gonsalves will have a dozen men on the water front. Unless you were followed, I think that we'll be safe here."

"I wasn't followed."

"Are you holding something back from me?"

"I suppose so." She turned toward the single window on the alley and stared blankly at the drawn shade.

"You suppose so."

"Jordan and I had connecting rooms. Were you blind?"

"I noticed. So what?"

"It wasn't a very—pretty arrangement. I threw myself at him."

"Maybe the guy had something you went for."

"I hated him. But I let him. I made him fall for me."

"Look, you're not shocking me. I never sized you up as strictly innocent."

She faced me sharply. "Thanks."

"What you did with Jordan is your business, and he's not going to do any talking about it. Why don't you forget it?"

She shrugged her shoulders gently and turned on a faint embarrassed smile. "I suppose you're right. Sorry."

"When I want to know anything, I'll ask."

"You're a nice guy. Bruce. I'll answer. But when you open that firecracker, don't expect me to read Dad's report to you. He used a code."

"I'd like a look, anyway."

"Of course." She moved away from the window and picked up her cigarettes. "As long as we're going to stay a while, I'm going to take a long, hot bath."

"In case I'm asleep when you get out, what side do you want?"

"Your choice."

"O. K., baby. And Donna, whatever Gonsalves' boys did to you in the room to get you to talk, I hope it wasn't too bad."

She turned on the bathroom light and managed a smile. "Ask me something, and I'll tell you." Then she closed the door.

I lit a cigarette, stood for a minute thinking, and returned to the bed. I heard the water tap start, and it had a funny, high-pitched sound. I examined the firecracker, then held it between my fingers and twisted until the bright red paper split.

Even as the shell broke, I told myself not to be too surprised if there were nothing inside but powder. After the last few hours I felt that nothing short of the second coming of Christ would actually catch me unawares.

I saw coiled paper inside the shell. I pulled it out and discarded the empty firecracker. When I unrolled the paper I discovered there were two pieces. One was covered with tight writing by pen, I looked it over carefully, but it didn't tell me a damn thing. The other made a little sense. It was a small, hand-drawn map of the colony.

It listed only a few details. There was the Porto do Cerco, the barrier gate at the neck of the peninsula that marked the end of Macao and the beginning of Communist territory. A graveyard was indicated on the Red side of the gate, and the name of a grave marked. It said: João Santos."

A straight line was penned from that grave along the length of the peninsula to an X mark. A notation explained the X. It said: "São Paulo catacombs."

I puzzled over the line that connected the two points, one in present Red territory, the other in the heart of Macao. It was too straight to indicate a road. What had Donna's father meant by it?

I put the stuff aside, finally, and tried to get something on the radio. I couldn't even get a buzz out of it; the damned thing was broken. I lit another cigarette and re-examined the papers. The only thing that São Paulo meant to me was that burned-out cathedral on the hill. It was one of Macao's relics, like the forts, the three-century-old remains of the colony's past grandeur.

But São Paulo catacombs was a new one on me.

There was no longer any sound from the bathroom. How many cigarettes was she going to smoke in there? I got my mind back to the papers.

I rolled them back up and wondered what to do with them. I returned to the radio and pulled it away from the wall. I poked around the dusty wires and spotted a repair where the extension cord joined the set. A splice had been wrapped in adhesive tape. I unwound the tape and found it still fairly adhesive. I went back to the bed and ripped the tape in two. With one length I made a tight unit out of the papers; with the other I taped the business to the outside of my ankle.

That, I said to myself, was that.

I put out my cigarette and wondered if Donna were ever going to get out of the bathroom. I looked under the four-poster and found the usual auxiliary. Then I stripped down to my shorts, turned out the light, and got into bed.

I took the outside.

I made a stab at falling to sleep. My body was a bunch of tired aches, but my head was full of ideas, and my ears picked up every small sound Donna made in the water. Circumstances were going to put us in bed together, but I'd be a lout for taking advantage of circumstances. I'd gone into casual love affairs on shorter notice than four hours, but Donna was different from the others. She stirred something basic in me. I'd always been content living in a world of strangers, but I'd known the second she called me in from the alley that I'd found something different. I wanted to make friends. I was tired of making my phony peace with strangers. I wanted someone to love, and this kid had what it took and I wasn't exactly sure why. All I knew was that for the first time a woman scared me. I began to dread her coming to bed. I was afraid I might take too much for granted, and louse up the whole business.

Hell, I thought, go to sleep.

I heard the plug lifted out of the tub and the water gurgle away. A gunshot couldn't have brought me wider awake. She was a long time drying herself, and I just lay there in a mental sweat.

Some drunk in the alley began singing in Portuguese and hammered with a bottle at our door. He stuck around for a couple of minutes and I was on the verge of getting up and bouncing him across the alley when he drifted away.

I heard the bathroom light snap off. My eyes were open, but it was so dark in the room that there was the same blackness, open or closed. Then I heard the door open with a small growl from the old hinges.

I couldn't see her, but I could sense her presence as she felt her way to the bed. One of her hands grazed my leg under the sheet, and it seemed to surprise her. Maybe she had expected me to take the inside, by the wall.

There was nothing for her to do but climb over me. She did it at the foot of the bed, pulled back the top of the sheet, and slipped underneath.

I lay very still and very straight. She got settled on the pillow and her breathing sounded very relaxed. I seemed to be hugging the edge of the bed with a mile of space between us. Maybe she was really halfway up the wall.

She rustled once, turning on her side, I thought. I don't know how much time passed before she rustled again, and I figured she had returned to her back.

Small sounds came to us from the alley, breaking the agonizing quiet in the room. Then, for a while, it was still out there and I felt as though I were in a black void. I strained to pick up some distant noise, anything to bring me back to reality.

Donna's breathing was almost inaudible. I kept waiting for the heavier sounds of sleep, dreading them as much as I was confused by my own reserve and indecision. I lay with my hands along my sides, waiting. Waiting for what?

A moment later she shifted again and our arms touched accidentally. The touch was fire. That was all it took. Our hands found each other and my fingers closed gently on hers.

"Are you asleep, Bruce?"

"Sure," I said. "I can sleep through anything."

Our hands remained locked, but neither of us moved beyond that.

"This is crazy, isn't it?" she whispered. "I mean, we hardly know each other."

"I know a lot about you. I know you flashed your eyelashes at me and told me to jump and I jumped. I know I want to keep jumping. That's all I need to know about you."

"I'm lucky, Bruce. I've never been this lucky before."

"Don't—"

"Don't tell me not to call you a sucker to your face. I'm sorry, darling, I just can't help being glad it was you. You're still mad at me, aren't you?"

"I'm still mad, baby, but with a difference. Don't ask me to explain it, I don't understand it myself. After four hours, I'm mad *about* you. It's the craziest thing that's ever happened to me."

"Bruce, don't turn this into a cheap conquest."

"Look, baby, I'm not trying to sell you a fast bill of goods. I don't like the idea of falling in love. Laugh it off if you want to."

"You're funny," she said, and was silent for the next few moments. "It's hard to laugh in the dark."

"Then I'm glad it's dark."

"Four hours—"

"I know. It's crazy."

"If we keep talking, it'll be five."

"And it'll get light."

I think we were both smiling, then, even in the dark. I pulled her arm in tight beside me and reached for her with my other hand. I brushed her breast and it was naked, and my hand brought her shoulders towards me. Our lips found each other and our bodies followed. My hand trailed down her back to her hips and found she had compromised with nakedness. She had worn only panties to bed. As my lips left her she pulled me back, burning herself against me with healthy passion, and I thought to myself, Rua da Felicidade. Happiness Street.

Our lips separated and she hooked her hands behind my neck.

"What color are they?" I asked.

"What?"

"The panties."

"Black. They're brand-new. Don't tear them."

I didn't. When they reached her ankles she kicked them free and they were lost somewhere between the sheets.

In another moment she whispered, "Darling, am I one of the crowd?"

"What do you mean?"

"I mean, have you— How many others have you had?"

"Go to hell."

I kissed her eyes and returned to her lips. She responded anxiously and pretty soon we weren't even whispering any more. The old four-poster picked up the conversation.

Chapter Eleven

I don't know what woke me up. But even in sleep I realized Donna was no longer curled against me. I rose on my elbows and fought against alarm. My God, did I still distrust her?

I looked between the footposts of the bed, and movement stopped, like something caught on film. Donna stood there, and she was fully dressed. The room was filled with a yellow light from the window shade, still drawn. Donna's lips parted with a sort of panic as she saw me looking at her. She had my shirt and windbreaker in her hands, and she was searching the pockets.

It was a couple of moments before I could get my mind to function. Then I said, "What the hell are you doing, baby?"

She got a fast grip on herself and tossed my things to the foot of the bed. She faced me with sudden coolness. "Don't look so hurt. Maybe I'm just a tramp."

"There's nothing in my pockets."

"I'm finding that out. I want the papers."

I threw back the sheet and got into my trousers and felt awkward as hell doing it. "You're not making sense this morning."

"What have you done with them, Bruce?"

"That stuff can wait. It's us that counts. We were in love this morning."

"That was this morning. It's past noon now."

I walked to her and took her roughly in my arms. "Listen, baby, I love you. I love you any time of day, any week, any year."

"Please—don't kiss me, Bruce."

"You're trembling," I said. "You're acting phony, and you're trembling."

She twisted away and moved to the window. "I've changed my mind about things. I'm no good for you. I'm sorry I got you messed up in this business."

"You're trying to say something, but I can't figure out what it is. Maybe if you try real hard you can make sense."

"Why bother with explanations?" she muttered softly, her back toward me. "It'll be better if I take the report to Hong Kong myself. You can find someone else to sleep with. We can forget we ever met."

"Sure," I said. "It'll be easy."

She turned, but her eyes wouldn't look into mine. I was getting angry and I was glad for that, because it would keep me off my knees. I wouldn't beg, even for love.

She had been fumbling with the cord of the shade, and suddenly the shade flew up and fresh light splashed into the room. "Where—"

"If you really want it, it's yours," I snapped. I walked to the window and pulled the shade down again. "I took you and the plans to bed." I raised my foot and ripped the adhesive tape from my ankle. I threw it on the bed and started for the bathroom. "Go on. Get out."

Her composure crumbled. "Bruce, for God's sake, get me a cigarette."

"They're on the radio cabinet, baby. Take all you want."

I stood in the doorway and watched her hands go to her face as though to hide the desperation I would see. My jaws tightened as I walked to the radio. I lit a couple of cigarettes and approached her slowly. What the hell had happened? I pulled her hands away and placed a cigarette between her lips.

She drew on it slowly. "Don't hate me, Bruce."

"I'm just a guy you slept with," I said. "We're strangers."

"It would have been easier to leave if you hadn't awakened."

"Sorry I fouled up your plans."

"It's not right to fall in love so quickly."

"That was this morning," I said bitterly. "This is afternoon."

"My God, Bruce, don't throw my words back at me."

"You know what you're doing, I don't. No explanations, if that's the way you want it."

"I don't want to hurt you."

"I'm hard to hurt, baby. Really hurt."

"Bruce—"

I snapped the cigarette out of her lips and took her in my arms. I kissed her viciously. In another moment she was clinging to me, her muscles no longer tensed. We stood together a long time.

"What's wrong, baby? What's happened?"

"Me," she said. "Just me."

"I'm dumb. Wise me up."

Her hands found my back, and held tightly. "I love, you, darling. I love you—but you've made me feel so terribly cheap. I wanted to get away. Doesn't that make any sense? I didn't want to have to face you again."

"We acted like human beings," I said. "Let's not be ashamed of it."

"It happened so fast. Us, I mean. Four hours, and then this awful room on this awful alley. When I woke up this morning I felt like a tramp."

"I never go to bed with tramps," I said. "Only strangers. I'm sorry about this place, baby. The rooms are nicer in the Hotel China Seas, but this one is a lot safer."

"I'd never been frightened that way before—about myself, I mean. What I had let Jordan make of me. I threw myself at him, but I had a reason. With you, I had only four hours and no reason."

"To hell with Jordan."

"Try to understand me, Bruce, please. I know I'm sounding like an idiot. When we were together last night I tried to find a reason. I tried to convince myself I was in love with you. But it wasn't until a few minutes ago that I believed it. When you told me to get out, I knew. I am in love with you."

"Then it's settled, honey."

She turned out of my arms, and I realized she was still wound up inside. I thought to myself, You were a bastard for setting her up in a situation like this.

"Funny," I said. "Today I like your bangs."

"I thought I could walk out on you," she went on.

"Why don't you get Jordan off your chest?"

She hesitated, took her cigarette back out of my fingers, and sat on the edge of the bed. "It's not very pretty. Jordan was the only lead I had after Dad died. I knew he was mixed up in the smuggling and Dad's murder. I made a play for him, and he fell."

"You pitch a mean pair of eyelashes when you want."

"He didn't know who I really was, but I think he began to suspect last night."

"Enter Bruce Flemish."

She nodded. "Before that, he wanted me for keeps. Gradually, I learned enough to know I had the right man. When I felt I had him hooked I told him I needed money, a lot of money. I told him I was being blackmailed. He didn't ask questions—he just said he knew a way to get a lot of money. He said he was tired of the thing he was in, and we could go back to the States and live like millionaires."

"The papers?"

"Yes. His idea was to get safely to the States, then blackmail Wilkerson. Wilkerson's enormously wealthy, and he couldn't risk exposure. I persuaded Jordan to let me take the papers to Hong Kong, so he wouldn't run the risk of being discovered with them here. We planned to meet there and fly back to the States together. But last night he demanded the stuff back."

"Someone tipped him off who you were."

"I suppose so. I knew all along Jordan might be Dad's murderer, yet I slept with him." She cringed. "Then, this morning with you, I asked myself what sort of person I had become. It frightened me when I opened my eyes to this cheap room, and saw a man I hardly knew sleeping beside me."

"I think I'd have died if you'd really walked out of here, baby."

"That helps, darling."

"Where does Gonsalves fit into the picture?"

She twisted her head. "I don't know. Don't laugh, but I'm inclined to trust him. I've been on the verge of telling him who I am. He might simply have forgotten me from the past. For all I know, he thinks I'm working for Wilkerson. He was Dad's friend, I know that, but there's so much I don't understand. I've simply been afraid to trust anyone. Anyone but you."

"If it's all the same to you, I'll keep Gonsalves on my list. What did his boys do to you in the room?"

She lay back on her elbows and looked at the cherubs painted on the ceiling. "Just took pictures. It didn't hurt."

"His boys are nuts about photography. What pictures?"

Her eyes fell, avoiding mine. "Nasty ones."

"Well?"

"They said the pictures would go into the pornographic market unless I talked."

"You didn't talk."

"No."

"If I didn't know you better, I'd think you were a tramp."

"The idea terrifies me—naturally. I'm trying not to think about it. After I refused I thought they'd try some sort of immediate torture, but apparently someone got a better idea, because they left me alone."

"Yeah. I was their better idea, but I don't enjoy the thought of any pictures of you floating around in the hands of old men and lonely sailors. Maybe I can figure a way."

"Please, no. We've gone through so much for Dad's report. That's the only thing that's really important."

"Any reason we couldn't cable the stuff from Macao?"

"It wouldn't get through. It wouldn't be safe to try."

"All right, we'd better figure a way to Hong Kong. Sorry, baby, but we're holed up in this room until nightfall. There's a slim chance Gonsalves, Wilkerson and Company figure we've already slipped through their water-front blockade. That ought to help a little. Meanwhile, we've got to eat."

She began to smile. "I'm starved."

"I ought to be able to rustle up some chow within a hundred yards of this joint." I taped the papers back to my ankle and found Donna's purse. "I'm going to take your dough. I want to be damned sure you stay put."

She came up to me, put her hands on my shoulders, and asked for a kiss without saying a thing. We kissed, but not too long. Not long enough for more than reassurance. "I'll stay put," she said. "Be careful, darling."

I was careful. I watched the alley from a crack in the door until I felt sure it was safe to walk out in the sunlight. Donna locked the door after me and I made the few steps to the Rua da Felicidade at a casual pace. The sky was a brilliant blue and the sun was enough past noon to throw warm, heavy shadows along one side of the street.

The sidewalks hurried with life while rickshas and honking cars competed on the street. I paused on the corner after I spotted a Chinese sidewalk kitchen halfway down the block, but I saw no danger. I worked my way toward it and made the browned Oriental understand that I wanted food to take out. He turned to the job with a happy grin when I agreed to buy his largest rice bowl to contain it. He lifted metal lids off his steaming caldrons of food, but all I could identify was the rice and the three turtledoves he'd probably had small hope of selling. I saw a wineshop a couple of doors away and went there while he completed our menu. I bought two bottles of Portuguese red wine.

The Oriental was wrapping newspaper over the picnic lunch when I returned. I paid him and moved off.

It was only a matter of seconds before I noticed it. Along one side of the newspaper, turning brown from the moisture of food, was the top of a picture that continued into the folds of paper in my hand. I didn't have to see it all to recognize it.

It was the one Nakov had taken in my dressing room. Of me. Of Bruce Flemish in the act of murder.

Chapter Twelve

I glanced back, and the Oriental at the kitchen seemed to have his eyes on me. I hurried past the alley, around the block, and entered from the opposite end. At least, all he'd be able to say was that I went "that way" along the street. I kept my head low until Donna let me through the door.

"Hello, stranger." She smiled.

I set the warm bowl on the radio, removed the newspaper, and spread it out. It was in Portuguese, and I couldn't make head or tail of the story. But the picture was clear, and even with my eyes shut, it was a good likeness.

"You're pale, darling. What's wrong?"

"I'm suddenly famous," I said, "because I let Gonsalves throw a curve at me. Read Portuguese?"

"No."

I left the newspaper with her and began moving about the room. How many hours before dark? Six, maybe. Six hours in this hole of a room, and then an outside chance of slipping through the water front. Had that Oriental really recognized me, or had he merely watched me walk away out of curiosity, because I was a new customer?

Donna looked up from the paper, her spirits faltering. "I don't believe what I see, do I, darling? Seeing isn't believing, is it?"

"Every damned cop in Macao will have an eye out for me." I told her about the photograph pressure Gonsalves had put on me to throw in with him. "I thought I'd burned the negatives, but he must have had prints."

"Bruce, you risked *this* just to help me?"

"Don't rub it in."

"Bruce—"

"And that bastard lectured *me* on the good old American double-cross. Hey, wait!"

I tried to remember exactly what I had seen on the film he had held briefly to the light for me. I had seen two forms, and an arm that I thought was mine. But had it been? Gonsalves may not have had prints after all.

"Listen," I said. "This is just a chance, so don't count on it. Maybe Gonsalves isn't completely rotten. Maybe he had no intentions of actually releasing those dirty negatives of you. How many did his boys shoot?"

"Two."

"That figures. He showed me a couple of negatives when we were making a trade for the firecracker. I was overanxious to get out of there and maybe I jumped to conclusions. He may have switched your films on me. The only thing I'm sure of is that I burned hell out of two negatives."

She touched my arms and looked up to my face. "Bruce, how can you love me after what I've done to you?"

I began to calm down a little. Hell, we were still alive, weren't we? "If you didn't do things to me, baby, I wouldn't love you. We're not licked yet. Let's eat."

She got on her toes and kissed me. "Can we get married in Hong Kong? Am I asking too much, darling?"

"I wasn't going to give you a choice," I said. "If marriages are made in heaven, we'll get it done either there or in Hong Kong."

"I love you terribly. Even in this awful place, I love you."

"Can you put up with this awful place another few hours?"

"You're a magician. Turn it into a palace."

"Hocus pocus."

"It's a palace."

"I forgot chopsticks," I said. "We'll have to eat with our fingers."

We ate with our fingers and tried to figure out what we were eating. We forgot everything but us, and split the third turtledove. We drank wine out of the bottles, and told each other about our earlier lives in the States. She had grown up in Reno, and me, I was a San Francisco kid, and that made us practically neighbors. I told her how I had got into the magic game because I liked to keep moving, but she said she didn't want to chase me all over the world. I said I'd tried to quit a dozen times, and she said she'd cure me. She told me about a small cattle ranch in Nevada her dad had owned, but I told her I didn't go for chaps and spurs and the only thing I knew about cows was that they gave milk, and I didn't like milk. She said, nevertheless, I had the makings of a sensational cow hand.

"We'll have kids, of course," she said.

"Someone's got to drink the milk. How many?"

"All you want. You can put in your order any time you want to."

We might have got on with it, but a knock sounded at the door and brought us back to the present. We stared at each other for a confused moment.

"Get in the bathroom," Donna said firmly. "My picture's not in the papers."

"I can handle myself."

"Please, Bruce."

I hesitated, but when the knock came again I decided she was right. I got the gun out of her bag and closed the bathroom door—but not shut. I left a crack to see and hear.

I watched Donna straighten her shoulders with forced courage. Then she answered the knock.

"*Bom dia, senhorita,*" I heard an old man's cheerful voice say. "I am Father Bello. I come to save you from this life of sin. You are new here, yes?"

"I've got a customer, Father," Donna said. "Maybe later."

"I understand, senhorita. I make the rounds each day. Ah, there is no air in the streets. I fear we are in for a typhoon."

"Thanks for dropping by."

"My pleasure. Tomorrow, perhaps, you will invite me in."

She closed the door, and leaned against it to catch her breath. I came out of the bathroom. "You're handy to have around," I said.

She came toward me, smiling, and kissed me lightly. "If we're still here tomorrow, darling, I'm going to ask him in—to marry us."

I didn't say it, because I didn't want to add to her alarm, and maybe I was all wet. But I played with the idea that Father Bello was a phony. A police wolf in clerical robes. Or maybe one of Gonsalves' pack taking up the scent of this morning's trail. Hell, I decided angrily, stop looking for goblins. You're getting like Donna—automatically distrusting almost everyone.

I kissed Donna back. "Sure," I said. "I always wanted to get married in a palace."

Later, I began tinkering with the radio, trying to get it to work. I poked around for about twenty minutes, got mad at it, and then discovered the trouble. It wasn't plugged in.

I plugged it in, growling back at Donna's comment, and went

through a couple of Chinese stations before I hit English on Radio Hong Kong. A woman was giving a lecture, and I shut it off.

"Man, it's hot," I said.

"Bored, darling? That's what people are when they talk about the weather."

I kept thinking about Father Bello. Donna's father had made a mistake somewhere, and it had finished him.

It was one thing to mark the priest off as a case of nerves—mine—but a risk to let the idea go unchecked. "I'm going out for a minute," I said.

"Bruce—"

"I'll be right back. Relax." I didn't want to put the idea in her head, and I didn't want to argue. I just walked out, leaving her slightly confused and angry.

Outside, the alley was deserted and burning with heat. I moved toward the back, where the small, glass-fronted office sat. There was no one inside, and I saw a wall telephone. I tried the door and it was open. I went in.

I called the operator for the number of the seat of the diocese. From there on out everything went in slow motion. I was finally connected and then got shuttled from voice to voice until we got languages matched. And eventually I found out what I wanted to know. There *was* a Father Bello who made the rounds of the Rua da Felicidade, and even as I was getting the information I saw him coming out of a crib across the alley. I described him over the phone as he shook hands with the Eurasian girl and moved on to the next door. The description checked.

I hung up the phone and grinned with relief. I looked at an old wooden clock on the wall. It was almost four. In another couple of hours, the alley would come back to life.

I hurried to our room. I stepped inside, and said, "Hocus pocus—I'm back."

The room was empty.

I stood there, held to the spot by the blank face of the bathroom door. I got across the room and snapped open the door.

She was stretched the length of the zinc tub.

"You might have knocked," she said, Her face rested on the back, one arm draped over the side, a cigarette between her fingers. Her breasts seemed to float through the quiet surface of the water. She looked beautiful and very much alive.

"Hell of a time to take a bath," I said.

"It's a habit I have. Are you angry, darling?"

"I'm sorry, baby. You gave me a scare. These days I scare easy."

"I've often wondered," she muttered, "what I'd do if a strange man walked in on me when I was taking a bath. I'm not even embarrassed. At least, I should be embarrassed."

"Why don't you scream?"

She twisted her head. "No. I'm not the screaming type. Think of something else."

"You're a crazy kid." We were both smiling by then, and I pulled a towel off the enameled rod. "Get up."

She dipped the coal of the cigarette in the water and it died with a thin sizzle. Then she rose from the tub like a mermaid, turning her back toward me, and held her arms up. I wrapped the towel around her, sarong-like. Her hands closed softly over mine as I tucked in a corner.

"I was mad at you when you walked out," she whispered, "but I like the way you walked back in."

I turned her around and kissed her lips.

"You're getting wet," she said.

"Stop talking," I said.

I picked her up under the knees and arms, and her feet trailed water into the room and to the bed. Her tanned skin looked fresh and radiant where her shoulders rose from the towel, and where her legs left it. The next moment her head lay deep in the pillow and I kissed the colors, the restless green eyes, the red lips, her tanned shoulders.

"Home," she said.

"There's no place like," I said.

The towel ended up around one post of the bed.

Chapter Thirteen

I got some music on the radio, later, and we lay on the bed listening and talking and waiting for night, and dreading its arrival.

We tried not to talk about the trouble we were in, or our chances of getting away free to Hong Kong. But as the sunlight softened against the drawn shade, I found myself wanting to talk about the things that puzzled me.

"Have you ever heard of the São Paulo catacombs?" I asked.

"A little. It's a local myth, like the tunnel that's supposed to lead from the cathedral ruins out of the colony."

"Your father drew a map of it."

"I know. But I don't understand what he meant by it. I've asked questions about the catacombs and the tunnel, but all I got were smiles. They consider it a romantic joke. There's a legend that the early Jesuits buried their dead down there. In case the pirates sacked the town, the tunnel was a way out. But if they really built it, they didn't need it for that—the pirates never took over."

"I don't think your father would be fooled by myths."

"Officially, no one appears to have been interested enough to dig and find out. They say an earthquake destroyed the original cathedral, and when it was rebuilt—"

"A fire left only the facade. I know that much local history. I wish I had time to poke around up there."

The radio music cut out suddenly, and a calm British voice entered the room and we fell silent. It was one of those moments. Even before he really got started, you braced yourself for bad news. "We interrupt, ladies and gentlemen, to bring you further word on the typhoon that swept northern Luzon early this morning. The Royal Observatory reports the storm has moved into the South China Sea and may strike the China coast in approximately ten hours. Vessels in this area are advised to move to protected anchorage, although it is hoped the tropical depression will arc northward and miss the Pearl River estuary. According to the Philippine Meteorological Bureau, the storm, traveling at thirty miles an hour, carries winds of seventy to ninety-five miles an hour. This is ZBW, Radio Hong Kong."

I swore, hard and loud, and when the music was resumed, I shut the radio off. "That's great," I said. "Just great."

Donna lit a cigarette nervously. "When Father Bello mentioned it, I thought he was just making conversation."

"Ten hours. A typhoon on the way, and we kill the afternoon in bed."

She stiffened. "I hope it wasn't a *complete* waste of time to you."

I wheeled and took her shoulders in my hands. "I'm sorry. baby. I didn't mean it that way. If we're going to get off this damned colony there's no time to lose. We can't wait for darkness. If we're lucky, maybe we can fast-talk some junk captain into making the trip before the typhoon scare gets all over the water front."

"Bruce, why can't we just stay here? Wait it out."

"Look, we've been lucky so far, but let's not press it. The police are looking for me, remember? Our neighbors are already probably gossiping about the two Americans who hardly come out for air. We've got to keep moving."

"All right."

"Give me an hour. If I can't set up passage by then, we might as well forget it."

"Bruce, don't leave me here alone—again."

"I'll be back for you, don't worry about that. But I've got to nose around by myself. If I run into trouble, I want to be plenty mobile."

We hashed over that for a few minutes, and she finally saw it was the best way. I left my windbreaker, kissed her quickly, and checked on the alley. It was clear.

I walked the short distance to the water front under a late, merciless sun. I didn't kid myself. Either I was going to have luck or I wasn't, and there was too much life on the streets for me to make a fetish of caution. Whenever I spotted a striped turban, I changed direction. That meant cop, and it was no trick to avoid them.

I followed through a lane that brought me face to face with the inner harbor. There was frantic movement on the wharves, and volleys of commands aimed at the coolies unloading the junks. Under the mysterious sunlight, the colors seemed sapped of vitality. Baskets of fish were being hustled off the wharves, but I already knew the answer to the fevered activity. Typhoon.

Riding the muddy water were clusters of junks, the larger ones looking like ancient caravels. Sampans worked around the surface like
wooden bugs.

I chose my moment, and then crossed quickly to a loading platform.
The fish odors were almost too thick to penetrate. I caught the eye of
a sampan coolie, a boy, climbed down to the water, and slipped under
the mat canopy of his boat. I pointed out a nest of junks in the stream
that looked seagoing and told him to take me there.

He grinned back and got the sampan moving.

As we approached, the junks looked listless in the water, their mat-
ting sails folded, brown fish nets hung from the masts to dry.

I climbed aboard the nearest one and caged ducks near the poop
began to squawk nervously at the intrusion. I stepped over a tangle of
lines and moved toward a low deckhouse, but no one appeared to
challenge me. There was a broken wooden door, and I opened it.

A small light burned below, and I saw three Chinese women. Only
one of them looked at me. She was on her back, her face contorted
with pain. The other women were midwives.

I started to close the door, with unspoken apologies, when I paused.
That woman, lying on a pile of dirty pallets, was smiling now. I smiled
back, while the midwives looked as though the end of the world were
coming, instead of the beginning of one.

When I closed the door I turned and faced the eyes of a stocky Chinese fisherman.

"Are you the captain?" I asked.

"This ship my ship."

"I want to go to Hong Kong. Now. In a hurry. I'll pay—"

He shook his head. "*Tai-fung* nearby. All boats come in. No go out.
Tai-fung bring on baby."

Typhoon bring on baby. These guys didn't need radios, and they
probably couldn't read a barometer. They had other ways of knowing.

I left him without arguing, and crossed to the junk tied next to him.

And then the next, and I got the same answer, with smiles, with suspicion, with finality. I returned to the waiting sampan and had the
boy taxi me to another group. I didn't lose time going aboard. I called
up for the captains. Some were deaf to English, but when I was understood I got the same answer—typhoon.

I was licked.

I told the boy to take me back in, and then he finally opened his mouth.

"Wanchee go Hong Kong?"

"You catch on fast."

"*Chinês Negro*—maybe him take you."

"The Black Chinaman?"

"Yes—proper name. Him smuggler. Velly good man."

And probably a cutthroat as well, I said to myself. "All right, take me to him."

The coolie nosed the sampan out across the harbor waters toward the worn shoulders of Patera Island. He skirted the low apron of land and brought us slowly to the far side of the island, out of sight of Macao. We moved along slowly, and so many minutes dropped away I grew suspicious. Maybe my coolie was only a smart kid chasing phantoms for extra fare.

Suddenly he pointed victoriously. *"Chinês Negro."*

I saw the pomegranate-red stern of a motor junk, anchored off a beach cove. It was narrow, like all junks, but the superstructure was low and sleek. Its wooden rudder, rising from the silted water, was cut through with diamond-shaped perforations. The junk appeared asleep, like some huge water animal floating lazily under the hot sun.

We scraped alongside and I climbed aboard. The first thing I saw was a Portuguese boy of about three, with a large gourd tied to his back.

"Tufão coming," he announced with childish friendliness, as though repeating idle gossip he had heard. The words made me grit my teeth. Even the kids were talking about the weather.

"Take me to the *Chinês Negro.*"

A small, dirty hand reached into mine and the boy began pulling me along the deck toward the poop. I stooped low through a wooden hatch and followed him down a short ladder. The air below was hot and stuffy and flavored with a heavy, sweet odor. I recognized it at once: opium.

The child pulled apart a rich lavender curtain and the smell billowed out with fresh fury. A small lamp, turned low, hung from the sloping bulkhead of the sleeping quarters.

I saw the Black Chinaman.

He lay curled on his side on a modem mattress flat on the deck.

Beside him a woman looked up startled from a small alcohol burner where a black pellet was beginning to simmer on the end of a long needle. She was obviously a Portuguese Eurasian, dark and striking. The Black Chinaman, his eyes closed, one hand outstretched as though waiting for the next pipe she prepared, was naked to the waist. Reddish hair covered his black chest and shoulders, and thick muscles stood out with quiet menace as he shifted impatiently on the mattress.

The woman barked at the child, who ran away laughing.

Something rustled behind me, and when I turned I saw an old Portuguese sailor with a very new gun in his hand, standing in the opening of the curtain.

"What do you want?"

"I want to do business with the *Chinês Negro,*" I answered.

The woman spoke. "He sleeps. No business now."

"No," I said. "His eyes are open."

They were half open, watching us through a dreamy grin. The eyes were completely Oriental, full-fleshed above, almost lashless. The pupils gleamed a leather brown. The nose was handsomely fine and sharp, the skin a rich black. "You are an American?" he muttered in a soft, resonant voice.

"Yes."

"Please sit down."

There were no chairs. I sat on a pallet and the Black Chinaman rose to a cross-legged position on his mattress. He motioned the sailor away with a curt flourish of his arm. He turned to the woman. "This smoke is of bad quality. It gives me a headache. We will resume later with Chandu."

She nodded and turned off the flame. She left the familiar pipe beside the mattress and retired silently from the compartment. I looked him over carefully. Where but in Macao would you find a black Chinese? I thought. He had the small angular frame of Portugal's China, with the muscular overlay of Portugal's Africa. His hair was thick and short-cropped and straight, the color of dark rust. I wondered how many pipes he had already smoked. The nauseous odor hung like a fog in the unventilated room. If he were too full of smoke, I'd be wasting my time on him. He'd never find his way to Hong Kong through an opium dream.

He was wearing dirty white trousers, his feet bare. "Sits before you *O Chinês Negro*," he announced hazily.

"I want you to take me to Hong Kong," I said. "Now."

"There is talk in the harbor *of tufão*."

"I know, but there's still time to make the crossing. I heard *O Chinês Negro* was very brave, afraid of no storms."

"My ship is good."

"So is my money. I'll pay five hundred Hong Kong dollars—passage for two."

He laughed deeply, his mind sharpening as we talked. "You take the steamer. It will save you money. I go back to my pipe."

"What is your price? Damnit, it's only forty miles."

He rested his hands on his knees; he delayed, he waited as though straining to force the fog out of his head. I had less than H.K. $800 of Donna's money, worth about $130 on the exchange, and I knew he'd bargain for every cent. In the dimly lit compartment, his white teeth shone behind a fragile smile. He was a young man, I realized suddenly, perhaps not yet thirty. "*Tufão* increase the price many fold."

"How much?"

He snapped his finger with finality. "Five thousand Hong Kong."

His mind had sharpened, all right. "Damnit, if you've got any speed in this junk, you could make it in three or four hours. My price would give you fast money."

"I prefer to remain in Macao. It is you who wish to go to Hong Kong."

"All I can spare is six hundred."

He chuckled warmly. "Then we both remain in Macao."

I let my anger show. "Hell, you're just like the others," I said. "All the river men here are scared silly of that typhoon. Even *O Chinês Negro*. I'm sorry I broke into your pipe dreams."

I started to rise. He grinned handsomely and held out a hand. "My skin is black," he said. "It came from Moçambique many centuries ago. A black skin makes a heart brave. Sit down. We discuss price, not courage."

"I don't have time to haggle with the Oriental in you. If six hundred dollars warm your blood, warm up your engines."

"It is the extent of your funds?"

"It's every damned cent I'm willing to pay."

"Who is the other passenger?"

"A woman."

"She is beautiful?"

"What's that got to do with it?"

He smiled pensively. "With a beautiful woman aboard, the *tufão* will make way for us. You carry the money with you?"

I moved to the drapes. "I'll bring her back. When Macao is out of sight, I'll pay."

"You do not trust me?"

'No'

"That is wise. We shall await your return."

When I got back to the alley, a few women were already sitting in their doorways looking for early customers. I reached our room, knocked quickly, and waited. No one answered. What the hell. I thought angrily, if Donna were taking another bath I'd drown her.

I tried the knob and was alarmed to discover the door was unlocked. I walked into the half-darkness of the room and the hair rose on my skin.

I didn't see Donna. I saw Josef Nakov lying comfortably on the bed, pillows propping up his back, and a gun in his hands aimed directly at me.

"Welcome home," he said.

Chapter Fourteen

"What have you done with her?" I growled.

The small Russian swung his legs off he bed, the gun and his heavy lenses following me. "The senhor, it is not easy to outwit him, my friend. Luck has been with us. We have kidnaped the girl—a very common happening in this part of the world. But we shall be kinder to her than the others were to the senhor. We will not remove her thumbs."

I started for him.

"Please, my friend, keep your distance. The senhor will not mind if I kill you. The police, also, will understand without much explanation."

"Where is she, Nakov? In the hotel?"

"She is safe—from all eyes. The place need not concern us at the moment."

I looked at his gun, and decided it was no time to argue. "How'd you find us? Father Bello?"

"Nothing happens in this quarter that he does not know, my friend. But his motives were quite innocent in helping us. A few questions from us, a few answers from him—it is enough. Do not blame the good father. But we thought you had slipped through our fingers— patrol boats are even now searching to bring you back."

"O.K., I'm here. Now what?"

"You are privileged, my friend. You will have the honor of ransoming the girl."

"What makes Gonsalves so sure I give a damn what happens to her?"

"A few papers make a cheap price to pay for such a lovely woman. You will pay."

I wanted to rip the adhesive tape off my ankle and throw it at him, but something held me back—wild, crazy anger. I *couldn't* give in to Gonsalves. "Go to hell. Tell the senhor to go to hell."

"Later, we will aid you both to get out of Macao."

"Sure, you'll ship us in coffins. You're not kidding me, Nakov. Gonsalves wants the papers *and us.* He figures we know too much."

Nakov brushed the accusation aside with a skin-deep smile. "It is a fine proposition—especially if you consider that I can shoot you at this moment and take the papers."

"Are you so damned sure I've got them?"

"No, but the gamble is in my favor."

"All right, take me to Gonsalves."

"You have a gun?"

"If I had a gun you'd be doing the Russian Cossack dance by now."

He approached and patted my pockets anyway. I kept telling myself: You're not the hero type, forget Donna. You'll both be goners, and the papers as well. Gonsalves takes all—unless you get back to the junk.

"Now, into the alley," Nakov said firmly. "I will walk directly behind you."

He opened the door for me, and I spun. My hand lashed the gun barrel as his finger pressed the trigger. The shot went wild. I blasted a fist into his face, and it snapped him sprawling against the wall. He was a little guy with a big gun, and it had taken only one good poke. He slipped along the wall to the floor. Out.

Out, get out fast. That gunshot would draw interest and cops. I paused only long enough to get Nakov's gun, and stepped into the alley.

Light was fading, but the heat held up. Doors were opening along the alley and heads poked out curiously. I forced myself to walk away slowly. Hell, maybe they'd figure a firecracker had exploded. Eyes turned on me, but I kept walking. When I reached the end of the alley, I somehow kept from running. I shouldered my way through the sidewalk life, and later I couldn't contain myself any longer. I began to run.

I got down to the water front where the sampan coolie was still waiting. He didn't need directions, and once I was under the canopy he shoved off. I kept asking myself, Can I leave Donna behind? Are the papers really *that* important? On the surface I knew I was doing what she would have pleaded for me to do, but inside I was beginning to die. I loved her, and I was walking out on her. I was being logical, not heroic.

A dozen times I was on the verge of ordering the coolie back, but what could I do? If Gonsalves didn't get me, the cops would. Why kid myself? I was licked in Macao. Get away. Get to Hong Kong. Don't let Gonsalves win all the prizes hands down.

The small engine was turning over with noisy impatience as we came alongside. I paid the coolie and crawled over the rail. It was growing dark, the air still and expectant. The captain came toward me from the poop.

"You are alone?"

"Yes," I snapped. "Shove off."

His eyes wrinkled along their ends, and for a moment he looked completely Oriental despite the black skin. A pair of binoculars were strung from his neck, and a palm hat with a small peak at the center rode jauntily on his head. "Too bad." He grinned. "I was eager to meet the American's woman, and my wife is jealous for nothing."

I saw his wife, holding the child near a mast, her eyes dark and suspicious as they watched us. Her black hair was very long and appeared freshly brushed. She had tried to make herself look pretty while I was gone. Not for us, but for *O Chinês Negro.*

He laughed when he saw her. "She loves this black skin of mine—and she makes a good pipe. Use my sleeping quarters, we have no others. The rest is for cargo."

"I'll stay on deck."

"Tie a gourd to your back, then," he laughed, "like the boy, in case the typhoon washes you overboard."

"What are you waiting for?"

"Please—show your money. It would be a pity to make a false start."

I let him look at it, and he was satisfied. Then he turned and leaped briskly up the ladder to the poop.

He shouted to the old Portuguese sailor at the bow, and a moment later the anchor was lifted and the junk began to cut slowly through the water. My jaws were clenched as I walked forward. I was doing what my reason said was right, but my heart said it was wrong.

The junk picked up speed and a few moments later we turned into the harbor. A few sea birds squawked at the sampans and junks crowding nervously around the water-front jetties, and their distant voices made the only sound around us. Lights were beginning to come on ashore and overhead.

I felt like a guy teetering on the edge of a high window, trying to talk himself out of jumping. It would be suicide for me to go back, yet

I had to keep the shout from bursting through my lips. Donna was somewhere behind that sprawling water front, and soon we'd be out of sight. Of Macao, and of each other.

They wouldn't kill her, I reasoned desperately—not until they abandoned hope that she could lure me and the papers to them. I still had time to think, to gamble.

I stood watching, but hardly seeing, as we passed the tip of the peninsula and headed sharply into open water.

Nakov's gun felt heavy in my pocket, and I decided to check it. There might be trouble before the trip was over, and I wanted to know what I had to back me up. Nakov said Gonsalves had patrol boats out looking for me. They were probably far ahead.

It was a revolver, and I threw off the cylinder. There were cartridges in all but two chambers. That left me four shots. I started to toss the cylinder back in place, when I looked again. One shot had been fired in the room, but the other empty chamber didn't look empty.

Something white was coiled up inside, something Nakov obviously meant to hide. I picked it out and unrolled a small square of photographic paper.

I moved close to the port running light. It was a contact print about the size of a match folder, a candid shot. Under the red glow I made out the figure of a stocky man walking between two armed Red Chinese soldiers along a deserted jetty. The camera had been snapped as the man took a despondent drag on a cigarette. He looked as though he were being walked somewhere—to his death.

The man was easy to recognize. He was Senhor Gonsalves.

But as I held the picture closer to the light, I wasn't sure I understood what I saw.

In this picture. Senhor Gonsalves had both his thumbs.

On the river in the photographed background floated several small boats decorated with dragons' heads at the bows. The whole scene appeared in a dawn light. Gonsalves with his thumbs, Gonsalves between Red soldiers. Had it been a political kidnaping six months ago?

Why had Nakov kept the picture hidden? Was it fodder for blackmail, or what?

I didn't recognize the background, but I could see it wasn't Macao.

I slipped the small print in my pocket and counted $600 for the Black Chinaman. We were losing sight of Macao.

I lit a cigarette and walked to the afterpart of the ship. I climbed the short ladder to the poop, where *O Chinês Negro* stood at the wheel.

"I expected you to be a little more anxious for your money," I said.

He laughed. "You can go nowhere with it. I am not worried."

I handed over the bills. "How long?"

"I am not a prophet. If the river and the wind do not get angry at us, four hours perhaps." He pocketed the dough without counting it. *"Obrigado."*

"How about turning off your running lights?"

"You have more to fear than the storm, magician?"

I picked out the whites of his eyes in the darkness. "All right, what else did you pick up from your seagoing grapevine?"

"Magician, in my business it is wise to know all things. I know you run from Senhor Gonsalves."

I felt my muscles tense up. "A friend of yours?"

"A good man, a patriot. But I, too, must often run from him. He makes trouble for us on the river who find profit in other than fishing. He is close to the governor general."

"So I've heard. In my book, he's a complete bastard."

"Since the famous kidnaping, he seldom bothers us. The occurrence broke his spirit, and now there is little trouble in running our cargoes."

He twisted the wheel as a swell caught us, and I planted my feet farther apart. "You know this river," I said. "What does it mean when the boats get dolled up like dragons?"

"You change the subject?"

"Not necessarily."

"It occurs in the dragon-boat festival."

"When?"

"During the Fifth Moon."

Did it make sense, I asked myself? There was a picture in my pocket that must have been taken only a couple of months ago. Gonvalves with his thumbs.

Blood rushed at my head. "Turn around!" I shouted. "We're going back!"

There was a small chuckle, but it wasn't coming from his lips. It was near, behind me, and I turned instantly. "On the contrary, my lad, we're going on to Hong Kong."

Coming up the ladder was the unmistakable bulk of Colonel Percy Wilkerson.

Chapter Fifteen

"A bloody night for a river trip," Wilkerson said, swinging up to the poop deck with exaggerated agility. "I say, my lad, you might have let the typhoon pass before pulling out on us."

I gripped the handle of the gun in my pocket and stared at him, only half believing what I saw. The baggy seersucker suit looked ectoplasmic in the darkness. "What brought you aboard?" I muttered stupidly. "A strong wind?"

"It was easy enough to manage. I say, you've got a gun."

"I'm aching to shoot someone—anyone. Maybe you'll do, Wilkerson." I turned to the Black Chinaman. "Get this tub turned around."

"Stay on your course, Captain," Wilkerson directed in an unruffled voice. "This lad is impulsive—someone must look out for him. I'll accept the responsibility."

The Black Chinaman looked between us, grinning, and kept the wheel steady.

"See here, my lad," Wilkerson said evenly, "put away the gun. If you shoot us both, you'll have a bloody time navigating this vessel anywhere in the dark. Shall we go below for a chat? I waited, but you didn't come down."

"What's your game, Wilkerson? How did you spot me?"

"You walked directly past my godown on the water front. You might have been more cautious, my lad. I had all but given you up. Figured you were up to a bit of a run, and me with a bad arm, too, thanks to your handy ways with a knife. No grudge, my lad. Followed your sampan at a distance and came aboard during your absence."

"We're going back," I said. "The captain seems to take orders from you. Tell him."

"My lad, I paid him a greater sum than you. You *were* a bit cheap." He started down the ladder. "Coming?"

I felt like a kid with a toy in my hand. No one seemed to consider the gun deadly but me. But if I were going to shoot, the time was now. I looked down at Wilkerson's white form and couldn't pull the trigger. The first puff of spray exploded from the bow and swept back along the junk. I looked at the Black Chinaman.

"I turn back," he whispered amiably, "for the woman, yes?"

"Yes."

"Go below, then."

I eyed him and suddenly I loved the guy. Wilkerson was already out of sight, confident that I would follow. I was going back to play a hunch, to pin down a legend, to tempt disaster, and I felt right about it. "Pull in off the Porto do Cerco," I said. "Is there a graveyard just beyond it?"'

"Yes, but that is Communist soil."

"That's where I want to go."

Then I went after Wilkerson. No sense in keeping him waiting.

The woman left the compartment as I entered. The child remained asleep on a pallet in a corner. The accumulated scent of opium clung to the swaying room, but at least the fresh smoke had been aired out. Wilkerson sat on the mattress, grinning as I entered.

"Now then, shall we lay our cards on the table and shuffle them into a single deck? I'm not a bad chap when you get to know me."

"Who are you, Wilkerson?"

"An honest businessman forced into violence by scoundrels. Put away the gun, my lad. It's quite useless."

"I like holding it," I said. "Makes me feel like a kid again. Why are *you* so damned anxious to get to Hong Kong?"

"The report that accident has placed in your hands would ruin me, as you doubtless know. What is your game, my lad? Reward from the customs service? I understand they pay handsomely."

"I'm just in it for kicks," I said.

"The girl is an adventuress, of course. Jordan, I expect, is sorry he ever met her."

"Look," I snapped. "Her father got a line on your smuggling, and it got him murdered. Chances are his blood is on your hands. Want to change the subject?"

The grin left his face. "Let's not. Are you *sure*? About the girl, I mean."

"Quite," I said.

"Now, that's bloody surprising, but I didn't kill her father, you know. My regret is he wasn't accurate. I rather suspect it was Jordan who did him in." He dipped into a pocket and brought out a handful of watermelon seeds.

"How are you doing it, Wilkerson? Exporting dope from your fire-cracker plant?"

"My lad, you jump to conclusions. I fear the authorities will do the same. That's why I consider it vital that *I* deliver the report rather than *you.*"

"What's the matter, don't you like the color of my eyes?"

"The report is in error and I think it imperative to the good name of my firm that I hand it over voluntarily. I shall then be in a position to bargain for my honor. So you see why I am as anxious as you so recently were to reach Hong Kong."

"I've never read the report," I said. "I'm still on a guessing basis over the whole affair."

His eyes fastened on me as he began to munch the seeds. "There are moments, my lad, when I am inclined to enjoy your company. You are disarmingly naive."

"Thanks."

"I have been victimized, sir, by a scoundrel."

"Jordan?"

"Exactly. An American, too, such as yourself. You did me a service, if one can believe the papers."

"Now *you're* jumping to conclusions," I said.

"Am I? That's delightful. As manager of my plant, Jordan was able to salt my shipments to your country with firecrackers of another make, but with my brand labels. As you guessed, capsules of opium were substituted for the powder within the shells. Where he obtained his narcotic supplies, I do not know. Since the end of the recent great war the bloody poppy has been outlawed here in Macao, and the governor general has tried hard to enforce the new laws."

"How nice," I said. I listened to the throb of the engine and wondered if the lights of the water front had come back in sight.

"I fancy," Wilkerson went on bitterly, "Jordan has been able to do his business within my business at a rate of perhaps a million American dollars a month."

"I heard he was broke."

"Without question he is but a cog in a larger machine. There is the smell of politics about the whole affair."

"The Reds?"

"Quite likely."

"Why is Senhor Gonsalves so interested?"

"A queer duck, that one, but very close to—"

"I know—the governor general."

"He has patriotic motives, I expect. A gambler, but gambling is legal. A man of alternate moods, a split personality, if I may say so."

"It figures," I muttered.

"The report, if I am to believe Jordan, names this old party as the head of the bloody smuggling enterprise. Only yesterday he attempted to blackmail me on that basis, but when I produced his price, he was unable to produce the report. It would have been the simpler way out for me, of course, and in business there are times when one must swallow his pride."

"How would Jordan know? Does he read code?"

"He claims to have provided the girl's father with the very information. His motives are obscure. Perhaps he saw the jig was up and decided it would be wiser to misdirect attention from himself. He was not an honorable man. My lad, I have spent thirty-eight years in the Orient, and I hope to survive another thirty-eight-as a man of honor. But I fight for more than face. I shall be ruined if your country bars all imports of my product. I depend upon U.S. dollars to balance my books, now that the Reds have closed the Chinese market to me."

"Everybody's got problems," I said. "We'll turn the report over to the authorities together."

"My lad, you still don't trust me."

"After what I've been through, I wouldn't trust the Chase National Bank. Nothing personal—I'm just not giving the report to anyone this side of the consulate in Hong Kong."

"I shan't let you out of my sight, then. I do apologize, my lad, for refusing to turn back. Is it the girl? Surely, now, you understand my anxiety to get the report out of Macao and out of reach of interested parties there."

I got up, and he smiled at the gun still in my hands. I was inclined to believe Wilkerson, but I couldn't dismiss the fact that destroying the report would be the easier way out of his troubles. He had admitted agreeing to Jordan's blackmail. It was apparently Jordan's itching palm that had caused him to try to get the report back from Donna, not the fact that he had caught on to her identity. "I'm going on deck," I said. "You want to stay here?"

He laughed broadly and brushed the residue of the seeds from his palms. "My lad, I don't intend to allow you from my sight."

He got up and I held the curtains apart for him. I was going to have to do it, and I was going to hate it. The child rustled on his pallet, turned on his stomach, and muttered in his sleep. Wilkerson moved through the curtains, and as soon as his back was toward me, I let him have the butt of the gun. I saw his head turn and surprise in his eyes, and I felt a little sick. His legs gave way as the junk rode a swell, and he fell heavily, overturning a dark wooden box within the cabin. A couple of modern hand grenades spilled onto the deck and rolled free.

I went after them, and then took a closer look at the box. The Black Chinaman's private arsenal—collected piecemeal, I reasoned, from the cargoes he smuggled. I placed a grenade in both front trousers pockets, and slipped the revolver through my belt. I still felt like a kid playing war, armed to the teeth and looking a little foolish. But I had a hollow feeling inside. I wasn't having fun.

I saw distant lights to port as soon as I got on deck. They were moving behind us and it took me a few moments to orient myself. They would be the lights of the outer harbor, edged by the busy Praia Grande. I came up beside the Black Chinaman, who was peering through his binoculars at the shoreline. The Portuguese sailor was at the wheel and the woman stood with her back to the low rail, watching me.

"There is Porto do Cerco," the captain said to me, handing over the glasses. "To the right, you will see the old cemetery."

I held the binoculars to my eyes. At first I could see nothing but blackness, but finally dim shadows cleared on the lenses. Thin lights were spotted about the massive brick arch, the Porto do Cerco, dividing Red China from Macao. I could see only the top of the barrier gate, but at its base I knew there were soldiers of different nations guarding either side. I edged to the right and gradually made out a dark hillside, broken with small patches of gray-white. The cemetery.

"How long can you wait for me?" I asked, handing back the glasses.

"An hour. Two hours—no more. That should be enough for a magician, yes?"

"Yes."

I noticed for the first time that our own running lights were off. The Black Chinaman cut speed so that we almost seemed to be drifting.

"We cross into Red Waters," he said. "I will take you as close to shore as I dare."

"Thanks."

"My woman and her old father do not like what I do. They say I am a crazy one. But it amuses me to see an American take more risks than I."

"Don't go away," I said. "I'll be back."

"With the girl."

Within another five minutes we had drifted to about three hundred yards offshore. The captain nodded his head. This was as far as he went.

I thanked him and started down the ladder to the deck. The woman suddenly began to chatter in Portuguese to the Black Chinaman. I thought it was a family argument starting up and was glad enough to get out of there. But he called me back.

"My woman says to let you use a rowboat."

"I can swim."

"The girl, perhaps, cannot."

I fell in love with both of them.

Within another five minutes we had silently lowered a flyweight dinghy to the water, and I shoved off in the darkness.

Chapter Sixteen

João Santos. A Portuguese name on an old Chinese grave, but in Macao even the Chinese had Christian names. Donna's father had marked the entrance to a legendary tunnel with that name, and I thought to myself that if he *had* made errors in his report, this had better not be one of them.

I rowed softly, and tried to convince myself I was acting with logic. After a couple of minutes, I gave up thinking about it. The stars were still out in that false calm before the storm. Two hours. Hurry.

I let up on the oars a few yards offshore and peered into the darkness. If there was any life on the hillside, I couldn't see it and I couldn't hear it. I continued rowing until the skiff felt the drag of bottom. I climbed out and pulled the boat to a firm purchase in the heavy silt of the shore.

Any boats that normally slept in these waters, I figured, had scurried to inner harbor to seek protection from the storm.

I straightened, took the gun out of my belt, and started to walk.

Within seconds I was on a weedy slope and began to climb. The darkness ahead of me was broken only by the faint whites of horseshoe-shaped graves. They lay in the hillside like so many miniature Greek amphitheatres, each with its own audience of family tombstones.

I had matches, but I dreaded showing light even though I felt myself the only living thing around. I tried reading a tombstone name with my fingers, and found it worked. I felt the carvings of Oriental ideograms running vertically. João Santos, unless he too were legend, I thought would read across.

I moved from grave to grave of varying sizes, slowed up by an occasional Christian name. I was losing time fast, but I could figure no other way. I *had* to have luck. If I didn't have it now, I wouldn't need it later.

I crouched in a small grave, and my fingers traveled back over the name letters for a fresh start. I had felt a J, and it brought me alert.

J as in João. My fingers worked nervously. S as in Santos. My hopes soared. Trembling, I picked out the date: 1641.

I straightened, João Santos, at least, wasn't legend. He was dead, and this was his grave.

I heard two voices suddenly above me on the slope, Chinese voices. I dropped quickly behind the horseshoe curve at the low vault doors. One of the voices was a woman's, and both grew quickly louder. I gripped the gun and peered into the darkness above. Two figures took shape only a few yards from me. I could make out enough to know both were in the uniforms of Red China. They were coming down the hill, hand in hand, and I crouched motionless as they passed the grave of João Santos. Their voices gradually disappeared along the hillside, but I was too tensed up to laugh about them. They'd picked a hell of a place to be alone.

I put the gun back in my belt and ran my hands over the small vault doors. They felt like brass encrusted with age. The lock plate was ornate to the touch, but old as the mechanism was, it held firm. I decided against wasting time trying to pick it. I would have to shoot, and I hoped I could be safely within before the noise attracted Reds within earshot.

I nudged the tip of the gun in place and fired. The explosion rolled up the hillside like thunder, but the doors gave. I rushed through and closed them again quickly. Let the Reds wonder what happened, and where.

Even though it was black in there, I could feel the smallness of the room. I lit a match. The coffin was inches from me, deeply carved and lacquered in brilliant reds and greens. I dragged it away from the wall when the match went out and shoved it against the doors to prevent them from swinging open under investigation from outside. When I lit another match, I saw that legend was fact.

I had uncovered the entrance to a tunnel.

The coffin had rested over the opening. I tested a foot inside, felt the rung of a ladder, and a moment later followed with my body.

It was only a few steps down to the tunnel itself. I lit another match and light flickered ahead of me: walls narrow and dry, the ceiling occasionally strengthened by old wooden beams. The steady current of air snuffed out the match, and I lit another. In the second moment of visibility I almost rejected as imaginary what I saw near my feet. A flashlight.

I picked it up and tried it. The batteries were fresh. I decided the

tunnel was well used, the flashlight left by the last person out for his
return.

I couldn't quite stand straight, but I tried to hurry in a bent position.
There had been a familiar odor in the air the moment I had entered;
now I pinned it down. Opium.

I scurried along, and the position I was forced into made me feel ani-
mal-like. Nothing changed in the beam of the flashlight: dark, low
walls and rotted beams, some of them fallen. I felt a charge of discovery, but my fears were larger. It was only a wild guess that I would
find Donna at the other end.

Despite the air current, perspiration rolled off my skin. I couldn't
gauge the distance I had come, but I knew I must be out of Red China
and under the outer streets of Macao. As I hurried forward I began to
notice the smell of opium growing stronger. Judging from the map,
the tunnel stretched about a mile in length, but it seemed as though
I had already come twice that.

Occasionally the beam of my flashlight sent a rat scurrying. My back
ached, but I couldn't straighten, and my head felt battered and raw
where I had scraped the rough ceiling in my haste. I don't know how
many black minutes passed before my nose and skin warned me I was
approaching the end. The opium fumes had almost imperceptibly
grown to powerful, dizzying strength and the air was becoming heat-
ed.

I stopped, catching my breath, and snapped off the light. Then I felt
my way forward for more minutes. I saw dim light ahead.

It flickered against the walls at a turn. I left the flashlight in the dirt
and got hold of the gun. I moved quietly to the end and exposed my
head cautiously to see along the traverse passage.

I saw several lighted kerosene lamps hooked from the ceiling beams
along a maze of catacomb cells. I saw two old Chinese, stripped to
their waists, tending rows of small charcoal ovens. A white vapor rose
from brass basins on each—opium cooking. I could hear the soft,
thick bubbling of the raw stuff as the Orientals moved silently from
basin to basin and stirred the dark, chocolate-like masses. The night
shift, I thought. I saw crypts along the walls, overhung here and there
with banner portraits of China's Red leaders.

I didn't hesitate. I stepped into the corridor and shot twice. One
Chinese, his eyes suddenly turned to me with amazement, stumbled

against the brazier nearest him as he fell. The steaming basin slipped after him and spilled the lava-like narcotic over his shaved head, choking off his terrified scream. I couldn't watch. The other didn't know what hit him. His back had been turned, and I didn't give a damn about chivalry when I fired.

But the explosions brought a third Chinese out of one of the connecting aisles, and we startled each other. He began to jabber in alarm. I pressed the trigger. I missed, and hated to use my last shot, but had to fire again. He twisted and fell. I waited. There were no others.

My nostrils felt thickened by the fumes, and the intense heat thrown off by the rows of ovens made my eyes burn and my head throb. I hurried through the main passage to the end—solid wall. I entered the side aisles looking for another chamber or a way out. I stumbled over raw supplies, boxes packed with large, rough balls of unprocessed opium.

I found a way out. At the end of a deep, closet-like burial passage I came upon new wooden stairs. I held onto the gun, even though it was empty.

I climbed high into complete darkness again. My head finally touched surface, and my hands explored it. Wood. I pressed against it, and it raised. I expected to see light, but I saw nothing. I pushed my hand through the open crack, and felt the close-ribbed underside of carpeting. I would have liked to see what I was getting into, but I couldn't stop to worry about it. I pushed the trap door up and climbed out.

It was still dark, but I made out windows on one side of the room. I walked quietly to the nearest and looked out. The silent, gray facade of the cathedral, like the last remaining wall of a gutted building, rose close on my right. Tile-roofed factory buildings and old living quarters were lit up at its base and along the shoulders of the hill.

I used a match to get my bearings in the room. I saw stock all around me—fireworks. Was this Wilkerson's place? I wondered. There was a door ahead of me, but no ray of light showed beneath it.

I turned the knob slowly. I entered a darkened factory room with rows of stools and littered tables. I cupped the match in my hands to narrow the light. I saw what would be the front door onto the street. I saw a stairway leading above.

I took the stairway. At the top I entered along a carpeted hall of living quarters. Then I saw light. It came through the bottom crack of a door at the end.

I heard the tired, faint sobbing of a woman long past hysterics. I heard the angry growl of a voice I knew.

I pressed my hand around the knob and turned it slowly. I felt the tongue draw back in the lock. The door was open.

I shoved it wide and stood with the gun in my hand as both of them turned.

Senhor Gonsalves was standing beside a bed. His face was swollen with rage. His expression could hardly make room for surprise. The woman on the bed, her body clearly bruised, wasn't Donna, and there were no others in the room.

It was Phebe, the stripper, and Gonsalves had been beating her.

For a second movement was suspended in the room. We looked at each other, and my hopes were sinking very fast.

Then Gonsalves grinned. "Come in, senhor. Your woman got away half an hour ago. Unfortunately, this one allowed her to escape."

Chapter Seventeen

I don't know where he came from. But he came fast behind me. I turned and caught the blow above the ear. It was Gilberto. He struck with a vengeance and the white tape across his nose poised as a single image in my mind before consciousness died. I must have gone down swearing, because when I awoke I had an unfinished curse on my lips.

It seemed only a split second of time to me, but it must have been long minutes. I was on the floor of the same bedroom. The first voice I picked out was Nakov's. He was bragging about something.

"All right," Gonsalves interrupted impatiently. "The American comes to."

"What a fool, to think he could outwit you, senhor."

One side of my face lay flat on the rug. I saw Gonsalves' thick legs across from me. His shoes, two-tone, were faultlessly polished, and for some reason it struck me funny as hell. I remembered then my own ankle, the adhesive tape, the report. I started to bend my leg to feel, but laughter stopped me.

"Do not bother, Senhor Flemish," Gonsalves said. "We have taken it from you, together with the grenades. *Sim, sim,* you have lost everything."

I closed my eyes and went on swearing again.

There was a quick rustle, and I felt someone crouch beside me. A warm hand touched my face as Gilberto barked something in Portuguese, but I knew the touch and I began to think I had gone mad.

I turned my head and saw Gilberto pull Donna roughly away from me.

"Hello, baby," I said.

"Hello, darling," she muttered.

Nakov laughed.

"It is not a pleasant duty, you understand," Gonsalves said. "You have both made it necessary by snooping into these affairs."

I was on my feet now and had a cigarette going in my fingers. Gilberto held Donna's arms behind her. Phebe sat on the edge of the bed, like an outcast, her head buried in her hands. Nakov held a fresh, big gun and looked supremely happy. "O.K.," I said, "so you're going to murder us."

"We can find another word," Gonsalves said, his hands stuck in his pockets. "Eliminate. Murder is for your Chicago gangsters. In politics, we eliminate. It is death on a higher social level."

"We'll appreciate the difference," I said, "but why bother? We're not very clear on what the hell your game is. You must be getting damned scared to want to murder everyone in sight."

"You play dumb, Senhor Flemish. It is not becoming. But the young lady *was* very stupid. She escaped us tonight and returned to the same alley where we first discovered her. You should be happy we found her and brought her back to you."

"'Bruce,' Donna cut in, as though she had to make me understand, "I thought you might come back."

"But it was I who came back." Nakov beamed. "As the good senhor said, she was very stupid."

I turned on Gonsalves angrily. "Make him shut up," I said. "If he licks your boots once more in public, I'll puke."

"Josef means well." Gonsalves smiled. "He is devoted to me."

I thought of the small photograph I had found in Nakov's revolver. If my guess was right, Nakov was ready to hang Gonsalves up by his missing thumbs. Where was that picture now? Had they discovered it in my pocket?

"We don't know anything," I said. I turned to Gilberto. "You don't have to twist her arms so tightly."

"Gilberto doesn't understand English," Gonsalves said. "Your concern for Miss Chandler is touching. I knew her father—a fine man, but he had a fatal curiosity."

"*You* killed him," Donna muttered in a small tense voice.

"No, senhorita, not personally. But the accident was arranged at my direction. *Sim,* he was a good man. He trusted me. I apologize that until last night I failed to recognize you. It was only from the tape recording between you and Senhor Flemish that I learned your identity. So you see, I cannot risk what both of you may have learned. It is safer to eliminate. We will get on with it below. The typhoon is not many hours off. I should like to be home in bed."

I knew it was useless to protest, but I wanted him to keep talking, and I protested again. We didn't know anything. I wanted time to size up the others. Nakov held the gun, and if I played it right I thought I could get him to turn it on Gonsalves. Phebe was silent as a mouse, but Gilberto was a real threat. I saw bulges in Gonsalves' coat pockets, and figured he had his hands around the grenades. Our chances were slim, but I kept talking.

"Is Wilkerson working with you?" I asked.

Gonsalves found the question amusing. He laughed. "Yes and no."

"His fireworks plant below?"

"Mine, senhor. It turns a nice profit. You say you know nothing, and it would be a shame to die innocent. I shall provide a good reason to kill you if I answer your questions."

"You use too much clay in your firecrackers."

"You persist?"

"I persist. You're Communists, I can guess that much. I'll bet your friend the governor general is being played for a real sucker."

"He is a fine man, but of the Old World. His friendship is of great value in my work. My blood is mixed, senhor. In Macao we Eurasians have always been less than the Portuguese. But in the people's new China, we have equality. The Reds do not mind that Portuguese blood flows through my veins. Once we tried to hide our Chinese blood, now we can be proud of it."

"Patriot of Macao—this is a hell of a way to live up to your reputation."

"I am a citizen of China. I prefer to think of myself as Chinese."

"What about your devoted assistants?"

"Dedicated members of the party, for reasons of their own. Except Gilberto, who is dedicated only to me. He doesn't question, he serves."

"He'd have a fit if he could understand what you've admitted."

"He is quite reactionary. It is a charming joke I share with you."

Nakov eyed Gonsalves and laughed again. It was a great little joke all the way around.

"Jordan was the link, wasn't he?"

"*Sim,* but a weak one. He was eliminated in time. Again, it was the tape recording that proved my suspicions. The American Communists are an unstable lot, senhor."

"American dollars are more reliable, aren't they? A million a month, Gonsalves?"

"We are stepping up the exports. The American hunger for opium buys the People's Army medicines and gasoline. You can appreciate that we spend your dollars wisely. Red China needs American funds to purchase American products. Your country attempts to keep both from falling into our hands, so we resort to cunning."

"I've had a look at your opium works underground. You're set up for big things."

"You shall visit it again."

"A guided tour, this time."

"*Sim.*"

"What was the routine, Gonsalves? Why did you have to get Wilkerson in the act?"

"We wanted the protection of a reputable brand. The Chan Tom name is above reproach with your customs service. The inspectors cannot split open every firecracker your country imports. So we have the protection of a good name, and in the event of accidental discovery, it is the Colonel who must take the blame."

"Then you change tactics, and keep exporting."

"Exactly."

I looked at Donna. "Her father found out you were processing the dope underground, filling firecrackers with the stuff, and then, through Jordan, getting them into Wilkerson's shipping room. Certain Stateside accounts had their orders filled with certain firecrackers."

"You agree, it was cunning."

"Sure, I agree. Wilkerson was paid for firecrackers, and you were paid for opium."

"The report, unfortunately, lists our friendly importers in the States. You can understand the great damage it would do if it were sent."

"Chandler did a thorough job."

"Not quite. He did not see my connection. He believed Wilkerson was responsible. He confided what he learned to me. I have long fought to suppress opium smuggling by others here. He expected my co-operation."

That figured, I thought. "Why did you *really* want me to load those Hong Kong dollars on Jordan last night?"

"Does it matter?"

"I'd like to know."

Gonsalves gave a passing glance to Donna, who looked almost too exhausted and defeated to draw any hope from what was being said.

"Jordan executed the details of Chandler's auto accident. The car burst into flame and Jordan told me the report was burned with Chandler's brief case. He lied. He kept it for himself. I suppose he hoped to break away and resort to blackmail. Jordan had an American sense of humor, even in matters of death. He sent Chandler an anonymous packet of worthless money as a warning that he would be killed. As you know, senhor, the Chinese burn paper money for the dead. It is meant to pay one's way through eternity. Perhaps Chandler did not get the point of this joke. Even before I learned that Jordan was conspiring with the girl, my mind was made up to eliminate him as a safety precaution. Wiring his apartment provided me with many reasons. I had hoped to pass on to him his own grim joke, but you failed me. It is a trifling thing."

"All right," I said. "I suppose we might as well get it over with. Are you going to let Gilberto watch?"

"He thinks you conspire against the government of Macao. But perhaps it would be best if he knows nothing of the plant of ours underground."

"What are you going to do—let him take up on Phebe where you left off?"

"It will not be necessary. She was careless in guarding the girl and has been disciplined. Both will wait here for me." He passed the word to Gilberto, who only nodded and released Donna's arms. She came toward me and we stood embracing each other in the center of the room, able to forget for a last moment that we weren't alone. She was trembling, and so was I. Nakov giggled, opening the door for us.

"It's not going to do any good eliminating us," I snapped. "Wilkerson knows about your opium smuggling. He's on a junk now, bound for Hong Kong." That was stretching the facts, but anything seemed worth trying.

"Senhor, he will not reach Hong Kong. I have long ago directed our Red patrol boats to intercept any junk attempting the crossing against the danger of typhoon. I hadn't expected you to walk back into my hands." His voice took on a bantering tone. "But of course, Americans all think of themselves as heroes. They cannot abandon a woman in distress. We Communists like to think of ourselves as heroes too, senhor, but for a greater purpose than the arms of a woman. Your performance has been an interesting one."

"I know," I said. "I'm a sensation. Let's go."

We walked. Donna and I led the way along the hall, down the stairway, and into the plant. Nakov stuck so close behind me with the gun that I could feel his overanxious breath against me. I kept warning myself to keep my nerve and my patience. Timing would be everything. I had a trump card—Nakov. But I had to play it right. Gonsalves had been silent on the candid picture of Gonsalves with thumbs, and his silence backed me up. Upstairs, I had been able to reach into the pocket where I had left it, and it was gone.

Donna started to whisper. "Bruce. My God, why did you come back for me?"

"You knew I would,"

"But I didn't want you to."

"For God's sake, let's not get involved in a family argument now."

We fell silent again and our feet did the talking. In the long, empty plant we sounded like a herd on the move.

We reached the stockroom and Gonsalves found a flashlight. He moved around ahead of us to the trap door and pulled it up. "I will go first," he said, "with the girl. Then Senhor Flemish, and Josef, stay close behind him with the gun. I will light your way. Shoot instantly if he attempts anything."

"Even if he thinks anything, I will shoot."

I sensed, then, that Nakov hadn't reported to Gonsalves our previous encounter off the Rua da Felicidade. He didn't want to be disciplined for carelessness. He wasn't going to be careless now.

Gonsalves lowered himself a few steps and turned the flashlight on Donna. She gripped my arm.

"Go on," I said firmly.

She looked up into my eyes, and for a moment I think she began to despise me for being so cold-blooded. I touched up her bangs with my fingers, and said it again, but softly. "Go on."

She broke away from me and started down.

"Now you." Nakov smiled.

Gonsalves aimed the flashlight toward us and he was invisible behind it. The wooden stairs were narrow and dropped sharply. The hot air stung my nostrils. Opium was still cooking, but no one was tending it now.

We reached bottom and Gonsalves led us along the short passage and stopped at the lighted main corridor of the catacombs.

"*Meu Deus!*"

He saw the three half-naked bodies. He stepped forward, and Nakov nudged me to follow. I saw then that one of the Chinese had crawled about fifteen feet after I shot him. He left a trail of blood.

Gonsalves turned to me sharply. "It is too bad you can only die once, senhor. We shall have trouble finding reliable opium workers to replace them."

"I'm sure you'll manage."

"Of course. We will manage."

"Where does your raw stuff come from, Gonsalves? Your Red pals smuggle it through the tunnel, sure, thanks to João Santos, but I thought you Commies outlawed it too."

"It is outlawed for Chinese. But there are poppy fields still cultivated in China—for export. History reverses itself, senhor. For a hundred years the British and you Americans have drugged the Chinese; it was the only way of balancing the trade. Foreign opium for our silks and teas and jades. Now it is a different balance of trade. We trade our opium for your dollars, senhor. You must admire our enterprise."

I didn't argue the point. I knew Britain had fought two special wars to force opium on the Chinese and create a market. I knew American ships had carried opium to market. Now, a century later, the Chinese were turning the tables, and our hopheads were helping to pay for the Red Chinese military machine. It was a vicious sort of historical justice.

"I suppose Josef will do the shooting," I said.

"He will not mind," Gonsalves remarked. "Both of you, walk to the opposite wall."

I tightened my jaw and took Donna's hand. It was wet with perspiration. Nakov followed a few feet behind. We turned, our backs against the rough dirt wall. Along the corridor on either side, the rows of braziers cooked opium, and they seemed like spectators whispering between themselves with the soft noises of surfacing bubbles.

Now, I told myself, play your trump.

Chapter Eighteen

"Who are you, Gonsalves?" I muttered. "Who are you *really?*"

I saw Nakov's reaction first. It was a subject I knew he didn't want brought up. He eyed Gonsalves curiously, standing between us, as though asking for an order to shoot—quickly.

Gonsalves stood in the opening of the dark passage above, and for a moment he didn't say anything. Then an uncertain smile played around his heavy lips. He passed over Nakov with a glance. "Senhor, Gonsalves is a respected name in Macao. Do you dare question it?"

"You're not Gonsalves," I said. "You can talk in front of Nakov. He's smart, he found out. But he's keeping your secret. The guy's dedicated to you."

The danger was in Nakov's losing his head and blasting me before I could get it out. He stood in the middle of the corridor, the grin off his face. "The American only wastes time," he muttered to Gonsalves. "I will shoot now, yes?"

Gonsalves looked him over with faintly amused eyes. "What do you know, eh, Josef?"

"Absolutely nothing, senhor, *absolutely*. He is trying to make trouble between us."

Gonsalves smiled broadly now, like a guy who already knows the punch line to a joke under way. *"Sim, sim,* you have found out."

"Senhor," Nakov sputtered quickly, "the party secret is safe with me."

Gonsalves silenced him with a flourish of the hand. "It is not an important secret—between party workers. So Josef knows. I do not mind."

Nakov began to smile again, but I was just beginning to force the wedge. "O.K., we don't count," I said. "Our mouths are going to be shut forever, so I'm still asking questions. I congratulate you on the impersonation. You're probably doing a near perfect job. Is the real Gonsalves dead?"

"Eliminated."

"Do you really look that much like him, that they should switch you into his shoes?"

"Senhor Flemish, the trouble was not so much our faces as our thumbs. Mine have been gone since childhood in Canton."

"Then the kidnaping was mostly a hoax."

"It was politics—on a practical level. The man I impersonate held a position of confidence with the governor general. My ears hear much that is meant for Gonsalves. You understand, it was an opportunity we could not pass up."

"Gonsalves was kidnaped, then, and his wife paid half a million Hong Kong dollars to get you back. You sent a couple of thumbs in advance so everyone would expect a thumbless Gonsalves—you."

"As one whose business is trickery, you must admire the cleverness of it. The wife, of course, I sent away immediately. For a year I devoted myself to *becoming* Gonsalves, learning his voice from recordings made secretly, learning his childhood, his friends, his handwriting. But to fool a wife—that is another thing."

"There was one thing you didn't learn—Chandler had a daughter and Gonsalves knew her well." Donna held my hand tightly. "You didn't recognize her."

"As you said, I can expect to be no more than near perfect."

"I have already congratulated you. Chandler, thinking he was talking to a patriotic Gonsalves who would cooperate in smashing the opium smuggling at its source, made the mistake of tipping you off."

"*Sim.* The poor man literally talked himself to death. I extend my sympathies to his daughter."

Donna wasn't the wilting type. She stood beside me, and she took it on the chin.

"O.K.," I said, "I'll ask it again. Who the hell are you?"

"My name is Santos. It is my ancestor whose grave you must have entered, but through which, unfortunately, you will not leave. He was an ancestor Gonsalves and I shared. The good senhor was exploring the old grave, and had only then happened upon the catacomb passage, when he was kidnaped. We immediately saw good use for the tunnel by not disturbing the legend. Chandler, I am sorry to say, discovered its use, and you followed his map. It is a pity, senhor, you have worked so hard only to die for your troubles."

"Yes."

"I am not a man without curiosity, senhor. How did you come to suspect the impersonation when even the governor general remains fooled?"

This was where I was going to kick the wedge, but his question puzzled and for a moment disarmed me. I assumed he had taken the picture from me; I assumed he knew what tipped me. I looked quickly at Nakov. Was he the one who had searched my clothes and got the snapshot back for himself? I could read Nakov's face now, and I realized suddenly my hand was strengthened—unless he got nervous and pulled the trigger too soon.

"The snapshot," I said.

"Senhor, I do not understand."

I don't know what kept Nakov from shooting me then, unless it was fear of his boss. His face was streaming perspiration. He was sweating out our conversation more than the overheated catacombs. I knew I had to reassure him fast, before he lost his control. "There's a picture floating around loose in Macao," I said quickly, to get Nakov momentarily off the hook. I watched his hand on the gun and it seemed to relax slightly. So did I. Nakov began to turn his smile back on. "It shows Gonsalves alive four months ago—a Gonsalves with thumbs. They were supposed to have been cut off six months ago. What did your comrades do, keep him alive for a couple of months to answer questions you ran up against on the job and didn't know the answers to?"

"Of course. He was finally eliminated during the dragon-boat festival in Canton. This picture interests me."

"It ought to worry hell out of you."

"I will look into the matter."

"How could a guy use it?"

"Blackmail, perhaps. I owe you my thanks. I was not aware such evidence existed."

I let it fly, and all my hopes went with it. "Nakov's got that picture in his pocket!"

The next instant was a blank. No one moved. No one breathed.

Then Nakov wheeled and the gun shot flame. He shot rapidly, like a man suddenly scared out of his wits. There were three quick explosions. He shot the guy he really feared—not me. The guy he had hoped to blackmail: Santos—alias Gonsalves.

He stood looking as Santos began to fall in the passage entrance, and fired another shot into him.

Donna held onto my arm and stopped looking. "Bruce—"

"Shut up," I whispered harshly. "Don't run until I tell you."

I got loose of her and took a testing step forward. Nakov brought up the gun. "For God's sake, don't shoot," I snapped. "You've got to get out of Macao. I can help you. When they find him dead you'll be a goner."

"No. Get back."

"Let's make sure he's dead." I walked quickly, then, and Nakov didn't shoot. He appeared more dazed than frightened. But I knew the trauma wouldn't last long. He'd shoot us both down—witnesses, revenge, fear.

I crouched beside Santos' body. "He's still breathing," I said, slipping my hand through clothing to his heart. The spot was wet, he was dead, but I continued the pretense. I undid his tie and opened his collar and worked my body into a position to conceal from Nakov what my hands began to do. "Can you spare another shot for him?"

There wasn't a sound from Nakov. My back was to him now, a hell of a target. What was Nakov trying to do, count his shots?

My fingers slipped in and out of Santos' pockets, and I found the report. The adhesive tape had been unwrapped from it—two curled bits of paper. "You're going to kill us, Nakov?"

"Yes." His voice sounded almost disembodied.

I palmed the report and began getting Santos' body to a sitting position against the passage wall. "I think he's trying to say something," I said. "He's asking for you, Nakov!"

I had a hand in Santos' coat pocket, where he had placed one of the two grenades.

"Get back to the wall," Nakov ordered, with a faint return of authority in his voice.

"He's asking for you!" I shouted.

To myself I was shouting, Come here, you bastard, come here.

I felt the tip of the gun against my back as I hovered over Santos. Five seconds, I told myself. You've got about five seconds if he doesn't pull the trigger on you. "All right, I'll get over there," I said.

"I will not even give you time for a kiss," Nakov muttered. "But I will let you die together."

I began to straighten. But when my hand came out of Santos' coat pocket, it carried the pin out of the grenade.

Five seconds to get clear.

I walked quickly, not sure which would come first—the gun or the grenade. I don't know how I got across the dirt corridor without running, but I counted. Two—three. I reached Donna. Four.

"*Run!*" I grabbed her arm and pushed.

The shot sounded like a whisper beside the explosion that instantly swallowed it. We ran blindly between the opium pots; it was like running through an earthquake. A cloud of earth quickly enveloped us. Donna stumbled; I pulled her up and we kept going. There was the clatter of a falling beam behind us, and the kerosene lamps from the ceiling swayed dizzily. "You hit, baby?"

"No."

We reached the end, the turn to the long passage, and we stopped there. The noises died away, and I looked back. It was like looking through a brown fog. The braziers still bubbled their basins of opium. The one grenade had exploded the other in Santos' pocket, but Nakov had squeezed out one shot before the two of them were blown apart. We had been lucky.

We stood there tight against each other, and a small echo of the explosion came to us from the dark tunnel. It had gone a mile and come back.

I picked up the flashlight I had left on the way in, and we started back together.

When we reached the shoreline, the stars had gone behind dark, advancing clouds, and a sharp wind had come up. If the junk was still out there waiting, I couldn't see it. I found the skiff, hurried Donna in, and shoved off.

The water was choppy, and Donna held onto the wet gunwales as I rowed. It seemed as if I'd struggled over a mile of angry water, when Donna shouted in the wind. "I think I see it—to the left."

I turned and looked. It was the junk, all right, about thirty yards away. But it was beginning to move under its own power.

I told Donna to start yelling, and she yelled and I rowed.

"Darling! It's turning toward us!"

In another few moments we were alongside, and the Black Chinaman's voice came to us from the poop. "Magician, I had given you up."

"Only reason we came back was to return your rowboat," I laughed. "Give us a hand."

He helped Donna over the side, and then we got the skiff on deck.

"Even in the darkness," the captain said after a quick introduction, "I can see she was indeed worth going back for."

We started below. "You still willing to try the crossing in this weather?"

"It will be a race, and I shall enjoy the gamble. The storm is still hours off."

"There are likely to be Red patrols out looking for us."

"You try to talk me out of the trip?"

"I just want you to know what you're getting into."

"All my life, magician, I have been dodging the patrols. Go below. I will tell you when the lights of Hong Kong appear."

They appeared yellow in the wind, and as we jockeyed closer through the water the rains came and blotted them out. The Black Chinaman hustled us onto a jetty and pulled out quickly for a storm anchorage. Wilkerson was seasick and we had a hell of a time getting him to a hotel. A few minutes later the typhoon broke open its real fury and the noise of whistling winds and rains driven through the streets was deafening.

I registered as Mr. and Mrs.

We got Wilkerson squared away in his room, and then got squared away in our own.

"Home," I said.

"There's no place like," Donna muttered, hugging me close.

"I've never been a hero before," I said. "I do all right?"

"Mind if I call you a sucker to your face, darling?"

"I know," I said. "You're glad you picked me. As a matter of fact, baby, so am I."

I had been afraid the typhoon was going to louse us up, but that's not the way it worked out. We enjoyed the typhoon. It isolated us in the hotel until late morning and gave us an excuse for breakfast in bed.

Later, we turned the Chandler report over to the authorities and Wilkerson got himself off the hook. I put in a call to the governor general of Macao, who didn't believe a word of what I told him, but at least he promised to have Gilberto questioned and Phebe sweated. A couple of days later, I learned I had been cleared of Jordan's murder. But I didn't get to first base convincing anyone of the catacombs and the mile-long tunnel that led to an old Chinese graveyard on Red soil. They only laughed. They found the trap door, all right, but the grenades had caved in the short passage, and Macao wouldn't believe it had led to anything but a cellar. As for the grave entrance, that was outside the colony. Let the Reds worry about it, and let us have our legends.

I got tired of sounding like an idiot, and decided to let it go.

Wilkerson offered to have my magic equipment sent to me, but I said no. It hurt, but I knew the only way to make the break was clean. And by that time Donna had explained to me how you ride a horse and I was taken with the idea of becoming a gentleman cow hand in Nevada. I was good at poker and was sure to make a success of it.

Two weeks later we had our plane reservations to the States on money Wilkerson had loaned us. But just before we left the hotel for the airport in Kowloon, we got a cable from the customs service. They had seized thousands of loaded firecrackers from three Stateside importers listed in the report. We were entitled to a 25-per-cent reward, with a top of $50,000. They'd let us know after the haul was appraised.

But the cable was anticlimactic. The only thing that really mattered to us occurred a few hours after the typhoon passed. I made an honest woman of Donna. We got married.

THE END

The Venetian Blonde

By A. S. Fleischman

Chapter One

A young blonde with wet hair sat in her bathing suit at the bar. After a while she got up and stood a long time at the jukebox trying to make up her mind what to play.

"Harley," she said, "what do you feel like hearing?"

The bartender gave her a dead glance. "It's your nickel, girlie."

"*Never on Sunday* makes me cry."

"Then play something else."

"I don't have a nickel."

Harley set up a beer in front of me. It was around four in the afternoon and I had just hit town. I figured Charlie Braque would never find me in a tide pool like Venice, Calif. "Crazy broads," Harley muttered. "This one's a leftover beatnik. Hangs around town looking to get knocked up."

She wore a loose, one-piece bathing suit that dripped sea water down her long legs and formed a broken mirror at her feet. The hair clung to her head like a dead starfish. "Harley," she said, "you ought to get some Ruth Olay records."

"Girlie," he said, "why don't you go home?"

"Did I tell you I dreamt about Lawrence Welk last night? A real nightmare. He was playing just for *me*."

I lit a cigarette and tuned them out. I had come a long way for a guy with nowhere left to go. I figured I was at least a dozen steps ahead of Braque's traveling gunman. He might look for me in Vegas, but not in Venice. They would expect me to run with the big rich, not the small change. They were hunting for Skelly, the high-living, fast-spending cardsharp in a Brooks Brothers suit. Skelly, the broadsman with instant fingers and the finest bottom deal around. What they wouldn't believe was that the cards had turned to Jell-O in my hands that night in Boston. And it had got me an invitation to a funeral. My own.

I glanced up at the bar mirror. The face looking back at me was gaunt and tired. My suit looked slept in, which it was, and my sandy hair kept slopping across my forehead. I had been trimming it myself and that's the way it looked. I was lean and long-legged, and I was almost tapped. Broke. Tap City. I was down to the threads on my back and forty bucks in cash. I had a silver cigarette lighter with my initials carved in it and a wrist watch, also engraved, and I wore the last of my monogrammed shirts so I wouldn't forget, I supposed, who the hell I was. I had changed names almost as often as socks.

But as a card mechanic I was finished. My hands wouldn't hold still for it any more. I wouldn't trust myself to deal a game of solitaire. But I was feeling too good, at the moment, to feel bad about it.

"Girlie, this ain't Union Station. Go home."

The wet blonde remained at the jukebox like a child fascinated with the bubbling lights. I ordered another beer and asked the bartender for a phone book. I began flipping the pages for Williams, Rinny Jim. I had come to Venice with the thought of dropping in on him. He had put the bite on me a couple of years ago; he had needed $500 to put together a horoscope scheme. Now that I was short of lines, of bank rags, he'd help me.

Like a hundred other towns, Venice was a kind of homecoming for me. My folks had been vaudevillians and sometimes, when I was a kid, we spent our summers in Venice. I remembered it as a gilded place, all beach and sunshine and papier-mâché buildings. We always put up at the St. Mark Hotel, the grandest spot in town. I remembered my father strolling along the boardwalk with a Malacca cane and a Panama hat. He had eyes like God, and I remember, the summer I was ten, he caught me diving off the end of the amusement pier for small change. He didn't consider it a respectable way to make a score; he was a stickler for responsibility and made me throw the bangers back into the sea for the good of my character.

I found Rinny Jim's name in the book and marked the address with my fingernail. I decided not to telephone. The Grand Canal, where he lived, was only a couple of blocks away. I paid for my drinks and headed for daylight. The girl at the jukebox turned with her wide green eyes to watch me go.

"Chow," she said.

I stopped. "What?"

"Chow."

She must have been old enough to hang around the local deadfalls, but there was a kind of glazed innocence about her. She had good legs, tanned and long. "Spindlelegs," I said, "I don't think we're on the same frequency."

"It's what they're always saying in Italian movies. Chow. Like hello or goodbye."

I shot a quarter in the air for the jukebox. "*Ciao*," I said.

I crossed the street to a magazine stand and bought a pack of cards. I hadn't touched the pasteboards in months. When I reached the beachfront I felt that I'd been tricked. The amusement pier had been torn down. The fun rides had vanished and even the boardwalk was gone. Hell, I thought, the past had been dismantled.

But the St. Mark Hotel was where I had left it, standing like a defiant museum piece. An old man in overalls sat in the window reading *Capper's Farmer*, and it turned me away. The bartender had already told me that the locals, the respectables, had rousted most of the beats out of town. From what I could see on the streets, Iowa had come to Venice-by-the-sea, and for all I knew the Nestors spent their retirement growing field corn in the hotel window boxes.

I started walking. An ocean breeze swept out the last heat of day along the grand colonnades of Windward Avenue. The town had been laid out and plastered over in a kind of daydream of Italy. Some real estate promoter had dug canals and lagoons, thrown up bridges and imported a fleet of gondolas. As the stories came back to me, he had even brought over the gondoliers. The rich built villas on the beach and the Red Cars from Los Angeles brought weekenders to the amusement pier and the boardwalk. By the time I got to know Venice the Italian gondoliers had apparently got homesick and abandoned the canals to the mosquitoes. Now, as I crossed the imitation Piazza San Marco, the town had the musty look of an old stage set left behind by some traveling opera company.

Rinny Jim Williams was a country boy from New Orleans. We had hustled cards together a long time ago, but he didn't have the hands for it. He was a mimic, a good actor, and he left the pasteboards for the short con. He had always had grand designs for money getting, and I hoped the horoscopes had paid off. I walked across town to the Grand Canal with a vision of five C-notes before my eyes.

The canal was lined with broken sidewalk, aging palm trees and mouldering California bungalows. But Rinny Jim's place turned out to be a doge's palace, give or take a few centuries. It stood on a watery corner, a kind of demented California Gothic with lead-glass windows, a hip roof and a spiked iron fence overgrown with scarlet bougainvillaea. A polished brass plate said:

INSTITUTE OF SPIRIT RESEARCH
Evangeline Ann Barlow
Director

I lit a cigarette and wondered if I had the right address. I walked up on the porch and stood around waiting for someone to answer the bell. I rang three or four times.

Finally I tossed away my cigarette and gave it up. There was no one home but the spirits.

I walked back to the gate feeling like a bill collector with no aptitude for his job. But I needed that $500 and I'd come back. I'd camp on Rinny Jim's doorstep until he showed.

A woman in Bermudas and a coolie sun hat was riding a bicycle along the narrow, broken sidewalk, and we had to stop for each other. She had a sack of groceries in the basket and a fresh copy of *Vogue*.

"Excuse me," I said.

"Excuse me," she said.

Her voice was soft and unhurried. She was somewhere in her early thirties, I supposed, and deeply tanned as if she had an option on the sun. Her beauty was languid and melting.

"I wonder," I said, "if you can tell me who lives in the corner house there."

"A witch," she said.

She said it with a kind of private amusement, like an in-joke, that tipped me off. "Are you Evangeline Ann Barlow?"

"I might be."

"A girl like you," I said, "could bring witchcraft back in style."

She smiled again, appraising me from behind her dark glasses. "What are you selling?"

"Sunshine," I said.

"Sorry. I'm up to here in sunshine."

"So I've noticed."

"My friends say I light up in dark rooms. Like radium."

"That must be something to see, Miss Barlow. I'm looking for a man named Williams. Rinny Jim Williams. He's in the phone book at your address."

"Imagine that."

"I'm an old friend of his. Name's Appleby."

"What does he look like?"

"Kind of a tall, lanky gent."

"Wavy hair and smooth talking?"

"Yes. I owe him some money and since I was passing through town I figured on squaring the loan, Miss Barlow. Is he around?"

"Appleby," she mused. "I never heard him mention anyone named Appleby."

"How well do you know him, Miss Barlow?"

"Quite well," she smiled. "He's my husband."

I absorbed that piece of information without batting an eye. I had known two of Rinny Jim's wives, and Evangeline made three. I wished her luck. "I've never met anyone named Evangeline before."

"It's quite a shock, isn't it?"

"When will Rinny Jim be back?"

"You can leave the money with me."

"I don't mind waiting."

"It's going to be quite a wait," she smiled, and I had an idea she was on to me. She knew I wanted to put the bite on her husband. "He's in Mexico on business. I don't think he'll be back in less than a week."

I kept my poker face intact, but my knees buckled a quarter of an inch. I had been counting on tapping Rinny Jim's bank roll. "Funny," I said, "I just came from Mexico."

"Ships that pass in the night. I'll tell him you called, Mr. Appleby."

"Oh, I'll be around," I said as airily as I could. I had just about enough in bank rags to get me through a week. "Goodbye, Evangeline."

"Goodbye, Mr. Appleby."

She smiled and I smiled and she rode off down the sidewalk to the gate. A black cat appeared out of nowhere and crossed my path. Pure witchcraft.

I kicked at it.

Chapter Two

I had dinner at a counter joint on the beach and checked into the Grand Metropole, an upstairs barn of a hotel with a permanent vacancy sign in the street door. I had no baggage and gave the clerk, who looked as transient as the hotel, a night's room rent in advance. I made a scribble for my name on the register and took my choice of rooms. The key rack was loaded.

My window overlooked the beachwalk and the ocean. By the time I showered at the end of the hall night had fallen and a blinking neon sign outside my window came on. It said BEER. The beachwalk below was deserted and even the tide was out.

There was a small round table and a pair of bentwood chairs to keep me company, and I sat down with the pack of cards I had bought. I broke the seal and shuffled them, but I was thinking about Rinny Jim's wife. She was nobody's folly. She knew the score and I wondered if I could expect Rinny Jim in a week, or if she had only been gassing me. It was clear enough that they had some kind of big con underway in the Institute of Spirit Research. If her name was Evangeline, my name was Appleby. The only thing I could be sure of was her sex. She was a lesson in anatomy. Hell, Rinny Jim had walked off with the textbook.

I turned over the top card and began dealing off seconds. I wasn't sure why I bothered to practice, except to work some of the rust out of my fingers. I wasn't going to sit in on any pasteboard action. I was through. I hadn't lost my skill, I had lost my nerve.

I straightened up the cards and tried the subway deal—off the bottom. I watched my hands doling out the cards like a pair of machines. You could hold my bottom deal under a microscope and detect nothing. I was great in a cheap hotel room dealing to an empty chair. Put someone in it and I couldn't whistle *Dixie*. I'd have the shakes so bad I could hardly light a cigarette.

It had come on me in Boston like the first sign of a head cold. I had flown up from New York to sit in on some heavy action. A money man named Charlie Braque had rung me in and bankrolled me. All I had to do was win.

"Kid," he told me, "it's like having Man o' War running for me. We can't lose, can we?"

Some thirty-eight hours and ten minutes later I had lost $125,000 of Charlie Braque's bale of hay. I excused myself to go to the john and crawled out of the window. I started running for the Mexican border. I knew Braque well enough to read his mind. He'd put in so many fixes himself he'd see one now like spots before his eyes. Even after six months I couldn't be sure one of his bookkeepers hadn't picked up my trail in order to balance the books.

But I had stopped looking over my shoulder. There was no record of my re-entry into the U.S. I had shed my luggage in Tijuana and walked across the border like a tourist. It was as easy as that.

The beer sign kept flicking on and off and by ten o'clock the state of my throat was dry, drier, driest. I put on my tie and went out.

I ended up at a stand-up bar along one of the side-street colonnades. A sign over the door said SINNERS WELCOME, but the sinners had gone somewhere else. There were three stand-up customers, and I made four. Fish net was hung from the ceiling and the floor was covered with beach sand. The place was a kind of narrow ash tray with a liquor license.

I hadn't noticed the girl when I walked in. She had her arm around a bull fiddle in the rear of the joint, and she seemed to be trying to pick out a tune for her own amusement. Chopsticks, maybe.

She was the green-eyed wonder. Nothing had changed but the bar and the hour. She was still barefoot, she still wore the loose black bathing suit, and her hair still hung in strands like a golden fright wig. The only difference was that she had stopped dripping sea water. She had dried in the night.

"Hey, Viola," one of the drinksters grinned. "Play something purty. How about the *Yella Rose of Texas?*"

She ignored him. She seemed to be humming to herself and getting a charge out of the stray sounds, deep and resonant, plucked from the catgut.

"Hey, bimbo," the next guy said. "You wannadrink?"

"She don't know she's thirsty unless you tell her," the first man laughed. "She's got sawdust for brains. Hey, Viola. Your mother know you're out?"

"Bimbo, you wannadrink?"

She had them tuned out, but they kept broadcasting. The third guy was too far gone in barley to keep the scene in focus.

"Hey, Viola. The cat got your tongue?"

"You wannadrink, bimbo?"

"Where did you sack out last night, mophead? On the beach again? Ain't you heard the beats has left town? They give the place a bad name. How come you ain't left town?"

I stood with my beer and wished the orator on my left would wise up, but he must have figured he was the floor show. The girl stuck with the bass fiddle; she wasn't reading him.

"Hey, Viola," he grinned. "Is that a bathing suit or are you just standing in the shade?"

"Ask her if she wansadrink."

"My friend here wants to know if them pointers are real or just for flash."

"Bimbo, you wannadrink?"

"I'll tell you what I'm gonna do for you, bathing beauty. We'll take up a little collection. I got a buck here says they're for real. Gordy, peel off a frogskin. That makes two. You other gents wanna fatten the pot?"

"Leave the kid alone," I said.

"You a Sunday school teacher, or something?" The jawsmith turned to the stoned drunk. "You in for a buck? Help the little girl earn her way through barber college." The drunk peeled off a five in the bad light, and the promoter held the bills folded between his fingers. "We got a big spender here, Viola. Seven greens in the pot. Money, money, money. It's all yours, honey. All you gotta do is settle the argument. Show us what you got under the suit. Maybe throw in a bump and a grind. How about it, Viola?"

Viola was listening now. She looked kind of angry and maybe a little scared. "Squaretoes," she muttered in a small voice that just carried, "you got a mind like an unflushed toilet."

"Look who's talking."

She came out from behind the bull fiddle and started through the beach sand for the door. I think she knew she wasn't going to make it. Squaretoes stepped out in front of her and blocked the way.

"A deal's a deal, honey. You ain't welshin'?" She stood there looking through him.

And then he waved the money slowly in front of her eyes as if the bills were supposed to hypnotize her. "Money, money, money," he grinned. "I bet you ain't seen a jackpot like this all summer. All we're askin' is to settle a little difference of opinion. Give us a looksee, Viola. I say they're real. You know what I mean, I'm on your side."

She just stood there.

"I mean, whaddya got to lose? Come on, Viola—*strip down.*"

That's when I grabbed his shoulder, spun him around and bounced him off the wall. The bills flew out of his hands and his eyes rolled. The jawsmith had a glass jaw. I left him in a heap on the sand and walked out.

I was five minutes away before I realized I had hurt my hand. I was too smoked up at first to pay any attention, and kept walking around. I ended up on the beachfront and held my hand under a drinking fountain. When I looked around I saw that the girl was following me, like a night shadow, in her bare feet. She stopped.

"Chow," she said.

"Let's skip the movie dialogue," I snapped. "Why do you hang around doggeries like that?"

"There's nothing else open."

"You must live somewhere. Go home."

"You hurt your hand?"

"Naw. I'm just waiting for hot water."

I pulled my hand out of the drinking fountain and wrapped my pocket handkerchief around the knuckles. She drifted a little closer. "You want me to tie it?" she murmured.

"Keep your mitts off," I said. "Go home."

I walked away, heading back for the hotel. An empty beach tram went by, like a night crawler in circus stripes, shuttling between Venice and the lights of Ocean Park in the distance. When I reached the corner I turned and she was right behind me.

"I thought I told you to get lost," I said.

"You own the sidewalk?"

"Don't follow me. Understand?"

"Chow."

I crossed the street and moved down a deserted section of colonnade, like a standing ruin, with a darkened art gallery called The Gas House. I scratched a match and lit a cigarette, and I knew she was still dogging me.

"Look," I said, "you don't have to thank me. That leather jacket was asking for it. Now beat it, Spindlelegs."

"My name's Viola."

"That's a nice name and I'll bet you're a nice girl, but I don't dig you beats."

She shrugged and just stood there, half real and half shadow. Her wide green eyes seemed to have a light of their own, a kind of animal light, beautiful and inscrutable.

Finally I said, "You want a cigarette?"

"I don't care."

"Well, do you or don't you?"

"It doesn't matter."

I stuck one between her lips to settle the argument. "Don't you ever comb your hair?"

"If you want me to I'll comb it."

"Don't do me any favors."

I lit her cigarette and she fastened those eyes on me as if I had just named her in my will. "You're not like the other townies around here."

"All right, now let's get it straight. I'm going this way and you're going that way. Ciao?"

"Chow."

"So long."

"So long."

"Goodbye."

"Goodbye."

I backed away from her and she stood there as if I had turned her to stone. Finally the lights in her eyes went out and I got on my way. I had all the problems I could handle without any help from this beachnik, or whatever she was.

When I got back to my hotel room I was ready for the sack. I opened the door and knew right away that something was wrong. Either the neon beer sign had gone out or my shade had been pulled. I snapped on the light, figuring I was already dead if it was a visitor from the East.

She was propped up on the bed as if she had paid the room rent. Evangeline. Rinny Jim's wife in a smile, a yellow dress and high heels as sharp as rapiers.

"Hello, Skelly," she said.

Chapter Three

I shut the door after me. "You're wrong," I said. "You don't light up in the dark."

"Maybe I'm not plugged in." She swung her heels off the bed and straightened her dress. Her hair was black and pulled in a chic French roll. She had green eyes, like the beachnik, but there the similarity ended. There was nothing lost about Evangeline. "I've been waiting for hours," she murmured.

"Why?" I slipped off my tie and hung my jacket on a hanger behind the door. She knew who I was. She wasn't guessing. She knew.

She said, "What happened to your hand?"

"Let's skip the openers," I said. "What are you doing here? How did you find me?"

"It's a small town." She spread the playing cards around on the table as if she could read them. "I telephoned around. You ask questions, you get answers. You're Skelly, aren't you?"

"Get to the point, Evangeline."

"That is the point. You're Skelly."

"Okay. I'm Skelly. How did you guess?"

Somehow the room seemed smaller with Evangeline in it. "I think I could have picked you out of a crowd," she smiled. "Rinny always talks about you. He says you're the best."

"The best what?"

"Rinny says you're the smoothest talking, fastest dealing, honest dishonest card player in the business. Suddenly I got the feeling that I've been waiting for you.... I like the best."

"Is Rinny Jim in town?"

"No."

"Did he happen to mention the half-grand?"

"No."

"I was afraid of that," I said. She leaned forward with a cigarette between her lips and held my wrist as she took a light off the stub between my fingers.

"And then," she murmured in that low, measured voice of hers, "about a month ago a man began hanging around the house. He said he was a skip-tracer. He was looking for you. He seemed to think you might show up."

She paused, waiting for my great stone face to slip, but I managed to hold the mask in place. Braque wasn't behind me. He was ahead of me.

"Ergo," she smiled, "when Appleby turned up today in a used haircut and a rumpled suit, I began to think it had to be Skelly. I have an intuition for things like that. In a way, you might say, we've been expecting you."

"Does that explain what you're doing here?"

"Doesn't it?"

"You just wanted to warn me."

"Yes."

"What are you trying to feed me? You could have sent Western Union."

She shrugged. "I thought we might have a drink."

"How did you get in here?"

"I walk through doors. It's part of my act."

I let it drop. "Level with me, Evangeline. Is Rinny Jim getting back next week?"

"I don't know."

"I'll bet."

"I mean it. I don't know. You know Rinny. He's off chasing bluebirds somewhere."

"What did the skip-tracer look like?"

"A kind of thick little man with a blah face. You wouldn't like him."

"What else?"

"He said he could make it worth my while. He told me who to call if you turned up."

"Who?"

"I've forgotten."

I had an idea Evangeline hadn't forgotten anything since kindergarten, but I let it go. In a way she was saying she could make out my death warrant, but I didn't think she had been sitting up in my hotel room just to rough out an obituary. Evangeline had something on her beautiful mind.

"How about a drink?" she said.

"Let's talk here and save money."

"How broke are you?"

"I was counting on Rinny Jim to dress up my bank roll."

"You should have known better." She spread the cards again. "How about these?"

"I'm out of practice."

"Would you accept money from a woman?"

"Evangeline," I said, "at the moment I'd accept money from Whistler's Mother."

"I can let you have a hundred dollars to start."

"To start what?"

Her eyes, green and soft and bewitching, were not entirely inscrutable now. She was past thirty and beginning to grasp at time. She ran her fingers through the sides of my hair as if she had just taken an option to buy.

"You can start with a haircut," she said. "And your suit needs pressing."

"That's not what I meant."

"And move out of this flea trap to my place. There's a bachelor apartment over the garage—sun deck and everything. You'll be safe there."

"From everyone but you."

"Possibly," she smiled. "In your spare time you can help me vacuum up a million dollars."

"A million dollars."

"Give or take a few thousand."

"Just like that."

"Real money. Used by a little ol' lady in Bel Air."

"And you're cutting me in."

"For a third."

"Why me?"

"Rinny says you know the score. Rinny says you think with your head. Rinny says you're a talent, and that's what we need."

Her fingers tied themselves gently at the back of my neck. "You're a friendly girl," I said.

"Yes."

There was a steady light in her eyes and the words just stood there. She was so near we seemed to be breathing the same air. "Tell me more," I said.

"The rich lady in Bel Air. Darling nephew—dead. We sit in dark room and make nephew's ghost walk and talk. She comes across with the money."

Her hands were still on my neck and under my eyes lay the summer cleavage of her dress forming an aggressive, sun warmed letter W. The next move was mine and I found myself slowly pulling her arms off me. Grave-robbing wasn't for me.

"Thanks for the invitation," I said. "But a third of nothing is nothing. Table-rapping went out with high button shoes. And if I moved into Rinny Jim's house I might not be able to keep my hands off Rinny Jim's wife."

She tilted her head a degree. "We could try the honor system."

"For the first ten minutes."

The gleam in her eyes became a smile. "You're a capital fellow."

"Yeah."

"The money's in my bag," she said. "Help yourself."

I swept the bag up off the bed and handed it back to her.

"No thanks, Evangeline. I'll stay on K-rations."

"My name's not Evangeline. Call me Maggie."

"Good night, Maggie."

"Aren't you going to walk me to my car?"

I walked her to her car. It was a yellow Caddie parked around the corner. She slipped in behind the wheel and rolled down the window. There was no one left on the streets but a wino leaning on a parking meter with his bottle hidden in a brown paper sack.

"Think it over, Skelly," she murmured. "All that money in Bel Air. It's just a matter of staking a claim."

"I'll be blowing town in the morning," I said. "So long, Maggie."

"Luck."

She drove off and turned the corner, and I figured she had marked me down for a chump. A chump I was. A capital fellow without capital. I could have been riding off in that Caddie instead of holding down the sidewalk with the wino. I had an idea Maggie was damaged merchandise long before Rinny Jim teamed up with her, but I wasn't going to jump his claim.

I returned to my room and went to bed.

Chapter Four

I didn't highball it out of town the next morning. I slept until ten and it was already getting hot. I pulled the flapping shade and gazed out at the beachfront and the ocean. The day was blinding. The surf was breaking slowly and casting up a kind of instant lace on the sand. The first person I saw below was a girl in a black bathing suit feeding bread crusts to a wheeling flock of sea gulls. It was a moment before I came awake and recognized her. Spindlelegs. The beachnik. Viola. I pulled down the shade.

Now here was a hell of a way to start the day, I thought. Ciao. I wondered if she had slept on the beach, and then I dropped the thought. I had other worries to worry. I shaved in the basin and tried to shut out the squawking of the gulls outside the window. My right knuckles were stiff and a little swollen. Sometime between going to bed and getting up I had handicapped the day. I didn't have enough getaway money to getaway. I had to pump up my bank roll. I would spend the day here in the room doling out cards. Taking the kinks out of my fingers. And tonight I would find a game to sit in on.

It was the only trade I had. My hands would have to hold still for it.

I cleaned my razor, wrapped it and slipped it in my jacket pocket. I had learned to carry my traps with me. I thought about Maggie and her lovely green eyes and all the bees and honey she had talked about. Even if she had cut the score in half, just for round numbers, it was still a big score. I could pay off Braque and have enough left to get well. In the bright light of day it was a temptation, a way out, a jackpot But I didn't play con games. It just wasn't my brand of fakus.

I didn't mind scoring at the card table. I had never met a cardplayer who wouldn't cheat if he knew how. I always figured it was worth the price of admission to be shorn by an expert. My subway deal was a thing of invisible beauty and a lesson in cards. I could stack a hand in front of a jury and walk away free. I never took a pot with anything but sheer skill. I have played against sleeve holdouts and readers and daub and shiners, but I never used them myself. That was for grifters. I considered myself an honest man whose trade was cheating at cards.

I put on my tie and went downstairs. Viola and the sea gulls had gone away. The colonnade was in empty shadow, and I wandered along the ocean walk looking for a cup of coffee. I found a glassed-in eat shop and went in. There was a short row of piano stools and I took my choice.

"Coffee."

I wondered about the man with the blah face. Maggie's description didn't help much. The counterman had a blah face. Where was Braque's thick-set little man now? Maybe he had got tired of waiting. Maybe even Braque had lost interest and I was running from nothing.

The coffee was hot and friendly, and I found myself replaying, almost hand for hand, the game in Boston. I suppose I had held a hundred post-mortems trying to figure out what went wrong. The first four or five hours were just friendly poker, a kind of reconnoitering. Two of the players were Boston locals, a cigar-chomper with watery eyes and a got-rich-quick real estate promoter. There was a redheaded player from Toronto, a joke-cracker and chain-smoker, and Braque. They were all high rollers—heavy gamblers. The strategy was that I was to deal Braque winning hands. He didn't need the money; he just wanted to win. It meant something to him.

After about ten hours of play I dealt him one barn-burner after the other. He had small, dumpling hands, and no one could accuse him of palming anything larger than a postage stamp. The whole thing looked like a winning streak, and he shot ahead fifty grand. Then I tried to pull out of the game; I figured we had made our score and had a train to catch. But Braque began to believe in his winning streak and got greedy. He wouldn't fold up.

We opened a fresh pack, ordered breakfast sent up, and played cards. I began dealing him sick hands and the Toronto man began to score. I planned to bail out Braque later, but when later came I went on the blue-ice cold. I dealt from everywhere but the top of the deck and couldn't bring Braque in a winner. As the deal went around the table I began to suspect there was another educated broadsman at work.

I kept asking for a new deck. The real estate man wore a British mustache and I watched for daub. He could be grease-marking the high cards by picking up daub every time he smoothed his mustache. I watched for crimps. I thought maybe we were being cold-decked, and then, as the day wore on, I began to lose touch with the game. My deal got heavy, like someone trying to talk with a thick tongue. I began to sweat. My hands were ice cold and Braque was sharpening his eyes on me. I got the inside shakes and my battery went dead. Braque was down more than a hundred grand and I couldn't rescue him. Half an hour later I excused myself and went to the donicker and got out of there.

Now I huddled over my coffee as if it were cold out. I had supposed at first it was just a case of nerves. But I knew better. The eyes of my old man were on me and he was still making me throw the bangers back.

I was hunched over the mug of coffee when a small sensation came over me, an awareness, a feeling that someone was watching me. I tried to shrug it off and looked up at the counterman. "Are there any poker players in this town?"

He was a high-pockets with reddish eyebrows and a kind of par-boiled complexion. "Bound to be," he said.

"I feel lucky."

"Where you from?"

"Yakima, Washington. Name's Appleby."

He gave me a final appraisal and he must have figured that anyone wearing a tie at the beach was either lost or a detective. "No sir," he said. "I ain't heard of any action around here. Except checkers. They got a checker house down the beach there. It gets real exciting some-times."

"Friend," I said, "is someone watching me?"

"Yes sir."

"A thick-set little man?"

"No sir."

I crushed my cigarette and gave a kind of inward groan. I didn't turn. I didn't have to. The beachnik would be staring at me through the window like the Poor Little Match Girl in a black bathing suit. "A kind of stringy blonde?"

"Yes sir."

I sat there and burned. What kind of togetherness kick was she on? She was beginning to stick to me like flypaper. I hunched over my cof-fee as if to make myself invisible. Maybe she would go away.

The counterman emptied my ash tray. "Is she gone?" I asked finally.

"No sir. But she don't bother nobody."

"She bothers me."

"Been hanging around the beach all summer. We got rid of most of the beats, but she just hangs on. Looks lonesome, don't she?"

"Flag her in."

A moment later she had moved up beside me on her bare feet. I kept my scowl straight ahead of me. I wasn't going to let her turn those large, gazing eyes on me and cool me off. "Chow," she said.

"Sit down."

She slipped onto the stool beside me. We sat that way, side by side, looking straight ahead. And then I told the counterman to pour her a cup of coffee and fix her something to eat.

"I'm not hungry," she said.

"I didn't ask you. Listen, Goldilocks, we'd better get squared away on the ground rules. Stop dogging me. Stop being there every time I look. Stay away from me."

"Why?"

"Because that's the way it's going to be. Understand?"

"I'm not hurting you."

"You're bugging me."

"Don't call me Goldilocks. My name's Viola."

"Where did you sleep last night?"

"At the Beverly Hilton."

"On the beach?"

"Sometimes. It's not hard to find a place to sleep around here. I pose a lot. I know a lot of artists."

"Do you always go around in that bathing suit?" I asked. "What kind of spook are you? Don't you have a dress?"

She just sat there letting me air my lungs. A moment later, in that half-whispering voice of hers, she asked, "You have a comb?"

I passed it along the counter. "Don't straighten your thatch on my account," I said. "I couldn't care less. What do you want to eat?"

"I ate."

"With the sea gulls? Stale bread?" I looked over at the counterman. "Fix her some griddle cakes and sausages."

He laid out the batter with a great hissing from the stove. She fussed with her hair and I peered ahead as if I were trying to see through a solid wall.

"Do you want a cigarette?" I scowled.

"I don't care."

I shoved the pack over. "Another thing," I said. "If you must feed sea gulls, must you do it under my hotel window?"

"Change your hotel."

"That's brilliant."

"You always grouchy in the morning?"

"Afternoon and evenings too."

She returned my comb, but I didn't look at her. In a way it was like trying to deny to myself that she existed. The griddle cakes came, giving off rising twists of steam.

"Now let's review," I said. "You're going to sit right here and eat your breakfast, and I'm going to leave. And you're not going to dog me. You're going to go your way, and I'm going to go my way, and we're both going to live happily ever after. Check? Okay? Right."

I got up. I left her sitting and walked to the cash register and paid the tab. I didn't look at her and I don't think she glanced at me. It was over between us. She didn't even say chow.

The counterman doled out my change and reappraised me. "Tell you what," he muttered. "Turn up around eight and maybe I can steer you into a friendly little game."

"You can count on me," I said.

At the door I found myself taking a fast look back; it was sheer reflex. In the beach sun her golden hair shone like a 14-karat artichoke. I was dazzled for a moment. I knew she had more in the attic than the locals gave her credit for, but I saw now that combed out and dusted off she might even be pretty.

She sat there giving her back to me, and I left.

When I got back to the hotel there was a phone message from Evangeline. Maggie. She wanted me to call her. I tore up the slip and told the deskman to say that Room 201 had checked out and left town if anyone called again. Then I paid for another night and locked myself in with the paste boards. I needed the money. I had to try once more.

I practiced for hours. I set up the wall mirror on the table and doled out seconds and bottoms. I watched my fingers in action; the illusion was perfect. I smoothed out my false shuffle and tried to work the stiffness out of my bruised knuckles. I crimped a card and practiced cutting to it. Finally I took down the mirror and played against the empty bentwood chair. I was peerless. If there was a nerve in my body I wasn't aware of it. Over and over again I stacked a good hand in the rapid gathering up of dead cards from the table. I top-palmed. I crimped. I peeked. But it dawned on me finally that I was kidding myself. This was talking to myself. With someone looking on, my hands might turn to Jell-O again.

I needed someone in the other chair. Someone to play against. I needed a kind of dress rehearsal, and I thought of the beachnik.

No, I told myself. Not her. Don't be a sap. Stick to the mirror.

Chapter Five

Around three o'clock in the afternoon I went out looking for her. I checked in at the local deadfalls and searched along the colonnades. Viola had taken me at my word. She was making herself scarce. I ambled along the beachwalk, my eyes tightened against the sun. Along the green benches stout women sat like public statues put out for the day and taken in at night. Viola was gone.

And then I found her. I had stopped for a loaf of bread and Italian salami and a couple of cans of cold beer for the room. I glanced in the window of The Gas House, and there she was. There was an old bathtub with claw feet in the center of the gallery, and she was in it.

I shifted the sack of groceries and walked in. The place had a cool tile floor and pictures hung around the walls. Some beatnik painter in sandals was on a tall stepladder, peering down at her and putting dabs on a canvas board. He had posed her with a concertina between her hands. There was water in the tub, and floating in it were tins cans and general refuse.

I walked around her, taking in the scene with a kind of glower. She didn't give me a flicker of recognition.

"Ciao," I said.

She held the pose as if she had been turned to alabaster. A pair of beer cans made small clinking sounds in the water. I looked up at the painter.

"What's this supposed to be?" I said.

"Lifesville, man."

I looked back at Viola. She was turning blue in the cold. "You coming with me?"

The vacant look went out of her eyes and her lips parted in a faint, sudden smile. She collapsed the concertina between her hands and rose out of the tub in her wet bathing suit.

I took her hand and hastened her toward the doorway.

"Hey, peasant," the beatnik snapped. "The chick is mine. Leggo. I've only got her half-painted."

"Man," I said, "that's lifesville."

We walked around the corner to my hotel. She thawed out in the hot sun, dripping water with every step and hanging onto the concertina. Once inside the room she took a slow turn around, her golden head at a tilt, and pulled the green shade.

"What's that for?" I said.

"Don't you want me to undress?"

"No," I said. I walked over and lifted the shade to let the sun back in.

"What did you bring me here for?"

"Do you know how to play cards?"

"Like steal-the-pack?"

"Like poker."

She gave a little shrug and kept making turns around the room as if she had missed something the time before. "We going to play cards?"

"By the hour."

"You some kind of freak?"

"I'm a gambler," I said. "Don't you own anything dry to put on?"

She gave another little shrug. "What's your name?"

"Appleby," I said. "What's with the squeezebox?"

"He said I could keep it."

"I'll go down and pawn it and you can get yourself some threads to wear."

She held onto the concertina. "No."

"You can't sit around here in a wet bathing suit."

"Why?"

"It doesn't look right."

"Who's looking?"

"Me."

In the end I persuaded her to go down the hall and take a hot shower and stay there until her lips turned pink again. I put together some sandwiches and opened a beer. I figured I was saving money. I was going to need all the bank rags I had to finance my comeback at the card table.

I knew I was a chump to let Viola hang around the place, but I couldn't help myself. It wasn't only that I needed a table partner. There was an open innocence about her that bugged me. At breakfast I had kicked her around like every one else and tried to forget her, but she wasn't that easy to forget. I was sorry I had been so heavy-handed about it, and I guess I needed to square myself. If I made a score tonight at least I would be able to put some clothes on her, stuff some bills in her pocket and put her in a taxi back to lifesville.

She made a little knocking sound at the door and I told her to come in. But it wasn't Viola at all. It was Evangeline Ann Barlow.

"Hello, Skelly," she murmured.

She entered in striped pants, sunglasses and sandals. She shut the door, leaned against it and lit me up with a kind of sly smile. I looked at her and she was beautiful as hell. "Hello, Maggie."

"They said you checked out."

"I did."

"They said you left town."

"I did."

"Can I come in?"

"You're in."

She smiled her cool smile and moved away from the door. After a moment she picked up the concertina and found a couple of leftover notes in it. I wished she'd go.

"I lied to you last night, Skelly."

"Did you?"

"Don't leave town."

"What did you lie to me about?"

"Rinny. "

"What about him?"

"He's not coming back."

"Where is he?"

"I don't know. We've split up. For good."

I put aside my beer, took the squeezebox out of her hands and tossed it back on the bed. "Don't con me, Maggie."

"I mean it. It's true, Skelly."

I wasn't really buying it. I figured she was laying down a story, and I thought I knew why. "Then that leaves the two of us," I said.

"Just the two of us."

"A team."

"There's a million dollars waiting for us, Skelly. Think of it."

"Don't feed me that fairy tale again, Maggie."

"I need you, Skelly. Help me."

My only thought was to hustle her out of there. It didn't make sense to me that Rinny Jim would part from a lusty package like Maggie—

and a million piastres. I had an idea she was trying to freeze him out and dump him. He had better hurry home before she swiped everything but the foundation. I had known women like Maggie who couldn't get through the day without laying down stories, putting the con on everyone from the milkman to the boyfriend. It was something in their make-up. As a cardplayer you learn to drop people in the proper slot, almost on sight, and there was no question in my mind that I had Maggie pegged. She was a peddler of fantasy. A liar.

I told myself to get rid of her. "I'll give it some thought" I said. "How about tomorrow?" I'd be gone by then. "I'll come by your place."

"What's wrong with tonight?"

"I'm busy tonight."

I opened the door to hasten her exit, but Viola was standing there. She had a bath towel wrapped around her like a dress that had shrunk to the knees.

It was an awkward moment. And then Maggie remembered to smile. "Who's the girl?"

"What girl?" I said.

"The one in the towel?"

"What towel?"

I told Viola to come in and Maggie gave me a final glance. "It could have been nice, darling," she murmured. "But don't give me jokes. You won't show up tomorrow. Goodbye, Skelly."

She left and I shut the door, and for a moment I stood there thinking. For a moment I even forgot that Viola was in the room. It had really been Maggie shutting the door on me. Striking me from her list. She had sensed that I had been giving her a story; we had been two pros trying to con each other. I supposed we had more in common than I cared to admit to myself. It was as if, on first sight, she had spotted the instinctive grifter in me. She had dropped me in the slot, and I didn't like the feeling.

I knew now that I would never lay hands on Rinny Jim's $500. I could forget it.

"The lady is beautiful," Viola said.

"What lady?"

"The one with the perfume."

"What perfume?"

I picked up my beer and saw that Viola was still dripping water.

That kid wasn't housebroken. She laid her bathing suit across the window sill to dry, and it suddenly dawned on us that there was nothing between us but a damp towel.

"Do you intend to sit around here in that thing?"

"Why not?"

"How old are you?"

"Twenty-two," she said.

"On the level?"

"No."

"How old are you?"

"Twenty-four."

I picked up my beer can and stared at her. "Turn around."

"Why?"

"You're skinny."

"Thanks."

"What kind of a beatnik are you?"

"I'm not a beatnik."

"What are you?"

"I'm me."

"What if I make a pass at you?"

"You won't."

"Why?"

"I'm not your type."

"What is my type?"

"The bundle who just left."

"A lot you know."

"Why did she call you Skelly?"

"She thinks I'm someone else." I opened the other can of beer and passed it to her. "Grab a sandwich and sit down."

"Do I really have to play cards?"

"If you're going to hang around here you do."

She slipped into the opposite chair, and I warmed up the deck while she ate. I cut and shuffled and cut and shuffled. My right knuckles bothered me like a gimpy leg when you're trying to run, but I had to ignore it. There was only one way I knew to make a score, and that was with a pack of cards. I should have known better than to try busting my hand on somebody's chin.

"Am I really skinny?" she murmured.

"Nothing that a few square meals won't fill out."

The next hour was bizarre. I packed the deal and dealt her an ace-full, but she accepted it as if she was entitled to a full house every time she played. It came to me that she had as much card sense as a wooden Indian. When I dealt her a bobtail flush she discarded it and tried to fill out a pair. She was hopeless. But my hands stayed dry and sure and relaxed. I'd make it.

"Is this what you do for a living?" she asked finally.

"Why?"

"I don't like gamblers."

I looked up from my cards. "Who asked you?"

She shrugged her bare, bronzed shoulders. With her back to the window the dying afternoon ran a soft, hazy light along her skin and ignited the ragged ends of her hair. It was like playing cards with a rag doll. "I'm bored," she said.

"Cut the pack."

"How did you get to be a gambler?"

"You wouldn't be interested."

She fell silent. I placed my cigarette on the edge of the table and doled out another hand. "My folks were out of vaudeville," I said finally. "A magician showed me how to back-palm a card when I was twelve and I was hooked." I wondered why I was beginning to tell her this. "After the war I put together a magic act in New Orleans and began loitering around the booking offices. It took me six years to figure out that I was starving to death. Magicians went out with vaudeville. All that's left to work are casuals and one-niters. How many?"

"How many what?"

"Pasteboards. Flats. Cards to fill out your hand."

She studied her hand for almost a full minute and then asked for four cards. I sighed inwardly and ran them out. "Anyway," I said, "there I was, sitting around cheap hotel rooms with a pair of educated mitts that could barely keep me eating. And then one day I got wise. I had drifted to Kansas City. I got myself some old clothes in a pawnshop, baggy pants and wide suspenders—the farmer bit—and got on a bus for the corn country. I scraped dirt under my fingernails and found a poker game. Listen, those farmers were driving Cadillacs. Anyway, I got well overnight."

"But you're still sitting around a cheap hotel room," she murmured.

I looked up and scowled at her. "A temporary embarrassment," I said. "Tonight I get well again."

The evening was a disaster. I left the hotel around eight and scraped dirt under my fingernails from a potted geranium at the door. I met the high-pockets and he steered me to a card parlor faced out with the trappings of a real estate office. I walked in with exactly $31.45 in my kick. I didn't try to get rich quick. For an hour or so it must have been old glue holding me together. My hands were dry and steady. I chipped along, neither winning nor losing, but all the while laying down a story. I was from Yakima, Washington. I had 500 acres of wilderness. Good hunting. Can't beat it for fishing. I was just in town for a few days, visiting a cousin. It was a story I had built up, piece by piece, over the years. It was Appleby, fleshed out and shod and tailored from whole cloth. There were times when I envied Appleby his 500 wild acres in the foothills of the Cascades. I had never seen the place and I never would.

The air was turning blue with layers of smoke. I was down to a dozen chips. I ran up a full house, crimped, and set the pack out for the cut. The mark cut to my crimp and I completed the cut with the full safely on the bottom. I dealt them from there. I took the pot and I was on my way. Within the next half hour I ran my winnings up around $200 and was telling a fishing story when my hands went dead. My eyes began to ache. I thought at first it was only the smoke. But it was the jimjams. The inside shakes. The sweats.

It came over me like the first rumble of summer lightning. I sat there. I made fists of my hands, trying to hold it off, but the shakes came in waves like nausea. I must have gone white. Were these locals reading me? I wanted to leave. Get out of there. But I was too far ahead. I had too much of their money, too early to quit. They'd kill me.

I was trapped and I sat there. It was like trying to see through the fuzz in a hangover. I played on. The pack in my hand felt as heavy as lead. I don't know how I sat through it. It was Boston all over again. I lost track of time. I could fell the sweat trickle down inside my shirt. I was no longer making sense out of the game. I pushed some chips into the pot as if I couldn't give them away fast enough, and finally, when I reached for more, they were gone. I was wiped out.

I picked up my cigarettes and got to my feet. "Easy come, easy go," I mumbled, and left.

I walked. The tide was out and the black ocean made small hissing sounds. I took in deep lungfuls of night air, and a slow rage came over me. I had conned myself. I had swindled myself into believing I could make it again, but I would never make it again. I was spooked. I had become card-simple. I was washed up.

It didn't occur to me for several minutes that now I was broke. Really Tap City. It didn't seem to matter. What mattered was that I had nowhere left to go. I had run my skills out to the end of the line and found a dead end. Twice. I had abandoned magic to make it as a card hustler, but now even that had curdled. Skelly's golden mitts had turned to glass. I was finished. Break them and toss them in the nearest ash can.

I kept walking. I passed the Grand Metropole and looked up at my window. The light was on and I could hear Viola fooling with the concertina. I walked away. Along the beachwalk the Mexican fan palms rustled in the offshore breeze. I crossed over to the canals. I needed a good stiff drink or even a bad stiff drink.

The house, at night, was an accumulation of shadows. The spiked fence, the shrubbery and the vines seemed to shore up the dark shape of the house itself. Through the lead glass windows an upstairs light fell on the canal waters in the broken shape of a mosaic. I rang the bell.

It was a long time before Maggie appeared. She gave a little smile and told me to come in. She wore mules and a pink robe. "I was just brushing my teeth," she said.

"Don't let me stop you."

"I didn't expect to see you again. I'm glad you changed your mind, Skelly."

She closed the door and we stood in the hall, in the half light, speaking in half whispers. "Did Rinny Jim turn up?"

"I told you," she said. "He's gone. For good."

I didn't really give a damn about Rinny Jim. Anyone who would leave a girl like Maggie unattended was light on common sense. "Do you think we could scare up a drink?"

"Easy."

"You have cats' eyes," I said.

"No," she smiled. "Cats have my eyes."

"Let's skip the drink."

"But that's what you came for."

"No," I said. "I wanted to find out if you really light up in dark rooms."

"Do I?"

"Maggie," I said, "you're positively incandescent."

Chapter Six

The next day the sun came up and the sun went down without any help from me. I sat around Maggie's living room on a gentle diet of whiskey and cigarettes, and Maggie sat around in golden sandals and a yellow muu-muu. I didn't waste time reminding myself she was the wife of an old friend. Last night, after tossing in the pasteboards, I had needed Maggie. I had had to reassure myself that I wasn't a total loss, and Maggie had been reassuring as hell. Maybe that was what old friends were for.

The living room was something left over from the twenties. Or maybe Maggie had gone to some pains to recreate an atmosphere of a time that had died. Resurrection was her business; it said so on the door. There were beaded lamps, a dark console phonograph and a large floor vase holding plumes of pampas grass. The parquet floor was almost obscured by a lush patchwork of Oriental prayer rugs. The room, which could be closed off by old-fashioned sliding doors, was paneled in golden oak. The centerpiece was a round pedestal table with claw feet and five grim chairs snugged up in place. "What's this room used for?" I asked. "Embalming?"

She smiled and closed off the sliding doors as if to shut out the twentieth century. "This is where I hold séances."

"You mean floating tables and talking trumpets?"

"Anything can happen in the dark, Skelly darling."

"That's show biz," I said. "I thought those routines went out with the Charleston."

"But they still pay off." She leaned over to take a light off my cigarette. Her black hair was loose and flowing, a silken shadow brushed to one side of her head. "I have a new angle."

"Maggie," I said, "you have angles and curves Euclid never imagined."

She arranged herself on a leather hassock, her suntanned feet arched in the sandals and her arms boxed across her knees. She studied me for a moment and then murmured, "Have you ever heard of Mrs. Edwin Ellicott Marenbach?"

"A friend of yours?"

"She doesn't know I exist." Maggie had a sense of timing. She tapped her cigarette over the ash tray like two beats of a metronome. "But I've made a study of Mrs. Edwin Ellicott Marenbach. What she eats. What she drinks—a small glass of Meier's cream sherry in the evening. Rich isn't the word for her. She's rich, rich, rich."

"Nice," I muttered with only preliminary interest. In a way I had been waiting for Maggie to make her pitch. I was prepared to say yes to anything; it didn't really matter to me what Maggie had in mind. A buck was a buck and I was Tap City. "Nice, nice, nice."

"Maybe fifty million. A widow. Home in Bel Air. Sound interesting, Skelly?"

"Fascinating, Maggie."

"The old man's been dead for twenty years. He held some industrial patents and the estate keeps paying off like a slot machine. He was a heart case." The metronome of Maggie's finger beat out a slow march. "But Mrs. M hardly spends a dime. She probably still saves short pieces of string. That type. She keeps only two servants—a personal maid and a chauffeur-handyman. She has the locks in the house changed almost every month."

"Why?"

"Suspicious of everyone. Eccentric. And domineering. The old man probably had to get her permission to have a heart attack."

"Is he the ghost you intend to lure back from the grave? He may not want to come."

"No," she murmured. "There was a nephew. Jamie Marenbach. He lived with them. He was the one she really loved—her own flesh and blood. She got the old man to adopt Jamie as a child. Jamie came to hate her. She wasn't home when the old man had his final attack, and Jamie never forgave her for it. She might have saved him, I suppose. The old man was as close as Jamie had ever been to having a father, and it hurt like hell when he folded up. But that was twenty years ago. When I met Jamie he looked like an underweight Greek god. He played the bongos. He used to hang around the beatniks for kicks. The old lady wouldn't let him have any spending money—he'd come home drunk if she did. He came home drunk anyway. He borrowed from everyone. Even Rinny. He liked Rinny."

"He's dead?"

"Stone, cold dead," Maggie said. "And Rinny was with him the night it happened. They had been boozing in the beat joints along the ocean. Jamie got tanked up on dago red and excused himself to go to the beach."

"And?"

"And the tide was pulling out. He sat himself in shallow water like a yogi and let the waves break over him. Finally Rinny went out looking for him. By then the breakers were rolling in over Jamie's head. He didn't budge. He just sat there in the lotus position. Rinny, who was not entirely sober himself, tried to get to him. But it was too late. An undertow dragged Jamie out to sea like a doll. A few days later he was washed up on the beach. The sharks had been at him."

Her voice had fallen to a whisper. She crushed the cigarette and let the sharks swim around our minds for a moment.

I said, "How long ago was this?"

"Last April. About four months ago."

"Did I hear you mention a million dollars?"

"I was coming to that."

"I was sure you would."

"Jamie let it drop once, to Rinny, that the old lady was sitting on a big lump of cash. Probably not in the house, but scattered around in her bank vaults. He thinks it must be nearly a million in big bills. The old man, apparently, had tucked it away more than twenty years ago—undeclared, untaxed and unclean. Mrs. M just sits on it."

Maggie rose and began casing the room, moving from vase to lamp to window. In the flowing muu-muu she had the preoccupied air of a stunning, black-haired sleepwalker. But even asleep, I was sure, Maggie was strictly wide-awake.

"Mrs. Edwin Ellicott Marenbach is no fool," she went on. "I've got to handle her carefully. She's not going to fall for Ouija boards and tea leaves and crystal balls. For all I know she bites half-dollars to make sure they're genuine. She's going to be suspicious of us from the word go."

"But you've got it figured out."

"Every move, Skelly."

I shrugged off any lingering sense of conscience. Here was my chance to learn a new trade. Don't fight it, Skelly. You can't hustle cards any more. How are you going to get well? Grab the money and run.

"We've got to sell her Evangeline Ann Barlow," Maggie said. "I need you to bait the trap and lay down the story. The smooth talk. And then, step by step, I think we can brainwash her into shelling out for Jamie's ghost."

"How's the booze holding out?"

"If you keep drinking you're going to have a hangover."

"Nonsense," I said. "I drink to keep sober. How do I bait the trap?"

She had been carrying a dinner ring in her pocket and now she produced it, turning it in the light to give off blue sparks. The stone was a sapphire: cold, enormous and dazzling. "This belongs to Mrs. M. Jamie was not above stealing his aunt's jewelry to raise money. He sold this to Rinny for $50."

Even from across the room I could guess that the ring's value was somewhere in the thousands. "What do you want me to do with it?" I asked.

"Return it."

"If I didn't know you better I'd think you were getting soft."

She smiled again, and came toward me and dropped the ring in my palm. "I mean it. Return it, Skelly. Hide it somewhere in the house. And I'll do the rest."

"Like what?"

"Like you'll see."

"But that's housebreaking, Maggie."

"For a good cause. And it's not as if you were taking anything. You'll be putting it back."

I bounced the ring in my hand. It had the feel of cold fire. "All right," I said, "I'll find a way. But I don't see the payoff."

"You will."

"Maggie," I said. "I don't think you really trust me."

"Darling," she said, "—with a hot little million waiting, I don't entirely trust myself."

That was a sentiment I could understand. We smiled and made up. "Then what?" I asked.

"A journey begins with the first step—Chinese saying. In the end Mrs. M will swear that Evangeline Ann Barlow works miracles. When she's really hooked I'll lead her by the hand to the bank and from the bank to Jamie."

"Jamie."

She drew one of the chairs from the table and slowly moved it forward again as if seating an invisible guest. "In the end, Skelly darling, I'm going to seat Jamie at this table."

I believed it. Maggie could lay down a snow job like the blizzard of '88. She had talent. She was a pro. She had already figured out that Mrs. M had only one blind spot—Jamie. The old lady would come across for Jamie's ghost.

I believed it. I even began to believe in the million dollars. What I didn't believe was that Maggie was going to cut me in for more than peanuts. At the blowoff she might be hard to find. I had an instinct about broads like Maggie, but it was too early in the game to look for wooden nutmegs. She had only begun to tip her hand; once I knew her bottom card I would figure some way to look out for Skelly. Meanwhile, she was diverting to look at, amusing to contemplate, and overflowing with the sap of life. Rinny Jim had walked away from a harem concentrated into one well-stacked dame.

Night came on with a smell of jasmine vines curling up outside the open window. Maggie told me a little about herself. She grew up in the carnies. "My mother was a mitt reader," she said. "An imitation gypsy. When I was thirteen she had me working in the cootch show. I looked eighteen."

"I can believe it," I said.

"I got my fill of gawks and farmers. I made up my mind that some day I was going to wear mink. How much mink will a million dollars buy?"

"About one square mile."

I burned cigarettes and lost track of time. Still in the muumuu, she said she wanted to go swimming. That sounded like a good idea. We went swimming. I brought along a bottle and two glasses and planted them in the sand. It must have been midnight. There didn't seem to be anyone else alive—just the two of us in the warm night with the surf breaking at our feet. The muu-muu fluttered in the breeze, sketching in her figure with quick, disappearing lines.

"We'll go to Mexico," she said, extending the thought like a promissory note.

"I've been to Mexico," I said.

"Paris. The Riviera."

"Just you and me."

"Us."

"Have a drink."

"You don't believe me, do you?"

"Of course I do, Maggie darling. Just stop conning me. We're partners, right?"

"Right."

She raised the muu-muu above her ankles to let the surf swarm about her feet. I rolled up the bottoms of my trousers and stripped off my shirt. She caught my hand and another wave washed in around us. I found myself pulling her against me and she gave a little laugh, the merest silken rustle in her throat. Then she broke away and flung the muu-muu to the sand and swam away, through the hiss of the breakers and into deep water. She was a hell of a strong swimmer. I was not too drunk to let a good thing get away. I dove in after her. She was naked as a fish.

I awoke late the next morning with a hangover. I left Maggie asleep and went foraging for a cigarette. All I could find were crushed packages from the night before. Not a gasper in the house. Finally I began going through the ash tray for a butt long enough to straighten, and that's when I noticed it.

We had been burning Pall Malls. The tray was full of them. I picked out the stub of a filter tip, an Alpine, and wondered how it had got there.

My head was knocking. I sat on the hassock, and like a simpleton I stared at the butt for a full minute. And finally it got through to my half-embalmed brain. Someone had been in the house. Someone had killed his cigarette in the tray. Maybe Maggie and I were not alone on the premises. And then the hair rose on the back of my neck. I had a feeling.

I had a feeling Rinny Jim was back.

Chapter Seven

I was in no mood for panic. I straightened the best butt I could find and lit it. Then I tried to remember where I had left my trousers. I listened. The house was silent. I supposed there was no one lurking in the morning shadows; maybe Rinny Jim had come and gone while we had been out. I got up and wandered back along the hall and dog-eyed the bedroom. Then I shook Maggie's ankle.

"Where the hell are my pants?"

She came awake with one eye. "Funny man."

"Someone's been here."

The other eye came awake. "What?"

"Cigarettes. What brand does Rinny Jim smoke?"

"Any kind he can bum. Why?"

I explained my theory to her, but she only sat up and began to laugh. She said she had found a leftover Alpine in the pocket of her muumuu and smoked it herself. "Skelly, you've got a hangover."

"Not me," I said. "Never felt better in my life."

"I'll fix you some coffee. You can put cotton in your ears when it begins to perk."

I found my trousers in the donicker, banging out to dry over the shower rod. They were still clammy from the sea. I must have been the best-dressed swimmer on the beach. It was a wonder I hadn't gone in wearing my necktie. I shook out the pants and crawled into them, thinking all the while that something Maggie had said didn't add up right. But the exact point kept eluding me. Then I remembered to shave.

The coffee helped. Maggie had brushed out her hair and sat in a quilted pink robe across the table from me. "Can I count on you to salt the gold ring in Bel Air tonight, Skelly?"

"The housebreaking bit is out," I said.

"But you gave me your word."

"You ought to know better than to take the word of a boozer. I don't think I'd be very good at burglary. I'll find another way."

She got up and poured me another jolt of coffee. "If the old lady gets a look at you, Skelly—that's it. You're dead. We can't be seen together any more."

"Do you know her routine?" I asked. "When does she leave the house?"

"She does her own grocery shopping. The chauffeur drives her into Westwood every afternoon after her nap. They hate to see her coming. She feels every peach and avocado in the bins."

"What time is the nap?"

"After lunch."

"Is there anything about her you don't know?"

"Nothing."

"Let me have the sapphire. And I'll take some cash on account."

"On account of what?"

"On account of I'm flat broke."

Her long fingers gathered the neck of her robe together in a kind of protective gesture. "How do I know you're not going to pick up your shoes and run?"

It was a real temptation. "Could Antony ditch Cleopatra?" I said. "Did Tristan cut out on Isolde? Maggie darling, I'm your obedient servant."

"Double-cross me, Skelly," she whispered, "and I'll poke you in the eye with a sharp stick."

I bought a pack of smokes and did business with the first clothing store I came to. I outfitted myself in faded denims and a cheap yachting cap. It helped to feel like someone else; anyone would do. But my head was calming down and I was able to keep a single thought for more than five seconds. I knew now that Maggie had lied to me. The awakening came over me like a delayed crack of lightning. Her lipstick was missing from the cigarette stub. She hadn't burned that Alpine at all. Someone had been in the house and she had covered for him. Rinny Jim? What kind of domestic peek-a-boo were they playing?

I floated along Windward Avenue, trying to push this line of thought to some conclusion, but I came up with less than nothing. I didn't bother my convalescing head with it. The sun was too strong and the day was too hot.

I dropped off my suit at a cut-rate cleaning shop, bummed a street map from the Standard Station and looked up the Windsor Canyon Road section of Bel Air. It was not exactly around the corner. Mrs. Edwin Ellicott Marenbach was hidden away in the residential wilds a few miles from Beverly Hills. I had already doped out my approach, and if I was seen at all I would be remembered as one of the faceless in yachting cap and sunglasses. A type.

I flagged a taxi and began my makeshift career as a confidence man.

It was practically a sleeper jump. Finally we joined the traffic along Sunset Boulevard and turned off into Windsor Canyon Road. The pearly gates couldn't have opened on greener pastures; the great fire had leapfrogged this canyon. Homes lurked behind shimmering trees; enormous lawns and fields of ivy softened the hillsides. I was surprised that they allowed anything less than a Mercedes on the road.

We stopped at the foot of Cadiz Way and I got out. I told the hackster to wait. Mrs. M lived on a steep residential spur. I walked up the hill. It was the last house, set back from the road; a large Spanish stucco with a red tile roof. The mailbox at the foot of the gravel driveway said MARENBACH.

Aging eucalyptus trees were everywhere, shading the grounds and filling the air with a resinous scent. It was a long walk to the door. I stepped on my cigarette and started along the driveway. It was one-thirty. Mrs. M would be asleep.

I knocked at the door.

I knocked again.

The maid came, opening the door a crack and giving me half her face. "Yes?" She spoke as if she hadn't raised her voice above a whisper in years. Her one eye was blue, timid and guarded.

"Excuse me, ma'am," I said. "My brakes have gone out on my car. It's just down the hill. I wonder if I could use your phone."

"No." The gap in the door began to shrink.

"But I just want to call the Auto Club."

"I'm sorry."

"But—"

"The phone is out of order. I'm sorry."

The door clicked shut and I stood there swearing to myself. The maid no doubt had standing orders not to let anyone in the house.

Maggie was way ahead of me; it was going to take dynamite to get past the front door.

I couldn't just stand there. I moved. I walked back to the road. The mail truck was working its way up the hill, raising red flags on the boxes. I slowed down. If there was mail for Mrs. M, the maid might come for it.

The truck passed me up and I watched it over my shoulder. But it didn't stop at the Marenbach box. It went on up to the circle to swing around, and started back down the hill.

What did I have to lose? I returned to the box, raised the flag and ducked into the eucalyptus trees. I kept my distance until I was on a line with the front door of the house, and then moved in closer. You could hide an elephant in the trees. I waited. I wondered about the chauffeur. The garage was somewhere behind the house. If I had a choice I'd just as soon not make his acquaintance.

Not more than a minute passed before the door opened and the maid started after the day's mail. I could hear her feet crunch in the gravel. She was a thin, birdlike figure in domestic whites. She had left the front door wide open. An inch would have been enough.

She was halfway to the box when I walked in. There was a tiled entry and two steps down to the living room. The house was cool and silent. I didn't press my luck. I already had the sapphire in my hand when I reached the furniture. I buried the ring deep behind the cushion of an overstuffed wing chair. I had an impression of heavy velvet drapes and a vaulted ceiling. I paused only long enough to steal a glance at a large oil painting, in an encrusted gilt frame, of a child with blond curls and one leg folded under him. I guessed that was Jamie before the world closed in on him. I left.

I doubt if I had burned up fifteen seconds. I was back with the eucalyptus before the bird lady reached the mailbox. It took her a long time to convince herself that it was empty. She reached in and looked in and reached in again. Then she gave it up and returned to the house.

I returned to the cab and told the driver to wake me when we got to Venice.

Chapter Eight

One of the first things I did was get rid of the yachting cap. It was giving my headache a headache. Then I checked back into the Grand Metropole. I got my old room back. It was beginning to feel like home. I paid a week's rent in advance. It was like putting down roots.

I pulled the green shade, to shut out the sun, and for the first time in a couple of days I thought about Viola. The beachnik. Spindlelegs. I supposed she would turn up in the morning, outside the window, feeding sea gulls. She had floated into my life and maybe she had floated out of it. It didn't really matter.

I went down the hall for a shower and then slept off the tag end of my hangover. I got up around six and remembered I hadn't got back in touch with Maggie. She was probably out looking for me with a sharp stick. I used the hall phone.

"Maggie darling," I said. "This is your obedient servant."

"Skelly—you long-legged bastard!"

"That's no language for a witch."

"Where have you been? I've been waiting all afternoon."

"Why don't you come by in your yeller Cadillac, and I'll take you to dinner and we can overhaul each other by candlelight."

"Where are you?"

"The Grand Metropole."

"I thought you were moving in here. With me."

Not on your life, Maggie darling, I mused. Spare me your little badger game—whatever it is. "The neighbors might talk," I said. "A nice girl like you."

"Skelly—"

"I'll be waiting for you."

"Did it go all right in Bel Air?"

"Splendid," I said. "I believe I have a talent for these parlor tricks of yours."

We drove up the coast to Malibu and pulled off at a roadhouse for dinner. It was a place with checkered tablecloths and fish down both sides of the menu. We ordered mahi mahi and I attempted light conversation. Maggie was not altogether friendly; I think she sensed that I wanted to make a few changes in our working relationship. I asked her if my cigarette lighter had turned up around her place; I had mislaid it. She said no. She kept asking where I had salted away the ring, but I kept putting her off.

"Aren't you going to tell me?" she murmured finally.

"Tell you what?"

"The sapphire, darling."

"But I told you," I said. "I got it in the house, just as you said."

"But *where?*"

"Is that important?"

"You know it is."

I shook my bead. "Maggie darling, that's just the point. You're playing this game so close to your vest—or should I say chest—that I don't really know the time of day. At some point in these proceedings you're going to have to make up your mind to trust me. That point is now. Trust me or let go of me. Cue me in or get yourself another partner."

She raised an impeccable black eyebrow and smiled. "I scratch your back—and you scratch mine?"

"A thing like that could catch on," I said.

"You're a doll."

"What's this ring bit all about? How does it pay off? Let's scratch, and we'll both be dolls."

I struck a match for her cigarette and she leaned into it. "The ring is the opening gambit, Skelly. It's going to get me past the front door."

"Not an easy thing to do," I said. "I don't think that maid would let firemen in the house if the kitchen was burning. I got the feeling she's terrified of the old lady."

"Yes. Mrs. M thinks everyone is trying to steal from her. Tomorrow I write her a letter. I say that in our researches at the Institute we have intercepted a voice claiming to be that of her nephew, Jamie. Anyway, this voice—I tell her—tells me that he had once taken one of her jewels, a sapphire ring, and hidden it from her. You tell me where, Skelly. When she reads the letter she's going to think it was written by some kind of creep. She doesn't really believe in the living, why should she believe in the dead? She's no fool. But I'll bet that before an hour passes she's unable to pass up that spot and have a look. When she finds the long-lost ring, exactly where Evangeline Ann Barlow said it would be—we crack her shell."

"Then what?"

"I think she'll call me. If not that day, the next. She won't be able to sleep, thinking about Jamie's voice. She'll want to hear it for herself. And that's when I get past the front door and make points. That's when she begins paying through the nose."

"How are you going to deliver Jamie's voice?"

She gave a small shrug. "Don't be a bore, Skelly. I trust you exactly as far as you trust me—just from day to day. I told you what you wanted to know. Where did you hide the sapphire?"

"In the sunken living room. Under a portrait of a kid with sausage curls."

"That was Jamie. She kept him in curls until he was six. He cut them off himself."

"Anyway, there's a wing chair under the picture. I stuffed the ring behind the cushion."

"Exactly where, Skelly?"

"On the left side."

"Did Mrs. M see you?"

"No. Just the maid. And she doesn't realize I got past the door."

"A square mile of mink," Maggie whispered, rubbing her arms in luxurious anticipation. "Think of it."

"Less my cut, Maggie darling," I said. "Don't forget my cut."

When I got up the next morning there were no sea gulls and no Viola. I was almost disappointed. Without quite realizing it I had looked forward to having someone to shout at. I missed her. In a kind of inside-out way I supposed I even needed her. I needed someone to make me feel a little better than I was. I was not entirely enchanted with the prospect of victimizing a grieving old woman—even Mrs. M. Still, I had not made the world the way it was and felt under no obligation to improve it. That was for the regulars. I was having enough trouble just making it from day to day.

But now, for the first time in months, I had a flash of hope. If Mrs. M loosened her purse strings, if Maggie's ghost-making worked, there was an outside chance that I could make a cash settlement with Charlie Braque and get him off my back. I would be free.

Later in the day I came across Viola's concertina hanging in the window of a pawnshop along the arcades. It gave me a small jolt. She had refused to part with it the night of my farewell to the pasteboards, but she had given it up after all.

"Did she give any address?" I asked the man. He looked up at me through a black loupe stuck in one eye as if all humanity were as suspect as a Swiss movement.

"I remember distinctly," he said. "She said the Beverly Hilton."

"Didn't she hock it?"

"She sold it."

"What do you want for it?"

"For you—$12.50."

I don't know where the next couple of days went. I kept checking with Maggie, but there were no communiqués from Bel Air. After three days the whole thing began to smell like sour milk and Maggie began chewing her nails over the phone.

"You're too impatient," I told her. "She's got to wrestle with sixty years of common sense. I'll bet she's stationed the maid at the phone to keep her from weakening."

I stayed away from Maggie. I was in no mood to find Rinny Jim skulking around. I killed time. I went to the library and read the out-of-town papers. I picked up *The Compleat Angler*. I read about the outdoors as if it belonged to someone else. Someone like Appleby. I had tampered with Clausewitz and the head shrinkers and Balzac and the Greeks. There had always been times when I needed to get as far away from the card table as possible, and in whatever town I was in there was always the book stacks. I had checked myself out on a lot of subject matter, most of it useless in my trade, but even Clausewitz on war had taught me something about poker.

Whenever I was on the street I had the feeling that if I turned suddenly I'd find Spindlelegs somewhere behind, dogging me. I asked here and there, but no one had seen her in days. She had done a fade. I guessed she had left town, and I was sorry. I was even a little burned. Like the sea gulls, I had got used to having her around.

Chapter Nine

On the fifth day the phone rang.

The waiting was over. Mrs. Edwin Ellicott Marenbach invited Miss Evangeline Ann Barlow to call on her that evening "for a little chat." I had to hand it to Mrs. M. She was a tough old party. She would still be looking for wooden nutmegs in heaven, or wherever it was she had made arrangements to go.

I spent the afternoon with Maggie learning how to work the traps she had rigged up. I discovered that electronics had come to the table-rapping set. When we left Venice, around seven-thirty, Maggie was wired up like NBC. She was a walking broadcasting station, with a transistor mike in her bosom and a transmitter not much bigger than a pack of cigarettes at the small of her back. She dressed in black and wore a hat with a black veil. The funeral march started going through my mind.

"They're playing our song," I said.

"What?"

"Forget it. You look enchanting, partner."

"I'm counting on you, Skelly. This has got to go right on cue."

"Don't worry about me."

"She's still suspicious. One false move and we're out on our ear. But when she hears Jamie's voice she ought to jump out of her shoes."

"If I know the type," I said, "she'll try to pay off in short pieces of string."

I drove up the coast as far as Santa Monica and turned right on Wilshire Boulevard. It was coming on dusk. I stopped in Westwood and we split up. Maggie took a cab into Bel Air. She carried a tambourine and a stout volume on the occult. She clutched it like a family Bible. I was to follow in the Caddie about five minutes later and park a couple of hundred feet down the hill from the house. That would put me out of sight, but I would be able to listen in for my cue on a battery-powered receiving set. Maggie would be broadcasting with her bosom mike. Even as she stepped into the cab I picked up her voice: "Bel Air, driver. Twenty-seven Cadiz Way."

I watched the cab vanish in the traffic. I could almost pick up Maggie's heartbeat on the transistor. I waited. And then I headed toward Sunset and the darkening green hills of the big rich. I slowed at the entrance to Windsor Canyon Road, where a night watch had come on. The nighthawk peered at me as I went by, but the Cadillac removed me from immediate suspicion.

The canyon was as silent as a museum. The day's army of Japanese gardeners, scratching up every fallen leaf and trimming every hedge, had retreated. Night was falling and I remembered to turn on the lights.

I followed the white line, thinking that the only thing that could disturb the timing was a flat tire. But I reached Cadiz Way and parked halfway up the hill under a giant pepper tree. Maggie's taxi came tooling down and was gone. I killed the lights.

I listened in on Maggie's bosom mike, keeping the receiver tuned low. I was barely able to pick up Mrs. M's voice, but even then there was the suggestion of a certain heaviness, like a voice rising out of a bottle. Apparently she had just come in, joining Maggie in the living room.

"Please be seated."

"Thank you," Maggie said.

"That will he all, Hilda." The maid, I supposed. And then to Maggie: "That girl is a bother. She thinks I'm going to name her in my will. They all think that. *Hilda, will you stop listening at the door. I know you're there.* Well let me look at you. What is it you want? Money, I suppose."

"Mrs. Marenbach—"

"I'll be blunt. I stopped believing in tea leaves and palmistry when I was a girl. I really don't know why I asked you to call."

"Then perhaps I'd better leave."

"You're a very confident young lady."

"I'm not a fortune teller, Mrs. Marenbach. I don't read palms and tea leaves."

"Why did you come?"

"You invited me."

"Yes. The ring." There was a pause. "What is it you expected? A reward? There was no ring behind the cushion. Nothing at all."

I did a slight take, scowling at the receiver. The old battle-axe wasn't going to admit anything. But Maggie was equal to her. "Then Jamie was just teasing us, wasn't he, Mrs. Marenbach? No, I'm not looking for a reward."

"Do you expect me to believe my nephew talked to you from the other side? My dear young lady, that is rubbish."

"I know how you must feel, Mrs. Marenbach."

"If such things were possible, why would he talk to a perfect stranger? He would talk to me. I brought him up as if he were my son. I'm the one he loved."

"Of course, Mrs. Marenbach. And perhaps he is trying to reach you. Our researches at the Institute are far from complete. We know so very little, Mrs. Marenbach. We are working on the frontier of darkness. I can tell you only that your nephew has come to us—to me. I have heard his voice. He has spoken through my lips. Good night, Mrs. Marenbach."

"Hold on. Sit down." There was a long pause. "My mind is not entirely closed, young lady. Dear Jamie was a dreadful boy. He stole from me. I know he did. But he was my own flesh and blood. Would you like a glass of sherry?"

"No, thank you."

"What is the tambourine for?"

"We have found that Jamie responds to the sound of the tambourine. Take it in your hands."

"My dear young lady, I think you are a very clever trickster."

"Of course you do."

"I suppose you'll want the lights out."

"One small light will be fine."

I had to credit Maggie with knowing her trade. She was a lesson in smoothness. I opened the glove compartment, where a small phonograph had been installed. Jamie's voice was on a record. I would broadcast it into Mrs. M's living room. The book that Maggie would now clutch to her breast as she went into her trance was nicely gimmicked. Pages had been hollowed out and a transistor receiving set installed. This whole bit of ghost-walking had been made in Japan. Everything but Jamie's voice. Rinny Jim, who could mimic anyone, had made the record.

I was picking up the tinny jingle of the tambourine. Mrs. M was giving it a try. I began warming up the record player. Any moment now, in the grip of an occult trance, Maggie would start calling Jamie's name. My cue. Everything was quiet except for the metallic whisper of the tambourine. And then it came.

"Jamie... Jamie..."

I had the arm of the record player in my fingers when headlights from below flashed up the hill. A car was coming. Some instinct warned me. I shut the glove compartment and killed the transmitter and receiver. There was nothing more suspect than a man waiting in a darkened car. I got out and walked across the road toward the nearest house. The headlights lit me up and I kept walking.

It was a private patrol on the cruise. I could feel the eyes of the fuzz on me. I started up a long flight of flagstones. The car ground its way to the top and made the circle. Then it started down. I reached the house and rang the bell.

After a moment the front porch lit up. That was fine. It made me look legit. A Filipino houseboy opened the door with a ready-made smile.

"Gold evening, sir."

"Would you tell Mr. Gwynne that Major Van Deerlin is here."

"I beg pardon."

"Mr. Gwynne."

The patrol car was below me now and almost stopped. It was as if the nighthawks were, defying me to get past the front door.

"No Mr. Gwynne live here, sir."

"You must be mistaken," I said.

"No mistake. Mr. Steven live here."

"I must have the wrong address," I said. "If I could check your phone book—"

I was in. The houseboy asked me to wait in the entry, and a moment later he returned with the directory. I supposed Maggie was going wild all tied up in her trance with no Jamie to pay it off. I killed another minute flipping pages. I scratched down a number, thanked the Filipino and left.

The patrol car had given me up. It was gone.

I made it fast. I warmed up the record player and transmitter, and tuned in on Mrs. M's darkened living room. The shimmer of the tambourine had stopped.

"That's quite enough," I heard the old lady say. "You can stop pretending, young lady. Please get out."

"Jamie..."

"You're in no more of a trance than I am."

I touched the needle to the record. After a moment Jamie was on the air.

"Aunt Orva... Aunt Orva... this is... Jamie."

The effect in the living room must have been electrifying. The tambourine began to rattle again. Maggie, with her arms crossed around the book, had practiced mouthing the words on the record, and the illusion had to be powerful. Jamie's voice would seem to break from her lips. The book she clutched was arousing no suspicion.

"Don't be... frightened... Aunt Orva. I'm happy... here. I... miss you..."

There was a pause in the recording. Maggie had expected Mrs. M to speak, to respond, to recognize Jamie, but she was keeping an icy silence. There was only the nervous flutter of the tambourine.

"I... miss you. I have... tried... to reach you."

And then Mrs. M broke the ice. *"Rubbish!"*

"The closet.... I didn't mean to do it. Don't punish me, Aunt Orva."

"Stop this nonsense!"

"Don't... punish me...."

"Damn you, Jamie!"

Her voice came rolling up like a menacing clap of thunder. The hairs on my neck stiffened.

"Goodbye, Aunt Orva..."

"Jamie!"

"Goodbye..."

"Jamie—I hope you roast in hell!"

Chapter Ten

It was as if we had stepped on the tail of a snake. I parked in West-wood and waited for Maggie with the hiss and rattle still in my ears. I didn't like this high-class grave-digging I had got into. But if I had any misgivings about swindling a dear old lady, they curled and blew away. She was not quite as gentle and kindly as a meat axe. Mrs. M could look out for herself. But we'd be lucky to come out of this fakus with our heads on straight.

Maggie came by in a cab, and I started the engine. I picked her up and headed back toward the ocean. She lit a cigarette. It was a long time before either of us spoke. Finally she slipped off her shoes and folded her legs under her and watched the lights of Wilshire Boule-vard swarm past. And then she gave me a smile. "We're in," she said.

"You're conning yourself, Maggie. She hates the kid."

"But she believes. She talked to Jamie. She believed it."

"Sure she did. But if Jamie were in Hell she wouldn't buy him a gar-den hose to put out the blaze. She's *glad* he's dead. She's not going to pay off to hold his hand again."

"I tell you we're in, Skelly. She turned white when she heard Jamie's voice. I told her we hold a séance at the Institute every Wednesday night. She's got to come back for more."

I stopped for a red light. "It'll serve her right if she does. It sounded to me like she was scared. As if Jamie knew something that frightened her. The closet bit. What was it between them? What did the closet mean?"

Maggie rested her head on the seat. "I didn't know it would set her off that way. I don't know what it means. Jamie was a crying drunk. When he was stoned, really stoned, he'd begin carrying on about a closet. 'I didn't mean to do it, Aunt Orva. I didn't mean to do it.' He kept saying that over and over again. Rinny remembered it and put it on the record. We figured it would be like Jamie's signature. It would have to mean something to her. She would have to believe it was him."

"Keep your figure," I said.

"What?"

"If she blows wise I'd like to think that you can always go back to the cootch shows."

I slept late the next morning. I lifted the shade on a blinding patch of white sand and blue water, and lowered the shade again. I was in no mood for summer. It was going to be a bad day. Something in the air. I shaved and showered and wondered how I had got into this ghoulish enterprise.

I stayed away from Maggie. I floated around and the day passed. I tried to stop looking for Braque's paymaster in every strange face along the colonnades. There were too many other towns where they might expect me to turn up. If anyone bugged me it was Maggie. She had rooms over the garage and she couldn't figure my staying at the hotel. There were moments when it wasn't easy to remember that she was someone else's wife. But I managed to keep the thought in mind. I couldn't buy her story that Rinny Jim had walked out on a million dollar score. Every time I walked in the house the feeling came over me that he was watching from the bushes. If he wasn't, he should have been.

There was an imitation sidewalk café along one of the arcaded side streets, a place called Chez Sam's, and around seven I fell into one of the outside tables. The specialty of the house, as well as I could determine from the menu, was canned spaghetti. I had nothing more in mind than to watch night fall on the sea at the end of the street, and eat cheap.

I noticed the guy first. I had seen him before. He was sitting with a girl at one of the other tables, a beer-drinker drinking beer. He was the jowly gent I had clouted on the jaw my first night in town. Either he didn't recognize me or he couldn't see that far. The girl was class. She was a slim blonde in a low-cut summer dress and green shoes. She wore dark sunglasses with the authority of a visiting celebrity, and it was a full ten seconds before I realized who she was. It jarred me. I stared at her and then put down the dog-eared menu and walked over.

"Chow," I said.

Viola glanced up at me. She gave me a look reserved for total strangers. "Go away," she said in a quiet voice.

"Whatever you've done to yourself," I said, "I like it."

The geek screwed down one eye and began to rumble. "Move along, friend."

I sat down and ignored him. It wasn't so much that Viola had changed herself into a beauty. I saw now that it had been the other way around. The beauty was there to begin with; the hemp-haired rag doll in the wet bathing suit was an imposter. It was as if she had been running away from the girl I saw now—a quietly stunning blonde in an expensive dress. "I looked for you," I said. "I asked everywhere."

"Leave me alone."

"Hey," the man said, "I thought I told you to get lost."

I stared into Viola's dark glasses and nodded toward her companion. "You with him?"

He answered for her. "You looking for a week in the hospital? The little lady's with me. We're going to get hitched."

It was like a blow to the side of the head. "He's putting me on, isn't he?" I asked Viola.

"No."

"Are you suddenly up for grabs?"

"Why don't you go away?"

"Listen," the geek said, rearranging his jowls along fighting lines, "I'm going to count to ten by fives."

"Viola," I said. "Tell this mathematical whiz to beat it. What happened to you? Where did you go?"

"Five. I said *five*, mister."

"You never came back," Viola murmured. "I waited for you. I thought you'd come back."

"*Ten!*"

I got up and put my hand in his face and shoved him back in the chair. "Blow wise, will you? Sit still and I won't have to break the furniture over your head. Viola—are you coming with me?"

"Where are you going?"

"Take a chance."

She picked up her traps and turned to the geek. "Thanks for the drink," she said. I took her arm and hustled her to the end of the street while he sat there making slit trenches of his eyes. But he didn't follow us. He was a born loser and he knew it.

A beach tram came by and I flagged it down. It was empty except for a kid with a peeling nose and a black violin case beside him on the seat like an unwanted friend. The tram was a pink-and-white confection shuttling between Venice and the amusement pier at Ocean Park. We took the rear seat.

"I missed you," I said.

"Did you."

"Where did you go?"

She gave a little shrug. "Home."

"Where's home?"

"Pasadena."

"Didn't it work out?"

"No."

"I'm glad you came back," I said. "I really missed you."

"You said that."

"Don't be sore at me, Spindlelegs."

"Do you have to call me Spindlelegs?"

"With your hair brushed and some threads on you, you're something to see. But you're still skinny. Is that the way they grow them in Pasadena? Look, Viola, I didn't run out on you."

"It doesn't matter."

"But it does. I couldn't come back to the hotel that night. I was beat. I didn't want to face you. At the time I didn't realize that you meant anything to me. Even then, somehow I couldn't face you. I think I figured you'd always be around. But when you didn't turn up it made me sore. When I got over being sore I was still sore. I'm glad you came back, Spindlelegs."

She turned and the sea wind began whipping her hair across her cheeks. Her face reflected the last blaze of the sun. She held back her hair with a hand and gave a little smile. She had a way of smiling that was somehow as private as the act of undressing. "Chow," she said.

We had dinner on the amusement pier. The evening was festooned with lights and the roller coaster roared through the air like a night-flying beast. We were two faces in the crowd, but we had never been more alone. As the evening spun itself out we drew closer together until, in the house of mirrors, we saw ourselves become a single, melting reflection.

"Marry me," she said into the mirror.

"Do you ask every guy you meet?"

"Starting today."

"I won't marry you."

"Did I tell you about my mother?"

"No."

"Always a bride, never a bridesmaid."

We left. I turned my pockets inside out. I had spent every thin one I had. We didn't even have tram fare back.

"We walk," I said.

"Okay."

We carried our shoes and started back in the wet sand, with the surf tossing up seaweed around our feet. We didn't speak for a long time. I wasn't thinking ahead more than a step at a time. I knew I was falling in love with this long-legged blonde, this beachnik, this green-eyed wonder, but how do you break a fall? We left our footprints in the sand, and I tried to keep a level head. I was in no position to take on extra baggage. I was living like a newspaper in a high wind—and yesterday's newspaper at that. I was an ex-card hustler. I had no business cutting into Viola's life. But I wasn't going to see her take up with geeks and scavengers. It wasn't that she didn't have enough sense to come in out of the rain. I had her figured out now; she wanted to get wet.

I said, "Do you have a place to sleep?"

"No."

"You're not coming home with me."

"Why not?"

"Stop trying to act like a broad. You don't belong in a place like Venice."

"Where do I belong?"

"What happened in Pasadena?"

"There's no place like home—except home. Spare me."

"What happened?"

"Mother's husbands keep getting younger all the time. Did I tell you? She's a beauty."

"I can believe it," I said.

"I mean a *real* beauty." The white surf rushed up and receded, lighting our way with foam. "When I was eighteen she was drifting through her late thirties and between husbands, and I think she began to hate me just for being eighteen. She tried to keep me in jeans and low-heeled shoes. If I charged any clothes she'd send them back. I'd find her staring at herself in the dressing room mirror—like the witch in the fairy tale."

" 'Mirror, mirror, on the wall—' "

"I couldn't care less. I loved horses and used to spend all my time around the stables. Finally I went away to Stanford and grew up, and here I am."

I gave her a glance. "Spindlelegs," I said, "I have a feeling you left out something."

"Let's skip it."

"Let's not." I cupped my hands around a match and we dipped our cigarettes into the flame like straws. "Did you meet a guy?"

"Yes," she said.

"What was he like?"

"Something like you, but nothing like you at all."

"Does that make sense?"

"He was from Louisville—accent and all. I loved it. I had gone out to USC to take some courses, and there he was. The teach. The prof. He was young and soft-spoken and he wore a vest to hang his Phi Beta key on."

"Are you in love with him?"

"I hate him."

"But you were in love with him," I said.

"Yes. I had it bad—like measles. I was even going to marry him. I finally brought him home to meet Mother. She was sweet and charming and chic and full of leftover blessings. I almost thought I had been wrong about her." Viola's voice dropped almost to a whisper. "You can guess what happened."

"I suppose I can."

We walked along and it was several moments before she could make up her mind to unload it all. "I found them together," she said, and the words were almost lost in the wind. "Funny. It was the first time I ever saw him without his Phi Beta key. It was broad daylight and she didn't even bother to lock the French doors. They were in bed."

A wave cracked and shot a white line through the darkness. I found her hand and it was cold. We just walked along. Mirror, mirror, on the wall, I thought, who's the fairest of them all?

"All that happened early last spring," she said. "I drifted to Venice. You don't have to be yourself in Venice. You can be anyone you want to be, and I wanted to be nothing. Zero."

"A stringy blonde in a wet bathing suit," I said. "I almost believed it."

"But you came along and I wanted you to like me—and then you were gone. I thought it must be that other woman."

"In a way, it was," I said.

"She's beautiful."

"Only on the outside. Don't start making like a dumb broad. She's nothing to me."

"I sold the concertina and went back to Pasadena in a taxi. In style. I walked in the house and Mother acted as if I'd never been gone. She was on her way to the hairdresser, and she gave me a peck on the cheek and drove away. I stood it for a week. It was no use. She's getting herself a new husband, and she introduced me as her sister. She couldn't wait to get me out of the house again."

"And here you are."

"Here I am."

"You don't want to get tangled up with a guy like me."

"Why not?"

"Don't be a broad."

"You keep telling me."

I said, "Marry me."

"Do you ask every broad you meet?"

"Starting today."

"I won't marry you."

"That's the right answer."

"There's your hotel."

I lifted her chin and then pulled her up close and kissed her. The surf washed up around our feet. I don't know how long we stood that way. Maybe the tide came in and maybe the tide went out. She clung to me with her head against my chest and then, when she tilted her face, I could tell she was smiling. "Chow," she said.

"You're not moving in with me," I said.

"You told me."

"But you've got to sleep somewhere."

"Yes."

"Come on."

We crossed the beach toward the lights of the Grand Metropole. For months now the future had been one damned minute after the other; suddenly, I wanted to see tomorrow come, and the day after and the day after. The future was Spindlelegs. If I could make it. If I could make Maggie and her ghost-walking tricks pay off. All I needed was traveling money and I could make some sense out of doubling up.

There was no one along the oceanfront walk but a short, bald-headed man sitting on a green bench with his back to the ocean. It was as if he were mesmerized by the word BEER flickering on and off at the bottom of the hotel sign. Viola and I stopped to put on our shoes, and turned into the hotel. I picked up my key. It wasn't Phi Beta, but it was a place to kip for the night.

I had left the shade up, and the beer sign was flashing in the room. I snapped on the light, and almost at once I stopped cold. It hit me. The blah face. The man on the green bench. He was watching the room. Waiting for me to get back. I hit the light, but it was too late. I had put out the welcome mat.

"What's wrong?" Viola asked.

"Don't touch that switch."

I looked down from the window. The beach was empty. The man had to be on his way up. I turned to Viola.

"Beat it," I said. "Go down the hall to the donicker. If you don't have to make the john, take a shower. Only stay out of here. Understand?"

I hustled her out and shut the door. The squat, bald-headed man could only be from the East. Braque's heavyman. The six months of waiting were over. He had finally caught up with me. This was the night Braque was going to close the books. Maybe.

There was a knock on the door and I told him to come in.

Chapter Eleven

I raised the bentwood chair over my head. The door opened, letting in a dim, yellow blast of hall light, and Maggie walked in. Maggie. I almost split her in two.

I lowered the chair. "What the hell are you doing here?"

"We've been waiting for you."

The bald-headed man was right behind her, sweating from the climb up the stairs and grinning like a Halloween pumpkin. He wore a tie like a noose and the points of his collar had curled up in the heat. He shut the door, and I looked at Maggie. I could see murder in her eyes. "Who's your friend?" I asked.

She seared him with a glance. "This is dear Mr. Noah Porter. Devoted husband, father of four and by trade a cheap, conniving s.o.b."

"At your service," Porter said, handing me his card with a great air of bemused satisfaction. He was a private detective.

"What do you want?"

"All I want is to help you two nice people."

"He wants a piece of the action," Maggie snapped.

Porter gave her a round, benevolent smile. "The little lady is overwrought. I don't blame her. Really I don't. But there's no reason why we can't talk this over and come to a very pleasant arrangement for us all. Very pleasant, indeed. Appleby—is that the name?"

Except for lipstick Maggie hadn't bothered with any makeup. She kept giving me dark glances as if she expected me to push the man out the window. "Mrs. M hired him," she said. "To run a check on us."

"A woman of strict procedures," Porter said. "A woman of wise precautions. Money, like an open garbage can, always attracts flies. Do you mind if I light a cigar?"

"Mr. Porter," I said, "I wouldn't stand by that open window."

"Good thinking, sir," he grinned. "Careless of me."

"Let's have it." I watched him light his cigar. "What do you think you know?"

"Nothing. Absolutely nothing. Everything. Absolutely everything."

"Let's start with nothing."

"Right, sir. My client, who is not a woman of prodigal spending habits, has retained me in this little matter at a reduced fee of fifty dollars a day and expenses. She tells me that Miss Evangeline here has brought the Great Unknown, the bourn from which no traveler returns—except by appointment, perhaps—into the old lady's very living room. A matter of the late nephew. Voice from the dead, I believe. Baffling. Puzzling. And the discovery of the sapphire ring. Astonishing. Clearly a major talent at work. I would be the first to confess that I haven't the faintest notion of your *modus operandi*. I know absolutely nothing. Why, I applaud you—there's no one with a higher regard for talent than Noah Porter, at your service."

"I can see that," I said.

"But in three or four days of nosing about—why, there's no telling what sordid information might come my way. Nothing could sadden me more than to have to tell that poor old woman that she has fallen into the hands of bunco artists. To puncture her dreams. A doting aunt who thinks she might once again brush the cowlick out of the eyes of her dead nephew. She pays me off—say, $200, which doesn't go far, believe me, with four kids at the trough. She's left broken-hearted, my kids go hungry, and you two fine people have to find another mark and start from scratch again. It doesn't make sense."

"But you could give us a clean bill of health," I said.

He rolled the cigar between his lips. "Yes."

"How much?"

"Like the lady said, a piece of the action."

"How big a piece?"

"How big is the action?"

"That depends on Mrs. M. We may have to settle for peanuts."

"I want a third."

I glanced at Maggie. "Is there anything he can dig up on you?"

She crushed her cigarette and exhaled sharply. "Only traffic tickets."

"Porter," I said. "Get out."

He gave a nervous little laugh. "Cut me in for a quarter. No point in being greedy. A quarter it is."

"Beat it."

"Why, I can be of genuine service—"

I grabbed him by the neck and the seat of his pants, and Maggie opened the door. I threw him out and his cigar went rolling along the hall. He picked it up, dusted it off and didn't seem to mind at all. "Must be a lot of money," he smiled. "A lot of money. Yes, sir, a lot of money."

I shut the door and looked at Maggie. For a moment we just exchanged static electricity. "The cheap vulture," she crackled.

"Not so cheap."

"You shouldn't have thrown him out."

"Then why did you bring him here?"

"I thought you might break him in two."

"Maggie," I said. "There's a corner of that mink-lined mind of yours that positively scares me."

"Are you going to let him queer it for us?"

"That's a chance we may have to take."

"I'm not going to take any chances."

"Do you want to cut him in?"

"No."

"Then forget it."

"But we could let him *think* he was in."

I gave her a long, steady look. In Maggie's book there wasn't even honor among thieves. If she'd cut Porter in and cut Porter out, she'd do me the same. The thought wasn't entirely new to me. In the end she'd be happy to pick up all the money and run—thumbing her sharp, lovely nose all the way to the bank. Maggie was a sly dog. But it wasn't banking hours yet.

"Forget it," I said. "He can't hurt us and I think he's too smart to try. The old lady hired him to tell her she was right—not wrong."

"Skelly, he's trouble."

"Listen. If Mrs. M really wants to believe she's going to believe. No one's going to talk her out of it. Not even Porter. He's not simple—he knows that. He'll be back and he'll settle for crumbs."

She went foraging in her straw bag for a cigarette. "Okay," she said, dismissing Porter from the conversation. I struck a match, and she took hold of my wrist.

"Speaking of expense money," I said, "how are we fixed?"

"We're not."

"I need another hundred."

She exhaled and gazed at me through the smoke. "Don't be funny. I've put everything I own into props. It's taken me months to get ready for this."

"All right," I said. "I'll take you home."

She rose, hooked her arms around my neck and looked into my eyes. "Where's the girl?"

"What girl!"

"The chippy. My car's parked at the end of the street. I saw you walk into the hotel together."

I pulled her arms off me. "Don't waste your time, Maggie."

"We're in this together. Just the two of us. You're mine, darling."

"You're Rinny Jim's wife. Or can't you remember back that far?"

"Get rid of her, Skelly."

I peered at her and let a couple of seconds go by. I was burning, but I managed to keep my straight face straight. "Maggie," I said, "you haven't been reading the fine print. Nobody owns me. I'm in this strictly for the payoff. The only thing that's holding us together is the million piastres you keep talking about. Now let's take that lusty body of yours out of here and stop pretending it's amateur night in Dixie."

She smiled. She gave the room a hard glance as if Viola might be hiding in the wallpaper. "You're mine, darling," she said. "Remember that."

Chapter Twelve

The next morning I pawned the concertina and Viola and I had breakfast. A summer fog had come in, lowering the skyline fifty yards from shore. Venice was beginning to give me the jimjams. Or maybe it was Maggie. Or Porter and the old lady. Or maybe it was me. Whenever I stopped to think, I had to remind myself not to think. Except of the money. A buck was a buck was a buck.

"Say something," Viola murmured. "Anything."

"Pass the salt."

"Are you always grouchy in the morning?"

"Only four days a week," I said. "The other days I'm a stick."

"If I weren't in love with you," she said, bending forward in the café booth, "I think I'd fall in love with you."

I looked at her. There was a smile and a mist in those summery green eyes of hers. I wondered how I could suddenly get so lucky. "I'll give you five minutes to change your mind," I said. "After that you're stuck with me."

"What's your name?" she asked.

"That's a fine question to ask after spending the night in a man's room."

"It's not Appleby, is it?"

"Does it matter?"

"It's Skelly, isn't it?"

"Yes."

"Are my five minutes up?"

"No."

"Who's Appleby?"

I flagged the waitress for a refill on the coffee. "Appleby?" I said. "He's a backwoods gentleman from around Yakima, Washington. The sun always shines for Appleby, even when it rains. You'd like him. Raises horses and runs a few head of cattle. He's got 500 acres with a stream rushing through it, and the trout bite for him even when they're not biting for anyone else in the whole northwest."

"Is he anything like you?"

"Nothing like me at all." I had laid down the story so often that one of these days I was going to start believing in Appleby myself.

"What about Skelly?"

"Skelly," I said, "is a figment of my imagination. You don't want to get mixed up with a guy like that."

"You said he was a gambler."

"That was the other night. Now it's all over. He turned in his checkered vest. Eat those sausages, Spindlelegs. They're fattening."

In the silence we could hear a foghorn further up the coast. After a moment I got up and went to the wall phone. I dug out Porter's card and rang him, but there was no answer. I hung on for a while and then gave it up. When I got back to the booth Viola was lighting a cigarette.

I said, "Did you ever run across a beatnik named Marenbach? Jamie Marenbach."

"I used to see him around."

"How well did you know him?"

She gave a small shrug. "I wasn't his type. He went for the housewives. But mostly he was drunk. Every so often a long black car with a chauffeur would turn up and a beefy little man would fish him out of the dives and take him home."

"A bald-headed gent?"

"Yes."

Porter, I thought. The old lady has made use of his services before. If she cared enough about the kid to pluck him out of low company, there was hope for us. She'd have a chance to pluck him from hellfire and brimstone.

I stood up. "Come on. We're going to find you a place to stay."

"What's wrong with your room, Mr. Skelly?"

"I managed to keep my hands off you," I said. "An arrangement like that can't last."

"Maybe I want to be a broad."

"Look. Some have it and some don't. You'll never make it, Spindlelegs."

"I'm not moving."

"Then I will."

"Are my five minutes up?"

"Yes."

"You're stuck with me. That was the deal, wasn't it?"

I took a bus into Santa Monica and found Porter's office over the merry-go-round at the foot of the pier. It was an old yellow building with second-story bay windows and a view of the coast. The fog was burning off and the day was looking up. Porter was in.

"Sit down, Mr. Appleby, sit down. No hard feelings. None at all. Business is business. Sit down."

There was an oak desk with a brass spittoon and a salt breeze coming in through the window. Porter sat with his back to the, window and his face to the door. The beat and thunder of the merry-go round rose up through the floor boards like a miasma. The walls trembled and none of the pictures hung quite straight.

"Listen to that," he smiled, cocking an ear. "I'm just a kid at heart. Wouldn't have my office anywhere else. Why, you'll go out of here whistling. Cigar?"

"Porter," I said, "I got a sudden hunch about you."

"Is that a fact?"

"You're bluffing."

"Is that a fact?"

"I don't think the old lady hired you at all. Not this time. You're trying to swindle us."

"Now what gives you that unkind idea?"

I stared at him. "That maid of hers has big ears. I'll bet there's not much that goes on in that house that you don't know. You were Jamie's keeper, weren't you? That's what she hired you for. You were supposed to keep your private eye on him, but you let him drown himself."

"I was fond of the boy," he said. "I feel mighty poorly about what happened."

"I have an idea that the old lady wouldn't trust you to mail a letter. Not now. Not any more. But someone once said—I think it was you—that a garbage can brings flies. Porter, it looks to me as if you've been buzzing around for a long time."

"Is that a fact?"

"You walked in last night with high cards. You walked out with low ones. I figured we might have to settle with you for ten percent of the score—and we're talking about a very large action. Maybe a million dollars. But this morning you're not holding any cards at all. You're not even in the game, Porter."

"An amusing theory, sir."

"All you have to do to make a liar out of me is pick up the phone and report in."

He turned his head and hit the spittoon. "Don't believe I'll trouble the lady. You come here just to tell me that?"

"I've got another hunch."

"Is that a fact?"

"I think you're loaded. You enjoy poor-boying it too much to be anything but loaded. But if I'm wrong I'm wasting my time and you'll do me a favor by throwing me out."

The air shimmered with the mechanical banging of cymbals from the monster below. "Sit still," Porter grinned. "You sound like a man with a proposition. Let's have it, sir."

"If you want to come in with us, that ten per cent is up for grabs."

"How much?"

"How fast can you lay your hands on ten grand?"

"Would five years be fast enough?" He chuckled and rolled the cigar between his lips. "Why should I trust you with a penny, sir?"

"Because you'd like to see us take the old lady, providing you come in for a share. Because we've run out of money and we've got to raise the scratch to stay in the game. It takes money to make money, and we're tapped out. If I don't get it from you, I'll get it from someone else."

"I daresay."

"Well?"

"I might consider a modest investment. I like the way you work, Mr. Appleby. Direct. To the point. A clear head. You inspire confidence, sir. A modest investment. Say, $500."

I stood up. "If you deal in pennies you'll get paid off in pennies. Forget it, Poorboy."

Behind him, through the window, the sun lit up twenty miles of coastline. "But you make me no guarantees," he smiled.

"There are none. You're betting on a horse race. If you can't afford to lose, save your money. Buy bonds."

He peered at me and went on rolling the cigar between his lips. I wanted that $500 so bad I was breaking into a sweat. "Ten per cent of the spoils," he mused. "Tempting. Very tempting indeed, sir. How does a crisp $1000 bill sound to you?"

"I can't hear it at all."

"Two."

"Speak up, Porter."

"Twenty-five hundred cash dollars and here's my hand on it."

It was a warm, pudgy hand. I shook it like the handle of a slot machine that was about to pay off. "Porter," I said, "you're in."

He went on the send for the money and half an hour later I walked out of the office just as he said I would. The sound of the merry-go-round was in my head and I was whistling.

I called on Maggie and split the money right down the middle. She was not happy about cutting Porter in, but she was not unhappy about the bank rags. Now that he had an investment in us, I told her, Porter would lay off. He could stop trying to figure an angle for himself. Then I returned to the Grand Metropole, rented a room across the hall and gave the key to Viola. She told me I was a stick. I gave her a pat on the keester and told her she couldn't give it away. I sent her out to buy a nightgown, a change of threads and a suitcase. Then I put $500 in an envelope, addressed it in her name at General Delivery, Venice, Calif., and marked it to be held for ten days. Case dough. Just in case.

There was nothing left to do but wait for Wednesday night.

Chapter Thirteen

Wednesday night came and Wednesday night went, and Mrs. M didn't show. Maggie was all got up in veils and beads, and I doled out eighty dollars for a black suit and a narrow black tie. I was to be introduced as the founding father of the Institute of Spirit Research. I had a reaching rod in my pocket and I wore a harness to tip tables. The two of us sat around in the séance room with the pampas grass and the fringed lamps like a pair of actors waiting for an audience. By ten o'clock we were avoiding each other's eyes. It looked like we were bust, and the curtain wasn't going to rise on our little drama. Mrs. Edwin Ellicott Marenbach had stayed home.

"Maybe she's sick," I said.

Maggie was eating smoke and trying to wear a smooth place in the rug. Her veils were flying. "That old bat hasn't had a sick day since she became a rich widow. We'll give her another half hour."

"Don't waste your time." I got up. "I'm leaving."

"Where are you going?"

"Maybe I can find a friendly funeral somewhere. It's a shame to let this black suit go to waste."

She shot me a deadly glance. "It's that girl, isn't it?"

"Don't get your quills up," I said. "If anything turns up, call me."

"Damn you!" She slipped off a shoe and threw it at me.

I left.

She called a little after nine the following night. Viola had shampooed her hair and I was watching her fluff that shorn, golden head with a towel. But I was thinking about Maggie. She had run up against a tough old lady—too tough even for Maggie. She was still no closer to mink than the nearest rabbit, and I was sorry. She would look great in Mrs. M's money. She would give it a real airing out. All I wanted was enough to pay Braque and get him off my back, and I was sorry about that too.

"I saw him the night he drowned," Viola was saying.

"Who?"

"Jamie. You were asking about him, weren't you?"

"It doesn't matter any more," I said.

"There was a woman, too."

I peered at her. "What are you talking about?"

"I was on the beach. In the dark. By myself. I saw the three of them."

The phone at the end of the hall had already begun to ring. "What do you mean—the three of them?" I said.

"Jamie was passed out. Another man and the woman carried him between them. I couldn't figure out what they were trying to do. I watched for a while and then wandered away. I think I was afraid. But it didn't mean anything to me until a couple of days later when the body washed up on the beach."

I looked at Viola and felt a tightening along the back of my neck like a sudden, cold draft. "Have you ever told anyone about this?"

"Nobody ever asked me."

The phone kept ringing and I think I knew it was for me. I think I knew it was Maggie. Why had she given me a different story? She had left herself out of it, pretending that only Rinny Jim had been with Jamie that night on the beach.

"Yes?"

"Skelly," Maggie said, breathing into the phone. "She's here. Come quick."

"Mrs. M?"

"Yes. I can't talk now. Hurry."

She hung up and I stood there at the dark end of the hall. This thing was beginning to smell of murder. That icy feeling stayed with me even as I got into my gimmicks and hurried toward the canals. If Rinny Jim and Maggie had killed the kid, I was dealing myself out. Tonight. Was that why Rinny Jim had cut and run to sit things out on the map of Mexico?

The summer fog was back, drifting through the palm trees and feeling its way into the canals. When I found the house I could make out an aging Rolls Royce pulled up in the driveway from the narrow street in the rear. A chauffeur sat there smoking a cigarette. The house, with its lights on, glowed in the fog like a jack-o'-lantern. I went in.

Maggie met me in the hall and there was no time to talk. I was angry, but it would keep. She brought me face to face with fifty million dollars. Mrs. Edwin Ellicott Marenbach, her back erect, had taken a chair under the beaded lamp, and looked as if she were sitting for her portrait. I had expected an old woman, but I don't think she was much past fifty. I had expected the face of a witch, but what I saw wasn't a face at all. It was sheer make-up. Her cheeks were heavily rouged and powdered, and she had painted a mole on her cheek; if she stood out in the fog too long, I thought, all those colors would run together. She wore a brown, snap-brim felt hat, and what I could see of her hair was a carroty orange. She was smoking a wheat-colored Mexican cigarette that had already filled the room with a strong, raw presence. Even in that first glance I could tell that Mrs. M had once been beautiful. Perhaps she still was. It was as if she were hiding even from herself behind the artificial colors and the brim of the hat.

"Well," Mrs. M snapped, "Let's get on with it. Where do I sit?"

"At the table," Maggie said. "Any chair you like."

I closed off the sliding doors. Maggie took the telephone off the hook so that there would be no interruptions, and lit a candle at the center of the pedestal table. I supposed Mrs. M had planned her sudden appearance out of a lingering sense of suspicion, to see what specters Maggie could call up at a moment's notice—if any. I pulled the brass chains on the lamps and a kind of darkness spilled into the room, filling up the corners and recesses. The candle flickered. Maggie had somehow managed to slip into her beads and veils, and now she took her place at the table. She sat there with the theatrical trimmings and the bearing of a high priestess.

"We will now spread our hands on the table," she said.

Mrs. M puffed on the cigarette and kept her hands to herself. "Rigmarole," she scowled. Maggie gave me a flash of eyes and it was clear enough that the evening was going to be a duel between these two women.

"Mrs. Marenbach," I said, taking the cigarette from between her fingers and putting it out. "If we hold hands we cannot accuse one another of trickery. Miss Evangeline is a gifted medium." I was speaking as Dr. Appleby, the eminent authority. "I am as interested as you are to see that this experiment tonight is scientific and aboveboard. It is surely very little to ask that you lay your palms on the table so that Miss Evangeline can proceed."

The candle burned like a miniature sun in a dark, oak-paneled universe. Mrs. M slipped her hands on the table. She had made her point, and permitted herself a faint, momentary smile. We touched hands, linking ourselves around the table. Her fingers were as dry as paper.

Maggie lifted her head and closed her eyes. "We will now meditate."

The candle was timed. Five minutes. I closed my eyes. Maggie had rehearsed me well; I found myself going through all the fakus. But the thought in my head was, This isn't merely a parlor game any more. What are you doing here, Skelly? Get out. They must have murdered the kid. Maggie and Rinny Jim. Get out, Skelly. Cut and run before it's too late.

But I sat there and the minutes passed. Then Maggie opened her eyes and began to speak again. "Jamie," she breathed. "Jamie... if you are here with us... make a sign. Let us know. Jamie... your Aunt Orva has come. If you are with us... make a sign. Blow out the candle. Blow out the candle and we will know you are here."

We stared at the flame. Mrs. M's eyes were hard, skeptical slits. We waited and the candle burned on. Then, as if in a ghostly breath, the flame went out. Mrs. M's hand jumped in mine. Our shadows vanished from the walls and we sat in total darkness.

"Welcome, Jamie," Maggie whispered.

The séance was underway. The candle was almost the simplest of Maggie's traps; it had been gimmicked with a short, faked wick to burn out within minutes. In the blackness Maggie and I separated hands. She had taught me how to work the "fountain pen" clipped to my outside breast pocket. It was a medium's reaching rod. Standard equipment. The insides pulled out like an automobile aerial. I held it between my teeth and silently drew out the tubing. With her free hand, Maggie found the tip and hooked one of her veils to it.

"Jamie..." she was calling. "Jamie, stay with us. Don't leave. Your Aunt Orva has come to see you. She believes now, Jamie."

But Aunt Orva had had a moment to think and she was trying hard to hold onto her sense of reality. "That was no more Jamie than the nearest draft, dearie."

"Jamie, can you make yourself known to her?"

By that time I had the reaching rod in my hand like a fishing pole. With the gossamer veil dangling from the tip, I passed it over Mrs. M's shoulders, touching her softly. In the pitch black it was the touch of the dead. Her fingers under mine stiffened. Then she pulled them free to reach out in the dark, but I was warned. I lifted the rod and veil away from her.

"My dear Mrs. Marenbach," Dr. Appleby said. "You mustn't break the chain of hands."

"Something touched me."

I was anxious to be finished with these routines. I wanted to get Maggie alone and sign my walking papers. A con game was one thing; murder was for creeps. And I was getting tired of pandering to Aunt Orva's fifty million dollars. It was as if she had come to persuade herself that Miss Evangeline had made a fool of her that night in Bel Air. If we weren't holding her hands to the table she would be capable, I thought, of striking a match in the dark.

Maggie kept a soft patter going as if to coax Jamie into a kind of reality. I was wearing a harness under my shirt, and now I hooked it under the edge of the table. I could have lifted an elephant. Maggie kept calling to Jamie, and as if in response the heavy table tipped sharply and the candlestick flew to the floor. Mrs. M gave a little gasp and immediately regretted it.

"What nonsense," she said sharply, but her hands were betraying her—they had turned ice cold. "My nephew Jamie would *not* spend his time knocking over tables."

With the harness I was able to raise the table off the floor in a sudden, rising movement that brought us all to our feet. And then the table settled slowly to the floor and Mrs. M was silent. The effect, in the utter blackness of the room, had to be eerie and unsettling.

"Jamie is angry with us," Maggie murmured.

Not a word now from Mrs. M. The mind, I was learning, abhors a dark room. The two spare chairs around the table had fallen over, leaving the three of us sitting in total blackness. The lowing of foghorns came to us.

"We will light the candle," Maggie said finally.

She had found it with her foot and pushed it toward me along the floor. We broke hands. I exchanged the faked candle for a duplicate, a good one, that I was carrying in my coat pocket.

And then I stopped. I froze. A sudden feeling came over me that there was someone else in the room. A sound. For a moment I thought I must be falling under the spell of Maggie's hocum myself, but it was there. A presence. There were four of us in the room. I could feel the hairs go up on the backs of my hands. Suddenly, it was as if death were standing at my elbow.

I struck a match and the candle flamed up.

It was a man.

He sat in the chair to my right. His long, narrow face and bony hands were chalk white. He stared out of avenging, deep-set eyes at Mrs. M across the table.

The moment jumped with electricity. Her face blanched, even under the mask of cosmetics. I glanced at Maggie and she gave me the merest flicker of reassurance. I thought during those first seconds that Mrs. M would pass out from the shock, but she was too tough for that. Her breath came hack and she passed a hand in front of her eyes as if to clear her vision. The young man was still there, white as powder, silent and forbidding.

"Jamie," she said almost voicelessly. "Jamie, dear. It's you."

I looked from one to the other trying to keep a clear head. Maggie was full of surprises. Jamie was dead but actors with long young faces were a dime a dozen. In the darkness Mrs. M's senses had been put through the wringer, and now she was seeing Jamie's long young face behind the chalky white powder.

Maggie had a sense of timing. She allowed Mrs. M this high-voyage glimpse of the Great Beyond and then blew out the candle. The séance was over. When I turned on the lamps the guy was gone.

Chapter Fourteen

The big con, I knew, was often as elaborately staged as a Broadway play. Maggie had a big talent and she knew how to use it. The Rolls pulled away in the fog and Maggie fingered a check for $200. "They'll get bigger," she smiled. "Much bigger, darling."

Mrs. M would be back for another séance the next night. She was hooked. She had seen Jamie. With her own eyes. And Maggie had rung down the curtain, leaving her wanting more. She would be back and the checks would get bigger. For $200 she hadn't even had time to chew the kid out. If she had come in like a lion, she had gone out like a titmouse, and I couldn't care less.

Maggie closed the sliding doors and kicked off her shoes. "Fix me a drink, Skelly darling." She threw herself against the colored pillows on the couch and stretched her arms in minor ecstasy. "I feel glorious, Skelly. Absolutely *evil*. I've got her in the palm of my hand, haven't I?"

I fixed myself a short one. "Where's the spook?" I said. "Get rid of him. I want to talk to you."

"Don't be angry. I was going to tell you about him, but there wasn't time."

I turned with her drink and she was pointing one leg in the air as if to reassure herself that she was not only evil but still beautiful. I pushed the leg down and put the drink in her hand. "Maggie, " I said, "I'm pulling out."

She looked up. "Make me laugh, darling," she said. "But don't make me laugh."

"What kind of a patsy are you playing me for?"

"You're going to ruin a perfectly lovely evening, aren't you?"

"As best I can," I said. "You didn't tell me you were with Jamie on the beach when he drowned."

"Was I?"

"You were seen."

She set her drink on the floor. "You don't say."

"I do say."

"Well, what difference does it make?"

"Maggie, you swim like a fish. I saw you the other night. Between you and Rinny Jim the kid couldn't have drowned. It doesn't make sense. I'm not even sure he was grogged up on Dago red when you two dunked him in the surf. I think he was already dead."

It struck her with the impact of a feather. "Skelly darling," she said, "you have an evil mind. We're two of a kind."

"Two of a kind doesn't win card games," I said.

"Who saw us on the beach? That cheap shamus?"

Keep Viola out of it, I told myself. "Forget it."

"Porter." She pulled off her earrings. "It must have been him. That squeaky shoe tried to follow Jamie everywhere."

Then her eyes settled on me again. "Have you any other bad thoughts, darling?"

I finished my drink. "Lotsa luck."

"You're not going anywhere."

"You don't say?"

"I do say. I still need you—Dr. Appleby."

"Get someone else to tip your tables."

"But I like *you*, partner. The moment we met out on the sidewalk I knew you were for me. It was as if I were waiting for a guy named Skelly to come along—like the man said. You and me. Two of a kind. I've even stood still while you amused yourself chasing half the beach broads in Venice. But don't talk like a chump. You're not walking out on me. I want you, Skelly. And I've got you."

I shot her a dark glance. "Say it very slowly," I said. "I'm a real thick-head." I knew exactly what was coming. Maggie had been holding my death warrant ever since I blew into town. All she had to do was sign it.

"That man was here again, Skelly."

"When?"

"A couple of days ago."

"With the same blah face?"

"And the same friendly offer. You must have got someone pretty sore at you back East, partner. He upped the ante."

"How much am I worth to you on a slab?"

She was on her feet now. "Peanuts, darling."

"What did you tell him?"

She began running her hands along my shoulders as if all that was left to do was kiss and make up. "Nothing. I said if you turned up I'd call him. But I wouldn't do a thing like that, Skelly. You know I wouldn't."

"Provided I stick around and stop thinking bad thoughts."

Her voice became a mere breath. "Providing you're nice to me, darling."

"You've got me right where you want me, haven't you?"

"You're mine, darling," she whispered. "You really are."

"Sure, Maggie," I said. This kind of bedroom blackmail was for geeks, and I pulled her hands off me. "There's the phone," I snapped. "Visit me in the morgue."

I'd take my chances. I crossed toward the sliding doors, but I never got that far. She was there ahead of me and it was going to be over her dead body.

"You're quite a guy, Skelly."

"I'll take your word for it."

"Jamie wasn't murdered."

"A hunch is a hunch," I said. "I play hunches."

"There's something you've got to know. It might as well be now."

"Make it fast, Maggie."

She put her finger to my lips. "Jamie wasn't murdered. He's not even dead. He's alive, Skelly."

I stared at her. "What are you trying to give me."

"I mean it. Jamie's alive. He's standing right behind you."

Chapter Fifteen

I turned. The guy with the powdery white face was standing with a cigarette in the far corner of the room. Jamie. The spook at the table. He stared at me with a mocking, bantering grin. Then he punched out his cigarette and walked through the wall.

He was gone.

I peered at the spot. Nothing that had made sense to me a moment before made sense at all now. Except the pivoting oak panel in the corner of the room. Jamie had made his entrance and Jamie had made his exit. It was rough carpentry, but it worked.

"He's been hiding upstairs for months," Maggie said.

The kaleidoscope had been given a violent twist and it was taking me a moment to absorb the new view. Jamie was alive. Mrs. M hadn't gazed on a spear carrier hired for the occasion. She had stamped the spook genuine, and I had sat there like a rustic thinking I had smelled out a murder. "Remind me to quit playing hunches," I said. I walked over to the ash tray and fished out the cigarette stub the spook had just crushed. It was an Alpine. Just like the other morning.

"Fix yourself another drink," Maggie smiled. "You look like you could use it."

"Why didn't you put me wise before?"

"I wasn't sure I could trust you."

"What makes you sure you can now?"

"Hunch."

"Never play hunches."

"You're a right guy. I just found that out. It's kind of new to me—I'm not used to right guys." She lit a cigarette. "I thought if I whistled, you'd jump."

"Is that the kind of guy you want?"

"I could have you stuffed and hung on my bedroom wall, Skelly."

"Maybe it's not too late to try."

"I'm not even tempted. We're partners, aren't we?"

"Are we?"

"Come sit down—partner."

"Maggie, you're quite a girl."
"I'll take your word for it."

The air was clearing. She had overplayed her hand earlier and she knew it. We were beginning to understand each other now. I fixed myself another drink. She was right; I needed it. The ground had shifted under me. If Jamie were alive I could begin to read Maggie's mind. And she had read mine; I was nobody's stud. We had both passed a point of no return and we were in this together to the finish. "I'm through fooling around in the dark," I said. "Smarten me up."

She began moving idly around the table. "It started almost by accident. Mrs. M had been rowing with Jamie for months. She found out he'd been stealing from her. It wasn't only the sapphire ring. It was anything he could lay hands on."

"Including short pieces of string?"

"Including. She wouldn't give him any money because he'd only buy wine with it. He's on the grape. The old lady has bugged him all his life. He's been a wino since he was fourteen."

"I can believe it."

"Jamie's half-stoned all the time."

"Including tonight?"

"Including. But in her own, tight-fisted way she loves him, I guess. In a way she thinks she caused his death and she'll give anything to undo it—even, maybe, a cool million."

"You've lost me."

"She'd put up with his stealing as long as she could. She blew the whistle on him. She told him that if he didn't round up the missing pieces she'd call in the cops and have him put in jail. This got through to Jamie. He had sold most of the stuff to that squeaky shoe—Porter. Porter had fenced the stuff and made himself a small fortune, and there was no chance of getting anything back. So Jamie got himself juiced up and waited for the axe to fall. Earlier in the evening Rinny tried to bail him out of one of the beat joints, and Jamie threw a bottle at him."

"Did he miss?"

"Someone called me and when I got there Jamie was gone and Rinny was nursing a cut on the head. Later, we found Jamie in the middle of Pacific Avenue trying to direct traffic—or get himself killed.

We grabbed him before someone called the cops, and walked him. We must have walked him along a mile of beach, trying to sober him up. And that's when we stumbled over the gimmick."

"The gimmick?"

"A body had washed up in the surf. It happens. It happened. The sharks had been at it and there wasn't an awful lot left."

"Someone thought fast," I said.

"Not that fast. We walked away from it. We had our hands full with Jamie. Finally, we got him here to the house and he opened up. He'd always liked Rinny and he was sorry about pitching the bottle at him. He told us that the old lady was going to clout him with the law. It was Rinny's idea to make the switch."

"Abra-cadaver."

"Yes.... They went back and salted the body. When it was found the cops made their identification by Jamie's ID bracelet on the stiff's wrist, a shoe, Jamie's coat and a few other things. It worked. Do you want all the details?"

"Everything, including the time of day."

"Rinny had already seen the possibilities. Jamie wanted to go to Mexico, but he didn't have a dime. Rinny showed him how we could all walk away rich. It was a matter of holding still for a few months while Mrs. M got used to the idea that Jamie was dead."

I gazed at her. "Then con her into a series of séances with Jamie as chief spook."

"Yes."

"It's got to work."

"It's working. She must feel guilty about Jamie's suicide—that she drove him to it. She's got a hard shell, but we've cracked it, Skelly. She can come here and square herself with Jamie."

"Or chew him out."

"Either way, she pays."

"You'll never make it big that way," I said.

"Wait and see."

"By the time you get it, you'll be too old to spend it. You've been talking about a million, but you're thinking in terms of hundred-dollar bills. You've been conning me, Maggie."

"Have you got a better idea?"

"Give me five minutes. Where's Rinny?"

"You keep asking."

"You keep giving me a different answer."

"Soon after it happened the police got a tip that just before Jamie drowned he and Rinny had had a beef. The bottle bit. They came here to check it out. It scared Rinny and he's keeping himself out of reach across the border in Tijuana. He's still in for a third, Skelly."

"Look, all I want is 125 grand, but I can't wait for my old age. I won't have an old age if your friend with the blah face catches up with me first. I'm in a hurry. Where's the spook? Upstairs?"

"Yes. Most of the time I keep him locked in. But when he's sober enough he can pick the lock."

"The voice on the record," I said. "You laid down a story. It wasn't Rinny Jim giving an imitation. It was the real thing. Jamie's own voice."

"Of course."

"Why all the production, Maggie?"

"I couldn't drive him out to Bel Air and put a microphone in his hands. I couldn't trust him to be sober enough. And what if he were picked up? It would blow everything. No. It was too risky."

"Do you mean he hasn't left this house in four months?"

"He likes it that way. I keep him in wine and cigarettes. He's happy. Sometimes he won't leave his room for weeks at a time."

He had it made for himself, I thought. A loaf of bread, a jug of wine and cigarettes. He had crawled into a hole and out of the world at large. No cops. No Aunt Orva. Just peace. "Introduce us," I said. "Let's go."

Had I said five minutes? It wasn't going to take that long; I already had an idea how to play our cards. How to play them for a quick jackpot. Jamie was a living royal flush. A barn-burner.

Maggie opened the sliding doors, but that was as far as she got. Porter was standing there. The squeaky shoe. His round face broke into a smile and his bald head caught the light. "Just protecting my investment, good friends."

Maggie turned incandescent. "How the hell did you get in here?"

"The porch light was on," he grinned. "I figured it was open house."

"How long have you been standing here?"

"Long enough, dear lady. I managed to overhear a word or two. Stunning news. So young Jamie is alive. Stunning. I couldn't be happier. I shed real tears for the lad. A fine doubt in my head about the spook, Porter could put an end to boy. A good lad. Risen from the ashes. Imagine. Like the phoenix itself. Ah, good evening, Mr. Appleby. You look positively disappointed to see me."

"Not at all, Porter," I said. If there was any lingering it. He would know Jamie on sight. "You're just in time."

"I try to be, sir. I try to be."

Maggie killed him with a glance, but he wouldn't take the cue. He merely chuckled and included himself in. I don't think Porter trusted us any further than he could throw his $2500.

We went upstairs. Maggie knocked on Jamie's door, and it was as if he were expecting us. He said to come in. Porter, beside me, was huffing from the climb up the stairs. "This is a moment, sir. A moment."

The room was painted black—floor, walls and ceiling. Jamie sat on a reed mat in the center, stripped to the waist, his back straight and his legs folded in a bow. The lotus position, I supposed. It was clear enough that he had a glow on.

"What's this?" he smiled. "A goddam stockholders' meeting?"

Porter traded him smiles. "Jamie, my lad—I congratulate you. You've swindled the Grim Reaper himself. Why, I saw you laid to rest, and I don't mind saying I never expected to see you alive again."

"The back of my hand to you, Porter."

There wasn't the faintest possibility now that Maggie had been laying down a story; Jamie was Jamie. "Maggie," I said, "take Porter downstairs and put a drink in him to get him over the shock."

She got him out of there and I was left alone with the spook. He was well-built, with light brown hair combed forward like fringe. He had a kind of natural good looks that were beginning to fray around the edges. My guess was that he couldn't care less. He had an easy smile, but his eyes were slack and maybe a little mean. He was watching me closely. "Anyone for Yoga?" he grinned.

I looked around the room. There was just the bed, an ash tray and the mat. The old lady had threatened him with jail, and in the end he had put himself in stir. "You've got a nice thing going for you, haven't you?"

"I'm seeking purity and harmony," he said. "I'm developing the delicate balance of body and soul. I'm a goddam lotus flower adrift in the silent grandeur of a still pond. Pull up a piece of the floor and join me."

"I can't swim."

"What did she tell you? That I'm on the muscadoodle?"

"Aren't you?"

"I'm drying out. Starting tomorrow." He changed positions, lying on his stomach and throwing his legs in the air. "This is the *Salabhasana*. The locust. Cures lumbago. Try it."

"I don't have lumbago."

"You never can tell."

"Jamie, I've got bad news for you," I said. "You're going home to Aunt Orva."

He straightened up and gave me a turn of the head. "What are you talking about?"

"You can't play dead forever."

"Why not?"

"You're the only heir, aren't you?"

"She'll go on for another thirty years. I can't wait that long."

"We'll get you a big down payment."

He lit a cigarette and stood up. "Don't think just because I'm drunk I'm drunk. She hates the sight of me. She always has."

"That's not the way it looked tonight."

"You know why she came?" he said viciously. "To ream me out in the heavenly kingdom—or wherever it is she thinks I reside. That's what brought her. She'll pay the price of admission for that. Only I didn't hang around long enough to let her find her tongue."

"I figured that much out for myself," I said. "But I only half believe it. Just as I only half believe she's as crusty and tough as she makes out. She turned white when she saw you. She was scared. But she looked relieved too, as if she'd found something she thought she had lost forever. I'll bet she shed real tears at your funeral."

He gave me a wink. "I don't know. I wasn't there."

"It's kind of a bum rap to let her think she drove you to it."

"She's been yakking at me ever since I was a kid."

"Why?"

"Ask her."

"You can't let her spend the next thirty years wondering who to leave her money to."

"Why not? She knocked me out of the will years ago. Figured I might croak her for it."

"Would you?"

He grinned. "If I did, they could never hang it on me. I'm legally dead."

I gave him a squint. His brain wasn't entirely embalmed. He had a license to commit murder. "It's all right for a hobby," I said. "But there's not a dime in it."

"Nothing's perfect, friend."

"Listen to it my way," I said. "I say your aunt will take you back under any terms she can get you. And we can work it to pay off—in a week."

"What's the hurry?"

"Your lease is running out."

"Forget it, friend."

"In a week Maggie will have your aunt so softened up she'll be afraid to wash sheets in case she might be putting you through the wringer. A séance every night. She sees you. She touches you. She talks to you. You're real. We talk about our experiments here at the Institute. We might be able to fix it with the next world to get you a return ticket to this one. She puts up an endowment. We deliver. You turn up in Bel Air—the soul of purity and harmony."

He shook his head. "I like it right here."

"The old lady gets what she wants—you. And that heavy pine box off her back. You get what you want—bank rags. Money. Scratch in your kick. You can buy your own vineyard. Maggie is dripping in mink and I get what I want—which is to get the hell out of here."

"I can't hear you. I bought myself a piece of the hereafter, friend, and I'm not turning it in. I'm staying right here." He opened the closet door and gave me a flash of his wine cellar. "You want a shot of muscadoodle? It's celestial."

I was in no mood for further debate. "Is that your last word?"

"That's it."

I swung him around and shot a right into the side of his face. He fell across the bed and then hit the floor in the locust position.

"Pack up your lotus pond, kid," I said. "You're going home next week."

Chapter Sixteen

I spent my days in the sun and my nights in the dark. Viola kept dunking me in the surf. She painted white zinc on my nose to keep it from burning; we would lie side by side on the hot sand and sometimes we hardly said a word all day. It was enough just being together—just knowing she was there beside me.

She asked me nothing. She had a kind of instinct going for her. I came and I went and when it was all over I would check her out on it. Meanwhile, I was losing my undercooked eastern pallor and beginning to pass for a native. Viola was filling out and if she kept it up I'd have to lay off calling her Spindlelegs.

"Love is a treacherous word," I said. "It isn't meant to be spoken."

"Who asked you?" she said.

At other times, just having her around gave me the jimjams. If I didn't score, if I didn't get Braque paid off, there was nothing in it for Viola but to wear black.

By Friday night Mrs. M could hardly stay away from the house on the canal. The chauffeur drove her out even before it was dark, and she sat around the living room smoking Mexican cigarettes. I walked in and almost blew the game.

The maid was sitting there.

Hilda.

Her timid blue eyes flew to me. I stopped breathing. I thought she had me cold. I was the man who had called at the house a few days before the sapphire ring turned up. I had tried to get past the door. If she had any intuition at all, she would blow wise to the hocum.

"Hilda," Mrs. M snapped, "sit up straight. This is Dr. Appleby."

If she had been sitting any straighter she would have been standing up. She was a scrawny bundle of nerves. She looked at me, but she wasn't seeing me. If I'd dropped a pin she'd have gone up through the ceiling.

I gave her a mellifluous voice. "My dear Hilda," Dr. Appleby said. "We're delighted to have you join us."

She kept a tight mouth. She didn't know me. Not in a white shirt, a bow tie and an eighty-dollar suit. If she remembered the guy at the door, he was a figure in a cheap yachting cap and sunglasses. Napoleon in a Brooks Brothers suit could stand in Macy's window and not draw flies. I relaxed.

Maggie closed off the sliding doors and we took our places around the table. It was clear enough why Mrs. M had brought Hilda along. For verification. She had the bait in her mouth, she wanted to swallow it, but it wouldn't go down. She needed someone to back her up, assure her that she wasn't seeing things in the dark and hearing voices that weren't there.

When the maid sees Jamie, I thought, she'll pass out.

She did. Cold.

We were in. Really in. On Saturday night I was ready to make my pitch. Mrs. M turned up, glowing with a kind of inner radiance. She was on speaking terms with the great hereafter and it wasn't a gift to be taken lightly. But Maggie tipped me off that things upstairs were not entirely peace and harmony. When I found Jamie, the muscadoodle was coming out of his ears. I locked the stuff up and propped him in the shower, clothes and all, while Aunt Orva waited for the witching hour in the living room.

Jamie hated my guts. Maggie was with me on going for a fast score, and that meant his romance with eternity was coming to an end. There was nothing he could do but rejoin the human race. We were closing the store.

I turned the cold water on hard.

"You crummy bastard," he growled under the shower head. "Anything I don't like it's a crummy bastard."

"Shut up or you'll drown."

"You're not kidding me."

"How fast can you get the flies out of your head? Your Aunt Orva's downstairs."

"You're not kidding me, crumb. You and Maggie, huh? Well, I got something to say about that."

"Save it."

"You figure on shacking up with Maggie?"

"Not in this world."

"Listen, crumb. It's me and Maggie. Keep your cotton-pickin' hands off Maggie. It's me and Maggie. I'll blow your cotton-pickin' brains out. Unnerstan'?"

"You listen to me," I snapped. "Your aunt is downstairs. You got that? It's important. We can't keep her waiting forever. You do your walk-on. Louse it up and I'll turn you out of here. You'll end up scrounging shoe polish to drink. Play it smart and you'll end up a country gentleman. That's your choice, kid."

"Crummy bastard," he growled. "Anything I don't like it's a crummy bastard tellin' me what to do."

I left him there. Maggie had coffee working and I spelled her with the old lady. It didn't come as a great shock that Maggie had been one of Jamie's housewives. That's what he was saying, wasn't it? But to her, I thought, Jamie had only been spare time. She went upstairs with the coffee, and I stalled Mrs. M. I discussed our work at the Institute, but I wasn't ready to make the pitch. She smoked her Mexican cigarettes and grew fidgety. Finally, around ten o'clock, Maggie joined us and gave me the office with her eyes. Jamie would behave. She laid a cheap mandolin out of reach on the couch, and killed the lights.

We went through the parlor tricks. You've got to set a mood. I flagged a piece of luminous cloth through the air with the reaching rod. It glowed in the dark, phantom-like.

"Jamie—is that you?" Mrs. M asked.

We ducked the cloth and all was still. Then the strings of the mandolin sounded; I scraped them with the rod.

"Is that you, Jamie?"

Jamie was right on cue. Maggie lit a candle and he was seated at the table with us. He was bleary-eyed, but he was there.

Mrs. M stared at him, and long years of habit were hard to break. "Sit up straight, Jamie."

"Yes, Aunt Orva."

"You look the way you used to look when you'd been drinking. You were a very bad boy, Jamie. You know that now, don't you?"

"Yes, Aunt Orva."

"I'm trying very hard to forgive you, dear."

"Yes, Aunt Orva."

"I'm sorry if you hated me. I tried to bring you up right, but you wouldn't let me. But that's all past now, isn't it, Jamie?"

"Yes, Aunt Orva."

"I miss you, dear. I didn't think I would. But I do. You're all I have."

"Yes, Aunt Orva." His responses were flat and disinterested. The candlelight danced in his eyes. He wore a black turtleneck sweater; his bony hands and his long, frozen face seemed disembodied.

Mrs. M's piercing eyes were dulled with a kind of sadness. "I wouldn't have called in the police, Jamie. I only said that to frighten you. I didn't think you'd—"

"Yes, Aunt Orva."

"I hope—someday—you can forgive me, dear."

Maggie cued him with a flash of eyes. "I want to go home, Aunt Orva," he said.

"If only you could, dear." Her eyes began to run, dissolving the make-up. "Everything would he different. You'd be happy. I'd make you happy, child. Do you remember how it was before your Uncle Edwin passed on? He loved you, dear. We both loved you."

He turned toward Maggie and clenched his teeth. "Christ, I need a drink."

If Mrs. M heard him, the words didn't penetrate. She was feeling pain of her own. "Your room, Jamie. It's just the way you left it. Your clothes are still in the closet. I haven't touched a thing."

He gave her a strange look. "What closet?"

"Your closet, dear."

Firecrackers seemed to go off in his head. Suddenly, that grapeshot mind of his released a cry from the past. *"I didn't mean to do it! I didn't mean it, Uncle Ed!"*

"Jamie!"

His fingers clawed at his eyes as if to blind himself. *"I didn't see it! Don't let them take me, Aunt Orva!"*

Across the table from me Maggie stiffened, her eyes two sharp candle-points of light; but Mrs. M was extraordinarily calm, as if she had seen this crack in his mind before. "Jamie, dear, it's just a nightmare," she said. "It's not real, child."

"I didn't mean it. Don't punish me, Aunt Orva. I didn't mean it."

I didn't like watching it. Jamie was in an agony of memory. The closet bugged him. I glanced at Maggie again, but she seemed, suddenly, lost—holding her breath for fear he would blow the bit. Then, as quickly as the terror came over him, it passed. It vanished. The air quieted and it was as if he hadn't heard a word he'd said. He smiled. He chuckled. "So long, Aunt Orva."

"Jamie—don't go."

"See you tomorrow night, old dear."

Maggie blew out the candle. She looked worried. We'd be lucky if the spook didn't start walking into walls trying to find the oak panel. Maggie gave him plenty of time.

"We will now meditate," she said. "Hands on the table and meditate."

I had to hand it to the spook. Whether he had meant to or not, he had turned in a peerless performance. Whatever the closet meant to him, it was private property and none of my business. Maybe five seconds passed and I was thinking that the old lady would swing for the full million. Jamie had softened her up like a pro.

That's as far as I got. Jamie hadn't made for the panel. He had come up behind me. I could sense it. Then his long hands slipped around my neck. Cold and silent, like reptiles.

Chapter Seventeen

I didn't make a move.

I sat still.

His fingers moved slowly in a tightening coil. I held that first breath. My hands, linked with Maggie's and the old lady's, stiffened on the table. I tried to think straight and fast. He's playing games with you, Skelly. Don't panic. Don't make a move. Don't blow the score.

"He was always a sweet child," Mrs. M sighed. "A good boy."

His hands locked in place and my head began filling up like a balloon. I had a quick vision of that narrow face of his gloating in the dark. If I made one wrong move he'd throttle me. He'd forget it was a game. This was for kicks. This was for laughs. If I grabbed and we went pitching around the room, the stage scenery would come crashing down on our heads. Someone would go for the lights and it would put us out of business.

He held on.

Mrs. M gave a final, meditative sniffle in the dark. "When his Uncle Ed passed over, the dear boy never got over it. He was only seven."

Drop hammers were pounding in my ears. I'd had it. Lights began pinwheeling in front of my eyes. I lashed up for him—and his hands melted away.

"It brought out a mean streak in the boy."

I choked on air. Magpie sensed that something was wrong. She held back on the light and my bellows began working again. I breathed deeply. The spook. I'd mop the floor with him.

When the lights came up he'd made good his exit. Laughing, I supposed.

I'd murder him.

Mrs. M looked in a compact mirror and repaired the flood damage to her eyes. The bitter, aging lines of her face were softened. Night by night the séances were giving her a beauty treatment. She and Jamie were reconciling in the dark. I poured her a glass of sherry. The waspish old woman was disappearing before our eyes. If life with

Jamie had been a kind of warfare, life without him had been lonely and conscience-stricken. But everything would be different now. It would be a new deal. She couldn't be happier. She had bought a piece of make-believe, and I hated to threaten it. I was beginning to like the old bat.

She held the sherry under her powdered nose and absorbed the fumes. "Tomorrow night at the same time," she said, as if it didn't need saying at all.

I glanced at Maggie and made the pitch. "No," Dr. Appleby said. "I'm sorry, Mrs. Marenbach. This is the last of our meetings."

Her eyes lifted. "What are you talking about?"

"Miss Evangeline's work here is finished."

"What?"

"We're leaving California."

"But you can't do that." She turned to Maggie. "It's not true, is it, my dear?"

Maggie lowered her eyes. "It's true, Mrs. Marenbach."

"But this is outrageous."

"I am taking Miss Evangeline to Switzerland," Dr. Appleby said.

The old lady thumped the wineglass on the table. "Don't talk nonsense."

"I don't have to tell you," Dr. Appleby said, "that Miss Evangeline is a woman of unique gifts. Requests from every corner of the world come to us—"

"How much do you want, young man?"

"I beg your pardon?"

"Plans can be changed, can't they?" She was simmering. She knew it was payday, and she knew we weren't going to settle for short pieces of string any more. "I could raise $10,000."

"My dear Mrs. Marenbach," Dr. Appleby said. "You misunderstand. Your gratuities so far have been very generous and kind. Our personal needs are modest, but the work of the Institute remains largely unexplored. We have much to do. It is very possible that Miss Evangeline's powers may fail her at any moment, like the ebbing of a great tide."

Mrs. M's hand crept up the neck of her dress. It had never occurred to her that Jamie, like some modern genie, could not always be conjured up. Night after night after night.

"That means," Dr. Appleby went on, "that we must hurry our work. There are great areas to be covered. There is a group in Zurich—educated men, men of science, Mrs. Marenbach—which has offered to endow the Institute so that we may push our work forward. We have decided to accept their offer."

Her eyes were as cold as dead stars. "How much?"

"I'm afraid you don't understand," Dr. Appleby said. "It's not a question of money now. We'll close up the house here and be leaving in a very few days."

"Dr. Appleby," she said, persisting, "I'm not entirely a poor widow."

I hated having to put her through the wringer like this, but it was the only way she was going to get Jamie back. "You're very kind, Mrs. Marenbach. But our work is in Zurich."

"I do not intend to let you take Jamie away from me!"

"I know exactly how you feel. Let me say—it may not be necessary."

Her antennae were picking up faint signals. "What do you mean?"

I walked slowly to the far end of the room. Mrs. M was picking up some idea of the kind of endowment in the air, but it seemed to me anything over $100,000 was going to knock her out of her chair. Every time she asked me how much and got no answer, the price would rise in her mind.

"Mrs. Marenbach, there is a faint possibility—"

"Will you stop playing cat and mouse with me? Do you think I'm a fool? You're fishing for an endowment, and I'm quite willing. Now that I've found Jamie I have no intention of letting you run off to Zurich. What have the Swiss offered you? Fifty thousand? I can have it for you in the morning. How much? How much?"

Maggie closed her eyes as if she never allowed thoughts of money to enter the purity of her mind.

"Mrs. Marenbach," Dr. Appleby said, "I should confess to you that we have only begun to investigate the depths of Miss Evangeline's strange powers. For more than a year we have been experimenting with a question of the ages— *'If a man die, shall he live again?'* Live, Mrs. Marenbach. Shall Jamie live again?"

The idea was enormous. "I—I don't understand."

"Shall I tell you that after a period of extended trance, Miss Evangeline was able to keep Jamie alive in this room for more than eighteen hours?"

The possibility was dazzling. "Alive?"

"Flesh and blood. If eighteen hours—why not eighteen days? Eighteen months? Eighteen years, Mrs. Marenbach?"

She was stunned, but she was also quick on her feet. "You want a great deal of money, don't you?"

"A great deal."

"How much?"

"It would demand a long and painful trance. Perhaps two or three days without letup. And if she succeeds, the cost to Miss Evangeline can be very great. Her gifts may be left impaired or even shattered. That is the risk. But if she is able to release this great power, Jamie will live again. You can take him home. Home, Mrs. Marenbach. He will have returned from the other side to live out his natural life."

She had been sitting as straight-backed as a school teacher, and now she began working her hands nervously in her lap. It was just a matter of naming the sum now, I thought. Miss Evangeline could offer up a dream and Mrs. M could afford to buy it. She'd even swing for the full million, I thought, but I found myself suddenly backing away from it. I didn't want to hit her that hard. Or maybe I didn't want to endow my partners with glory rolls that large. I was taking a dislike to everyone, including myself. There had been million-dollar scores before, but I couldn't do it. All I wanted was enough scratch to stay out of the grave. My end of the touch had to run $125,000; I'd square myself with Braque and be sweet to rich widows for the rest of my life.

"Dr. Appleby," she said, trying for a kind of desperate composure. "I think we've talked quite enough. We understand each other. I am really quite a wealthy woman. If there is any chance that Jamie may be brought back—I intend to take it. What are those Swiss people of yours putting up?"

The moment had come to spring the price, and I was very calm. *"Five hundred thousand dollars,"* Dr. Appleby said.

Maggie's eyes came open. That wasn't the figure I'd been reaching for and she knew it.

Mrs. M was staring at me. "I'll match it," she snapped, almost with a sense of relief, and my heart gave a leap. We were in. "I'll arrange to have a check made out."

"But your check is no good," Dr. Appleby said. I had to swing her to cash. A large check was too easy to stop and too hard to cash, and a check left a legal memory.

"What *are* you talking about?"

I glanced at Maggie and she communicated. This was where I earned my fee. This is what she thought she had seen in me the day we met. "Mrs. Marenbach, I don't have to tell you that the moment you withdraw half a million dollars from your estate—to underwrite experiments in occult research—it's going to raise every eyebrow in every bank you do business with."

"Never mind that."

"But it's important and you know it is. They will attempt to stall you, to persuade you to reconsider. We haven't the time. In the end, you will be subjected to great embarrassment. There could be publicity. It would not only be humiliating for you, but damaging to Miss Evangeline and our entire program of research. It's something you shouldn't risk and, on reconsideration, it's something we cannot risk. While we appreciate your own generous impulse, Mrs. Marenbach, I think you will agree that it simply cannot be done and we must go to Zurich as planned. I am sorry. I wish we could have helped. Good night, Mrs. Marenbach."

But she just sat there. She had to be thinking of all that cash salted away in bank vaults. Silent money. Quiet money. And it took her only a moment to spend it. "Dr. Appleby," she said firmly, "there is no reason why anyone need know. I could round up the cash, you know. It's really no problem at all." She rose and took a breath and smiled at Maggie. "It's settled, my dear. I hope you can begin your deep trance at once. Now we can meet again tomorrow night, can't we?"

"Yes, Mrs. Marenbach."

"Good night, my dear." She turned to me. "Give me until Tuesday, Dr. Appleby, and tell those foreigners that Miss Evangeline is remaining here. I'll have all the money for you. In cash."

She was completely brainwashed.

Chapter Eighteen

The moment the old lady was gone, Maggie turned on me like a swinging door. "You oily bastard," she said. "You went back on us. She would have said yes to a cool million. Maybe two."

"Maggie, don't be greedy."

"It was right in our laps!"

I started for the stairs. "That junior partner of ours tried to throttle me tonight. I'm going to break his skull."

She hurried along behind me. "Don't be a fool."

"He's a punk and someone's got to put him wise."

"But he wouldn't do a thing like that, Skelly."

"If that wasn't him, there's a real spook loose in here."

I reached his door and rattled the knob. He'd locked himself in.

"Jamie!"

He was probably sitting on the floor with his legs folded like a pretzel. "I can't hear you, friend."

"Open up!"

"There's no one here but us goddam lotus petals."

"Skelly," Maggie cried, "you'll ruin everything!"

"I'll hardly leave a mark on him."

I threw myself against the door, but the lock held. Then it occurred to me that I had turned the key on the bottles in his closet and taken the key with me. I fit it in the door and it worked.

He was seated under the light with his arms limp at his sides. He was grinning. "Hit me, daddy," he said.

"Skelly," Maggie snapped. "Leave him alone!"

"Get up, Jamie!"

But he didn't move. And he had no intention of defending himself. He just kept grinning. "Hit me, daddy."

I stared down at him and I couldn't do it. I uncoiled my fist. He was looking for punishment and I was in no mood to do him any favors. I opened the closet and began pouring his grapejuice down the drain. "You're drying out, punk," I said. "Starting right now." Then I tossed the key to Maggie. "Lock him in and don't buy any more of that muscadoodle."

I left.

Around midnight I chased Viola out of my room. She was wearing a green wrapper. The stuff was so thin that every time the red beer sign lit up it went through her like an X-ray. "Go on, beat it," I said, "before I unwrap the package."

"So?"

"Look, you may be big in Pasadena, but you're just blocking the door in Venice." I gave her a kiss on the tip of her nose and a rap on the keester. "Go on, beat it."

"Chow."

I checked in on Maggie around noon the next day. She was sunning herself on the fenced roof-deck over the garage. She wore a coolie hat and a short terry-cloth robe. Day or night she looked like a million dollars—and I couldn't touch it.

"You're supposed to be in a deep trance," I said.

She stretched her legs and turned her face to the sun. "How's that?"

"Better. What's with the spook?"

"He's quiet."

"Maggie," I said, "I woke up with a bad thought this morning."

She opened one eye. "I don't figure you, darling. You could be scoffing the flash, but all you have time for is bad thoughts."

It was an in-joke, and she knew I spoke the language. When the garbage workers—the fakirs pitching vegetable cutters—got hungry they could feed on the display. Scoff the flash. Maggie had grown up on the midway. A carnie always liked to work the broadie top—the girlie show. He could scoff the flash.

"It's never out of my mind, Maggie," I said.

"Light me a cigarette."

"Let's get back to my bad thought." I stuck a cigarette into the orange lipstick and lit a match. "You made a slip the other day, Maggie, and it woke me up this morning. Kind of a delayed reaction."

"That sun feels good, doesn't it?"

"We were talking about cutting up the score. And you said— remember that Rinny Jim was in for a third. A third, Maggie."

"It doesn't take much to wake you, does it?"

The surf was booming a couple of blocks away. "It leads me to a whole alarm clock of bad thoughts, Miss Evangeline."

"Like what?"

"Like you and Jamie never stumbled over a dead body washed in from sea."

She kept her eyes closed. "Go on."

"Like Rinny Jim is dead."

"Is he?"

"Like it was his body that you gaffed to pass for Jamie's."

"I thought you gave up hunches."

"Is it a hunch? If Rinny were alive you'd have said to keep him in for a fourth—you, me, the spook and Rinny. But you were faking, Maggie, and in your own mind there are only the three of us—not to mention Porter and his ten per cent. Rinny Jim is dead, isn't he?"

She turned her head and opened her eyes. "Yes."

"What happened?"

She looked at me for a long time. "Does it really matter any more, Skelly? He's dead. Not even Miss Evangeline can bring him back to life." She took a sharp drag on her cigarette. "That's almost funny, isn't it? Mrs. M is getting the best of it. She's getting Jamie back."

"How did it happen, Maggie?"

"The bottle Jamie threw at him. It didn't seem serious. He was fine. About an hour had passed, I guess, and we were walking Jamie along the beach. That's when it happened."

"What do you mean?"

"He collapsed. I think he must have died before he hit the ground."

"What did you do?"

"Jamie sobered up enough to understand what had happened. He begged me not to turn him over to the cops. And why should I? It wouldn't bring Rinny back to life. Jamie hadn't meant to hurt him. It had just happened."

"Then what?"

"It was my idea to put Jamie's ID bracelet on Rinny—and his shoes and coat. And together we pulled him out into deep water and let go."

"You always keep a cool head, don't you?"

"Yes."

Maggie had a quick eye for the main chance, I thought. Rinny Jim had never been anything but a charming, smalltime grifter. Jamie might be the muscadoodle kid, but he was solid gold. And she owned him. That's what fit. She owned him and she could whistle him into stir. That was a powerful gimmick.

"You'll look great in mink," I said.

"You bet I will, darling." She buried her cigarette in a geranium pot. "We could have a ball, Skelly."

"Thanks for the invite, Maggie."

"In a couple of days it'll be over. We'll have nothing but money to spend. Why split up?"

"We could send each other postcards. Keep in touch."

"I'm serious, darling."

"So am I."

"We go together like Scotch and soda." The sun plated her legs with fool's gold. "You're not the kind of guy I like, Skelly—you're the kind of guy I fall in love with."

I got up. "I'll treasure the thought."

The day turned suddenly cloudy. "You cheap, two-way sonavabitch. You think I don't know you've got that broad stashed away in your room!"

"Half a dozen of them," I said. I had nothing to fear from Maggie, not until we scored. And once we scored I'd pay off Braque and I'd be clean. All I had to watch was my timing. "See you in the dark, Maggie."

Venice on a Sunday night was skid row with seaweed. If you kicked a paper sack you might break a bottle. Sand blew in from the beach, laying a grit along the colonnades. The windows in the second-story hotels were lit by bulbs a couple of sizes too small, as if electricity had just been invented. In another two days I'd clear out. Tuesday. I was beginning to count the hours. Mrs. M would walk in with all the money in the world, and I'd sherry. Beat it.

Around ten-thirty I picked up Viola and we ended up in the stand-up bar with the fish net and the sign that said SINNERS WELCOME. My monogrammed cigarette lighter had never turned up, and I asked the bartender. I must have dropped it somewhere; I missed it. We weren't in there five minutes before a pair of sinners walked in, and Viola turned white. These two weren't local; they were slumming. "Do you know them?"

"Slightly," Viola whispered. "She's my mother."

Mother wore her blonde hair in a beehive and a black dress put on with a spray gun. She didn't look old enough to drink. The guy with her had on a cashmere jacket and a red vest. He looked bored.

"Take me out of here," Viola breathed.

"Not a chance," I said.

"Please—"

Even in the murky light the beehive made right for us. "Viola, darling. I thought that was you. Coming out of some hotel, wasn't it?"

Viola took a grip on my hand. "Hello, Mother."

"Have you met your father?"

"Hello, Father."

"Enchanted," he said.

"Who's this young man, Viola dear?"

"I don't know. I never ask their names, Mother."

"That's very funny, darling. But I'm serious."

"My name's Skelly," I said.

"Enchanted," the man said. He turned to the barkeep. "A gin pahit."

"A what?"

Viola kept tugging at my hand. She wanted out of there, but I wasn't quite ready. "Madam," I said, "I'm going to marry your daughter."

Viola gave me a kick at the ankle. "Don't believe him, Mother. He's just making small talk."

"But he sounds entirely serious."

"Never more serious," I said.

"He is quite handsome."

"Goodbye, Mother," Viola snapped. "We're late for a party."

She pulled me out of there and never looked back. Once outside, she turned her face to the wall and let go a few quick tears. She was scared. Now that I had seen the beauty in the family, what would I want with an imitation? She couldn't compete. I made her face me and wiped the tears with my thumbs. I'd seen her laugh, and now I'd seen her cry, and that's all you needed to know to know a woman. "You don't have to marry me," she said.

"Who asked for your advice?"

"She'll be back. You'll see. She'll be back and she'll let you chase her once around the block—and then she'll catch you!"

I lifted her chin and kissed her. "Stop worrying, will you? And keep your traps packed. In a couple of days we're lifting the feet and moving on. Until then, do me a favor, Spindlelegs. Keep your door locked. I don't want to damage the merchandise."

Chapter Nineteen

Maggie could whistle up my executioner, but by nine o'clock Monday night I still had my health. Once I got my hands on the money, another twenty-four hours, the only thing Maggie could whistle for would be a dog.

As far as Mrs. M knew, Maggie had been sitting in a trance for two days. The room was kept dark except for the candle burning in the center of the table—in case of a sudden visit. When the doorbell rang Maggie struck a pose like Whistler's Mother, and I let Mrs. M in.

She wore the same snap-brim hat, but the face had changed. She had left off several layers of make-up, and the effect was startling. It was obvious that she had once been a very beautiful woman. Her looks hadn't faded; they had deepened. She had been wearing a mask, but now the heavy eye make-up, the rouge and the beauty mark were gone. It was as if she hadn't shown her face in public for twenty years.

"I hope I'm not disturbing Miss Evangeline," she said. Her skin was clear and white, and there seemed to be a great calmness in her eyes.

"She's expecting you," Dr. Appleby said.

"I brought a gift for Jamie."

I opened the sliding doors. It was like parting the curtains on a stage set. The pampas grass, the rich oriental rugs and the beaded lamps existed in the shadows. Maggie, lit up by the yellow flame, sat with her eyes closed and her head back as if she were poised in some half-world between the quick and the dead.

"Miss Evangeline hasn't eaten in two days," Dr. Appleby whispered. "Nothing but a special herb tea from India."

"Poor thing."

Mrs. M, hardly daring to breathe in the great silence, took her place. Maggie made no sign of recognition. I excused myself and closed the doors.

I stopped in the kitchen to put a tea bag in a cup and light a fire under the kettle. Then I went upstairs and turned the key on Jamie's room.

He was lying on the bed, somewhere between the quick and the dead himself. He hadn't had a drink since Saturday, and his skin must have felt shot full of quills. The light hurt his eyes when I walked in, but he pasted a smile on his face. He looked shaky as hell.

"If it ain't my favorite crummy bastard," he said.

"How you doing, Jamie?"

"I got it licked, friend. And I owe it all to you."

I threw him his shirt. "You're on."

He didn't move. "Why, I'm so dry I'm afraid to snap my fingers. Might start a fire."

"How are you on your legs?"

"I've been a dissolute young man, but I see the error of my ways. I been thinking about all that loot and the good life it's going to buy me. Why, I might even lecture on temperance, friend. The idea intoxicates me—if that's allowed."

"Get up, Jamie."

The smile kept coming unpasted. He'd been out of the sunlight for so many months that the only color left in his face was the blue of his eyes. "Look, friend," he said. "I'm not facing the old bat without a drink. Man, I'm unglued. So you run out and fetch me a bottle of the old muscadoodle, and we'll put on ye olde spook show."

He looked so bad I wondered if he could get through the séance. "Get up."

"Man—I need a drink."

"Look, kid, I don't give a damn whether you embalm yourself or not, but I'd like to see the old lady get a fair shake. You're going home tomorrow and you're going home sober. I'll check you out on something. Whatever it was between you and the old lady is dead. You're getting a fresh deal. It's a new deck. Play it smart."

"Goddamit—get me a drink!"

I stared at him and wondered why I had bothered. There was only one way to get him through the séance. "Okay, punk," I said. "She's waiting. Behave. When she leaves you get a drink."

Nothing happened for the first ten minutes or so. I had returned with the cup of tea, and Maggie made a ritual of it. She breathed the fumes like there was sustenance in them, and then held the cup between both hands and drank. Sarah Bernhardt couldn't have made more of a production of it.

Jamie had come after that drink like a greyhound after a rabbit. Once he had joined us his eyes kept blinking in the candlelight. He was shaky. He fidgeted in the chair. He kept swallowing. He was counting the seconds, I thought, and avoiding Mrs. M's gaze from across the table. With money in his kick I supposed he'd get a plumber to pipe grapejuice into the house so that it would never be any farther than the nearest faucet.

"Jamie, dear," Mrs. M smiled. "Everything's ready for you at home. I cleaned your room myself. You are coming, aren't you? I mean, there's no chance—you won't disappoint me."

Dr. Appleby said, "Tonight Miss Evangeline will attempt to keep Jamie here in this room. Naturally there are forces trying to pull him back to the other world. The eternal conflict between life and death, Mrs. Marenbach."

"Miss Evangeline will succeed, won't she?"

"We'll know tomorrow," Dr. Appleby said. It was a comfort to be rich, I thought. Money could buy immortality. Jamie was barely holding himself together, and I knew I had to get her out of there. "You really must go now, Mrs. Marenbach."

But she wasn't ready to leave. "Jamie, dear, I brought something for you." She laid a square mahogany box on the table. "Do you remember this?"

He stared at it. "No."

"I found it in the garage today. There are lots of your old things packed there, dear. Don't you remember this box? It was your first toy after you came to live with us."

His shoulders began to twitch with the effort of holding himself steady. "No."

"You'd sit with it by the hour. You must remember."

"No."

As she pushed the box closer to him, some worn spring let go and the top opened. A harlequin jumped up, smiling.

The effect shot through Jamie like a charge of electricity. His hands lifted and his face drew back in sudden terror, but what he stared at wasn't the jack-in-the-box. "Uncle Ed," be gasped. "Please, Uncle Ed! Don't die! I didn't mean it! I didn't mean it!"

Mrs. M's eyes opened wide. "Jamie—"

The smiling harlequin had set off some frozen vision of the past. He clutched his face as if to shield himself and to hide, and racking sobs came over him. It was a child crying. "Don't die, Uncle Ed. Please get up. Please. It was just a game. I didn't mean to scare you. I didn't mean it. Don't die, Uncle Ed."

Mrs. M reached out a hand as if to touch him. "It's just a bad dream, Jamie. You mustn't—"

After a moment he looked up as if seeing her there for the first time. His eyes were glazed and empty. "No. I remember now, Aunt Orva."

"Please, dear—"

He looked at the tears on his fingertips and crushed them slowly. It was as if he hadn't seen them since the age of seven. He glanced at the jack-in-the-box and then carefully shut the harlequin back in. "Yes, Aunt Orva," he said. "Just a bad dream."

When Mrs. M was gone I brought up the lights and gave Jamie a belt of sherry. There was a tremor in his hand, and I damned near felt sorry for him. He was bugged. His face was slack and he couldn't sit still. He even said thanks.

Maggie just stared at him.

The drink seemed to take some of the slack out of him. "I don't suppose you could spare another teaspoon out of that bottle?"

He held up the glass and I filled it. "Make it last, Jamie."

He hunched his shoulders and let the glass sit on the table like a life preserver within reach. "You know, I killed the old man."

"Is that what you saw?"

"Like a silent movie. I've been carrying it around in my head. Funny. I didn't even know it was there." He tried to light himself a cigarette. It wasn't easy. "I was just a kid. I liked him. Hell, I really liked the guy. I mean—he was great."

"Sure."

He didn't look at me. The memory had been bottled up so long it had to come out, and I happened to be standing there. "I didn't know about his ticker. I was just a kid. The night it happened Aunt Orva had gone out. I don't remember where. I had been put to bed, and he figured we were alone in the house. It was raining. I remember now. I got up for a drink and saw that he was coming to bed. I cut into his bedroom. I hid in his closet and waited. I can remember giggling. I thought it was going to be funny. I'd jump out at him. I'd scare ol'

Uncle Ed. But I killed him. Man, I killed him."

That was as far as he got without reaching for the life preserver. He didn't look at the color. He didn't sniff the fumes. He poured it down and shut his eyes, waiting for the fluid to embalm his mind. The memory, the silent movie, had been dark for twenty years, but there was a kind of murky light now on the bottle he had crawled into and the cork he had pulled in after him.

"Warden," he smiled, "lock me up for the night."

Chapter Twenty

When I got back to the Grand Metropole there was a white Jaguar parked across the street, and the broadie at the wheel tapped the horn. For me. There was a night chill in the air, and all I saw at first was a sable elbow and a pair of red lips caught in a slant of light. It was Spindlelegs' mother. I walked over.

"Waiting for Viola?" I asked.

"Waiting for you."

"You're a doll." I was in no mood for the graces. All I wanted was for tomorrow to come. Tomorrow and Mrs. M and that half-million pias- tres. I'd be off the hook with Braque, Porter would get a ten per cent return on his investment, and Maggie could cut up the rest with Jamie any way she wanted.

"Can we talk?" the voice asked.

"Say it."

"Get in."

"Why waste the petrol? Do you want to come up to my room?"

"What's in your room that could possibly interest me, Mr. Skelly?"

"Me."

"You're very direct, aren't you?"

"There's nothing like a pretty girl—unless it's a prettier one."

"That's a charming thought."

"Upstairs," I said. "That corner room. The door will be open. Just walk in."

I left her sitting there and I didn't stop walking until I was halfway up the stairs and Viola was halfway down. She carried a cheap card- board suitcase in one hand and the concertina in the other.

"Where the hell do you think you're going?" I snapped.

"I'll find somewhere."

"You know she's down there, don't you?"

"Yes."

"So you're just giving up. Is that it?"

"I knew she'd come back. I could tell the way she looked at you.

"Are you going to run away from her all your life?"

"I'm not running. I'm walking. It's more dignified."

"What about me?"

"You're a nice guy. But a guy is a guy is a guy."

"They all tumble, huh? Wise up, kid. Who told you it was no contest?"

She gave me a dark look. "Mister, I've been through the Olympics." She moved, but I blocked the way. "She's coming up, isn't she?"

"By personal invitation."

"Have fun—Appleby or Skelly or whatever your name is. Play it smart and some day you may turn out to be my father."

I picked her up and carried her to the top of the stairs and along the hall. I got the door of my room open and pitched her inside. "You lovely blonde nitwit—undress."

"What?"

I sprung the suitcase, dug out the green wrapper and threw it at her. Then I locked the door. When I turned she was still standing there in all her threads. "I told you to strip."

She couldn't seem to get it through her head. "But—"

I caught her wrist and pulled her to me and kissed her until her toes began to curl, and then she knew she was winners. I unbuckled the belt she was wearing and she took it from there, stripping with soft, rustling sounds. She smiled. She was winners and she knew it now. "If she knocks at the door—"

"She'll have to break it down," I said. I set a chair under the knob and gave Viola a wink. Then she hugged me tight. Her head smelled of the sun and the sea. Her hands crept along the buttons of my shirt, undoing them like small acts of love, and finally I picked her up in my arms and killed the light switch.

The sound at the door came. A soft knocking. A turning of the knob. She tried again and whispered my name. "Skelly?"

Viola put her finger to my lips and the neon glow kept trying to press through the green shade, igniting her eyes and the soft gold of her hair and the bronze of her legs.

"Skelly?"

It was a long time before the sounds at the door went away. It was a long time before she got the message: I was going to let her stand in a sleazy hallway with sable hanging from her shoulders until she knew she was losers. Mirror, mirror on the wall—

Finally she walked away.

Around two in the morning the door started rattling again. Someone was there. It didn't wake me until Viola was already sitting up and pulling on the wrapper. "That's Mother," she whispered. "She's back." Then she was out of bed and at the door as if she were going to tear it off by the hinges.

But it was no visitor from Pasadena. The door opened on Maggie. She had thrown a kerchief around her hair and a dark bulky knit around her shoulders. She looked like she had just got out of bed herself.

When she saw Viola she turned cat-eyed. But she didn't have time for it and she didn't say a word. "Tell him I want to talk to him."

I came to the door and Viola faded into the dark. "What's the matter?"

"It's Jamie," Maggie said in a sharp whisper. "He's gone."

Chapter Twenty-one

I told Maggie to wait for me downstairs. I got dressed. Without Jamie we were paddling without a canoe. I'd be right back where I started—Tap City. Tapioca. Broke. Viola stood watching me with her arms crossed, and smoked down a cigarette. Her feet were bare and her hair was mussed and it wasn't going to be easy to walk out. Finally I put a kiss on her lips and a pat on her behind. "Don't hang around here," I said. "Move it across the hall."

"You're kidding."

I had seen the look in Maggie's eyes. "Across the hall," I said. "I don't want any cat fights in here."

"I'm just in the mood—*meeow!*"

I left and picked up Maggie downstairs. We walked to her car. "You've got lousy taste in dames," she snapped.

I got in behind the wheel and started up the engine. "Don't waste your time, Maggie," I said. "Where do we start looking?"

"Out the window."

"That's a big help. He doesn't have any money, does he?"

"Look, he's beat it," she said. "He's really gone."

"The first thing he'd go after is a bottle."

"You should never have tried to dry him out."

"Let's skip the broadsides. Does he have any money?"

She nodded. "He's got money," she answered. "He took it from my bag."

"How much?"

"Three or four hundred dollars."

I shut my eyes. With that much in bank rags he could finance a six month tour of the wine country. I turned on the lights and backed up. If we didn't find him the cops might. They'd get a real jolt if they checked his fingerprints. That would be the blowoff.

"How long has he been out?"

She shoved in the cigarette lighter. "I don't know."

"You're a big help tonight." It was easy enough to read her mind. A square mile of mink. If Jamie didn't turn up, what then? Back to some cootch show? A big score like this comes up only once, and if you blow it you've had it. I thought, If we find Jamie she'll kill him on the spot; if we don't find him, maybe I'll do.

"Stop simmering and tell me what happened," I said.

"I didn't know he was gone until about twenty minutes ago. I got up for a smoke and found my bag emptied on the rug."

"What are some of his old hangouts?"

"He wouldn't go back to them," she said. "Anyway, it's after hours. Look at the time."

There wasn't a bar or liquor store left open, but Jamie had had plenty of time to buy a jug. I cruised along Pacific, past the dark antique shops, the arcades and the self-service laundry on the corner. The shadows were piled up in every doorway like the day's refuse. "Watch that side of the street," I said.

She didn't say another word. I covered the alley behind the business block and glanced up at the iron fire escapes bracketed to the second-story hotels. He might be anywhere and he might be nowhere. I shot out to the oil derricks at the edge of town and then cruised up one black canal and down the other. Nothing. I crossed a wooden bridge. We raised a few dogs. And I kept thinking, It can't be happening. All those big ones, those thousand-dollar bills, are set to fall like autumn leaves. Without Jamie we're dead. Without Jamie I'm back doing hide-and-seek with Braque's traveling hoodlum.

I suppose half an hour passed before I thought of Porter. This was his trade. I stopped at an all-night gas station to use the phone. I dug Porter's card out of my wallet and dialed off his home number. I got no answer. I tried the office and drew another blank. This was our night. I gave it up.

"We'll try the deadfalls," I said. "He might be loitering around like a homing pigeon."

But everything with a liquor license was boarded up for the night. The coffeehouses were black. I parked in sight of the ocean and got out. "He could be out there curled up around a sand dune. Come on."

Maggie took the beachfront walk and I cut down to the water, and together we began to comb north toward the pier. I checked out every shadow that looked any larger than a Coke bottle. The sea had washed up dead humps of kelp, and at twenty feet each of them looked like Jamie. It seemed hopeless. It *was* hopeless. The salt wind tugged at my hair and my mind kept turning over. What was it between Maggie and Jamie? Something she had told me the other night no longer stood up. The night Rinny Jim had checked out here in the sand, Jamie had begged her not to put him in stir—she said. It made sense for anyone else, I thought, but not for Jamie.

The ocean at my left kept turning up at the edges. I sloughed through the cold sand. Jamie made his own kind of sense, I thought. Any bartender could hand down an opinion on him. He was on a punishment kick. He'd been on it for twenty years. Since the night he had jumped out of the closet and watched the uncle double up. That was so awful the lights went out in his skull, until tonight. But he had committed a kind of murder, and there were twelve men, tried and true, sitting in the dark of his head saying: Guilty, Jamie Marenbach. You did it. And you've got to pay for doing the old man in.

I kept an eye on Maggie; it was as if all the beachfront lights had been turned on for her. What was it between them? Jamie had to be a bad boy. A real bad boy. He had to goad his Aunt Orva into punishing his hide every day. He needed it. Hell, it was his daily purification. But after twenty years of trying to lash the punk into line, the old lady couldn't face herself any more.

But drunk or sober, the way it added up, Jamie wouldn't have pleaded with Maggie to save him from the cops. Hell, his idea of a great Christmas gift would be the electric chair. There was that mouldering memory of the old man to be paid for. If killing Rinny Jim had been the same thing, sheer accident, Jamie would have broken down the door of the nearest police station. His idea of living is to die. That would have been made to order.

No, I thought, it hadn't happened that way. There had never been any talk of saving Jamie from the cops that night. Maggie had lied. Rinny Jim's death had to be made to order.

I peered at Maggie again.

Forget it, I told myself. Find Jamie, grab the money and run.

We didn't find Jamie. We were still at it when dawn lit up the dark corners, and finally, around ten o'clock, I dropped myself at the hotel. We had half a day's slack before Mrs. M turned up with the money. "Get some sleep," I said.

"Don't talk like an idiot."

"He may turn up before tonight."

She lifted her eyes. "He hasn't known what time it was for four months."

"He's got all day to find a clock."

"He'll louse it up," she said. "He's jealous of you."

"Is he in love with you, Maggie?"

She gave me a brittle look. "Isn't everyone?"

"What did you promise him? An exclusive option on your services?"

"I want that money, Skelly."

"So do I. And so does he. I think he'll show."

"If he doesn't?"

"Stall the old lady. And see if you remember your old dance routines. You can always go back to that."

"Thanks."

"He may be waiting on the front porch," I said. "Unless he's got himself arrested, which is likely, or got himself killed, which is possible. Get some sleep."

"Skelly?"

I turned back. "What?"

"Don't go back to that girl."

"What girl?"

She gave me a quick, cloudy look and raised a cloud of pigeons off the street. The car almost scraped the buttons off my shirt. I stood there a moment, thinking, and then went upstairs. Maggie had been beating me over the head with olive branches, but she finally seemed to get the message. Our partnership ended the moment we laid our hands on the money. Maybe tonight.

Viola had cleared out, but she had left the green wrapper hanging on the back of the door. I was beat. I pulled the shade and went to bed.

I smelled muscadoodle. I heard the shade flapping in the afternoon breeze. I turned and opened my eyes. A knife was taking an option on my throat.

Jamie was back.

"Hello, friend," he said.

Chapter Twenty-two

I didn't move. The blade was cold and sharp, and Jamie's hand was not exactly steady.

"Man," he grinned, "I could serve you up on a platter. I should have brought an apple to put in your mouth. If a thing's worth doing, it's worth doing right. That's what Aunt Orva used to tell me."

His breath was twenty per cent alcohol, but he didn't look drunk. He just looked happy. All he had to do was lean on the knife. I lay still, hardly breathing, and stared up into his bright blue eyes. I became aware of sea gulls outside the window, milling and squawking, and I supposed Viola was down there.

"Let me see you sweat," he said.

"I'm sweating," I said.

He winked. "You know where I been? I been having a ball. But all the time I keep thinking of you, and that keeps me laughing. I mean, you're funny. You listening?"

"I'm listening," I said.

"But you don't get the point, friend. The real yock is coming up."

His hand was getting heavy, and I tried not to swallow. The shade kept flapping, letting in small bursts of sunlight.

"I mean, I've bought you a piece of the hereafter, friend. That's the joke. You listening?"

The hereafter was suddenly a quarter of an inch away, and I wondered if I could make a grab for his wrist and live through it.

"Man, you're sweating." He eased up on the knife. "You got something to say?"

"I'm listening," I said.

"You know where I been? I lit out for the big time. L. A. Main Street. I been cruising Muscatel Alley in a taxi. Man, that street never closes. I been setting up drinks for every bloodshot eye looking for a friend. With all that money you know what I'm going to do? I'm going to open a Rescue Mission for the dries."

"All what money?"

"Now what kind of a question is that? Man, this is the night. She pays off like a slot machine."

"And you'll be there for yours, won't you?"

"I wouldn't let Maggie down."

"Is that all you stopped by for? To cut my throat?"

He laughed. "You got it wrong. If I was going to cut your throat, friend, I'd have brought a hatbox. Of course, if you try to get up, I won't have a choice. But that would ruin the yock I got all planned. Take the fun right out of it."

"What are you talking about?"

"Man, don't move that way. Hold still."

"What did you come back for?"

"Why, I ran right out of money. And the old lady isn't due for hours. I thought you might loan me a little of the green to get me through daylight."

"There's money in my billfold."

"I already got that. How about the wrist watch?"

"What about it?"

"Take it off. Easy does it, friend."

"It's yours."

I undid the leather buckle and the watch came off. I thought for a moment he only wanted to be on time, but he straightened me out. "I can always raise a few last drinks with a timepiece," he grinned. The grin vanished. "You listening?"

"I'm listening, friend," I said.

"You sweating?"

"I'm sweating."

"I know what you're figuring. You think you'll stick me away in Bel Air and shack up with Maggie. No, man. I warned you not to entertain the notion. I warned you to keep your cotton-pickin' hands off the lady."

"She's all yours, kid."

"You're the guy who made time with her. I picked up your cigarette lighter. With your big fat initials on it, man. It was you."

His time sense was bollixed up—he had passed out the warning after the facts—but he had me cold. Hadn't he caught on that Maggie was an alley cat? "What did she promise you?" I said. "All the bedroom stories in the book?"

"I had it made, friend, until you came along. It was her and me. I could make shark bait out of you with this knife, but I don't have to.

Man, I tied a time bomb on you a couple of days ago and it's going to go off with a real loud bang."

"What are you talking about?"

"I'm talking about the late Mr. Porter."

"Is he dead?"

"May he rest in peace—but not too long."

"Put away the knife."

"You haven't heard the best part yet." Jamie cut off my voice again, and I just lay there trying not to swallow. "Maggie said he had some loony idea that we dragged Rinny down the beach and put him out to sea. You can't have madmen running around loose, can you? I mean, a girl like Maggie's got to think of her reputation. Right?"

Right. I tried to think back. The last I had seen of Porter he had been sitting beside the vase of pampas grass with a drink in his hand. The night the fog had come in.

"So I did him in," Jamie grinned. "It was the gentlemanly thing to do, friend. He drove a little Renault, and I waited out there for him in the fog and pinned him to the seat. Then I tooled the car along the canals looking for a good spot and dropped the machine over the bank. It's still there. But you know what happens? When the canals start smelling they drain 'em out to sea, and there that Renault's going to be high and dry with Porter sitting in it. And here's the yock, friend—you know what I clamped in his hand? That cigarette lighter with your big fat initials on it."

The gulls seemed to break out laughing. I stared up into Jamie's slack, grinning eyes. He knew better than to let go with the knife. He had set me up for a patsy.

You lousy punk, I thought.

You goddam winehead.

You scaly bastard.

He watched me turn color. That's what he had come for. "That's the tale, friend," he said. "You won't be around for Maggie. You'll be shacked up with the police department. They'll trace you down, man. They've got your signature."

Suddenly he let go with the knife, but in the next second I saw a brown grocery sack in the air; it came down on my head—and broke like glass.

The sun went out like a match.

Chapter Twenty-three

I don't know how long I lay there in the dark. The first thing I heard was the shade flapping in the breeze and the sea gulls on the beach, and when I opened my eyes the sun was still shining. My skull felt split in two.

Broken bits of glass lay on the pillow like shrapnel. I raised myself and lurched to the mirror expecting to see a bloody mess for a head. I stared at myself. All I saw was a headache. The throbbing almost knocked the mirror off the wall.

I stayed on my feet. I had an idea that if I lay down again I would die. I filled the basin with cold water and slopped my head. The wine bottle had raised a knot where I used to part my hair, and the muscadoodle had run down my neck and chest.

It was a long time before I was able to think, to pick up the pieces. I had a vague feeling that I was in a hurry, that I ought to he running somewhere

Porter was dead.

I was set to take the rap.

I turned away from the basin and looked around. What was I looking for? Jamie. The lousy punk. The goddam winehead. The scaly bastard. I had to find him. I had to get that cigarette lighter out of the canal.

I wondered what time it was. Mrs. M would show up around nine o'clock. For the blowoff. Jamie would be there for the blowoff, but I wasn't going to wait that long.

I lifted the shade and peered out. Viola was on the beach with the gulls and she gave me a wave. I supposed she had been waiting for my shade to go up. She started back toward the hotel, and I turned away. The sun was hot and saucy and still a long way from the horizon. Maybe it was four o'clock.

I brushed the glass and paper sack off my bed and hoped I could pass it off as if nothing had happened. But I had to get rid of Viola. I had to get her out of Venice. If Maggie blew wise that it was Viola, not Porter, who had watched them dump Rinny Jim into the sea, the situation would turn ugly—fast. Maggie was no one to leave loose ends.

I pulled on my shirt as if it were spun out of pins and got into my pants. Get rid of Viola for good, I told myself. You were a sap to let her hook up with you. You're marked one way or the other. If Braque doesn't get you, the cops will. Your luck began to curdle six months ago, and there are times when the harder you run the slower you walk. Skelly, you're crawling. Get rid of her.

She came into the room like a gust of wind and threw her hands around my neck. I almost blacked out again.

"Kiss me, you brute."

I peeled her hands off and opened my eyes again. She wore beach pants and a blouse tied at the midriff. "How fast can you pack?"

"Thirty seconds."

"You're leaving."

She gave her blonde head a tilt. "You mean *we're* leaving, don't you?"

"Hold still."

She held still and I lifted her chin with my fist and kissed her. "Thanks, brute," she said.

"That's hello and goodbye," I said. "Pack your traps and take the first bus out of town. Stop at the post office. There's a letter addressed to you. It's got travel money in it."

"I'm not going alone."

"I'll meet you." I had to lay down some kind of a story or she'd never go. "Run up to San Francisco and wait for me. Check into the St. Francis. I'll meet you."

A mist shot into her eyes. "When?"

"In a couple of days."

"Why can't I wait for you here?"

"Look, don't argue with me. We're splitting."

"Don't make me go, Skelly."

I'd never see her again. I could feel it and it was like taking gas. "I told you I'd meet you," I said.

"You're not giving me the brush-off, are you, darling?"

"You know better."

"Do I?"

I took her in my arms and I made it last. "You dumb broad," I smiled. "You're extra baggage. I keep stumbling over you. There's no one I'd rather stumble over, but not here and not now. Will you do me a favor

and get a room in the St. Francis, and in a couple of days I'll be there
and I'll break down the door."

"Honest?"

"You bet."

I kissed her and I made that last too. Then I shuffled her out of there,
and she wiped her eyes. When I got to the end of the hall I turned
and we looked at each other, and I think she knew, somewhere
behind the exchange of smiles, that I was walking out of her life.

Jamie knew better than to get in my line of vision. I was sure he
wouldn't be sitting in the local deadfalls, and yet I made the rounds.
The only place I knew he wouldn't be was Muscatel Alley. A drunk
can be crafty, and Jamie wouldn't have told me he had been there if
he intended to go back. He had taken my billfold and all I had left in
my pocket were a few bangers. I spent them for booze: a double shot,
fast, to either kill me or cure me. I didn't want to think about Viola. It
was cutting too deep. Keep moving, Skelly.

I crossed to the canals. I didn't waste much time trying to get lucky
and spot the Renault. The water was dark and murky, with a surface
like an antique mirror. Still, if I could locate the car I could wade in
and fish out my lighter. That would change my luck. Jamie had been
right; the police could trace the lighter back to the mountain they dug
the silver out of. Unless I got my hands on it first.

I looked along the Grand Canal, but the search seemed hopeless
without Jamie. There was hardly a ripple as far as the eye could see.
And he might have dumped the Renault in any of the side canals. I
walked only as far as Maggie's place and found her smoking up the
hall with a cigarette.

"Did Jamie show up?" I asked.

"What do you think?"

"Sit down. I want to talk to you."

"Talk to me standing up. Mrs. M called about half an hour ago. She
has the money. She said she would be coming over a little early
tonight."

"What time is it now?"

"Where's your watch?"

"Jamie borrowed it."

"Don't be funny."

"What time is it?"

"Almost five."

"Sit down."

She felt me out with a quick glance. "Is he dead?"

"No."

We had reached the staircase and she settled herself on the bottom steps, leaning back on her elbows and staring at me. "Where did you find him?"

"He paid me a social call," I said. "Right on the side of the head."

"What are you talking about?"

"He's a cat-and-mouser. He'd have killed me, but it would ruin his fun. He needed to gloat over me."

"Where is he?"

"Where's Porter?"

"How the hell should I know?" she snapped. "Make sense."

"Look, Miss Evangeline, this isn't amateur night in Dixie any more. I know the squeaky shoe is dead. *Spill it.* Where did Jamie park the Renault?"

She didn't bat an eye. "Ask him."

"I'm asking *you.*"

"Jamie killed him—not me."

"Did he tell you where he dumped the car? Did he tell you he set me up for the Arbuckle?"

She raised an eyebrow. "Did he?"

"If I take any pratfalls, partner, the scenery is coming down with me."

"What are you talking about?"

I hunkered at her feet and looked along her tight black Capris to the jade spots her eyes made in the half-light of the hall. "When the cops start passing out murder raps, doll, they're going to start with you."

"If I thought you were serious I'd laugh."

"You knitted together Porter's murder with your two little hands. All Jamie did was kill him." I leveled my fingers under my chin. "You're in it up to here, Miss Evangeline."

"Is that what you're peddling?"

"All the pieces have finally dropped in place for me, Maggie. You've been looking for the big mark all your life—and Jamie was it. The prize Arbuckle. The kid with a pipeline to fifty million dollars. I'll bet you lay awake nights for months trying to find an angle. Poor Jamie never had a chance. Hell, you've got the best educated navel in town. You must have made the other housewives on the circuit seem like furniture."

"You should know."

"I'll write you a testimonial. Jamie may think he let a bottle fly at Rinny Jim in a muscadoodle mood, but you know better, don't you? There was as much murder as muscadoodle in that accident. Rinny Jim was in the way. You wanted it to happen. Jamie wanted it to happen. It happened. I don't think you could have cued Jamie into outright murder at that point. But outright accident—why not? All you had to do was turn virtuous housewife and withhold the golden navel from Jamie until something happened, and it did. And suddenly you had the angle you'd been looking for. You could work a death certificate for Jamie, and you worked it. You could put together a foolproof, Jim Dandy spook swindle and big con, and you did. How am I doing?"

She glared at me and said nothing.

"But that night on the beach," I went on, "you thought Porter saw you and Jamie dragging a dead man into the sea. You and Jamie. You and the spook. What else were you afraid Porter had seen? The way you prepared Rinny Jim for the sharks?"

"Shut up."

"Shark bait. That's what Jamie kept shouting in my face. Shark bait. And it fits. You had to make sure that when the body washed up on the beach, it was beyond recognition. Blood is for sharks. You got him out in deep water and cut him into bait. You thought Porter had seen everything; that keeps unreeling in your mind whenever you shut your eyes. You couldn't risk that, so you turned the screws on Jamie. The spook may have killed him, but I'll bet you held Porter down."

"You can't prove it."

"I don't intend to try. Porter is sitting behind the wheel somewhere at the bottom of the canal, and all I want is to get my hands on Jamie. Hell, you've got him so brainwashed he thinks he's going to move this little love nest to Bel Air—or Paris or London or Mexico City—the same places you tried to con me with. He's in for a big surprise, isn't he? The moment you lay your hands on the money he won't he able to find you in the yellow pages. That's the blowoff for Jamie." I stood up and her eyes followed me without seeming to move at all. "If you're thinking there's always room in the canal for one more, don't bother. Because all I want out of this is the money. The scratch. And then I do a fade. Now you scratch my back and I'll scratch yours. Where did Jamie dump the car?"

Her voice was steady. "I don't know."

"If the cops get hold of me, I may develop a singing voice."

"*I tell you I don't know.*"

I stared at her and I had an awful feeling that for the first time all day she was telling the truth. "Miss Evangeline," I said, "if I get my hands on Jamie I'll beat it out of him. And when I finish with his face his Aunt Orva won't know him from raw meat. She's not going to pay half a million dollars for hamburger. You listening?"

"I'm listening."

"And I'm not taking any raps. I'll give you first crack at Jamie—I think he'll tell you. Play it smart and we'll all come out of this with glory rolls the size of toilet paper. You listening?"

"I'm listening."

I left.

Chapter Twenty-four

I had to keep moving. I lurched up and down the canals until the light faded, and I damned Jamie under my breath. He had dealt me a hand from the bottom of the deck, and I supposed it was my due. I damned him anyway.

I crossed rickety bridges and followed dirt banks and ribbons of broken sidewalk. I kept pushing Viola out of my mind. She'd wait at the St. Francis maybe a week. And then she'd know for sure. The only thing I'd ever give her was the weeps. For once in my life I'd done the right thing—and it cut like hell.

I kept peering into the canal waters. Nothing. Nothing but upside-down bungalows with their lights coming on. I reached the locks, where the Grand Canal dead-ended against concrete. I stared for a moment at the row of iron cocks, standing like cork-pullers, that drained the canals into the ocean. How long, I wondered, before I'd have the police on my tail? The water already looked ready for flushing. Did I have a day? A week?

I wandered back into town and figured there was nothing to do but kill time. When he was ready, Jamie would make his entrance in a taxi, all smiles and muscadoodle—if he was still in shape to read time. Another hour, maybe. Maggie would be getting into her beads and veils and wondering how dangerous I was. Once the money turned up I'd start glancing back over my shoulder. But she ought to know better. Jamie was her mark. If it came to that, he might even volunteer for the chair. If he was looking for punishment, he would finally make the big time.

A Greyhound bus went by with its headlights on, and I found myself scanning the dark windows. I didn't know where the bus was going or even if Viola was on it, but I gave a wave.

"So long, Spindlelegs."

I watched the taillights shoot away. I stood for a while watching the ocean come in and listening to the palm trees rustling their dry, dead petticoats in the breeze. Then I turned and decided to play my cards as best I could.

That's when I ran into Jamie.

I had walked about a block, to Pacific, and there he was, lit up in the headlights of a passing car.

"Toro!" he laughed. "Hey, toro!"

He had a sheet of newspaper between his hands like a cape and he was making passes at the cars. "Eh hey! Eh hey, toro!"

A blue station wagon slammed on the brakes and went corkscrewing around him and almost into an oncoming car. There was a cross fire of horns.

"Eh hey, toro!"

He stood on the white line taking the bulls from either direction, and it shot through my head that he was trying to kill himself. Really knock himself off. I ran.

Car horns were trumpeting like elephants. I thought of Jamie on a slab and Porter at the bottom of the canal. I dodged a pickup truck and reached the white line and followed it like a tightrope. Jamie turned his back to take on an MG.

"Hey toro! Toro!"

"Get out of the street—you bum!"

I heard a woman laugh and I swung Jamie around by the shoulder. "Come on."

He gave me a chicken-grin and threw a poke at me. I drove my knuckles into his chin, and that was enough. He bent and I caught him by the shirt and lifted him across my shoulder. I tried to get out of there before the cops came. There was another squeal of brakes. Headlights blinded me and I spun. Somehow I reached the curb and kept going. I was a block from the Grand Metropole and I hurried along the dim colonnades, past the dark, empty store windows to the hotel stairway. Then I stopped for breath and I could hear a police siren back on Pacific. I carried Jamie to my room and threw him on the bed.

He looked dead, but all I could think about was Porter. The fingers of one hand touched the floor, almost as if a breeze would set them in motion, and his jaw hung over to one side. But he was breathing and I tried to shake some words out of him. "Come on—wake up!"

He was breathing, but that was all. He was going to sleep for hours. I stared at him. His coat sleeves were wet almost to the shoulders.

Finally I went out into the hall and phoned Maggie to come get him with the car, but her line was busy. I dialed again and again, but I couldn't get through.

I went back to Jamie and tried to bring him to with the back of my hand. I was tired and I was sore and I was short on temper. "Come on, open the eyes! Where's Porter?"

There was nothing in his head but straight muscadoodle. I couldn't bring him to. For the first time I noticed that Viola's green wrapper still hung from the back of the door. Hadn't she cleared out yet? I crossed the hall and knocked; I opened the door and looked in. Nothing. The room was an empty bird cage.

That was what I wanted, wasn't it?

I tried Maggie's number again and had to give it up. She must have the phone off the hook, I thought. The old lady has turned up for the blowoff. I'd get the car myself.

I could feel a change of luck in the air. I had Jamie, didn't I? What was bugging me? Maggie? It was like curling up with a black widow, but I needed her. She needed me, and that put us at a standoff. If we got Jamie's eyes open—one minute alone with him and Maggie'd get him to crack on Porter. And there was the score. All the money in the world. I was too close to the teller's window to lose my place in line. Braque would sell me back my life, but I had to have those big bills.

I tried once more to rouse the spook. He was limp as dough and just about that pale. There was nothing to do but lock him in the room and get Maggie's car. I gave him a last look. His sleeves were wet and I wondered where the hell he'd been. I turned the key on him and cut across town toward the canals.

The porch light burned, spilling a yellow stain onto the surface of the water. Mrs. M's Rolls was parked on the street behind the house, and the chauffeur waited against a fender.

Maggie would be in the séance room, I thought. I straightened my collar and went in the front way. The sliding doors were open and I found Mrs. M smoking her Mexican cigarettes at the table. She was alone and she seemed relieved to see me.

"Good evening, Dr. Appleby. Is everything all right?"

"Everything is fine, Mrs. Marenbach."

"Miss Evangeline said it would be perfectly all right if I came a little early."

"I understand."

Her voice was only slightly above a whisper. "Naturally, Dr. Appleby, I'm anxious to—"

"Of course you are."

She lifted a tapestry knitting bag and let me see the money. My heart must have stopped beating for at least five minutes. There it was. The score. All the money in the world. Half a million dollars. I was surprised to see how light the bundle was. The bills were big ones. Green. Very green. Maggie had got Jamie to kill for them, and if I wasn't careful who stood behind me, I supposed I might be next.

"Where is Miss Evangeline?" Mrs. M asked, and suddenly I wondered how long she had been sitting alone. Hadn't Maggie only left on some excuse—maybe to call me? "The lights were on and the door was wide open," she added, "but no one came so I took the liberty of seating myself."

I tried to keep my eyes off all those bank rags. "I'm sure Miss Evangeline is upstairs with your nephew. You'll find that he's quite— weak. I know you'll be patient, Mrs. Marenbach. Excuse me, please."

I stepped out and closed off the sliding door. Where the hell was Maggie? I had to have the keys to her car. I don't know why I thought she'd be upstairs; I looked in the rooms and wasted time. I came back down and turned into her bedroom. The light wouldn't come on. I struck a match and I could see she wasn't there. The door to the donicker was shut. I lit another match and knocked softly.

"Maggie?"

I opened the door and flipped the switch but got nothing. The fuse in the back part of the house had blown. I struck another paper match and held it in the cup of my hand, and Maggie came up out of the darkness.

She was lying in the bathtub. Her black hair drifted like seaweed across her submerged face. She was stark naked. She was dead.

Chapter Twenty-five

I flinched. The match burned down to my fingers and went out, but I still saw her. Poor, deadly, beautiful Maggie. All she bad been able to buy with that lovely golden body of hers was a square mile of Hell.

I lit another match and touched the water. Cold. She had been lying in the tub for hours. Then I saw the electric coil heater at her feet. It had blown the fuse. The cord was still plugged in.

But she hadn't died by accident. The heater hadn't fallen in the tub and electrocuted her. That was for the cops to believe.

Jamie.

Jamie had held her under. It had to be. His arms were still wet to the shoulders. Some desperate agony had moved him to kill her.

I backed out and closed the door Had Jamie been in the house late in the afternoon, listening to us argue at the foot of the stairs? Maggie had hardly bothered to deny anything. Once she had her hands on the money, Jamie wouldn't be able to find her in the yellow pages. Had he heard that? Had it finally cut through the fog in his skull that Maggie was playing him for a mark?

I stood in the dark of the bedroom. Some fleeting instinct for self-preservation must have risen in Jamie's head. The crafty drunk had taken over long enough to plug in the heater. He was in the clear. His sleeves would dry off by morning. And then he had gone out in traffic to kill himself. Not so much for Maggie, I thought, but finally to knot the score for Uncle Ed.

I moved. I tried to find Maggie's purse. The car keys—that's what I had come for, wasn't it? Nothing had changed. The time bomb Jamie had dropped in my hip pocket was still ticking away—and Mrs. M's money was still waiting for me on the table. The jackpot was mine, wasn't it?

Nothing had changed, but everything was different. I found the keys and tried not to think about the old lady. Jamie was a murderer now, the real thing, and how could I palm him off on her? Easy. You just do it, Skelly. You don't think about it. You lift the feet and move. You grab the money and run.

My hands were suddenly cold and chills started along the back of my neck. I knew the feeling. I'd had it before. I got to the garage and started up the Caddie. I sat there for a minute trying to get a grip on myself. This is the way it had been that night in Boston. With the jackpot on the table I had started coming apart at the seams. Like now. Like tonight. As if I couldn't win for kicking myself. As if I had to blow the score in order to get clean.

My collar weighed on my neck like hemp. I loosened it. I backed out of the garage and had to work at it to keep my vision in focus. If I fell apart I'd pick up the pieces and keep going. I wasn't going to blow this score. I had to get free of Braque. This was the only way, wasn't it? But if Braque doesn't get you, Porter will. There's still a chance, Skelly, if you don't fall apart. If you can get Jamie to talk.

I swung the car around and was vaguely aware of the chauffeur in my headlights. For a moment I couldn't think which way town was. Finally I found myself on Pacific and turned right. In the aching pits of my eyes all the lights seemed far away. I wondered how long I had left Jamie alone.

Another wave of chills came over me and I buttoned my collar for warmth. Then I turned off Pacific toward the Grand Metropole at the end of the street.

And I stopped short.

I saw the flashing red light first and then the ambulance and the crowd that had gathered like a fence around the entrance to the hotel.

I left the car at the curb and got out. I stood for a moment in the dark of the colonnade, bracing myself, and then moved closer. The crowd parted for the stretcher and I stopped in the shadows, my eyes tightened against the flashing lights.

"I heard the blast."

"Shotgun, it sounded like to me."

The stretcher came through and my mind froze. Viola's green wrapper was thrown over the body. The breath caught in my throat.

Jamie.

I stared at the shapeless mound on the stretcher and couldn't move.

"Who was it?"

"Some transient."

"The cop said they're going to have to scrape the rest of him off the wallpaper. Skelly, his name was."

Skelly?

I began backing away. Jamie had died in my place. Braque's gunman had caught up with me. My head was whirling. No—Maggie had fingered me. It had to be Maggie. Settling with me for Viola; if Miss Evangeline couldn't carve her initials on me, no one would. Hours before Jamie had held her jealous head under the bath she had set this up. She had called the skip-tracer and given him my room number, and the gunman had blasted away at a drunk sleeping it off in the flashing neon of a beer sign.

The ambulance went by and I hung back in the doorway of a vacant store. Braque hadn't got me, but Porter would. I threw my coat collar up against the chill in my bones. The shotgun had blasted any hope I had of finding the Renault.

But the kaleidoscope had been given a violent twist, exploding the colors into another view, and suddenly I saw it and didn't know whether to laugh or to cry.

I was dead.

I was dead as hell.

They couldn't hang any more raps on Skelly. Not even when they drained the canals. The cops must have scraped my billfold or the engraving on my watch off the wallpaper. There would be no one at my funeral. Not even me.

I didn't have a banger left in my pocket, I was naked—I didn't have a name any more. But I was free.

Suddenly, it was a hell of a good feeling.

Mrs. M was still waiting, but she knew something was wrong. Her face looked drawn and tired from the strain of expectation. "Well?"

"Mrs. Marenbach," I said, "you're an old fool."

"I beg your pardon?"

"Jamie's dead. He's been dead for four months. I'm not going to let you grieve for him again."

"Dr. Appleby, what are you talking about?"

"My name's not Appleby. It's Skelly."

"What?"

"Skelly. I live at the Grand Metropole." If she read tomorrow's paper she could send any further inquiries to the morgue. She would put me down in the hereafter. "And I said you're an old fool."

Her sharp blue eyes flashed with some of their former brilliance. "Now see here, Dr.—"

"Skelly. Mr. Skelly." I looked at the tapestry bag. Grab the money and run, I thought. But I wasn't even tempted any more.

"But Miss Evangeline promised—"

"Miss Evangeline is after nothing but your money. So was I. You've been suckered into a confidence game, Mrs. Marenbach. We can't deliver Jamie to you. No one can. He's dead, dead, dead."

"But I saw him."

"You saw an actor. You saw an impersonation. You saw tricks and gimmicks. You're too old to believe in ghosts—wake up. You've been tricked." I kicked open the oak panel. "That's where the spook came from. You bought a ticket to a three-act play. It was all make-believe. Do I have to explain it all to you?"

She stood up slowly. I was sorry to hit her so hard so fast, but the old can be very tough. Tears welled up in her eyes, but her voice remained steady and controlled. "Maybe I'm an old fool," she said, "but I wanted Jamie back. And I feel that I did have him back—for a little while."

"I'm sorry, Mrs. Marenbach. I'm sorry if we hurt you."

She adjusted the snap brim of her hat. "I think I knew all along it was make-believe. But it made me happy. I feel as if I have finally made a kind of peace with Jamie—is that nonsense too? Is make-believe so contemptible, young man? I'd turn this money over to you right now if I thought there was still a chance—"

"There isn't."

She began closing the tapestry bag, and I took a final glance at all the money in the world, and knew I had at last squared myself. "When you become very rich," she said, "you find it easy to accept the notion that money will buy anything. Even—anything. Good night, Mr. Skelly." She turned at the door, paused to look at me and added a strange remark. "Thank you," she said.

After a moment I heard the Rolls drive away. I checked the phone. It was still off the hook and I left it that way. I walked into Maggie's bedroom and put back the car keys and took a dime from her purse. I glanced at the closed door to the donicker.

Goodbye, Maggie.

I left.

I stopped at a public phone and reported a number out of order. The operator promised to check into it, and I hung up. In time, I supposed, they'd have to enter the house. They'd find Maggie and it would pass for accidental death.

I crossed to the dark of the beach and figured I'd walk north until I'd put the yellow lights of Venice far behind me. The tide was booming in, igniting the coastline. I turned and gave the Grand Metropole a last look. It rose behind the beach with most of its windows black and empty. A flock of gulls were swarming in the air and I thought of Viola. I kept walking.

I might have gone a couple of hundred yards. I turned and watched the sea gulls again. It was almost as if Viola were there with some crusts of bread. And suddenly I couldn't walk away.

I cut slowly back across the sand, peering along the beachwalk lights—and she was there. Viola. And everything within me took a leap. She was sitting on the curb at the foot of the hotel, with her suitcase to one side and the concertina fallen in the street. She was crying and the gulls were milling around overhead. I looked at her, a skinny blonde with her head buried in her arms and her knees drawn up, and I wanted to rush to her. But I held back in the shadows.

"Spindlelegs. "
She raised her head.
"Spindlelegs!"
She got up then. She couldn't see me, but she heard me—and it had to be me. She didn't understand, but that didn't matter; who called her Spindlelegs but me? She rushed into the dark and we found each other.
"Skelly—"
"Skelly is dead—"
"But they said—"
"I told you to go to San Francisco."
"I missed the bus."
"You mean you changed your mind."
"I'll stay out of your way. Honest. You won't trip over me."
"But I want to trip over you."

"But you said—"

"Never mind what I said."

"You're *alive.*"

"Of course I'm alive."

"But they said—"

"Never mind what they said. Come on."

"My concertina."

"I'll wait for you."

She went back for the squeezebox and the suitcase, and then we turned our backs on Venice.

"Where are we going?"

"Did you pick up the money?" I asked.

"Yes."

"Would you like to get married?"

"Yes."

"We could grab a bus for Nevada. Instant matrimony. Okay?"

"Okay."

"How do you like the name Appleby?"

"I like it fine."

"We could go to Washington. Yakima. I've always wanted to see that part of the country."

"Me too."

"We could make a down payment on some of that wilderness. Good hunting. You can't beat it for fishing." I'd been laying down that story for years, and suddenly I believed it. I *was* Appleby. Why not? Skelly the card hustler was dead. I was Appleby. Maybe that was who I had always wanted to be.

The tide was coming in and we kept walking.

THE END

Stark Houʌe Preʌʌ

FANTASY/SUPERNATURAL

ALGERNON BLACKWOOD
0-9667848-2-0
Incredible Adventures $17.95
0-9667848-5-5
Pan's Garden $17.95
0-9749438-7-8
**Julius LeVallon/
The Bright Messenger** $19.95
1-933586-04-4
**The Lost Valley/
The Wolves of God** $19.95

STORM CONSTANTINE
0-9667848-0-4
**The Oracle Lips:
A Collection** $45
0-9667848-1-2
Calenture $17.95
0-9667848-3-9
Sign for the Sacred $24.95
0-9667848-4-7
**The Thorn Boy & Other
Dreams of Dark Desire** $19.95

MYSTERY/SUSPENSE

BENJAMIN APPEL
1-933586-01-x
The Brain Guy/Plunder $19.95

MALCOLM BRALY
1-933586-03-6
**Shake Him Till He Rattles/
It's Cold Out There** $19.95

GIL BREWER
1-933586-11-7
**Wild to Possess/
A Taste for Sin** $19.95

A. S. FLEISCHMAN
1-933586-12-5
**Look Behind You, Lady/
The Venetian Blonde**
19.95

ELISABETH SANXAY HOLDING
0-9667848-7-1
Lady Killer/Miasma $19.95
0-9667848-9-8
**The Death Wish/Net of
Cobwebs** $19.95
0-9749438-5-1
**The Strange Crime in
Bermuda/Too Many Bottles**
$19.95

DAY KEENE
0-9749438-8-6
**Framed in Guilt/
My Flesh is Sweet** $19.95

STEPHEN MARLOWE
1-933586-02-8
**Violence is My Business/
Turn Left for Murder** $19.95

MARGARET MILLAR
1-933586-09-5
**An Air That Kills/
Do Evil in Return** $19.95

E. Phillips Oppenheim
0-9749438-0-0
**Secrets & Sovereigns:
The Uncollected Stories of
E. Phillips Oppenheim** $19.95

Vin Packer
0-9749438-3-5
**Something in the Shadows/
Intimate Victims** $19.95
0-9749438-6-x
**The Damnation of Adam
Blessing/Alone at Night** $19.95
1-933586-05-2
**Whisper His Sins/
The Evil Friendship** $19.95

Peter Rabe
0-9667848-8-x
The Box/Journey Into Terror
$19.95
0-9749438-4-3
**Murder Me for Nickels/
Benny Muscles In** $19.95
1-933586-00-1
**Blood on the Desert/
A House in Naples** $19.95
1-933586-11-7
**My Lovely Executioner/
Agreement to Kill** $19.95

Robert J. Randisi
0-9749438-9-4
**The Ham Reporter/The
Disappearance of Penny** $19.95

Douglas Sanderson
0-9749438-2-7
**Pure Sweet Hell/
Catch a Fallen Starlet** $19.95
1-933586-06-0
**The Deadly Dames/A Dum-
Dum for the President** $19.95

Harry Whittington
1-933586-08-7
**A Night for Screaming/Any
Woman He Wanted** $19.95

FILM

Kevin McCarthy
& Ed Gorman (ed)
1-933586-07-9
**Invasion of the Body Snatchers:
A Tribute** $17.95

If you are interested in purchasing any of the above books, please send the cover price plus $3.00 U.S. for the 1st book and $1.00 U.S. for each additional book to:

STARK HOUSE PRESS
2200 O Street, Eureka, CA 95501
(707) 444-8768 griffinskye@cox.net
www.starkhousepress.com

Order 3 or more books and take a 10% discount. We accept PayPal payments.